About the Author

VOLKER KUTSCHER was born in 1962. He studied German, philosophy and history, and worked as a newspaper editor prior to writing his first detective novel. *Babylon Berlin*, the start of an award-winning series of novels to feature Gereon Rath and his exploits in late Weimar Republic Berlin, was an instant hit in Germany. A lavish television production aired on Sky Atlantic in November 2017. There are now six titles in the series, most recently *Lunapark* in 2016. The series was awarded the Berlin Krimi-Fuchs Crime Writers Prize in 2011 and has sold more than one million copies worldwide. Kutscher works as a full-time author and lives in Cologne.

About the Translator

NIALL SELLAR was born in Edinburgh in 1984. He studied German and translation studies in Dublin, Konstanz and Edinburgh, and has worked variously as a translator, teacher, and reader. He lives in Glasgow.

ALSO BY VOLKER KUTSCHER

Babylon Berlin
The Silent Death

GOLDSTEIN

GOLDSTEIN

BOOK 3
of the Gereon Rath Mystery Series

VOLKER KUTSCHER

Translated from the German by Niall Sellar

PICADOR

NEW YORK

GOLDSTEIN. Copyright © 2010 by Volker Kutscher. English translation copyright © 2018 by Niall Sellar. All rights reserved. Printed in the United States of America. For information, address Picador, 175 Fifth Avenue, New York, N.Y. 10010

picadorusa.com • instagram.com/picador
twitter.com/picadorusa • facebook.com/picadorusa

Picador® is a U.S. registered trademark and is used by Macmillan Publishing Group, LLC, under license from Pan Books Limited.

For book club information, please visit facebook.com/picadorbookclub or email marketing@picadorusa.com.

The translation of this work was supported by a grant from the Goethe-Institut, which is funded by the German Ministry of Foreign Affairs.

Designed by Steven Seighman

The Library of Congress Cataloging-in-Publication Data is available upon request.

ISBN 978-1-250-20634-3 (trade paperback)
ISBN 978-1-250-20635-0 (ebook)

Our books may be purchased in bulk for promotional, educational, or business use. Please contact your local bookseller or the Macmillan Corporate and Premium Sales Department at 1-800-221-7945, extension 5442, or by email at MacmillanSpecialMarkets@macmillan.com.

Originally published in Germany by Verlag Kiepenheuer & Witsch GmbH & Co.

First English translation published in Great Britain by Sandstone Press Ltd

First U.S. English translation published as an ebook original by Picador

First Picador Paperback Edition: February 2019

10 9 8 7 6 5 4 3 2 1

Remota itaque iustitia quid sunt regna nisi magna latrocinia?
Quia et latrocinia quid sunt nisi parva regna?

AUGUSTINUS, *DE CIVITATE DEI, LIBER IV*

PART I

CRIME

Saturday 27th June to Saturday 4th July 1931

1

The place smelled of wood and glue and fresh paint. She was alone with the darkness and the silence, with only her breathing and the faint tick of the watch in her jacket pocket for company. The man seemed to have disappeared again, yet she decided to wait a little longer, stretching to get the blood flowing through her arms and legs. At least there were no coat hangers on the rail; she could see a chink of light through the crack in the door. She took the watch from her jacket pocket. It was just gone nine. The night watchman would soon be completing his rounds on the sixth floor.

Confirmation came with the grinding of the lift, echoing so loudly through the darkness that she gave a start. It was time. He was on his way back down, and in the next few hours would only be concerned with the roller grilles in front of the doors and display windows, with making sure that everything was locked and no one could break in.

Alex carefully opened the wardrobe and peered out. Better safe than sorry, Benny always said. The neon signs on Tauentzienstrasse shone so much colour through the windows there was no need for a torch. She could see everything: the luxurious show bedroom, with a bed wide enough for a whole family and a carpet so soft her feet sank into it. When she thought back to the scratchy coconut matting in front of the bed she had shared with her little brother, Karl, when she was still living with her parents, in digs that were as murky as they were cramped . . . What had become of Karl? She didn't even know if the cops had gone looking for him after Beckmann's death. She didn't miss her family, but she'd have liked to see him again.

Alex spun around at a movement on the edge of her vision. The big mirror on the dressing table reflected an eighteen-year-old girl staring defiantly back, legs in baggy trousers and hair held in place by a coarsely woven linen cap. She gave herself a wry grin.

Pausing at the end of the elegantly decorated plywood panel that served as a makeshift bedroom wall, she peered around the corner. It was hardly necessary. The night watchman wouldn't make another round of the shop floor before morning, towards the end of his shift. She knew that from Kalli. There wasn't a soul around and it was a nice feeling, knowing that all this belonged to her for the next few hours. Her and Benny.

Alex found her way without difficulty. The restless, dappled light from outside, flickering constantly between one colour and the next, was more than enough. She had committed the most important things to memory a few hours before when the place was full of people. Behind her were the doors leading to the southern stairwell and, to the left, past the wall of curtain fabrics, was the access to the escalators.

Everything was calm. Traffic noise was muffled, almost unreal, a dull murmur from a different world that had nothing to do with its magical counterpart inside. She entered the deserted curtain section that seemed like a fairy-tale castle, long drapes hanging from ceiling to floor in silk, satin and net. As a little girl, she had often stood here in astonishment, clasping her mother's hand. Young Alexandra soon understood that her mother never came to buy, only to dream. Take it all in, she had said, we proles may not be able to afford anything here, but they can't stop us from looking.

They had never had enough money to buy things in the west, not even when Father was still in work and Mother had her cleaning job. In fact it had been rare for them to venture outside of Boxhagener Kiez. The Ku'damm, KaDeWe and Tauentzienstrasse—for her father these places were a symbol of wasteful capitalism, the west of the city a hotbed of vice to be avoided like the devil avoided holy water. If not for Mother the stubborn old man would never have allowed himself to be talked into those occasional summer visits to the zoo, but even Emil Reinhold understood that you shouldn't deprive working-class children of the wonders of nature. Alex had never cared to see creatures suffering behind bars, however, and by the polar bears she would already be thinking of the return journey. The Reinhold family was accustomed to strolling the length of Tauentzienstrasse before boarding the U-Bahn at Wittenbergplatz and heading back to the east. At the first shop windows Emil Reinhold would begin his recurring sermon about the excesses of capitalism, even if Alex and her mother had their eyes fixed on the displays. The KaDeWe displays held a kind of magic for Alex. In Mother's eyes, too, was the sparkle of long-forgotten dreams of a better life, a life which the dictatorship of the proletariat could never hope to provide. Father never noticed, or never wanted to notice. He continued his sermon to the captive audience of his sons, above all to Karl, who took everything so seriously. Karl, the prince of the proletariat, the staunch Communist, who was now in hiding from the cops just like his thieving sister.

Alex had almost reached the escalators when a noise brought her back to the present, a hard *clack*, more immediate than the padded roar of traffic. She crouched behind two giant rolls of cloth and listened: something was banging against the glass, clattering and scratching against one of the windows. She tried to place the sounds. A fluttering, then a cooing. Venturing from her hiding place, behind the neon-lit pane of glass she saw the silhouettes of two pigeons resting on the window ledge.

She took a deep breath to still her beating heart. First the mirror and now this! Benny would kill himself laughing if he could see her. When had she become so easily startled? When she realised her messed-up life was more important than she cared to admit?

With a loud flap of wings, the pigeons swooped back into the night and Alex continued on her way, the nervous tension accumulated during those long hours in the wardrobe all but evaporated. She enjoyed her night-time stroll through the silent department store more with each passing step. It was as if everything had fallen into a hundred-year sleep, and she was the only person awake in this enchanted kingdom. KaDeWe outstripped all the other department stores they had shut themselves in until now; Tietz for sure, but even the enormity of Karstadt on Hermannplatz paled against the magnificence of Tauentzienstrasse.

She left the curtain section and reached the escalators. The metal steps stood deserted and motionless as if an evil fairy had turned everything to ice. It was five storeys down to their agreed meeting point on the ground floor: the tobacco section, as always. It had become a kind of ritual, to stock up on brands they could never otherwise afford. Benny had a nose for the stuff.

She had met him on a freezing cold day in February, quarrelling over a cigarette butt that some snotty-nosed, rich little upstart had thrown half-smoked onto the pavement in front of Bahnhof Zoo, a few weeks after all that crap with Beckmann. Alex had already spent the money she had stolen from that fatso at the Christmas market. She was hungry and hadn't had a cigarette in two days.

They pounced on the butt in the same instant, she and this slender, almost dainty blond boy, who, despite his awkward appearance, wasn't afraid of getting his hands dirty. He moved quickly, but not as quickly as Alex. He glared at her, a look she had returned with interest, so much did her body crave the nicotine. It was a miracle they had managed to make peace and share the cigarette butt. No doubt it was his eyes that did it.

Right from the start Alex felt she had to look after this skinny boy with the melancholy gaze, and soon developed almost maternal feelings towards Benny, who was still not yet sixteen. At the very least, she felt like an older sister to him, yet it was Benny who, in the weeks that followed, showed her how to survive on the streets; Benny who taught her how to steal wallets, open doors without a key and drive cars belonging to other people. Useful knowledge for a girl who, when night fell, was never sure where her next meal was coming from.

For the whole of spring they made ends meet with pickpocketing, small-scale burglaries and a few assignments they took care of for Kalli while they survived from hand to mouth. Until they discovered department stores.

The first time at Tietz, on Dönhoffplatz, was pure chance. Alex and Benny were in the store just before closing to shelter from the rain. The idea came to them of its own accord as customers were politely ushered towards the exits. They only needed to exchange glances before spending the next few hours huddled tightly together in an enormous wardrobe trunk. When everything around them fell silent they ventured out, every bone in their bodies aching, to empty the jewellery cabinets, and whatever else they could lay their hands on. They filled two small cases from the leather goods section, just enough to carry comfortably without drawing attention to themselves. No one stopped them when they were back outside on Krausenstrasse or had any idea what they were carrying in their cases. They boarded the next train at Spittelmarkt, calm as you like, and passed unnoticed there too, a couple of youths with suitcases, who looked like exhausted street traders returning home after a long and fruitless day.

The next morning Kalli was astonished, and only too happy to cough up. They had never scored so much before, at most a pocket watch taken from a drunk, or a few odds and ends stolen from a car. After Tietz they stopped dealing in bits and pieces. Pinching wallets on the U-Bahn or fleecing drunks was scarcely worth it, being risky and always a matter of chance. The department store ruse was more lucrative, easier too. All they had to do was shut themselves in, raid the display cabinets and get the hell out. By the time the night watchmen noticed the empty displays, Alex and Benny were long gone.

They had worked over four department stores by now, and last time, at Karstadt, had made away with some really nifty pieces. It was Kalli who had suggested Berlin's finest establishment. Alex and Benny would never have thought of it themselves, out of sheer respect. In KaDeWe, they could really make hay, Kalli said, why not try their luck there? The place would be no better guarded than Tietz or Karstadt, guaranteed. He knew someone who worked there.

Now she was teetering over escalators making her way down floor by floor. The feeling of having KaDeWe all to herself suddenly overwhelmed her. She couldn't help thinking back to Tietz, where together with Benny she had moved from section to section, savouring the fact that they were alone with such treasures. They had tested any number of things, even paying the toy section a visit, a little coyly at first since, in spite of their friendship, they mostly concealed their childish sides from each other. In the second department store, however—Tietz again, this time at Alexanderplatz—they had got straight down to work.

The great hall on the ground floor opened out in front of her. To get to the tobacco products she had to go through gentlemen's fashion, where a line of mannequins with wax faces looked down on her rigidly, arrogantly, just like the snotty little upstarts who wore these clothes on the outside and could scarcely move for their conceit. Alex hated their kind and took pleasure that it was exactly these types who stood here now, condemned to spend the rest of their days as KaDeWe fossils. At the end of the army of mannequins she could already sense the wood panelling and shelves of the tobacco section.

Benny didn't seem to be here, but there was something in the weak light flickering outside. She froze, rooted to the spot. Had one of the mannequins at the end of the row moved? She took a closer look, but everything was as before. A red neon sign flashing outside was making the shadows in here dance. There was no night watchman among the mannequins, not a single peaked cap in the line, just casual fedoras, bourgeois bowlers and elegant top hats. She continued with her heart still pounding; it seemed as if every beat must be audible in the silence.

The mannequin that had so startled her stood right at the end of the line, just before the entrance to the tobacco section. She stuck her tongue out and it tilted its upper body slightly forwards. Terror coursed through her like an electric shock.

'Come right in, my lady,' said the dummy in an operatic Hungarian accent, 'don't be shy!'

'Are you trying to give me a heart attack?' Alex punched the snow-white dickey.

Benny took a bow, removing his top hat and waving her through the door like a fairground barker. 'Come in, my lady! And don't be cowed by the prices. There's something here for everyone!'

'You're a right one, you are,' Alex grinned. 'You look like a trainee ring-master!' She immediately regretted her choice of words when she saw his face. He had expected amazement, wonder, applause—anything but a joke at his expense.

'I thought since we were here, why not get all dressed up,' he said, trying not to let his disappointment show.

'Looks damn elegant,' she said. 'I've never seen you in anything like it.'

'Why would you have? This isn't made for the likes of us. Yet here I am!' He opened a canvas bag. 'I got you something from ladies' fashion,' he said, lifting out a red silk dress. 'What do you think?'

'We should stick with jewellery. Kalli can't get rid of clothes.'

'Just try it on.' He waved the red silk.

'Now?'

'It's an *evening* dress, isn't it?' He held out the shimmering, dark-red dress.

'Isn't it a bit too . . . classy?'

'The question is whether you like it.'

She held the dress against herself and looked in one of the mirrors. The size was right, and she really liked it. She wouldn't have thought Benny had such an eye for fashion. He'd never bought himself anything to wear, nothing, not even with the money that Kalli gave them last time, enough for half a dozen new suits. He had only noticed that she had bought herself a new coat some days later.

Benny fetched a silver tin from his inside pocket and took out a Manoli Privat, a six-pfennig brand. He didn't look so ridiculous in that get-up at all, she thought, it was just a little unfamiliar; she had only ever seen him in coarse linen trousers and his faded leather jacket.

'Do you want one?' he asked.

'Just a drag.'

Benny lit the cigarette and passed it on. Alex took two deep drags and returned it.

'It looks good,' he said, pulling gloves and a little hat out of the bag. 'You should put it on.'

Alex stepped behind a pilaster and changed into the dress, donning the gloves and placing the hat on her head, heart pounding. She'd never worn anything so elegant before, and felt good yet insecure at the same time. It was a strange sensation, but Benny must be feeling the same way. She could have spared him that stupid remark.

'Da-da-da-daa,' she trumpeted as she emerged. The boy who usually couldn't keep his mouth shut didn't say a word, and she knew immediately he was impressed. He looked so elegant, especially now, bowed ever so slightly before her.

'Will you dance with me?' he asked.

Alex laughed. 'Do you hear music?'

'Yes.' He took her right hand and clasped her left shoulder. 'Don't you?' He hummed a little melody and swayed her slowly back and forth in three-quarter time.

'I don't know how to dance.'

'Leave that to me.' He began to waltz, sweeping her along with him. His grip was firm and she abandoned herself to his movement and the rhythm of his song. They reeled past the mannequins with their arrogant faces, past the shelves and clothes stands, past the dappled light gleaming in from Tauentzienstrasse. Only when they came to a halt did she realise that they had danced halfway across the floor. She felt a little dizzy and out of breath, but happy nevertheless.

'Where did you learn that?' He never ceased to amaze her, this skinny boy with the child's face that sometimes appeared so terrifyingly serious and grown-up.

'In the home. The kitchen girls used to dance when the nuns weren't looking. They showed me—do you like it?'

She nodded, and he grabbed her again, spinning in the opposite direction this time. Alex was overjoyed. If her father knew that she took pleasure in such bourgeois frippery as the Viennese Waltz, he'd no doubt have condemned his wayward daughter even more than usual.

When they arrived back at the tobacco section she was unable to stand on her own. 'That was great,' she said, out of breath. 'We should have done it sooner. I could use the practice.'

'Maybe we should go dancing properly sometime. Somewhere real swish, I mean, like a dance hall on the Ku'damm . . .'

Alex laughed. 'They'd kick us out!'

'We'd just need to be dressed like we are now.' Benny paused, as if finding it hard to utter his next sentence, as if the words had to overcome a few hurdles first. 'You're beautiful, Alex,' he said, and it sounded as if he'd been meaning to say it for a long time. He stroked her cheek with his fingertips, startling her with his unexpected tenderness. She gave a little start, but he didn't notice, simply closed his eyes and drew nearer. Only when his lips brushed against her mouth did she react, pushing him away gently but firmly.

'Benny! You can't . . .'

He didn't seem to understand, or want to understand.

'I don't know. You're only fifteen.' *Shit, Alex, be nice to him!* 'Don't get me wrong, I like you. You're my friend.'

'Why can't I kiss you?'

He looked so sad and awkward she couldn't help taking him in her arms and stroking his head. 'I like you, Benny. But . . . we can't. Especially not now. We've got work to do.'

'True,' he said. 'Enough of this nonsense.'

He let go and unpacked the second canvas bag, into which he had stuffed his old clothes, but she could see she had hurt him for the second time that evening, only this time it had gone deeper. He was trying not to let it show, and she pretended she hadn't realised, but the atmosphere between them was soured. Moments before they had soared across the KaDeWe floor; now, in evening dress, they looked like two children who had been rummaging secretly through their parents' wardrobe. At least that was how Alex felt, and Benny too by the look of him. He rushed to get back into his old clothes, and Alex returned behind the pilaster to change.

'Let's get to work,' he said, passing her the second bag. Silently they went on their way.

The jewellery section was also on the ground floor, the glass of the display cabinets shimmering in the half-dark. Alex felt her nerves jangle again. The most expensive items would be stored in the vault, and, since the display cabinets contained only replicas, Alex and Benny could ignore the swanky rocks and concentrate on simple items that were bound to be genuine: plain rings, bangles and earrings, but mostly watches, any number of them, golden pocket watches and elegant wrist watches. Kalli always paid good money for watches.

Benny took off his leather jacket and wrapped it around his arm. 'Alex,' he said, 'I promise you, in two, maybe three years, I won't need to do this anymore. I'll spend the day wearing expensive suits, drive a car, and live in a nice house with servants. And then I'll ask you again if you want to go dancing with me.'

Before she could reply, he drew back his elbow and shattered the glass with a clatter that was loud enough to wake the whole city.

They moved quickly, not exchanging a word, Alex collecting wrist-watches from the shattered display cabinet and stuffing them into her bag, while Benny shook shards of glass from the leather of his jacket and prepared for the next assault. The second time, the clatter didn't seem quite so loud. She took care not to stuff too many glass fragments into the bag with the watches, which proved trickier with the next display cabinet, where a number of low carat diamond rings rested on the velvet between the splinters. Alex was concentrating so hard on these little splinters that she overlooked the sharp edge of glass in the brass frame and cut the back of her hand.

The wound bled profusely. Without saying a word Benny tore a strip of fabric from his shirt to bind it before emptying the third display cabinet. With her bandaged hand, Alex wasn't much use.

'I'm sorry.'

'It doesn't matter. We—' Benny broke off, turning to stone mid-sentence. 'Did you hear that?'

Alex shrugged, but then heard the noise too. Somewhere in the building a door had slammed shut.

'He's on the move again,' she whispered. 'That can't be right. He must still be doing his rounds outside; he won't be going over the shop floor a second time.'

'I wouldn't bet on it.' Benny grabbed another handful of rings. 'Maybe we were too noisy. Let's get out of here.'

He closed the two canvas bags, taking the heavier of the pair, and they started to run, with Alex, who was more familiar with the layout, leading the way. In the meantime, there were scores of night owls out and about on Tauentzienstrasse, its windows and doors barred to keep late-night window shoppers from temptation.

They had to find a rear storeroom or office window so that they could reach the access yard and get onto Ansbacher Strasse, before joining the crowds and taking the next U-Bahn train east. Same as always, except something happened that threw their plans into disarray.

The door to the southern stairwell opened, and a wedge of light fell on the shop floor. Alex jumped for cover, dragging Benny behind a wall draped with silk neckties. She thought she had seen a uniform in the door. Not the red-brown of the KaDeWe watchmen, but the dark blue of the Prussian Police.

Judging by the noise, it must be a whole squad of uniformed officers. Benny silently mouthed a word she'd have preferred to scream from the rooftops. *Shit!*

They would have to go via Tauentzienstrasse after all. They had no other choice. What the hell were the cops doing here anyway? Alex gave Benny a nod and led the way. Hunching slightly, using the shelves and clothes stands for cover, they worked their way through the half-dark, stretching the distance between them and the cops.

'Police!' someone cried. 'We know you're in here. Give yourselves up. You're surrounded on all sides!'

For a few moments a light flashed, then it was bright as day. Alex ducked behind the shelf they were passing and peered around the corner. It didn't look good. The officers had divided themselves into several groups and were systematically combing the entire floor.

She looked at Benny, who gave a helpless shrug. Not much time left. They had to do something. The lifts! The middle one was on the ground floor. Alex gestured towards the lift doors a few metres to their left and Benny nodded. It was their one chance to gain a head start; a little more time to hatch a new plan. They bent low, crawling past a long rack of trousers. The lifts were now almost within touching distance. All they had to do was break cover.

Alex heard a male voice close by. 'Look at that mess. Let's hope they haven't escaped.'

'They're still in the building somewhere,' said another. 'I can feel it.'

The cops had discovered the display cabinets, distracting them for a moment. She took a deep breath before stretching an arm towards the button.

The door slid open with a soft *pling*. Not soft enough.

'Stop, police!' someone shouted. 'Put your hands in the air and show yourselves!'

Alex pulled Benny into the open lift and pressed one of the top buttons. At least she knew how these things worked, thanks to Wertheim. The cops were already coming around the corner, shouting something like 'stay where you are', when the door finally closed and the lift began its ascent.

Thank God!

First things first, get onto a higher floor, distance themselves from their pursuers. It would take time for the police to get another lift down to the ground floor. She looked at Benny. At last they could talk again.

'Shit,' he said. 'What are the pigs doing here?'

'Maybe we set off an alarm.'

'More likely they were expecting us. Waiting to catch us red-handed.'

'They'll have to find us first.'

'True,' Benny grinned. 'I always knew you were a whiz at escaping, Alex, but where did you learn how to use a lift?'

'There was a lift boy at Wertheim who had the hots for me.'

He nudged her in the side and laughed, even though it hadn't been a joke. She had almost paid for that episode with the job she had lost half a year later anyway.

The lift came to a halt and the doors opened. 'Ladies and Gentlemen, we have reached the fifth floor,' she said.

'Shouldn't we go up one?'

'Yes, but via the stairs. Then the pigs will start looking on the wrong floor.'

Benny nodded. 'It's best we split up. You go up one, I'll go down one.'

'Split up?'

'We don't know how many there are. To have any chance, we need to separate.'

He sounded like a general before battle. If the situation hadn't been so serious, she would have laughed.

'Fine,' she said. 'And then what?'

'No idea. Get out of here somehow. There must be a few options in a place like this.'

'OK. When shall we meet?'

'Not till we're outside. The Märchenbrunnen. At the top of every hour.'

'Good luck, then,' she said. 'See you on the outside.' She looked at him for a final time before running upstairs to the sixth floor. Their footsteps sounded further and further apart.

At the top of the stairs she paused in front of the lift door. It was only a matter of time before the night watchman switched on the sixth floor lights but, for now, it was still dark. For the first time that evening she made use of her torch, shining a light on the numbered displays above the doors. The lift on the far right was already on the way up, now passing the second floor. They were on the move. No time to lose.

Alex burst onto the shop floor in search of another escape route or, at the very least, a place to hide. Her torch beam passed over red-white floor tiles and empty glass counters: the KaDeWe snack bar, heart of the new grocery section. She crossed the floor, moving past shelves full of jam jars until, suddenly, there was nowhere else to go. She looked for an opening in the whitewashed plywood wall whose flimsiness was disguised by rows of shelves. Finally, behind a sales counter, she found an inconspicuous little door with a simple ward lock that was easy to open. She slipped inside and found a stack of planks. The place looked like a building site. She crossed the room and found a door behind which was a staircase leading upwards.

She didn't know which way to turn, only that she couldn't fall into the hands of her pursuers. That had been her number one rule since living on the streets: never let the cops get you! For half a year she had been scared stiff they might pick her up and hold her responsible for Beckmann's death. Or, worse still, give her a good grilling and, in the process, discover it was her brother Karl who had shot that fucking Nazi dead; that she had just stood by and watched. Sometimes she thought it was all her fault: that *she* had turned her brother into a murderer, only to feel every fibre in her being protest. Because if it wasn't for all that Red Front bullshit, Karl would never have owned a gun in the first place.

But he did own a gun, and he had fired it.

Alex switched off the torch and listened. Voices, no doubt about it, and they were growing louder. They were combing the sixth floor. Of course: they weren't so stupid as to be deceived by the lift below. There was a flicker and then the light came on here too. Instinctively Alex eschewed the cover of the building materials and retreated inside the dark stairwell. What must the pedestrians on the street below be thinking, seeing all the floors in KaDeWe lit up just before midnight?

She put her bag over her shoulders and climbed the narrow, dark staircase, desperate to get away before the cops discovered the plywood wall and decided to look behind it.

Climbing through two attic floors she came upon a locked door that posed no problem for her skeleton key. A cold wind blew in her face. She was outside again, on a roof garden above the city. The Gedächtniskirche rose dark out of a sea of houses, and lights flashed in all colours from the urban canyons below. Traffic noise was no longer muffled by the walls of the store. The beep of a horn reminded her that life was waiting below, freedom too. How to get there? The wind was still blowing in her face, letting her know that she had ventured onto foreign terrain, and the cut on her hand was throbbing. She leaned over the parapet and looked down. The KaDeWe logo lit up the darkness, casting neon light on a steep roof with dormer windows. No chance of getting down that way. She prayed that the cops wouldn't get it into their heads to look up here. Who would be stupid enough to escape onto the roof? Well, Alexandra Reinhold, for one, but the cops couldn't know that.

Somehow she had to get past them, go down, right down to the bottom and out. She returned to the stairwell, closed the door behind her and stayed still for a moment, listening. Nothing. Everything was still dark. Only when she was certain that the coast was clear did she slowly descend

the stairs, step by step and, having arrived below, opened the door leading back into the light. The voices could no longer be heard. Had they left?
There was no one by the stack of planks, but it was strange that they weren't
looking here. They had left the light on. Alex crept towards the plywood
wall and peered through a narrow crack.

There was someone by the lifts. The cops didn't even have to search the
whole building, it was enough to monitor the exits.

She retreated towards the rear of the construction area. Carefully she
opened one of the windows on the western side and was startled by how
loud the noise suddenly was. Hopefully it wouldn't reach the lifts. She
stretched her head out into the night air, which smelled of petrol and rain-
clouds, and looked around. Four metres below she could see the balcony
that extended around nearly the entire fifth floor of the building, and beyond it the gaping chasm of Passauer Strasse. She could hang on to the window ledge, lower herself down as far as possible and then jump. She could
make it. As she was assessing the risks, she saw a figure huddled in a window recess on the balcony. Benny.

The cops had driven the poor boy outside too. He didn't see her, simply
crouched in his hiding place, keeping the door in view. Alex closed the
window. How were they going to get out of here in one piece?

The cut on her hand was still throbbing. She opened a door on the south
side. Again, it was dark. Only when she was certain that she couldn't hear
footsteps or voices did she switch her torch back on and enter a long corridor.
An office wing, everything new, the walls smelling of fresh plaster. Slowly she
made her way along the corridor, ignoring doors on both sides, before reaching a turn to the left, perhaps leading to another stairwell. She switched off
her torch after noticing a faint gleam of light from a window at the end of
the corridor. Outside she caught sight of a firewall, which must have looked
out onto the access yard.

*Excellent work Fräulein Reinhold, just like you planned. Only a few floors
too high!*

It had started to rain, but Alex longed for nothing more than to stand
outside in the middle of it. She stared through the window and said a quick
prayer.

Dear Lord, if you should be out there somewhere listening, please get me out of here, I don't care how, just get me out, and I'll pay any price, even if it means going to church.

She closed her eyes and listened to the drumming of the rain. Something about the sound made her hesitate and open the window. It was making an unspeakable noise, as if someone were striking a hammer against an anvil again and again. Alex poked her head outside and thought she must be dreaming. At that moment, she believed she had her prayer to thank for it. A fire escape! Iron steps led down floor by floor to the yard.

She packed her torch, shouldered her bag, stepped onto the grating and looked down. A fleet of lorries and delivery trucks was parked in perfect formation, otherwise the courtyard was empty—not a blue uniform in sight. The cops had overlooked the fire escape.

Alex gripped the damp, cold handrail and descended the wobbly steel staircase step by step, keeping the windows and yard in view. The wind blew rain in her face and the steel structure swayed and squealed under her feet, but she inched ever closer to the ground. She was dripping wet, with her bandage soaked through and her bag growing heavier by the minute until, at last, she reached the bottom.

If only she could tell Benny about the fire exit, but hopefully his luck would be in too. Using the delivery trucks as cover, she made her way to the entrance onto Passauer Strasse. The great iron gate was locked, but she'd been expecting that. She took out her picklock and, though she was shivering slightly and needed a little longer than usual, soon had it cracked.

The gate squeaked as she opened it just enough to slip through. And then she was outside. Free at last!

Never had she enjoyed listening to traffic quite so much. She sucked in the air greedily, as if only now could she breathe again after surfacing from a long dive. The rain had stopped. There wasn't much happening on Passauer Strasse, just a few hurried pedestrians snapping shut their umbrellas, and two or three cars splashing through puddles. No one paid her any attention. She tilted her head back and looked at the department store front, the crowning feature of which was the giant neon sign here on Passauer Strasse. Lit up at night like this, the store had a festive, almost Christmassy feel. She thought of Benny and, in the same moment, saw him clambering on the balcony's steel railings. What on earth was he doing there? He didn't seem to have moved very far from his previous hiding place, where she had caught sight of him moments before.

He stood on the balcony ledge, outside the railings. Alex caught her breath. The ledge could only be a foot wide. Surely he wasn't thinking of climbing down, not with the heavy bag on his shoulders. But that's what it looked like. Quick as a flash Benny crouched, facing inwards as he gripped the ledge with both hands, gradually lowering his body until he hung, legs dangling, a dark shadow against the narrow, illuminated windows. His feet were too far from the next ledge; he'd never make it down. A gasp of horror made her turn. Behind her stood a thin man with metal-rimmed spectacles and bowler hat, craning his neck.

A police officer appeared in silhouette above the railings, the star on his shako flashing briefly in the light. Benny was hanging from the balcony to hide, not to escape. The building's front was his final resort, but the cop must have seen him. He was leaning over the railings as if he knew someone was there.

Alex ought to have fled, but couldn't, and stood on Passauer Strasse as if rooted to the spot.

'The cops are there already,' Alex heard the man in metal-rimmed spectacles say. 'Why on earth would you jump from *KaDeWe*?'

Alex couldn't see exactly what was happening, only that the officer was now next to Benny, having also climbed over the railing. Did he mean to help him up? It seemed not. He tilted his head forwards as if speaking. Benny seemed to be saying something too, though Alex couldn't make out what.

Benny gave a cry, making her start. Was his strength deserting him? Surely not! Give yourself up, she thought. Climb back up and turn yourself in.

The cop's head was still tilted forwards and, for a brief moment, Alex made out his face in the glow of the sign. He was grimacing furiously. What on earth was going on? Had Benny shot his mouth off again? For a second time she heard him cry, more drawn out now, and desperate. He sounded like the boy he was, rather than the man he wanted to be.

She was holding her head at such an angle that her neck hurt, but, still, she couldn't look away. Why had he let go with his right hand? How was he supposed to hold on, with just one hand plus the heavy bag on his shoulders? She stared and stared and couldn't believe what she saw. Until at last she understood.

No scream, no cry. He fell silently through the night.

There was a thud like a sack of potatoes falling from a truck and, at the same time, a mighty crack. Then everything was quiet.

She snapped out of her trance to see Benny not ten metres away, painfully contorted and motionless on the ground. She rushed to his side. Hardly any blood, strangely. Benny's eyes were closed. There was someone wheezing behind her. The man with the metal-rimmed spectacles was staring goggle-eyed.

'Call an ambulance!' she hissed, but the man shrugged his shoulders helplessly and made himself scarce.

Alex leaned towards Benny and heard him rasping. He was still alive!

She kneeled on the pavement, laid his head on her knees and stroked his hair. He opened his eyes; his breathing became quicker and quicker.

'Alex,' he said.

'Try not to talk. There's an ambulance on its way.'

'I'm sorry, Alex, I messed up.'

'No!'

'I couldn't . . . I couldn't hold on any longer. He was standing on my fingers.' There was a wheezing sound as Benny tried to catch his breath. He was finding it hard to speak.

'Don't talk so much, Benny, don't talk so much.'

'Get out of here . . . or they'll catch you. These are bad people . . .'

She looked skywards to where the cop was staring down. He said something to his colleague and gestured towards her, towards Alex and Benny on Passauer Strasse below. The other cop began speaking animatedly, seeming to curse his partner. That wouldn't do any good now.

Benny took another breath and, again, there was a wheezing in his lungs. Dark blood suddenly streamed from his mouth.

'Benny!' she cried. 'Hold on. Hold on!'

He tried to smile. 'Promise you'll go dancing with me sometime.'

'I promise.'

The interval between his breaths became shorter and shorter. Alex wiped at the blood with her sleeve. Benny gazed at her wistfully the whole time, as if preparing to say goodbye. He closed his eyes.

'Don't give up, do you hear me, don't give up! The ambulance will be here soon.' Benny's wheezing became more and more frenetic until suddenly it stopped, as if someone had switched off a machine. 'No,' Alex screamed. 'No! You can't just die! I won't let you!'

She let his head sink slowly onto the pavement and looked around. A few rubberneckers had made their way over from Tauentzienstrasse. The man with the metal-rimmed spectacles hadn't reappeared, nor was there any sign of an ambulance, but a group of uniformed officers emerged from a discreet side door of KaDeWe.

She swallowed her tears and ran.

'Stop that boy! He's one of them!'

Alex didn't turn around. She knew she was being chased. She had to steer clear of pedestrians, screaming at an elegant lady to move aside and forcing her into the window grilles, before running towards the throng of people surging down Tauentzienstrasse. Find cover there and disappear. A whistle sounded behind her, and someone shouted.

'Stop! Police!'

She kept running, straight across the pavement onto Tauentzienstrasse past tooting cars. A taxi screeched to a halt, but Alex paid no heed. After what had happened to Benny, she feared for her life. She threw herself sideways in front of a tram, whose driver sounded the warning bell, crossed the central reservation, and followed the electric train as it juddered eastwards. Her gaze fell on the warning sign, which strictly forbade passengers from jumping aboard while the train was in motion. She leapt onto the moving platform and squeezed herself into the car. The windows on the other side were more or less obscured by her fellow passengers, but not quite completely. There they were, her two pursuers, waiting for the tram to go past as it took the bend on the Wittenbergplatz approach.

Alex jostled her way inside and looked at the sign: the number six, going towards Schöneberg. Not ideal, but if she got out again at Wittenbergplatz there was a good chance they'd spot her. The tram stopped, with more people getting off than on, and her cover grew thinner. She kept glancing out of the window, but could no longer see any blue uniforms. The last passenger to board was a fat man, whom she moved towards straightaway, taking cover behind him, keeping the doors in view.

A bell sounded and the train moved off. As it picked up speed, metre by metre, Alex felt her tension dissolve. She had shaken them off!

Suddenly she felt the cut on her hand throbbing again. The blood had already seeped through the temporary bandage Benny had tied an hour or so ago, and grief came over her like a wild animal. Tears streamed down her face and soon she was crying uncontrollably for the first time in years.

Only when she wiped the tears on her sleeve did she realise that everyone in the car was staring at her. 'What are you looking at?' she shouted, and the people, who had been gazing at her in sympathy, returned to whatever it was they were doing before.

2

That's what you got for being punctual: a wait. Rath's gaze flitted between his fingernails and the pictures on the wall. He spotted a grease stain on his jacket. He had been wearing the grey suit for too long. If he had known he was being summoned he'd have chosen the brown one, since it had been freshly laundered. At least his fingernails were clean.

Renate Greulich hammered at her typewriter as if she were the only person in the room.

'Dr Weiss is still in a meeting. Please take a seat,' was all she had said. So Rath had taken a seat, feeling as if he were in a doctor's waiting room about to receive bad news. He didn't know what exactly, only that it was sure to be bad.

When the bosses sent for him, it was usually trouble, although Rath couldn't remember a single occasion in the last few weeks when he had flouted the rules. He had only been back on duty for a week, after a fortnight's summer holiday. A few days in Cologne, then a week on the Baltic Sea with Charly. He—they—could have saved themselves the bother.

The telephone rang and Renate Greulich picked up. 'Yes, Herr Doktor,' she said, reaching for the file on her desk. She disappeared with it behind the padded door.

Rath gazed after the secretary and picked up a newspaper from the makeshift table. He leafed indifferently through the day's political issues, reparations disputes, austerity measures, until alighting on a headline in the regional section.

Late-night police chase in KaDeWe. Young intruder plunges to his death.

This was the case Gennat had mentioned at briefing: two jewel thieves caught red-handed in KaDeWe at the weekend, one of whom had launched an unsuccessful bid for freedom via the façade. The young lad, no more than sixteen or seventeen, was still to be identified. His accomplice had escaped with a portion of the spoils.

The way the article read, you'd think the police had hounded the boy to his death. That the pair had shut themselves in a department store to empty the jewellery displays didn't seem to concern the paper.

The door opened once more, only it wasn't Greulich who emerged, but a police officer, picture perfect in his freshly ironed and spotlessly clean blue uniform, shako wedged under his arm. The man knew how to appear before a deputy commissioner. Rath laid the newspaper over the grease stain on his suit as the officer nodded his head in greeting.

'What's the atmosphere like in there?' Rath asked.

'OK.' The officer gestured towards the paper. 'Have you seen the news?'

'Just looking now.'

'Then you can picture Dr Weiss's mood.' The officer appeared at a loss. 'I was in charge of the KaDeWe operation the night before last.'

'Nasty,' Rath said.

'A nightmare.'

'Don't take it to heart. Things like that happen every day.'

'Thanks, but I still need to go to Homicide.' The officer put on his shako. 'Why have you been summoned?'

'If only I knew.'

The officer tipped the peak of his shako by way of goodbye and disappeared into the corridor. Moments later, Renate Greulich reappeared and bade Rath enter. The deputy commissioner sat behind his desk, noting something down. His expression gave nothing away.

'Please take a seat,' he said, without looking up.

Rath sat and looked out of the window while Weiss calmly finished his notes. The crane in front of Alexanderhaus gleamed in the sunlight, leaving a cluster of reinforcing bars hanging weightless in the sky. Weiss snapped his notebook shut and gazed at Rath through thick lenses, like a senior teacher surveying an exam candidate.

'Inspector, am I right in thinking you have a brother in the United States?'

Rath had reckoned with all sorts of possibilities, but not this. 'Pardon me, Sir?'

'If my information is correct, your brother, Severin Rath, lives in America . . .'

'That's true, but . . .'

'. . . and you visited him there once . . .'

How had Weiss come by this information? No one knew about that trip, not even Rath's father, Engelbert, the police director, and he wasn't a man you kept secrets from. In the spring of 1923 Gereon had spent three months in the USA looking for his brother; his parents had thought he was on an exchange semester in Prague, thanks to the letters his friend Paul had posted from there. 'You're well informed,' Rath said.

'It's what I'm paid to be,' Weiss replied, without a trace of irony. 'You've heard of the Bureau of Investigation?'

'The American Federal Police . . .'

Weiss nodded almost imperceptibly and opened a thin file. 'I have a job for you, Inspector. A special assignment in which knowledge of American customs could be a distinct advantage. How's your English?'

Rath shrugged. 'OK, I think. The Yanks understood me anyway, and I understood them.' What the hell was Weiss driving at?

The deputy commissioner pushed the file across the table. 'This came through the ticker a few days ago,' he said.

Rath skimmed the first page. ABRAHAM GOLDSTEIN, PLACE OF BIRTH: BROOKLYN, NY. A profile. Weiss continued: 'Our American colleagues have warned us about this man. The Bureau believes he is a member of a New York gangster syndicate.'

'OK, but how does this concern us?'

Weiss raised his eyebrows before responding. 'Abraham Goldstein, nickname *Handsome Abe*, is on his way to Berlin. He went through customs at Bremerhaven yesterday evening.'

'If he's so dangerous, why did the Yanks let him leave in the first place?'

'Because they don't have a case against him. Goldstein was put on file a few times in his youth: larceny, criminal damage, grievous bodily harm, but since then nothing, not even a parking ticket. He's thought to be responsible for a number of underworld killings. Our American colleagues believe that he kills on behalf of Italian and Jewish gangster syndicates. The one thing no one disputes is that he has links to underworld heavyweights. Only, that isn't a crime.'

'Goldstein's Jewish?'

'Yes.' Weiss didn't bat an eyelid. As if it were unimportant—though of course it was anything but. A Jewish gangster in Berlin, that fact alone would be grist to the mill of the anti-Semites. Newspaper reports about the Sklarek Brothers' fraud had been full of anti-Semitic undertones. Suddenly Rath understood why Weiss himself had intervened.

'What's Goldstein doing in Berlin?' he asked. 'Any ideas?'

'None. The one thing we know for sure is that he *is* coming, on a tourist visa. Perhaps it's only to visit the Wintergarten or the Sportpalast, or he means to throw himself into the local nightlife, like the other tourists who come here because it's so cheap. Anything's possible.'

'Could he be taking care of a contract in Berlin? Eliminating someone who's making problems for the New Yorkers?'

Weiss adopted a sceptical expression. 'Links between local criminal circles and American gangster syndicates are not particularly well developed. Mostly drug-smuggling or alcohol. I can't believe that an American underworld feud would reach Europe.'

'Things aren't exactly peaceful here at the moment,' Rath said. 'If you think back to the last few weeks. Maybe one of our lot sent for him, to carry out a job . . .'

'There is tension in the city,' Weiss agreed. 'The Ringvereine know about Goldstein. Even before the Bureau got in contact, our underworld informants heard rumours that an American was expected in Berlin.'

'What are we supposed to do if the Yanks don't have anything on him?'

'Round the clock surveillance, and we want him to know it too. Make it clear he is being watched, that he can't so much as move without our knowledge. If he really has come to Berlin to kill someone, we have to show him that the best thing he can do is return straight home. Empty-handed.'

'With all due respect, Sir, isn't this a job for Warrants?'

'I'm certainly not about to discuss whose jurisdiction it falls under with you.' Weiss's voice took on a shrill, piercing tone like something from the parade ground. The man had served as an officer in the war and would brook no arguments.

'As you yourself have just observed,' he continued, 'we are talking about preventing a potential homicide. That alone ought to underline the importance of this assignment.' Rath nodded like a schoolboy. 'You're in charge of this operation. Round up a few men and get on your way. Goldstein has reserved a suite in the Excelsior. I understand you're familiar with it.'

Rath had stayed in the Excelsior for a time after arriving in Berlin two years before, but in the cheapest available single room. Weiss appeared to have done his research there too.

'Do you want me to greet him off the train with a bunch of flowers?'

'I don't care whether it's on the platform or at the hotel, so long as you make it clear that he is to behave himself in our city. He should . . .'

The telephone rang. Weiss picked up. 'What is it,' he said, annoyed.

Rath wasn't sure whether his audience with the deputy was over. He remained seated.

Weiss adopted a serious expression. 'I'll come out myself,' he said. 'Send for a car and let Heimannsberg know.' He hung up. 'I think we're finished here, Inspector. Now, get to work, and report to me tomorrow morning in person. I have to go to the university.' Clearly Weiss had been intending to leave it at that, but he must have registered Rath's quizzical expression. 'Student riot,' he said. 'The rector has requested police assistance.'

3

The Germans were strange, he decided. Everywhere he went, they wanted to see his passport: on the boat, in the harbour, on the train, and now in the hotel too. The head porter carefully entered his name, address and passport number into the big, black-leather guest register.

'We didn't expect you so early, Mister Goldstein,' the man said in English. His parting was so straight it might have been made with a ruler. 'But suite three-o-one is now ready for you.' He pronounced the name *Gollt-schtein*, like everyone in this country.

Goldstein pocketed his passport. 'Very kind, thank you.'

'You speak German!' The head porter raised his eyebrows as he waved a page boy over.

'Sure.'

The head porter handed the page the keys to the room. 'Three-o-one,' he said, and the boy stowed the suitcases onto a trolley.

'If you would care to follow me, Sir,' said the page, setting off for the lift. In his ill-fitting gold-braided livery, he looked like a monkey escaped from his organ grinder. Goldstein wondered why they hadn't given the boy, who wore a golden number thirty-seven on his cap, anything in his size.

It reminded him of his mother, Rahel Goldstein, who had made her only son wear his trousers for so long even the tramps would realise they were too small. The same Rahel Goldstein who left her dingy flat only to go to the synagogue or the market, and refused to learn the language of her adoptive country. Abe never understood why his parents had gone to America in the first place. Their existence had played out over such a tiny area that he wondered why they had chosen so big a country, so big a city, in which to live. He could never stand the confinement and, even as a little boy, had left the flat as often as possible until his mother's illness drove him onto the streets for good.

While Mother battled typhus and Father prayed for her salvation, Abe started hanging around with Moe and his gang by Williamsburg Bridge. They respected him, even if he was a few years younger. After Mother died, his father tried to pass him into the care of friends, then into a home, but Abe had resisted. Moe's gang was his family, and he didn't need anyone else. At fourteen Abe Goldstein earned his first paycheck, more in a single day than his father could scrape together in weeks. People in the neighbourhood had already started talking about him after Mother's funeral, which was the last time he had been to synagogue, and all the more when, on the occasion of Father's funeral, he had appeared drunk at the cemetery. They were *still* talking about him, too, though these days with respect, which was the only thing that mattered.

The lift sped upwards, barely making a sound. They made two stops, but only when the liftboy announced the third floor did number 37 turn his attention to the luggage trolley. Suite 301 wasn't too far from the lifts, just around the corner. The page opened the door and Goldstein stepped inside. Everything seemed to be in order. Exactly the level of comfort one would expect from the price category. A spacious, bright living room, big windows pointing towards the enormous station roof, immediately in front of them a large desk, and a comfortable, upholstered corner sofa against the wall. On the table was a fruit bowl, and, to the right, a double leaf door that led into the bedroom. The page had set the luggage down and was now waiting expectantly in the door, the flat of his hand facing discreetly upwards. Goldstein pressed a dollar note into the boy's hand—he still hadn't got around to trading his dollars for German money—and waited until the page had wished him a pleasant stay and departed.

At the window he lit a Camel cigarette. Clouds were building over the station roof, but the sun had fought its way through and was shining on the crowds in front of the round brick arches. People were streaming outside, with and without suitcases, waving taxis over or heading for the bus stop and tram. So, this was Berlin. He blew smoke against the glass and gazed across the city. Not knowing exactly what awaited him filled him with unease. Had he really made the long journey just to see a man about whom the only thing he knew was his name?

Hearing a noise from the bedroom he pressed the cigarette into the ashtray and reached for his waistband, still not accustomed to being unarmed. He took the paperweight from the desk and tiptoed towards the connecting door, bronze bird ready to strike. It seemed unlikely that it was one of Fat Moe's boys. The man's influence didn't stretch this far, but Abe Goldstein had never lost anything by exercising caution when the situation demanded. He looked through the half-open door. Against the end wall was an enormous bed, covered with a champagne-coloured satin duvet and flanked by two night-tables. To the right, next to the dressing table, a door led to the bathroom. It was open, and in the frame he could make out a nicely rounded ass belonging to a stooped figure in a black dress and white apron. A chambermaid, running behind schedule, was draping white hand-towels over a stand. He savoured the view for a few seconds before audibly clearing his throat. The maid wheeled around, but Goldstein could see from her eyes that she had wanted to be caught. She was out for a tip.

'My apologies, Sir.' She curtseyed and gazed at the floor, but there was a cheeky glint in her eyes when she looked up again. 'Excuse me, Sir. I'm Marion, your chambermaid,' she said in English. 'Ihr Zimmermädchen.'

She clearly knew that this latest guest was American, and her English wasn't bad.

'I appreciate chambermaids who go about their duties conscientiously,' he said in German. 'Don't let me keep you from your work.'

'Actually, I'm finished here.' She gave him another of her perfectly innocent glances. 'If my services are no longer required.'

He fetched his wad of dollar bills and handed her three notes. 'I'm sure I'll call on you again.'

'Ask for Marion. I have to go now.'

She pocketed the notes as if a tip of that size were the most natural thing in the world, and wedged a stack of hand-towels under her arm. Her profile wasn't bad either. She brushed casually against him as she squeezed past, and Goldstein felt the blood pulsing between his legs. He followed her into the drawing room, but she had already opened the door to the corridor.

'Marion!' he said. She came to a halt in the doorframe and waited. An elderly gentleman passed behind her along the corridor and squinted over curiously. To be on the safe side, Goldstein switched to English. 'May I see you again, Marion?' he said. 'You know, I could use some company in this town . . .'

She stood in the door and gazed up at him with her big blue eyes, in such a way that he was suddenly very aware of his erection. No doubt she could see it too. Not that he minded.

'I have to go, but I finish at four.'

'I'll be here. Just give me a knock.'

4

Rigaer Strasse was not a pretty street, but this was its ugliest point, right here. It was as if Kalli had deliberately chosen the lousiest spot in a district not famed for its charm. Alex had taken the 9 to Baltenplatz and walked the rest of the way; now she put down the heavy bag and stood in front of the display window. EBERHARD KALLWEIT BOUGHT AND SOLD was painted in white across the glass. All manner of junk was gathering dust behind the windowpane: a gramophone, a typewriter, an electric vacuum cleaner, a telephone, four chairs that weren't part of a set, and a rubber plant. None of it had been sold in the months Alex had been coming here. Kalli made his money from items that weren't on display, and didn't show up in the accounts.

There were no customers inside. She picked up her bag and climbed the stairs.

A rasping, high-pitched ring announced her as she pressed down on the door handle and entered. Kalli was lurking behind the counter in his grey overalls. His best shopkeeper's grin froze when he recognised her. For a fraction of a second, he seemed paralysed by the shock, but then he said quietly, as if afraid somebody might hear. 'Are you mad, coming here like this? What if I have customers?'

'You weren't at Krehmann's yesterday.'

'You've got some nerve! You went to Krehmann's after everything that's happened? After that monumental cock-up of yours! The police are after you. You realise that, don't you?'

'Cock-up?' Alex couldn't believe it. Kalli was an arsehole. 'A cock-up, that's what you're calling it? Benny's dead for fuck's sake.'

'What's he doing scrambling about on department store fronts?'

'Trying not to get caught. If that pig hadn't kicked him off, he'd still be alive.'

'What the hell are you talking about?'

'There was a cop after him. He stepped on Benny's fingers until he couldn't hold on anymore. That's why he fell. That pig killed him, and I had to stand by and watch.'

Kalli shook his head. 'I should never have let myself get involved with you kids.' He seemed to be speaking to the cash register. 'I ought to have known it would go belly-up.'

'*You're* the one who sent us to KaDeWe,' she shouted. 'We've never had any trouble otherwise. There were no cops in Tietz or Karstadt. It was *you* who insisted we turn over KaDeWe.'

'What are you trying to say?'

'That you sent us in because you wanted the goods.' She placed the bag on the counter. 'And we got them for you.'

Kalli snatched the bag from the counter. 'Are you crazy, walking around here with that? Coming into my shop?'

'Since you weren't at Krehmann's, I thought I'd bring it round. Jewellery and watches, as agreed.'

'The agreement was you wouldn't get caught.'

'They caught Benny. They didn't catch me.'

Kalli gave a rueful shrug. 'What am I supposed to do with all this? It's worthless after all the commotion. No one can shift it, not even me.'

'Commotion?' Alex shouted louder. 'Benny died for this and you're telling me you don't want it? Am I hearing you right?'

'Don't get so worked up, Alex. Let's take a look, but not here, out back.'

The little room behind the shop smelled of onions and beer. Kalli cleared away a plate and two bottles and laid the bag on the table. From the breast pocket of his jacket he fetched a battered leather case, opened it and fumbled out a pair of glasses. In his overalls and crooked wire-rimmed spectacles he looked like a mad chemistry professor. He sat at the table and held each watch in front of his lenses.

'Only watches,' he said after a while, sounding disappointed. 'No jewellery?'

'The cops have it. It was in Benny's bag.'

Kalli shook his head. 'That stuff about the cops killing Benny. Is it really true?'

'I saw it myself. And . . . he told me before he died. Benny told me the man trampled on his fingers until he couldn't hold on.'

Kalli considered a moment. 'Better keep it to yourself. You shouldn't spread that sort of story around; the cops won't stand for it.' He stood up so unexpectedly that Alex gave a start. 'Come on,' he said. 'I don't want things to be awkward between us.'

She followed him back into the shop where he pulled a lever on the cash register. The drawer sprang open with a loud *pling*. He fumbled a brown note out and passed it across the counter. 'Here! Because it's you, and because of the business with Benny.'

'A twenty?' she said. Werner von Siemens was staring back at her. 'You can't be serious. You gave us more for the junk from Tietz!'

'I'm doing you a favour. No one else will take it off you. Not after everything that's happened. Do you know how hot it is? It'll probably get me into trouble, but since it's you . . .' He waved the twenty. 'Come on, take the money and that'll be that.'

Twenty marks. Kalli would probably get that much for a single watch when he sold it on, and there were at least fifty in the bag. On the other hand, he was right. If he didn't take the watches she'd have to sit on them. She swallowed her rage, took the twenty and sneaked a peek inside Kalli's cash register. It was full. Maybe she could get the money due to her by other means. She stuffed the note into her jacket, and saw Kalli looking on in satisfaction. She wasn't finished with him yet.

'One more thing,' Kalli said, grinning like a hyena as Alex reached the door. 'I really don't need any more trouble with the police. So . . . do me favour and don't show your face around here for a while.'

We'll see about that you arsehole, Alex thought and nodded, we'll see about that.

5

Rath stood before a half-naked man, which so confused him he was no longer certain he was in the right place, although reception had given him exactly this room number. The man had an extremely muscular upper body which he seemed to enjoy showing off. Naked save for a hotel towel wrapped around his waist, he looked at least as surprised as Rath himself. He had clearly been expecting someone else, someone whom it was OK to meet clad only in a towel and with hair still wet from the shower. Had he already been accosted by one of the whores at Friedrichstrasse station, or did he have a girlfriend in Berlin?

Hand in front of his mouth, Rath gave a slight cough, an irritating habit in embarrassing or unpleasant situations that had been drummed into him as a child. Somehow he couldn't rid himself of it, even if it made him feel like a butler who has surprised his master in the throes of lovemaking.

'Abraham Goldstein?'

'Gold-sstiehn.'

The man in the towel didn't look dangerous exactly. He appeared athletic, and there was an ironic glint in his eyes, as if he didn't take life entirely seriously.

Rath flashed his badge. 'German police. May I come in, Sir?'

Goldstein stepped to one side and opened the door fully. Rath entered and looked around. The suite was elegantly arranged: damask wallpaper, mahogany furniture, soft carpets, and roughly four or five times bigger than the four-mark-fifty room Rath had taken some two years before. Probably five times as expensive too. At least.

Rath cleared his throat, continuing in English: 'Well, Mister Goldstein, I have to inform you that the German police are legitimated to . . .'

Goldstein, lifting a packet of cigarettes from the table, interrupted. 'I was hoping you were room service.'

Rath was surprised. The man spoke almost accent-free German, sounding nothing like the American tourists who seemed to chew, rather than speak, the language. 'I'm afraid I must disappoint you there,' he said. 'I come bearing neither food nor drink.'

Goldstein placed a cigarette between his lips and offered the carton to Rath. Was this bribery or could he accept? *Camel* read the inscription, and Rath was too curious about American cigarettes to turn him down. Goldstein gave him a light.

'So, Officer,' the American said, 'what brings you to me?'

'Inspector,' Rath corrected. 'Inspector Rath.' He almost added *Homicide*, as was his custom, but realised, just in time, that he was here in a different capacity. 'You speak German?'

'Thanks to my mother.' Goldstein shrugged. 'So, please explain what the Berlin Police wants from me.'

'Fundamentally it wants the same from you as it does from anyone else: that you behave yourself accordingly in our city.'

Goldstein exhaled smoke through his nostrils, the smile at the corner of his mouth having suddenly disappeared. 'Do you make this request of everyone, or is it just Americans?'

'You are one of the chosen few. I hope you appreciate the honour.'

'Speaking of behavioural codes, I'm just out of the shower. You'll permit me to get dressed? Take a seat.' Goldstein disappeared into the adjoining room.

Rath remained standing, keeping an eye on the bedroom window through the half-open door. He wasn't expecting a bolt for freedom, and he certainly wasn't expecting Goldstein to shoot his way out of trouble, but he decided, nevertheless, to unfasten his shoulder holster and take out his service weapon, a Walther PP, issued as a replacement for his Mauser the year before. He released the safety catch and placed it, together with his right hand, in his coat pocket. Just in case. Smoking with his left hand felt a little unusual, but it was fine.

He had just stubbed out the Camel when Goldstein reappeared in a thin, light-grey summer suit. Rath kept his hand tight on the pistol, finger poised over the trigger, but the American seemed determined to keep things peaceful.

'So, here I am. Won't you have a seat? You haven't even taken off your hat.'

'I prefer to stand.'

'I don't know what you've heard about me or my country, but rest assured you can take your hand out of your pocket. I'm unarmed.' Rath felt like a schoolboy who hadn't concealed his crib sheet properly. 'You still haven't told me the purpose of your visit,' Goldstein said, lighting a cigarette. This time Rath declined.

'I'd like to ask a few questions, that's all.'

'You do like keeping people in suspense. Ask away.'

'You are Abraham Goldstein from New York?'

'Williamsburg. It's part of Brooklyn.'

'Why are you in Berlin, Mister Goldstein?'

'Why don't you look in the guest register at reception?'

'I want to hear it from you.'

'I'm a tourist, exploring Germany's beautiful capital city.'

'There are no other reasons for your visit?'

'Such as?'

'Perhaps you've been hired to kill someone.'

Goldstein, who had just taken a drag on his cigarette, looked as if he had misheard. 'I beg your pardon? You have too much imagination, Officer.'

'You've been implicated in five separate murder investigations in your home country.'

'Yet I'm standing here before you now. What does that tell you?'

'That you have a good lawyer.' Rath opened the brown briefcase and removed an ink pad and fingerprinting sheet.

Goldstein stared at the form with the ten consecutively numbered boxes. 'What the hell is that?' he asked, switching to English.

Well, my arrogant friend, Rath thought, it seems as if we've thrown you after all. 'Herr Abraham Goldstein,' he said, formal as a bailiff, 'the Berlin police commissioner has invested in me the power to take your fingerprints. Perhaps we should sit down . . .'

'Do you behave like this with every foreigner?'

Rath opened the ink pad's metal lid. 'No.'

'To what do I owe the honour then?'

'Mister Goldstein, if I may speak openly, Berlin is not exactly thrilled at the prospect of your visit . . .'

'You shouldn't believe everything Hoover's men tell you. Do you think I'm a gangster?'

'It doesn't matter what I think. Your convictions justify police measures of this kind. I came here to spare you any unpleasantness. If you like I can pack everything up and order you to appear at the station tomorrow. The waiting times in ED are notorious. You'll want to take a few puzzle books with you.'

Goldstein grinned. 'I see you know all the tricks.' He took off his jacket, rolled up his shirtsleeves and sat at the table. 'OK, let's get it over with. But if you're planning to do this sort of thing in future, come a little earlier. Then I won't have to shower twice.'

'Cleanliness is a virtue,' Rath said, taking the American's right hand and pressing the thumb first on the ink pad and then inside the appropriate box on the form. A good, clean print. ED, the police identification service, would be pleased, even if Rath hoped they'd never have to use it. The fingerprint business was meant to show Goldstein who was in charge, not that he seemed greatly impressed.

'What happens to that sheet when we're finished?' he asked, sounding like a patient who wants to know his blood pressure.

'It's added to our collection,' Rath said, taking the next print. 'And if your prints turn up on anything even halfway suspicious, you'll be behind bars. Simple as that.'

'As I said, I'm a tourist, here to explore your city.'

'Then you'll have no objection to police observing you as you go about it.'

'Pardon me?' Goldstein pulled his hand away before Rath could press his already blackened pinkie onto the page.

'No need to get worked up. We're keeping an eye on you for your own safety. It shouldn't put you out in the slightest, so long as you've nothing to hide.'

'What if it does put me out?! Fucking unbelievable! Is this some sort of police state? I thought you'd driven your Kaiser out and founded a democracy!'

'The safety of our . . . tourists matters a great deal to us.'

Goldstein gazed at Rath as if sizing him up. 'So, I have my own babysitter, is that right? One with a piece, to boot.'

'If you like.'

Goldstein shook his head. 'What happens if I give you the slip? Will you shoot me?'

'You won't.'

A smile reappeared on Goldstein's face. 'Finally, an offer I can work with,' he said, stretching out a blackened right hand.

6

The number of people passing through these revolving doors! Just looking made you dizzy. For a while Rath had counted bald men, then moustachioed men. When that became boring he counted bowlegged women. You had to do something to pass the time—and he had already read all the papers. He still had to keep an eye on the hallway, of course, in case the Yank took a stroll, but it seemed as if Abe Goldstein was happy as Larry in his suite.

Every few minutes some helpful soul would change the ashtrays, so Rath lost track of how many cigarettes he had smoked. His supplies, at any rate, were dwindling. Only two were left in the packet, but the Excelsior housed a good range of tobacco products.

His attempt to intimidate the show-off Yank had failed spectacularly, and he was annoyed. Goldstein had made fun of *him* instead, by proposing a wager. As if they were playing chase, hide-and-seek or—more appropriately—cops and robbers.

Things weren't looking good. Rath lit his second to last Overstolz. The coffee in the gold-rimmed cup had long since grown cold. He took a sip and leafed through the *Vossische Zeitung* without reading it, until he grew tired even of that and placed the paper next to the cup. A boy immediately sprang forth, smoothing and folding the crumpled newspaper so that it looked as good as new, and replacing it beside the others. Rath stubbed out his cigarette and stood up. The porter gazed at him expectantly.

'Ah, Inspector.' His voice dripped with kindness turned sour. 'What can I do for you? Would you like to take another glance at the guest register? Or might I reserve you a room, since you are clearly intent on staying a little longer?'

'Don't put yourself out. Your hallway is perfectly agreeable. Very comfy chairs.'

'Where the comfort of our guests is concerned we spare neither trouble nor expense.'

'I should hope not.'

The porter leaned in a little and lowered his voice. 'Inspector, won't you please tell me what Mister Goldstein has done to attract the attention of the police?'

Rath leaned in too. 'I'm afraid that isn't any of your concern.'

'If one of our guests is suspected of a crime, we ought to know about it. I shall have to inform our in-house detective. We're talking about the safety of our hotel here!'

Rath nodded. 'Quite right. Fetch your detective here, but first, I'll make a telephone call.'

'Should I put it on your account?'

'If you would be so kind,' Rath smiled pleasantly. Four coffees, a sandwich and a telephone call. Driving up his expenses bill was about the only pleasure left to him, and there was still a big carton of Overstolz to be added.

A short time later, he stood in one of the telephone booths, staring through the glass door, listening for the connection. He still had the lifts in his sights, as well as the great revolving door leading onto Stresemannstrasse. No one was home at Spenerstrasse, so he asked to be put through to Lichtenberg District Court and Fräulein Ritter.

'Good thing you called,' Charly said. 'There's trouble.'

'What sort of trouble?'

'Weber's just back from holiday . . .'

Special Counsel Albrecht Weber was Charly's superior at the District Court.

'So?'

'Weber isn't quite so taken with your dog's charms as the rest of them here . . . Gereon, I can't take Kirie into work anymore. From tomorrow you'll have to start taking her to Alex again.' That was all he needed. 'Let's talk about it at dinner. There's something I need to speak to you about anyway. Will you be home on time?'

'That's why I'm calling,' he said. 'I'll be about an hour late. Weiss has lumped this surveillance on me.'

'The deputy himself? Go on, I'm all ears.'

Charly couldn't hide her curiosity. Once upon a time she had worked in Homicide too. As a stenographer, nominally, but Gennat and Böhm had been only too happy to rely on her investigative acumen, and had deployed the prospective lawyer accordingly.

Rath told her about Goldstein and his assignment.

'Sounds like a punishment,' she said.

'I didn't do anything, honest.'

'Perhaps Weiss wants to make you atone for your youthful misdeeds.'

'I thought I'd already paid my dues.'

About a year before, Rath had been subjected to disciplinary proceedings. He had got off lightly, mainly because Gennat had put in a good word, but his scheduled promotion to chief inspector had been temporarily put on hold. Not even political support from the Prussian Interior Ministry, prompted by Konrad Adenauer, a personal friend of his father, had been able to change that.

'I have to hang up now, Charly. I'm wanted here. See you tonight.'

There was a man at reception, whose appearance didn't quite match the elegance of his light-brown summer suit. Although the suit looked tailormade, it flapped at the edges whenever its bearer moved. He didn't look anything like the veteran cop Rath had been expecting, more like a starving, unemployed bookkeeper. The porter pointed with his chin towards the telephone booth. Rath left the booth and went over. The man's handshake was firmer than expected.

'I'm the hotel detective,' said the hotel detective. 'Grunert. And you're from the . . . CID?' He spoke the last word quietly, as if it were something to be ashamed of. 'Could I see your identification?'

'Certainly.' Rath fumbled the document out of his bag.

The hotel detective unfolded it with nimble fingers and compared the photograph with the man, declaring himself satisfied and returning it to Rath. 'You understand that we have a legitimate interest in knowing why the police are here. Herr Teubner tells me that your attention is reserved for a particular guest. The American in 301?'

'That's right. Abraham Goldstein. But don't worry, the man knows that the police . . .'

'Herr Rath?' Teubner, the porter, interrupted them. He stood behind his counter, holding the receiver in his hand. 'My apologies. Telephone for you, Herr Rath. It seems to be rather urgent. A Herr Gräf . . .'

Rath took the receiver. 'Reinhold?' he said into the mouthpiece.

'Gereon, you were right!' The detective sounded a little harried. 'Goldstein has taken the lift downstairs and is heading for the tunnel.'

7

It took Kalli a moment to realise what had happened. The pain in his skull was resounding, like the noise of the S-Bahn if you stood directly under the bridge. Then he noticed that someone was singing. He recognised the voice, but couldn't see who it was and, when he opened his eyes, saw nothing but a blurry, undefined, dirty grey. He had to force himself to focus, at last making out the familiar grey overalls he wore in the shop, covered in blood. He was staring at his own lap. A record was playing, and now he recognised the song thundering from the loudspeakers, much louder than he was accustomed to.

A blue figure was sitting on the sofa next to the record player, where he usually took his nap. With the face, the memory came flooding back.

A cop had appeared in his shop, someone he had never seen before, neither here nor in the neighbourhood—and Kalli knew all the cops who walked the beat. A newbie, he thought at first, who would learn in time that it was best not to sniff around in here if you didn't want to make trouble with Berolina. He had taken a wristwatch from the shelf, a cheap piece of rubbish, nothing like as elegant as the pieces Alex had lifted from KaDeWe. The cop hadn't responded to his friendly greeting, merely held the watch in his hand, gripping the strap so that the dial now faced him, and gaping at the inert clock-hand as if this piece of crap, whose provenance Kalli knew absolutely nothing about, was the most valuable item under the sun, before drawing closer to the counter.

'Bet this is stolen,' were his precise words as he arrived, nothing more, and Kalli felt his hunch confirmed: a greenhorn who needed to be taught some manners. One phone call to Lenz, and the matter would be resolved. Berolina would cut this big mouth down to size, no need to feel intimidated, but then something unexpected happened.

The cop, now standing right in front of the counter with an indefinable grin on his face, struck him without warning with his right hand, using the watch as brass knuckles. The first blow landed in the middle of Kalli's face, and the shopkeeper heard his nose break and felt blood streaming out of him. He tumbled against the shelves, still not sure what had happened. The cop pulled him up brutally by his overalls and struck him again on the point of the chin. After a brief flash of pain, everything went black.

He couldn't say how long he had been unconscious. Light spilled in from the shop through the crack in the door, so it must still be daytime. He lifted his head slowly, carefully, to avoid exacerbating the pain. The cop had made himself comfortable on the sofa, having removed the shako from his head and placed it beside him. This man sitting on his sofa, in his back room, listening to his music, did he have any idea what Berolina would do to him when they found out?

Kalli couldn't believe he had let himself be caught unawares like this. He thought he knew all the tricks, thought himself better than all the ne'er-do-wells here in the Samariterviertel. No one would dare rob his little shop. It was no secret that he kept a loaded war pistol underneath the counter. This cop either didn't know or didn't care.

Kalli tried to speak, but his tongue stuck to his gums. He could only utter a squelching sort of groan.

'Well, you bent Jews' sow,' the cop said. 'Awake at last?'

Kalli had to gather enough spit to get his tongue moving again. 'I'm not a Jew,' he protested, as if that was the most pressing issue to clarify. He was still thinking about the stupidity of his response when the cop planted himself in front of him.

'Then what are you doing in a goddamned Jew shop?' Kalli could smell the sweat in the fabric of his uniform.

Again, the blow came without warning, this time to the solar plexus. Kalli felt like he was going to choke, and instinctively tried to protect his stomach with his hands, but couldn't move. The man must have bound him.

'What's the big idea?' he gasped. 'What the hell is going on?'

The next blow struck him in exactly the same location. The gag reflex turned Kalli's stomach upside down and a part of its contents landed in his mouth. He swallowed the sour-tasting gruel and suppressed a fresh urge to choke. What kind of arsehole was he dealing with here?

'First rule: only speak when spoken to,' the cop said.

Kalli waited to be spoken to, but the man moved silently to the record player, removing the needle so that a violent scratch echoed through the loudspeaker.

Then a question did come, but not from the cop who had retaken his seat next to the shako. It came from a man who must have been standing at the door leading out back.

'Why do you think we're here, Kalli?' said a familiar voice.

Kalli turned as far as he could, but it wasn't enough to see his interrogator. The thing that startled him most was that they knew his name, even his nickname. All at once, Eberhard Kallweit knew he was in serious trouble. He had misread the situation. The cop was just muscle. Kalli's real problem was the other man, the owner of the voice. The nameless man, whom Kalli had always called *Stephan*, after the telephone exchange through which he contacted him. How the hell had he found his shop?

Lenz or Berolina must have ratted him out, otherwise he'd never have been listening to that voice within his own four walls, unless through a telephone cable. He didn't know anything about *Stephan*, didn't know what he looked like or what he was called, but he had to be a cop, a cop that Berolina trusted and probably even paid.

Lenz had given him the number to get rid of Alex and Benny, and Kalli had called it. *Stephan* hadn't identified himself on the line, and Kalli hadn't divulged anything, not even just now, when, after Alex's surprise visit, he had gone straight over to the S-Bahn station, and asked to be put through again: *STEPHAN* 1701. It was the only link to *Stephan* he had. He almost gave a start when the man picked up after the first ring. Then, drawing courage from the fact that he couldn't be seen, he proceeded to kick up a fuss. He had been shocked by the news of Benny's death, putting two and two together that morning as he leafed through the paper. Alex had merely confirmed his suspicions with her version of events later that day. He hadn't wanted the boy to die; nor, surely, had Berolina. No, it was the fault of the cops alone. It was they who would have to pay!

Stephan had been angry from the start, but seeing as he was invisible, Kalli didn't care. 'Why the hell are you calling me?' he had said. 'It's over. You don't know this number anymore.'

'That wasn't what we agreed! They were supposed to end up behind bars. No one said anything about killing them.'

'What was *supposed* to happen is none of your concern. The boy died. It was an accident.'

'It was no accident, it was murder. I've got witnesses. I know reporters who'd pay a pretty penny for a story like that. *Police officer murders minor!*'

The momentary silence at the end of the line confirmed what Kalli knew already. Alex must have been telling the truth.

'You've had your money, now you're out.'

'Maybe it wasn't enough.'

The voice was silent for a moment. 'Let's talk about that,' it said meekly, as if assailed by a guilty conscience. 'Where shall we meet?'

'Meet? You must be joking. I'll call you.' With that, Kalli hung up. There was still time to decide how much to ask for, and how it should be delivered.

If he had known the consequences of that brief telephone conversation, he'd have closed his shop for a few weeks and driven to his brother's place in the country. Instead, he was tightly bound in the backroom of his own shop, cursing the day he had ratted on Alex and Benny for a few measly pennies. All because they had become a nuisance to Berolina: two street urchins who had grown too big for their boots, cleaning out the city's department stores, making the fuzz jumpy and forcing prices down. Berolina was a more important business partner than Alex and Benny. A few years in the can wouldn't do them any harm, Kalli had thought.

'I've never known you so quiet, Kalli. Normally you'd talk the hind leg off a donkey. Or do you need a telephone to speak? You should have bought yourself one, then you wouldn't have to traipse all the way to the S-Bahn station.'

The voice was now directly behind him, just as calm as it had been on the telephone but a thousand times more threatening.

'Your friend here smashes my face in if I say anything. Is this a new police tactic?'

'The police *are* experimenting with new tactics, but I'm not about to discuss them with you. I assume you know why I'm here.'

'My telephone call just now?' Kalli shook his head indignantly, as if in denial of this whole scene, this whole situation. 'It was just a little fun.'

'I didn't hear you laughing.'

'I'm not about to rat anyone out. I've never blabbed. Ask anyone in the neighbourhood.'

'You're joking, aren't you? Should I be laughing?'

'Those two brats. That was different. They were criminals. I've got no intention of talking, believe me. I'd be getting myself into all kinds of trouble.'

It took a moment for the voice to respond. 'Do you know what?' it said. 'I actually believe you. You won't go to the papers, I'm one hundred percent sure of that.'

Kalli felt almost euphoric. 'No, I won't. Absolutely not. I don't even know anyone there.'

Stephan fell silent again, and Kalli felt as uneasy as he had at the start of the conversation. 'What else do you want from me?' he asked. 'Untie me. I'm thirsty.'

'One last thing, then you can have something to drink.' By the sound of his voice, *Stephan* must have been back by the door. 'You mentioned a witness. Give me a name, and you'll be rid of me. My friend here too.'

Kalli gazed confused at the cop, who had got up from the sofa again and started looking at the photos on the wall.

'You meant the other boy, didn't you?' the man at the door continued. 'The one who escaped. Did he come here? Try to make some money? Is he the one who's been spreading these tall tales?'

They didn't know Alex was a girl. Stupid cops, so full of their own importance! Kalli would've liked nothing more than to laugh out loud, but was prevented by the feeling of helplessness growing inside of him. Why didn't they untie him? It wasn't as if he was going to escape!

'The other boy?' he said, shrugging his shoulders—so far as he could with his hands tied. 'No, he hasn't been here. He probably knows not to show his face.'

'Why is it I don't believe you?' Though Kalli couldn't see him, he was certain that *Stephan* was shaking his head. 'Not that it matters. Just tell me where I can find the boy. That's all I need to know.'

'No idea. I don't know the brats myself. They only sold me stuff that one time. It's not as if they left a forwarding address.'

The man behind him said nothing more. The cop, however, ceased looking at the photo and moved towards the record player, dropping the tone arm on the record so that it made a hideous sound as it jumped up and down, before locating the groove. The bastard! Destroying his records! And so damn loud! Finally the cop found the volume control. Only, he didn't turn it down, as Kalli had expected, but up, until it couldn't go any higher. *Adieu, mein kleiner Gardeoffizier, adieu, adieu* . . . Kalli had never heard Richard Tauber sing so loud. The cop drew nearer and grinned.

8

With its tooting cars and rumbling buses, the cacophony on Strese-mannstrasse was a thousand times preferable than the soporific murmur in the hotel hall. Behind the trees on Askanischer Platz the brick colossus of Anhalter Bahnhof rose into the grey-blue sky.

Rath crossed over, keeping the two stairways that led onto the street in view. One of them was right outside the hotel, the second by the southeast corner of the station. They weren't steps down to the U-Bahn station, but exits from the pedestrian tunnel, which connected the Excelsior with An-halter Bahnhof. The tunnel was the hotel's pride and joy. No brochure omit-ted it, and Goldstein had discovered it on his very first day . . . well, good for him, but luckily Rath had stationed Gräf there.

He was wondering where Goldstein might have got to, when he emerged from the ground on Möckernstrasse, right by the station. The Yank was wearing the same outfit as before, a light, sand-coloured suit, matching hat and pale trenchcoat. Having reached the top of the stairs, he came to a halt and looked around. Rath made no attempt to conceal himself. If Goldstein saw him he would perhaps give up and return to the hotel.

The American was already making for the taxi stand outside the station when Gräf emerged, a little out of breath, searching for his target. Rath in-tercepted him.

'Looks like our man's about to take a taxi,' he said. 'I'll stay on him, you go back to the hotel. Plisch and Plum will take over in just under an hour.'

Gräf nodded and made an about-turn.

When Rath turned to face the taxi stand, Goldstein was gone. At the same moment, a premium-class taxi detached itself from the line and rolled towards Stresemannstrasse, where a number of cabs were filtering into the moving traffic. Rath made out a sand-coloured hat in the backseat; indeed, thought for a moment that Goldstein had briefly raised his hand, as if waving.

He made a note of the taxi number and sprinted for his car, which was parked by the station. By the time he'd started it, Goldstein's taxi was turning onto Stresemannstrasse, going towards Potsdamer Platz. Rath overtook an Opel looking for a parking spot and followed the taxi. He had a vehicle in his sights without quite knowing if it was Goldstein's taxi or not and, metre by metre, was drawing nearer. At Potsdamer Platz they stopped at a red light. Rath was so close he could read the number: 7685.

The light jumped to green, and on they went down Bellevuestrasse, across Kemperplatz and into Tiergartenstrasse. Rath stayed with them until, just as he decided that the American must be heading for the west, the taxi turned right, without indicating, towards the Grosse Stern. Goldstein had seen him.

They tried to lose him at the roundabout, first going all the way round several times, only to turn suddenly onto Charlottenburger Allee. Rath stayed with them, and caught them again by the Brandenburger Tor. How much was Goldstein paying the driver, he wondered. Refusing to be shaken off, he followed the crazed taxi further east, both drivers flouting every traffic regulation under the sun.

After three-quarters of an hour and an odyssey through Weissensee and Pankow, the wild chase was suddenly over. Having just turned onto a side street in deepest Wedding, the taxi came to a halt so abruptly on the kerbstone that Rath almost kept driving. He parked on the other side of the road, keeping the taxi in view. The meter must have clocked up an astronomical sum. Goldstein got out, and looked around, as if checking he was in the right place, before putting on his hat and marching purposefully towards a pub on the corner. He opened the door and disappeared inside. The taxi stayed where it was, engine running.

Rath got out and crossed the street, keeping the pub door in view, and held his badge against the taxi window. The driver wound down the window.

'Yes, Inspector?'

'Did your passenger say how long you had to wait?'

'He did.'

'So, when's he coming back?'

The man shrugged. 'No idea.'

'Did he or didn't he tell you how long you had to wait?'

'Take it easy, man. He said I should wait until the meter shows twenty.'

'What the hell does that mean?'

'Beats me. Only thing I know is it's at twelve fifty. He's already paid, so here I am waiting, and that's that.' Rath slammed the roof in rage and turned away.

The name of the pub hardly inspired confidence: Rote Laterne. The Red Lantern. A fug of beer met him as he entered the half-darkness, making out a lounge that stretched into infinity, a dark tunnel in which the bar shone like a promise. A few male guests sat in silence. One of them was barely capable of keeping himself upright, but even he turned his head to look. Rath couldn't see the Yank anywhere. The woman behind the bar continued to tap beer without looking up.

'A man must have come through this way,' he said. It wasn't a good idea to show his badge here. He turned to the barmaid. 'Did a man come through here?'

The woman, who seemed a little fragile, gave a slow, almost imperceptible nod. 'A while ago.' She gestured towards the back. 'Asked for the toilets.'

The narrow, dark corridor reeked of piss. Rath held his breath and flung open the toilet door, not expecting to find Goldstein by the urinal. He quickly made sure the cubicle was also empty and continued on his way to the courtyard. No trace. He hurried through a large archway leading onto *Reinickendorfer Strasse*, a wide street with lots of pedestrians, and spotted him there. The light-coloured hat was too elegant for a neighbourhood like this, where most people wore plain caps. Goldstein was making for Nettelbeckplatz, crossing the motorway just before the railway bridge. For a moment, Rath thought he was headed for the S-Bahn station, but he turned into Lindower Strasse, which looked just as run-down as the street where the taxi was waiting. Had he taken a wrong turn?

Yet Goldstein didn't seem like a lost tourist. He strode purposefully towards Müllerstrasse and descended the steps to the U-Bahn. Rath had to increase his pace to keep up, and saw him again on the platform, just as a train was approaching.

Goldstein grinned without, however, making any attempt to climb aboard. Rath stayed close to a door, ready to jump in if he had to. The stationmaster's 'Keep back!' came through the loudspeakers and had the effect of a starting pistol on Goldstein. He dived into the train, and Rath did likewise, just making it into third-class as the train started and the doors engaged.

'Are you daft or something?' grumbled an ill-tempered worker, whose foot Rath had trampled. 'Pay attention, can't you?'

'Sorry,' Rath mumbled. The next station was *Schwartzkopffstrasse*; they were heading south. Rath poked his head out of the door, but Goldstein didn't get off. There was no other way of keeping the Yank in view. He was sitting in second-class and there was no connecting door. He still hadn't got off when the 'Keep back' sounded. Only at the last moment did Rath pull his head in.

'You're a strange one,' the worker said. 'Don't know whether you're coming or going.'

The man got out at Stettiner Bahnhof, leaving Rath in peace. The rest of the passengers looked at him quizzically when, with each new station, he moved to the door, blocking the path of those boarding and alighting and earning himself a few shoves. Goldstein didn't dismount until Kochstrasse.

Goldstein waited for him at the foot of the steps. 'Well, Inspector,' he said. 'This Berlin of yours is a lovely city.'

They climbed the stairs, gangster and police inspector together.

'If you want a guided tour,' Rath said, 'I'd recommend one of Käse's travel buses. You'll see more for less money.'

'I'll remember that. Will you be joining me?'

Rath gave a sour smile.

They reached Friedrichstrasse. Dusk was falling and the first shops had switched on their neon signs.

'Will you escort me back to the hotel?' Goldstein asked. 'It shouldn't be too far from here, the taxi driver said.'

'I'll do anything I can to make your stay in our city as unpleasant as possible.'

Goldstein shook his head. 'Is that the famous Berlin hospitality?'

'We don't like your sort here. This isn't Chicago.'

'So I'm a bogeyman and this is a city full of angels. Is that it?'

'All I want is for you not to get away. As long as I manage that, I'm happy.'

At Wilhelmstrasse, Goldstein stopped at the corner outside the Prinz-Albrecht-Palais. He tapped a Camel out of the carton and lit it before replying. 'Who says I'm trying to get away, Officer?'

9

The sun disappeared behind the roofs and sent a final glimmer over the horizon. How peaceful the city seemed from here, how spectacular the view. The palace dome, the cathedral and the tower of City Hall seemed within touching distance, though not quite as close as the dark roofs and brick walls of the women's prison. To the right, the Friedrichshain treetops towered over the roof ridges and swayed gently in the breeze.

Alex sat next to the skylight, smoking a Manoli, drawing so deep it was as if she wanted to absorb everything; to keep all the fumes inside. She was smoking to quell her anger, but it wasn't working.

They had shared the first cigarette from that tin only two days before, but already it seemed like an image from another life: Benny standing before her smiling, so uncertain and so in love. His shy overtures, the failed kiss . . . And she had turned him down. Damn it!

Every evening they spent in Flat B they would sit here on the roof and share a cigarette before going to bed. They had to smoke it outside as cold cigarette smoke could give them away.

Flat B was really nothing more than an abandoned hovel in a Büschingstrasse attic, located in a rear building in which the majority of flats stood deserted. A perfect hideaway, perhaps a little too warm on hot days, but otherwise ideal. Benny had found it, God knows how, but he'd always had a good nose for a bolt-hole, and only very seldom in the last few months had they actually been forced to sleep outside. Whenever they had, there'd always been something to smoke, even if it was rolled together from the stubs of other cigarettes.

The last of the daylight shone over the roofs in the west. In the courtyard below it was already dark. Most people were in their beds. Alex flicked away the cigarette butt and watched it descend like a drunken firefly. Its embers corkscrewed into the night.

Yes, they had been damn lucky these last few weeks, but somehow she had sensed that fate would make them pay. With so much luck, something was bound to go wrong and, indeed, something had. Benny had died. It was as if all their luck was merely borrowed, and the repayments were far too high.

Kalli, that rat, had fobbed her off with a twenty, a measly twenty! Well, the skinflint would be sorry. Her mind was made up. It had to be tonight. In an hour's time it would be dark enough and she could get on the tram and head back out. Without cigarettes, there was no reason to sit on the roof any longer.

Their alarm system was a few tins on a washing line that Benny had connected to the door at the foot of the attic stairs. She was about to climb back through the window when there was a high-pitched, hollow clatter and footsteps on the stairs. Shit! Who was trying to get into the attic at this hour? She pulled her legs back and moved away from the window opening. Not a moment too soon. The door to the attic opened, and she heard a man's voice, so loud it was as if he was standing right next to her.

'What is it this time, Frau Karsunke? Everything here's dark.'

'Little brat, coming up here like that. She doesn't even live in the building.'

Alex scarcely dared breathe. The attic's forty-watt bulbs came on and cast a yellowy shimmer on the roof tiles.

'Are you sure? Doesn't look like there's anyone here to me.'

'I saw her. Not for the first time either. Something's not right.'

Alex had never heard the caretaker say a word, but knew it was him; she could picture his red face. He began to shout: 'Hello? Is there anyone there?'

'She must be hiding. You need to take a look-see, Herr Ebers.'

The abandoned hovel with the number fourteen was situated right at the end of the corridor. During the day, they would stand the mattresses against the wall, pack their sleeping bags away, and pile all their junk in front so that it looked like the last tenant hadn't cleared the flat when they left. One by one Alex heard the doors creak open.

'Guard the stairs, Frau Karsunke, so that no one can get away.'

The thought of escaping down the stairs past the two of them disappeared no sooner than it arrived. She stood stock-still on the roof, right next to the dormer window. Just stay calm. In half an hour they'd be asleep in their beds, and she could exit the building.

A few days ago she had asked Benny if it wasn't time to look for a new hideout. He had played it down, saying that this one still had a few days in it. Soon they'd rent a proper flat with the KaDeWe money Kalli had promised. She had let herself be convinced, but still had a funny feeling about Flat B. If only she had listened to her instincts.

'I told you, there's no one here,' the caretaker said. 'Perhaps she really is with the Grünbergs, like she said.'

'They're all asleep. She went upstairs two hours ago and never came back.'

'There's no one here, anyway.'

'Then maybe she's in one of the empty flats.'

'They're all locked. Listen, Frau Karsunke. You got me out of bed. I've come up to take a look, but that's it now. There's nothing here.'

'What about the window?'

'What about it?'

'The skylight. It's ajar.'

'Someone'll have opened it while hanging the washing.'

Alex heard footsteps approaching. Hopefully he wouldn't come onto the roof. She stood rigid. If he wanted to see her, he'd have to climb out. She heard the window hinge creaking but, from the sound of the bolt, it was being closed rather than opened. The idiot caretaker had locked her out and she could scarcely hear their voices.

A few minutes later the light in the attic went off. They were gone. She poked her head around the corner. Darkness everywhere. Perhaps it was a trap? Perhaps the caretaker was still there, waiting for her to show herself. Whatever, the main thing was that she had no idea how to get down.

In the meantime, what light remained had been swallowed by the night.

10

The red-black Horch parked next to the silo seemed out of place. The corner of Stralauer Allee was chock full of lorries and small delivery trucks. Hugo Lenz got out of the car and stretched his considerable frame into the night, feeling the blood course through his body. He liked the air here by the harbour, the smell of the river, mingled with the smell of petrol from the nearby tank. He didn't lock up. This was his kingdom; no one would think of stealing Red Hugo's car, not here. He had worked at the Osthafen many years ago prior to the war, before he started earning money by more dangerous, though far more profitable, means. The two and a half years in prison seemed a fair price, all things considered.

Things weren't running so smoothly at the moment, however. The Nordpiraten had been making serious trouble ever since Rudi the Rat had returned from the clink. Only this morning some hooligan had smashed up Fritze Hansen's kiosk, one of the most reliable earners Berolina had on their lists. It was a brazen insult. Well, what do you know, it said, Berolina can no longer protect their own. What are you still paying them for?

If Marlow didn't react soon, things would get out of control. Until now he had preferred to sit back, reluctant to do anything that might bring the cops into play and disrupt business.

Dr M. was perhaps not entirely wrong, but doing nothing wasn't the answer. The Pirates were becoming bolder by the day, and it was only a matter of time before somebody snuffed it. They had thrown Kettler out of the window, leaving him in a wheelchair, but it could have been worse. Lenz had wanted to strike there and then, but Marlow kept him in check. They had been allowed to torch a Pirate betting office on Greifswalder Strasse, but that was his only concession to his men's desire for revenge.

The good doctor had no idea that feelings were running so high. If he allowed this to continue, people would start jumping ship. Something had to give. The Pirates had to be taken out of circulation in a way that was sanctioned by the cops, and Hugo Lenz knew how to make it happen. His new allies would help him; they'd even pay for it.

He could already tell they were serious. The department store brats had been neutralised at the weekend. One of the little bastards had even been killed, not that Hugo had wanted that. All he wanted was to give those urchins, who had been making the cops nervous for weeks and ruining Berolina's business, a little warning. He hadn't wanted anyone to die, although a dead body was a damn good warning. The other brats would keep away from the city's department stores for a while, and Kalli knew that Berolina were better business partners than a couple of snotty-nosed street urchins. If there should be further deaths Hugo wouldn't complain. After all, Berolina wouldn't have anything to do with it.

He crossed the railway tracks that ran parallel to Stralauer Allee and connected the Osthafen with the wider world. He had suggested the meeting point himself. One of the warehouses next to the big cold-storage depot belonged to Berolina. Not officially, of course, no one rented a warehouse to a Ringverein. Officially, it was the firm *Marlow Imports* who used the almost two thousand square metre space, as the sign above the loading bay indicated. Lenz had seen to it that none of his men were present. Who the boss was meeting was none of their concern.

He moved along the quay, past the cranes that shifted goods by the ton, and the ships moored on the Spree, waiting to be loaded. There wasn't much happening. The crews were asleep, and the few workers he met had tired faces.

There were two men waiting at the loading bay. They were a little too well dressed for the neighbourhood, even if their suits were off the rack. Typical cop suits, Hugo Lenz thought. So, they were serious. Satisfied, he breathed in a gust of Spree air and grinned. He didn't need Johann Marlow to keep those Nordpiraten rats at bay. Things would be different now, and Johann Marlow, the arrogant prick, could go hang once and for all.

11

The house lay in darkness as Rath opened the main door. Everyone was asleep and no wonder: it was almost midnight. He felt as if he should have been in bed hours ago. Yet the rage in his stomach would make sleep hard to come by. He switched on the light in the stairwell and climbed the stairs, past Brettschneider's door. She looked at him in a funny way whenever their paths crossed, couldn't get it into her bourgeois little head that a man came and went in a flat shared by two young women. The landlord accepted that while Fräulein Overbeck was in Uppsala for two semesters, Rath sometimes spent whole nights and even had his own key. Frau Brettschneider, a single, retired teacher, did not. It simply didn't fit into her worldview.

He was tempted to ring her doorbell before disappearing into Charly's flat but, in the interests of domestic peace, resisted. It was Charly who'd bear the brunt, not him.

As quietly as possible, he opened the door and groped his way into the kitchen without switching on the light, only doing so once he had closed the door behind him. There was a note on the table. He removed his hat and read as he shrugged off his coat.

Dear Gereon,
I did wait up for a while, because I was hoping to see you, but now I'm too tired, almost too tired to write these lines. And tomorrow I have to leave early again. Annoying about your car. Tell me what happened in the morning.

C.

P.S. There's an open bottle of red wine in the cupboard. I wanted to share it with you, but we'll do it some other time. If you like.

He opened the cupboard door. The bottle was more than half full. Charly must have drunk two glasses on her own. He imagined her sitting there, some legal book or other open on the table, wine glass at hand, growing more and more weary as she waited for him. He would have liked nothing more than to take her in his arms, but she wasn't there, she was in bed sleeping and he couldn't wake her.

Next to the wine stood the bottle of cognac he had brought from Luisenufer. He only had to think for a moment, before leaving the wine untouched. It was a long time since he had drunk cognac before going to bed, and not just because Charly complained about the smell. He no longer needed it; sleeping by her side was enough to banish those nightmares that, for a time, had haunted his dreams. The smell of her body was enough to keep the demons at bay.

There was a pitter-patter across the hallway floor, and a scratching at the door. Rath opened it and a black dog looked up at him. 'Did I wake you, Kirie?' he asked, letting her in.

By the time he fetched the glass from the cupboard, she had curled up under the table as if she knew exactly where her master was going to sit.

Kirie was the living reminder of a murder investigation. She had belonged to a victim, and no one wanted to take her, not even the parents of the deceased. Rath had adopted the sweet little neglected pup who had been trapped in the flat of her dead mistress and, since then, had turned into a rowdy chit of a hound.

'We'll need to think of something for you,' he said. 'Your mistress can't keep you anymore, so you'll have to be a police dog again.' Kirie pricked her ears up, and tilted her black, canine head to one side.

Rath opened the bottle of cognac and sniffed its neck before pouring. The familiar smell recalled the times he had sat alone in his Kreuzberg flat wrestling with the day's problems before taking himself off to bed. Charly could grumble all she liked, today had been hard, damn it, and cognac alone offered the solution.

He felt his anger rise, rapid as a thermometer in boiling water. He cursed Abraham Goldstein, and he cursed Bernhard Weiss for foisting the assignment on him in the first place.

Czerwinski and Henning had been waiting an hour and a half when he and Goldstein finally reappeared in the Excelsior. However, Rath didn't know the extent to which Goldstein had ruined his evening until later, after he had left the Yank with Plisch and Plum and gone back out to Wedding to retrieve his car. He had travelled by taxi, determined to drive his expenses higher still, so furious he couldn't even look out of the window. The Buick was parked where he had left it: Kösliner Strasse, a notorious Communist area, and a neighbourhood in which sports cars were seldom left on street corners. Someone seemed to have guessed that the car belonged to a cop, or had taken it for a capitalist's plaything. Either way, they had serviced it good and proper.

Despite the flat tyres and smashed headlights, Rath was most annoyed about the scratches in the paintwork. Sheer vandalism and envy, nothing more. That jobless rabble! Rath had gone to the Rote Laterne on the corner, the same bar he had visited or, rather, passed through, hours before. It was already closed, even though it wasn't yet ten o'clock. He felt sure that Goldstein had recruited the people who had wrecked his car here. How, he wasn't sure, but money seemed the likely answer.

Then came the problem with the tow truck. He had had to run to the S-Bahn, to Senefelder Platz, to find a public telephone, which of course was out of use. After hailing a taxi on Reinickendorfer Strasse he found a late-night garage which could tow the defective Buick. By that point, however, the hands of his wristwatch already showed half past ten, and the garage was somewhere out in Reinickendorf.

He poured himself another cognac, then a third. He would charge the repairs to the Free State of Prussia, that much he had already decided in the taxi to Charly's place.

Meantime, Kirie had fallen asleep. Listening to her snore quietly, he rinsed his glass and placed it in the sink. In the bathroom he brushed his teeth extra carefully and downed two large glasses of water. The last thing he needed was trouble at breakfast. Charly mumbled something as he lay beside her, turning to place an arm around his shoulder, and he nestled close to her warm body, carefully, so as not to wake her. As the scent of her skin reached his nostrils, that scent which belonged to Charly alone, he closed his eyes and fell asleep.

12

The shop lay quiet and dark, the gas lamps on Rigaer Strasse were switched off, and moonlight shone dimly through the clouds. There wasn't a single light on in the building. Alex had been watching the street for almost an hour, but since the last S-Bahn spat out its half a dozen or so passengers she hadn't seen a soul.

It was late by the time she reached Rigaer Strasse, much later than anticipated. She ought to have been exhausted, but her rage kept her awake: rage at Kalli, rage at the cops, rage at that stupid caretaker who had forced her to climb over all those roofs until she finally located a skylight in the front building.

After today's incident, Flat B was too dicey. Alex would return for a final time, but only to pick up her stuff. She hadn't wanted to run the risk earlier. First, she had to take care of business in Kalli's shop.

Although certain that the street was deserted and no one was watching from the window, she took a final, precautionary, glance in all directions before emerging from the dark entrance, crossing the street and heading towards the shop. The carefully drawn letters on the sign told her it was closed. As she set about the door with her skeleton key she realised it wasn't locked. She pushed it open as slowly as possible, to avoid triggering the bell which announced new customers. A shy *pling*, then everything was still. She listened into the darkness. The open door made her suspicious. *Better safe than sorry!*

Alex couldn't help thinking of Benny, and the memory pained her. She saw his laughing face, then the grimace of the cop who killed him, his boots stamping on Benny's fingers as if he were treading out a cigarette, and her rage rose once more.

She was surprised that Kalli had forgotten to lock up. True, he was prone to getting drunk, and sometimes slept on the sofa in the back, which was why she had brought the knife. She wasn't scared of him, having dealt with far worse in the past. If need be she would extract the money by force.

The thought of a snoring Kalli in the backroom made her proceed as quietly as possible. Not daring to switch on the light, she groped her way forwards until she found the counter, following its contours with her fingertips to the cash register. She didn't know how much he left in the till overnight, but her plan was to take whatever money she could lay her hands on. There had been quite a sum in the drawer when she visited at lunchtime.

Thinking of how to unlock it without making too much noise, she hesitated. It was already wide open, the big cash drawer pulled out as far as it would go. And it was empty.

A strange feeling took root in her stomach. Even if he had been drinking, which seemed more than likely, a schlockmeister like Eberhard Kallweit would hardly forget to close the cash drawer. Or had he already taken the money out and locked it in the cash box, which he took with him every morning to the bank? She knew where he hid the box: on the bookshelf in the backroom. She had seen him once heading out back to fetch his cash, not realising that the display cases in his shop, dirty as they were, made for perfect mirrors.

Alex opened the door slowly and carefully, straining as she listened. No sound, not a snore, not a breath, just the ticking of the wall clock. Inside, she closed the door behind her. It was darker here than in the shop, pitch black in fact, without a window in sight. She searched for the light switch but, after a while, gave up, getting down on her knees and groping her way forward on all fours.

Here was the edge of the carpet, so that must be the table, and behind it the sofa. The bookshelf hung above the sofa. Alex continued crawling across the carpet, which hadn't been beaten in a long time and had crumbs and dirt everywhere, until she felt something sticky, instinctively pulling her hand away. What a pigsty! At first she thought Kalli, the messy bastard, had knocked over a bottle of spirits and failed to clean up, but then she recognised the faintly metallic smell.

She had waded into a pool of blood!

God damnit! She needed light to see what had happened.

She crawled back and edged open the door. In the meantime her eyes had grown so used to the darkness that the little light entering from the shop was enough to get her bearings. There was something big on the floor under the table: a body, a human body. Stay calm, she told herself. Finally she located the light switch on the other side of the door. Suddenly she felt curiosity and fear in equal measure. Her right hand gripped the handle of the knife, as her bandaged left hand stood poised over the switch, but there was no one else there.

Eberhard Kallweit lay in his own blood, which by now was seeping into the carpet. His body was in a horrific state, worse than Alex had ever seen, the face a crusty, bloody mess. She had to look twice to recognise him at all, but the grey overalls left her in no doubt. Her knees grew weak as she threw up the little she had eaten that evening against the wall.

13

Rudolf Höller trudged through the Brandenburg March sand. He was in good spirits, even if early morning wasn't his best time. He could have remained in the car, but wanted to see what had become of the dump. He stepped on a branch by the entrance and a flight of crows fluttered into the early morning mist. Apart from the beating of their wings, their cawing, and the rustle of the wind in the pines, there wasn't a sound. At this hour the garbage trucks were still out and about; they wouldn't roll up with their load for a while yet, but, when they did, there would be a continuous stream of rubbish flowing into the former clay quarry until late evening.

The wood on the other side of the hollow was part of Greater Berlin, but the dump lay beyond the four-million-strong city. Berliners didn't like to bury their rubbish within the city walls, and Schöneiche was an excellent place to dispose of things that had outlived their purpose. No one knew that better than Rudi Höller.

The fact that they had designated the dump, of all places, as the meeting point, seemed like a sign. He knew his way around here. It was, so to speak, his home patch. A few years ago, Rudi had worked as a garbage man and discharged his load here every day. Increasingly, however, he had used his rounds to nose out properties for a break-in, and ultimately to deliver packages of drugs. At some point he had ended up with the Nordpiraten, eventually elbowing his way to the top of the organisation, and not just in a figurative sense. Now he had reasserted his leadership claim after spending two years in the can at Tegel with Hermann.

The Pirates were crying out for strong leadership. Since the catastrophe at Reichskanzlerplatz, where half the Ringverein had fallen into the hands of the police, the organisation was fighting for survival. In the meantime, those bastards at Berolina had grown stronger.

It was time to put a stop to it. Soon the Pirates would no longer be limiting themselves to regaining lost ground. Today's meeting could change everything. He had managed to get to someone who, though still loyal to Red Hugo, had long been a thorn in Johann Marlow's side. And, make no mistake, Berolina were headed by Marlow, not Hugo Lenz. Without Dr M., Berolina would crumble like a dry leaf.

Yes, this was his chance to finally get even with Dr M., to show that arrogant upstart who was in charge of this city. Rudi Höller knew who he had to thank for his prison years. They had been shopped. The pigs had been waiting for them in the vault when he and Lapke and a few others broke into the bank on Reichskanzlerplatz. When Berolina worked in conjunction with the police, you could be sure Johann Marlow had a hand in it. He had half of police headquarters in his pocket, although they wouldn't be much use when he was in the ground.

Rudi the Rat had no qualms when it came to bumping people off. That was how he had earned his nickname, with a nod to his former profession. There were thousands of rats at the dump, many more than there were crows. Only, you couldn't see the rats. They didn't caw like the birds, but kept themselves hidden, striking mercilessly, quick as a flash—when the situation demanded.

Surveying the dump's expansion as if it were his own work, Rudi turned around. When he returned to his car, he saw a black sedan parked on the edge of the wood. Behind the windscreen were two men. He ran his hands over the old war pistol in his waistband as the first garbage truck rumbled slowly towards the entrance. The truck was early, he thought. On the one hand it was disrupting their meeting, but on the other it made him feel safer. He turned his face towards the wood in case the driver recognised him.

They hadn't mentioned there would be two of them. The caller had explicitly said it would be a private meeting.

The garbage truck had now passed, and was rolling slowly onwards. The doors of the black sedan opened and two well-dressed men got out. Rudi moved towards them. He'd give them a piece of his mind! He didn't like it when people broke arrangements.

Then he heard the air brakes of the garbage truck hiss, and turned around. It had halted a few metres behind him, and the driver had climbed out of his cabin. Rudi turned back to face the dark sedan and the two men, feeling calmer now, more secure. They would hardly gun him down in front of a witness.

Something rustled behind him. He turned again and realised his mistake. He had been concentrating too hard on the men in the sedan and ignored the truck driver. Now he understood what had so confused him about the man. He was wearing neither an elegant suit like the other two, nor the BEMAG uniform. Strangely, what most confused him was that the pistol in the man's hand was a make he had never seen before—and Rudi Höller knew his pistols. Without much time to think, he suspected the model into the barrel of which he was staring would be his last. Possibly American, he thought, then the muzzle flashed. He didn't hear the bang.

14

Andreas Lange had slept badly. He was still shaken by yesterday's events, even though things had turned out better than expected. Interrogating your colleagues was a thankless task, no matter the subject. No doubt that was why Gennat had lumped it on him, the new man from Hannover, whom no one at Alex took seriously anyway. True, he had been on duty at the weekend and was among the first CID officers at the corpse, but that also applied to Reinhold Gräf and *he* had been given some special assignment for Rath. Requested, it was said, from on high. Meanwhile Assistant Detective Lange had worked his first case as lead investigator.

It was little more than a show for Gennat, a case in which the worst you could do was make yourself unpopular at Alex. Buddha didn't have to alienate any of his favourites, but could observe how the assistant detective from Hannover had developed this past year.

The interrogations hadn't been nearly as bad as Lange feared. Even uniform knew what details were essential for the purposes of a statement. You didn't have to squeeze it out of them. Everyone had cooperated. No stalling, wisecracks or protests, so that Lange already had more or less everything he needed. It just had to be written out neatly and filed away. In a few days, he'd hand over the file to the public prosecutor, who would draw things to a predictable close.

It looked like there was no blame attached to the operation command. The KaDeWe intruder had recklessly tried to escape down the store front and fallen in the process. These things happened.

'One less for us to worry about,' a few colleagues had said in the canteen. Lange saw things differently.

A human life was a human life, and the deceased from KaDeWe looked like he was still a child. They still hadn't identified him. The operation commander, a young police lieutenant, regretted the fatal incident more than anything and had been so full of remorse that Lange almost had to comfort him. No wonder: it was a lot of responsibility for someone so young. Lieutenant Tornow wasn't even two years older than Lange, and the assistant detective had no idea how he would have coped in the circumstances.

Then, yesterday evening—Lange had already packed his things and was about to leave the office—Dr Schwartz had telephoned. It was this call that would haunt his dreams. 'I need to show you something,' the pathologist said. 'Could you come to Hannoversche Strasse early tomorrow morning? Best before the start of your shift.'

So here he was standing on the steps of the yellow-brick building with a queasy feeling in his stomach and an increasing sense of regret that he had eaten breakfast. At the top of the stairs, just outside the entrance to the morgue, he hesitated. Until now he had always visited the building with a companion, usually an investigating officer, which gave him the opportunity to stand to one side and not look too closely. Now, however, he had to go in and face whatever awaited him behind these walls, aside from a cynical doctor and dissected corpses.

The porter nodded as he showed his identification and entered the tiled surrounds of the morgue.

Lange had been racking his brains over why Schwartz had asked for him in person, rather than simply delivering the forensic report through internal mail. By now he could have been at his desk in the Castle, reading it over quietly with a cup of coffee before pinning it to the files. The boy had fallen from the fourth floor and died. Did it make any difference what bones he had broken, which internal organs he had damaged? Wasn't it enough for the information to be in the files? Why did the investigating officer need to look himself? Perhaps Schwartz just wanted to show him his own little tunnel of horror, to shock the green assistant detective. A number of colleagues had said the pathologist enjoyed playing such tricks on young officers.

Lange pushed the swing doors of the autopsy room, eyes fixed on the floor and mentally preparing himself to see some freshly severed limbs or heads, a dissected abdomen or, at the very least, an open thorax. The worst thing he had ever seen in the morgue was a head whose skull-pan had been neatly detached, making the deceased seem like one of those clay beer steins displaying Bismarck's countenance, the lid made up of a spiked helmet you could lift when you drank. Lange had managed to look away, but this time he was the investigating officer.

At last he dared to look up and was surprised. No chamber of horrors. There was a corpse on the autopsy table, but it was covered by a sheet. The pathologist hadn't even fetched any disgusting samples from his selection— his *canning jars*, colleagues called them—to put on display. Dr Schwartz sat at his desk making notes. When he saw Lange, he stood up and stretched out a hand.

'Ah, there you are. Also an early riser?'

'Out of necessity.'

'My assistant has just made coffee. Would you like some?'

'Thank you.'

'Thank you no, or thank you yes.'

'Thank you no.'

'Shame. You're missing out on the best coffee in Berlin. Strong enough to wake the dead, they say. Pity they can't drink it.'

Lange met the pathologist's tired quip with a shy smile. Schwartz, who hadn't batted an eyelid, pushed him towards the corpse. 'I wanted to show you . . . how can I put it? . . . something a little odd. I can't mention it in the report without having spoken to you first.'

'It wasn't the fall that caused his death?'

Schwartz shook his head. 'No, there's no doubt about that. He sustained such serious injuries upon impact that the internal bleeding filled the thorax. The poor boy choked on his own blood. Or more precisely: drowned.'

Lange swallowed.

'How old was he then?'

'Very young. Somewhere between fourteen and seventeen at a guess. But that isn't why I summoned you.' Schwartz grabbed a corner of the sheet, and Lange feared the worst, but the pathologist exposed only the deceased's right hand. 'That,' he said, pointing towards it, 'is the big surprise.'

Lange glanced down. No one finger seemed normal; instead each was unnaturally contorted, swollen and displaying all the colours of the rainbow.

'Breaks to the index, middle and ring fingers,' Schwartz said. 'The whole hand covered in haematomas and contusions.'

'So? He fell onto the pavement from the fourth floor.'

'He didn't sustain these injuries in the fall. The left hand is similar, but not nearly as bad.'

'If it wasn't the fall, then what?'

'That is precisely the question, and I'm afraid it isn't so easy to answer. Or, put another way: if you accept the most obvious answer, you could be in serious trouble.'

'I'm afraid I don't follow, Doctor.'

'In my opinion, and I have been doing this job a long time, the nature of these injuries leads me to conclude that they were sustained shortly *before* the boy fell. Since discovering them yesterday afternoon, I've been trying to imagine what could have happened, and . . .'

'Fortunately, it isn't your job to draw conclusions,' Lange said, realising straightaway that he had made an error. The pathologist seemed mildly peeved as he continued.

'Take my words as a discreet attempt to spare you the use of medical terminology that would mean nothing to you,' he said, looking at Lange like a professor eyeing his most unworthy student. 'Anyway, assuming the boy's fingers weren't beaten by a hammer shortly before his death, which, I must say, seems unlikely . . .'

'. . . then someone else must have broken his fingers,' Lange finished the sentence. All of a sudden he was wide awake, the fear of macabre jokes or unpleasant sights a distant memory.

'As you said. It isn't my job to draw conclusions,' Schwartz replied, 'but it looks like someone stamped on his fingers pretty hard. Perhaps even struck them with a blunt instrument. The poor boy lost his grip. With breaks like that, no one could have held on, it's just not physically possible.' Lange began to understand why the pathologist hadn't wanted to put it in writing.

'You're saying that in all likelihood we're not dealing with an accidental death . . .'

'. . . but with a murder. Correct.' Schwartz cleared his throat. 'That's what I'd call it when someone is sent flying from the fourth floor.'

'And it looks like the perpetrator is a policeman . . .'

'That's your conclusion, not mine.'

15

'Anyone else without a ticket?'

Charly showed the walrus-moustached conductor her monthly pass as the house fronts of Warschauer Strasse flitted by outside. The tram was squeezed tight with people on their way to work.

As usual, she had packed a book for the journey. Heymann's *Principles of Criminal Law* lay open on her lap, but she had too much on her mind to read. She preferred to look out of the window and think. Gereon's mood at breakfast!

She had only half listened to his story. His car had been wrecked by vandals in Wedding, and then he had had to get it towed to a garage in the middle of the night. She hadn't understood a great deal, only that it was his excuse for coming home so late without calling, and for being unable to drive her to work. She'd had to leave early as a result. Though the S-Bahn took barely twenty minutes to reach Warschauer Bridge, she had to take the tram the rest of the way, the 90, which stopped at every letterbox.

The secret still burned inside of her, even now when she was alone again. She had thought he would notice something in her expression at breakfast, that something in her eyes would give her away, but he was consumed by anger over the car. She hadn't even said anything about the riots at the university, so wary had she been of straying anywhere near the subject. Her plan had been to talk things through over a glass of wine, but he had kept her waiting so long she'd ended up going to bed. Now she was almost glad. What could she say to him when she wasn't even sure what she wanted herself?

Yesterday, Heymann had asked to speak to her in person, had even sent a car, and she had travelled to the university full of nervous anticipation. What could be so important that her former professor would send a chauffeur to pick her up?

The atmosphere was hostile when she stepped out of the car onto Dorotheenstrasse. People were demonstrating again, loudly and in the form of songs: "Die Fahne hoch," the Nazi party anthem. A few Communists tried to combat it with "The Internationale" and the result was a dreadful cacophony. She managed to make it to the building's north entrance unscathed, but the demonstrators had spread here too. Students in brown shirts tore messages and signs from the noticeboard and the few who tried to intervene, by no means all Communists, had been clubbed to the ground. The Nazis had brought batons.

By the time she reached her favourite professor's office, fighting had broken out below too. Heymann had stood at the window, shaking his head in disbelief. Friedrich-Wilhelms-Universität as the scene of such political vulgarity was simply too much for the old Prussian. Things were getting worse, especially in the legal faculty. You could almost assume that any first semester student would be a Hitler acolyte, and the younger they were, the more fervent. The brownshirted students didn't shy away from violence, they thrived on it. *Student unrest* was how the papers described it.

She had been so unsettled by the commotion that she didn't understand the professor's request at first. Half a year, and he wanted *her*? She had asked for a few days' thinking time, and still had Heymann's reaction echoing in her ears. 'Don't take too long, Fräulein Ritter, opportunities like this don't come around often.'

She couldn't keep Heymann waiting long, she knew that, but nor could she agree without speaking to Gereon, and thinking it over some more herself. The truth was, she had other plans. Her goal had always been a senior role in the Prussian Criminal Police. That was the reason she had taken up her legal studies, and why she had knuckled down and crammed like anything after flunking the state examination. *Failed* was the terse judgement of the exclusively male board of examiners, no further explanation given. Half a year later she had overcome that hurdle, albeit without distinction. *Satisfactory*. The main thing was that she had passed.

The electric train crawled out of the shadows of the Ringbahn Bridge onto Möllendorfstrasse and overtook a swarm of cyclists pedalling uphill; the army of workers on its way to the Lichtenberg factories. Seeing them she remembered how much she enjoyed holding down a regular job. She had felt the same way at Alex, where she had worked as a stenographer in Homicide and earned money to pursue her studies. Against that was the year she had spent almost exclusively at university, hunched over her books . . . Suddenly she wasn't sure whether Heymann's offer was quite as attractive as it sounded. On the other hand, it would provide her with opportunities she could never dream of otherwise, certainly not as a woman, if she were to continue stubbornly with her legal preparatory service.

Make your mind up time, Fräulein Ritter.

Meanwhile, the tram had reached Normannenstrasse. She snapped Heymann's book shut. Why was she so scared of discussing all this with Gereon? Because she knew it was about more than just these six months? It was about what would happen to them. That was it. Not that it made her feel any better.

16

Her eyes blinked and searched for him, as they had almost every morning since they met. His face was the first thing she saw, sitting cigarette in mouth, gazing into the new day. It felt all the more painful knowing he was gone, that he would never again smile and ask 'Breakfast?' and hand her a cigarette.

Suddenly, daylight filtered through the clouded windowpanes and made them seem dirty and grey. The day before her felt as bitter as the taste of night lingering on her tongue.

Alex sat and pulled her jacket tighter around her shoulders. In Flat A there was no blanket or sleeping bag to wrap herself in, and there was a strong draught besides. They had only used it in emergencies, or when they couldn't find anywhere better, but she didn't like sleeping here. There was far too much rubbish, shards of glass crackled underfoot, to say nothing of the rats, who were becoming more brazen. Barely a windowpane was intact and, on some nights, depending on which way the wind was blowing, you could hear the cries of the animals from the stockyard, their one final act of rebellion before death.

Flat A was a decommissioned axle factory, abandoned over a year before, and still standing only because the owner couldn't afford to have it torn down. Unfortunately, it was no longer much of a secret, and people came from all around in search of a free place to stay. She didn't like being here, certainly not without Benny, but after last night she had needed a refuge from the nightmare her life had become.

She wouldn't forget the sight of Kalli's corpse in a hurry. She'd never been able to stand the man, but now she felt something akin to guilt for intending to rob his till. Who on earth had made such a mess of him, and why? Wasn't the money in the cash register enough, or had he tried to hoodwink Berolina and found himself on the receiving end of Red Hugo's revenge? She had considered these questions on her long, night-time journey to Roederstrasse. At some point she had grown too tired to think and all she wanted to do was sleep.

She hadn't encountered a soul on her way to the flat, not even Kralle, the rat. The dirtbag had his eye on her and, on one occasion, she had only managed to fend him off with the help of her knife.

Only a few rooms were taken. It must have been well after midnight when she arrived, and everyone was asleep. She had sought out one of her usual places, as far away as possible from the stairs, covered herself with her jacket and pulled her cap over her head. Despite everything going on in her mind, she had briefly fallen asleep. And danced with Benny.

Stretching her arms towards the ceiling she yawned, still exhausted. She couldn't have been asleep for long, the floor wasn't exactly soft. She had to go back to Flat B one final time to pick up her sleeping bag and a few other things before finding a new place to stay. How, she wasn't sure. Benny had always known where, but she had no idea where he picked up his information. Somehow, he had just always known. If it came down to it, there was always the factory. Despite having so many things to take care of, she couldn't get up. Her body felt so stiff and heavy it was as if it were made of lead.

What a shitty day! What a shitty month! What a shitty time to be alive!

Something scraped over the floor and the door creaked on its hinges, pushing forward a mountain of junk. Suddenly wide awake, she fumbled for the switchblade in her pocket, feeling immediately more secure when she had it in her grasp. If it was Kralle, that stupid, puffed-up bastard, then he'd be in for a nasty surprise.

At the crack in the door appeared a dishevelled, dark-haired creature, her face crumpled with sleep. 'Morning, Alex. Do you have a cig for me?'

Alex let go of the knife and sank back. 'Vicky! You gave me a real fright creeping in here like that. I thought you were Kralle, or some other arsehole.'

'I heard something and thought I'd take a look. I didn't see you last night with the others.' Vicky came towards her. She had a pretty face under her unkempt locks, and big eyes that made it seem as if she were permanently gawking at something, even when she was as sleepy as she was now.

'I didn't get here until the middle of the night,' Alex said. 'Who's all here?'

'Oh, Fanny, Kotze, Felix and a few others. Not many. Most of them are gone already. Where's Benny?'

Alex was speechless. She had assumed the whole world must know about Benny's death, at the very least her friends—if you could call the people in Roederstrasse friends. But, of course, Vicky didn't know. How could she? Alex hadn't told anyone and, since Benny's death, hadn't spoken to a soul except Kalli. It was perfectly natural that Vicky was asking after him. Alex had always appeared with him in tow, every goddamn day these last few months.

'Didn't you hear? The thing in KaDeWe? Benny's dead.'

'That was you?' The news took all the strength from Vicky's legs. Her knees gave way, and she slid down the wall beside Alex. 'Fuck,' she said. 'Benny of all people. He was always so careful.' She slammed her fist against the wall and then again a second time, and started to cry softly, hardly making a sound.

Alex took the quivering girl in her arms. How could she comfort her? By saying what she scarcely believed herself? That the cops had killed Benny as if he were a rat, a parasite, vermin. She could imagine there were any number of people, and not just cops, who would be only too glad to treat her and Benny and Vicky the same way. Just do away with the dirty little brats who were ruining Berlin's streets with their begging and stealing, who shot off their mouths when a respectable citizen told them they should be at work instead of loitering around town.

If only they knew what real life was like. There were far too many people in this city, and far too few jobs. More than enough to eat, but far too little money to pay for it. People had to live somehow. The idea of going on the game, as Vicky and others she knew had sometimes done, repelled her. That someone like Kralle could do whatever he wanted with her body, for money, made her furious. The only thing a guy like him would see was her knife. You could earn your money that way too, Alex had discovered, thinking of the fatso at the Christmas market whose trousers she had pierced before robbing his purse. She hadn't known then that the money would be her start-up capital for a life on the streets.

Vicky stopped sobbing, and wiped the tears away with her sleeve. 'Sorry,' she said. 'But Benny . . . I liked him, you know?'

'Of course. I liked him too.'

'It was you in KaDeWe!' Vicky's eyes grew even larger. 'But then the cops are looking for you. You know that, right?'

'They're looking for a boy.'

'You're injured as well,' Vicky said, pointing towards Alex's bandaged wrist.

'A memento, nothing serious. Benny bound it.'

Vicky didn't ask any more questions. She seemed to recognise the rag from Benny's shirt. 'I could really use one now,' she said.

'One what?'

'A cig. Do you have a cig?'

Alex fetched the Manoli tin from her jacket. There was only one left.

Vicky whistled through her teeth. 'Nice,' she said. 'Where did you get that?'

'Benny.'

'Oh, I didn't know!' Vicky looked horrified. 'I don't want it.'

'They need to be smoked. I don't want to look at them anymore.' Alex turned the tin on its head, and let the last Manoli drop out. 'Come on, we'll share it,' she said. Share it like she always did with Benny. A fitting end for the last cigarette he had ever stolen.

Vicky produced a carton of matches and lit the cigarette for her. Alex took two drags and passed it on. The two girls smoked in silence. Gradually, Alex started feeling better, less alone. The desolation that had threatened to overwhelm her on waking had vanished.

'When's he being buried?' Vicky asked.

Alex hadn't thought about that. Benny was dead. His corpse was lying somewhere, most likely a police station, and at some point would need to be buried. 'How should I know when he's going to be buried? I can't exactly stroll into the police station and ask. They probably don't know his name. The paper didn't even get his age right.'

'Will they bury him with no name?'

Alex shrugged her shoulders. 'They'll get hold of it somehow. They're cops.'

'The cops I know are pretty fucking stupid. Besides, they don't give a shit if they have to bury one of us without a name or a gravestone.'

'You mean, Benny won't even get a proper grave?'

'What do I know, but wouldn't it be better if they knew his name?'

'Wouldn't that be like . . . snitching?'

Vicky suddenly seemed very certain. 'Someone has to tell the cops who he is. As a favour. It's the last time we'll be able to help him.'

'I don't know . . . I can't . . .'

'If you give me ten pfennigs for the telephone booth, I'll do it. I'll call the cops and tell them who Benny is. So that he at least gets a proper grave with his name on it.'

Alex felt tears welling in her eyes and had to pull herself together to continue. 'I don't even know his surname,' she said.

Vicky comforted her. 'Don't worry. I'll find out. I think he and Kotze were in the same home.'

17

It was impressive, the desk in the corridor, more imposing even than that of Police Commissioner Grzesinski. A real whopper. Rath had noticed it yesterday by the lifts on his way to Goldstein's room. He spread his things across its spacious, intarsia-decorated top. Alongside his cigarette case—this time he had come prepared with a dozen Overstolz—lay two well-thumbed newspapers, a cup of coffee, a glass of water and a half-full ashtray.

After yesterday, he had changed tactics. Weiss, to whom he had reported that morning, wasn't prepared to assign more men, despite what had happened. Thus, a new plan was required.

If it no longer mattered whether they were seen or not, there was no reason why they couldn't station themselves outside their target's door, and the desk made a perfect observation post. The service might not be quite as good as in the lobby—the ashtrays weren't emptied every three minutes— but Rath had managed to order a coffee along with copies of *Tageblatt* and the *Vossische Zeitung*, and he felt perfectly content. Especially since he could take turns with Gräf, and no longer had to spend the whole day in the same place.

The lift door opened with a soft *pling*. An elegant lady, who had linked arms with a smallish man, glanced at his desk curiously as she passed. Rath gazed after her; any distraction was welcome, especially one with such a nice rear end. The sound of someone clearing his throat made him spin around. Next to him stood the hotel detective, who must also have emerged from the lift.

'Good morning,' Rath said, and stood up.

Grunert gave a sour smile and shook his hand. 'Our conversation yesterday was interrupted,' he said. 'I looked for you in the lobby, but your colleagues said you were up here.'

Rath nodded. 'It's the best view of room 301.'

'If not exactly inconspicuous.'

'It isn't about being inconspicuous, it's about being effective.'

Grunert smiled his pickled smile. 'I would be most grateful if you finally explained why you are here.'

'You're aware that any information I do give must remain between us, and is subject to the utmost discretion?'

Grunert nodded.

'Good. The matter is quite simple: Abraham Goldstein, your esteemed guest, is strongly suspected of being a member of an American criminal cartel, and for this reason has been placed under surveillance by the Prussian Police. We don't want Berlin turning into Chicago, do we?'

Rath had hoped to lighten the mood a little with his final remark, but Grunert continued to look as though he had a bad stomach ulcer. Perhaps he did, too.

'And what is this . . . strong suspicion based on?'

'You'll understand that I can't tell you that. It's confidential CID material.'

'I just hope your suspicions aren't based purely on the fact that Mister Goldstein is of Mosaic faith.'

'Rest assured,' Rath said. 'The order to place Mister Goldstein under surveillance comes from Deputy Commissioner Weiss himself.'

Grunert gave a satisfied nod. Accusing Bernhard Weiss of anti-Semitism would be laughable.

They took such things seriously in the Excelsior. The hotel was thought to have once ejected Adolf Hitler out of consideration for its Jewish guests who, it was said, could not be expected to share the same roof as such a crude anti-Semite.

'Inspector, we have no objection to your monitoring Mister Goldstein, although I doubt your suspicions are warranted. Nevertheless, while I fully understand the need for this operation, I must also ask for *your* discretion . . .'

'Of course.'

'. . . and viewed in such light, your surveillance post is a little too conspicuous. At least for the remainder of our paying guests, who must be asking themselves why you need to spend the entire day seated at this desk.'

'We'll have to give them a story then. I certainly don't intend on leaving my post for the sake of a few guests.'

'A story,' said Grunert. 'Exactly what I was going to suggest. I'll have a few books brought to you from the library, along with a pen and paper. You'll be an author staying at our hotel, drawing inspiration from his surroundings . . .'

'An author?' Rath looked sceptical. 'Who's going to believe that?'

'I'll put the rumour about in the lobby, and soon the whole hotel will know. Old Teubner can be relied on there.'

'I don't know the first thing about writing. I hunt criminals!'

'Then you're a crime writer. That fits. And your new novel is set in our hotel.'

When Reinhold Gräf exited the lift half an hour later, accompanied by a black dog wagging its tail, he was a little taken aback by the pile of books and notepad.

'Are you keeping a record of everyone who emerges from the lift, or just copying the wallpaper pattern?'

'Don't you see? I'm a famous author, setting down his latest work. Incognito, naturally.'

Gräf glanced over Rath's shoulder. 'Looks more like wallpaper to me.'

The only things on the page were stick men and abstract patterns.

'I'm seeking inspiration,' said Rath. 'How did it go outside?'

'Kirie was a good girl and did a wee-wee, if that's what you mean. And Goldstein hasn't tried to climb down the façade, though I did see him at the window, I think. I'm not sure he recognised me though. What about you? Has our friend put in an appearance?'

Rath shook his head. 'So far just the hotel detective. This was his brainwave. But Goldstein must be awake; he let in the chambermaid.'

'Has he had breakfast?'

'He's had the chambermaid. Nothing's been brought to his room otherwise.'

As if on cue, the door to room 301 opened and the chambermaid emerged, throwing the two officers a brief glance and vanishing into the corridor. No sooner had she disappeared than the lift doors parted and the room service waiter rolled out a trolley, which he then wheeled into room 301.

'Maybe he really did have the chambermaid for breakfast,' Gräf whispered.

Rath shrugged. 'He's certainly enjoying himself.' He looked at Gräf.

'You shouldn't stand here the whole time. People will think you're my secretary. Leave the dog here and go and stretch your legs. Keep the hotel front in view. The last thing we need is for Goldstein to start climbing hand-over-hand across the balconies.'

Gräf nodded. 'When should I relieve you?'

'Let's say at one. I'll need to go walkies with Kirie then anyway.'

The detective had been gone perhaps quarter of an hour when Abraham Goldstein appeared in the doorframe of room 301 and carefully locked up. He hesitated when he saw Rath sitting at the desk, then burst out laughing.

'Good morning, Detective, have you transferred offices?'

'To be close to you,' Rath said, snapping shut his notepad of doodles. 'Sleep well?'

'Very well, thank you.' Goldstein pressed the button for the lift. 'Looks like it's going to be a nice day. Shall we then? I say *we*, since I assume you'll be joining me.'

Rath grabbed the dog lead.

'Police dog?' Goldstein asked, gesturing towards Kirie.

The lift door opened and both men stepped in.

'More dangerous than she looks,' Rath said. 'Trained to go for New Yorkers.'

'Didn't I say I was from Brooklyn?'

'The dog doesn't care.'

A lady inside looked the pair up and down; the lift boy gazed stoically into the distance.

'What's the latest on your car?' Goldstein asked. 'Repaired already?'

That hit home. Rath swallowed his rage and fell silent. Don't let the arsehole provoke you.

'Ground floor,' said the boy and opened the door for the woman passenger. Rath and Goldstein continued down to the basement, where Goldstein made a beeline for the tunnel.

'What have you got against daylight?' Rath asked.

'I prefer the underworld.'

Kirie, however, was not so keen, and Rath had to pull on her lead to keep up. Only when they began climbing the stairs, back up towards the daylight, did her pace quicken.

Goldstein headed for the taxi stand.

'I hope you won't mind if I don't invite you to *travel* with me,' Goldstein said as he waved over the first taxi from the rank. 'That would be breaking the rules.'

Rath took the second taxi, the driver reluctantly interrupting his reading of the paper.

'Where to, then?' he asked, as Rath manoeuvred the dog onto the back seat with some difficulty. Kirie had never willingly got into a car yet.

'Follow that taxi,' Rath said.

'Seriously?' The driver gazed disbelievingly into the rear mirror.

'Do I look like I'm kidding?' Rath showed his identification.

'Alright, alright.'

At the same moment, Goldstein's taxi moved from the verge onto the motorway, and Rath's driver accelerated. The inspector looked to the side, towards the pavement, where a baggage handler was struggling with several large items. At the last second he saw a familiar-looking coat. Shit! The Yank! Goldstein had either never got in or had got out straightaway! At any rate, he had sent the taxi on its way without a passenger.

'Stop,' he said.

'Pardon me?'

'Stop, damn it!'

'After three metres? I thought I was supposed to tail my colleague?'

'You did. Now stop the car!'

It took half an eternity for the taxi driver to pull over and accept a mark as payment—'Now I have to start again from the back! You won't be getting a receipt!'—before Rath and Kirie could finally get out. There was no sign of Goldstein. He must have disappeared inside the station.

Rath cursed, and dragged Kirie into the great entrance hall of Anhalter Bahnhof. Countless heads, countless hats. He gazed around and, at last, caught sight of a light-coloured fedora in the throng. He breathed a sigh of relief; Goldstein was in the queue at the ticket counter. Before he could disappear again Rath fetched up beside him.

'You really aren't so easy to shake off,' Goldstein said.

'I did warn you.' Rath was trying hard to hide the fact that he was gasping for breath.

'Is that why you've got the dog? So that it picks up my scent if I manage to give you the slip?'

'You didn't give me the slip.'

'Do you know something? You're starting to get on my nerves.'

'Then I'm doing my job.'

'I can think of better things to do than traipse around this city with you in tow. I'd rather stay here.'

'You do that.'

Goldstein exited the queue and made for the main entrance. A short time later, they were back on Askanischer Platz. Gräf, who was sitting on a bench under the trees, spotted them and adopted a quizzical expression. Rath gave a discreet hand signal to let him know the situation was under control.

'Your colleague?' Goldstein asked. 'I noticed him yesterday.'

'Then I'm sorry I didn't introduce you.'

Goldstein strolled across the square, taking a look at the neighbourhood. Rath followed. The workers were busy again at Europahaus, having erected a giant scaffolding around the entrance to the multistorey building. Over the next few days they would install one of the largest neon signs in the city. Curious passersby kept stopping to look upwards, where workers were scrambling about on the scaffolding and screwing in the neon strips. Goldstein gazed open-mouthed towards the sky.

'I must say, the building sites in Manhattan are more imposing. You'd need a good head for heights to work on those.'

'These will do me just fine,' Rath said, annoyed at himself. Why was he so talkative around the Yank? Especially when no detail escaped the man. He registered his surroundings with razor-like precision, and paid heed to even the most trivial detail.

'Vertigo?' Goldstein asked, quick as a flash, and Rath said nothing more, didn't even look up at the workers. When would Weiss take him off this damn assignment? When would he get to investigate a real murder again?

'Fancy a cup of coffee?' Goldstein asked. 'It's on me.'

'No, thank you. I can't possibly accept.'

Goldstein grinned. 'But if I were to have a cup somewhere,' he said, 'then you'd sit with me. If you're absolutely set on paying for your own, that's fine.'

A short while later they sat in Café Europa, where Rath had spent his first evening with Charly. There was no dancing at this hour, but a great deal of commotion on the roof garden. Two pots of coffee stood on the table in front of them, and Rath was secretly pleased that the American ran into the infuriating German custom of serving watery coffee in leaky pots. You either scalded yourself on the first cup, or drank the second cold, usually both.

Goldstein left the pot unremarked. 'I don't have anything against you personally,' he said, after serving himself, 'but it would be better for us both if you left me in peace. Perhaps if you had, you wouldn't have needed to take your car to the garage.'

'What do you know about that?'

'Only that I wouldn't be leaving *my* car unattended in a neighbourhood like that, particularly not such a nice model.'

'I'm forbidden to leave you in peace. Sometimes you have to make sacrifices.'

'You know, I'm an American.' Goldstein stirred his coffee, which was still far too hot. 'Perhaps, as a German, you won't understand this, but for me the most important thing is freedom. My freedom. If it's taken away from me, I can get pretty nasty. Just so you know.'

'Are you threatening me? We're not in America now. You can't just gun police officers down.'

'I think you have the wrong idea about our country. You ought to go there.'

'I know your country.' Rath was annoyed. He kept allowing himself to be provoked into making comments that were none of the Yank's business. He fumbled an Overstolz out of his case.

'Interesting brand,' Goldstein said. 'May I?' Rath hesitated. 'Come on. Just because I take something from you doesn't make it bribery. Besides, you cadged a Camel off me yesterday.'

'Help yourself.'

The men smoked in silence for a moment and drank their coffee.

'I still don't understand what I've done to warrant this kind of treatment.'

'Wrong tense. It isn't about what you've done, but what you might *do*.'

'Strange working methods, the German police. So, there's nothing I can do to get rid of you?'

'On the contrary. You can leave town.'

'Do you know what? I have a better idea. I'll wait until your bosses realise how ridiculous this operation is, and call you in.'

18

Alex stood in Büschingstrasse, checking the lie of the land. She had left her pocket watch in Flat B with the rest of her things, but the smell of onions and cabbage and bratwurst told her it must be about half past twelve. Time for lunch. A few scruffy figures gathered outside the entrance to the male Salvation Army hostel, but otherwise Büschingstrasse was deserted. Hopefully the same was true of the courtyard leading to Flat B.

She had used the last of her money to buy Vicky a coffee at the Grossmarkt, before treating herself to a six-pack of Juno and taking the number 66 out to Büschingplatz. In by night, out at lunch was the best way of avoiding the caretaker and that old snitch Karsunke, especially if you didn't want to field any stupid questions. Like the time he had asked her where she was going. She had given the answer Benny had drummed into her: to the Grünbergs in the rear building. They had the name from the mailboxes.

That wouldn't work now the caretaker was keeping a close eye on her. So, in for a final time to collect her things, and that would be it for Flat B. The caretaker could turn the place inside out for all she cared. He wouldn't find her.

From the opposite side of the road she peered through the entrance to the courtyard. It wasn't just her sleeping bag up there, but also the personal items she kept in a little tin, as well as Benny's pictures, which he had guarded like treasure. The yard seemed deserted, even the children who had been playing under the carpet hanger had vanished. Time was getting on. The queue outside the Salvation Army hostel had dwindled to three, reminding her that lunchtime didn't last forever. She took a deep breath, wished the caretaker and his informant Karsunke *bon appétit* and crossed the road. She had just reached the archway when the door from the neighbouring house opened and a cop stepped out.

The blue uniform, and the face, seemed like a bad dream. What was he doing in Friedrichshain, damn it? KaDeWe was in the west.

Flat B was too risky now, that much was clear, but she wasn't sure if the cop had recognised her. Thinking quickly, she switched directions, to make it seem as if she had come from the yard, then veered sharply, turning her back on him and making her way down the road as inconspicuously as possible. This wasn't anywhere near his precinct.

'Hey, wait!'

She turned only a little so that he couldn't see her face. 'Who, me?'

'You've just come from the building, haven't you? I'd like to ask you a few questions.'

Even if he had only seen her in boy's clothing three days ago, he'd recognise her. 'Sorry, I'm in a rush,' she said. 'My boss hates it when I'm late.'

'Hang on a minute there, little Miss.'

As he drew nearer she accelerated without turning around, not daring simply to run off. His hand fell on her shoulder. Instinctively, her fingers clasped the switchblade in her coat pocket.

'I just want some information,' he said. 'It's about a boy from the neighbourhood. Two boys, actually.'

She kept her eyes fixed to the ground, as if she were a shy, country innocent, and turned towards him. 'I don't know any boys here,' she said. 'Mother doesn't allow it.'

He grasped her chin and turned her face upwards. 'Don't I know you, little Miss?'

Now she saw his face, close as never before, and watched the penny begin to drop. 'Oh, my shoe,' she said, and bent down.

He'd recognised her, hadn't he, or would at any moment, the arsehole, the murderer! She fiddled with her shoe with her left hand, using the right to spring open the knife in her coat pocket.

Show no mercy now, she thought, this is the bastard with Benny on his conscience!

Again she felt his hand on her shoulder and knew there was no going back. She had one chance. Shooting up from her squatting position, she slashed him once across the face, and broke loose. The cop cried out, more in surprise than pain, she thought, and for a fraction of a second she stood rooted to the spot as he passed both hands across his face, gazing in disbelief at his blood-smeared palms.

He's let go of you, now run! But she couldn't, she kept staring at him.

Blood ran down his right cheek and the bridge of his nose. He looked at her with the same furious grimace she had seen at KaDeWe until, finally, she ran.

She didn't know if she had any chance against him, but she ran, ran, ran as fast as she could.

'Stop! Police!'

Fuck you, she thought, if you want to catch me, you'll have to work for it, fatso!

He called after her, but the distance between them had grown. Had he stopped running? Then she understood what he was saying.

'Police. Stop or I'll shoot!'

She carried on running, ducking instinctively as a shot flew across the road. The sound of a ricochet roared through the air. The cop had only hit a lamppost—but he had fired, he had actually fired, in the middle of the city, in broad daylight.

There wasn't a soul around.

No witnesses, not even anyone outside the Salvation Army. They were all eating inside.

Come to the windows, damn it, Alex thought, untie your napkins and come to the windows. Come outside, so that he can't just spray bullets everywhere. But, no one came, and if anyone *had* still been outside, they'd have fled after the shot. The city had painful memories of gun-toting cops.

Alex darted from side to side, zigzagging towards the traffic on Landsberger Strasse. Crossing Barnimstrasse, she looked around. The cop had come to a halt, a hundred metres behind her perhaps, and was taking aim for a second time. She threw herself to the ground as a shot rang out. She thought she heard the bullet whistle past her, but it was probably just the wind. She rolled over and got straight back to her feet. Her injured left hand was aching. She must have landed awkwardly, but it didn't matter now. He was trying to gun her down.

At last she reached Büschingplatz, and people. Jostling her way through the pedestrians, she hurried across Landsberger Strasse, dodging the cars as best she could. A man with an imperial beard, whom she almost knocked over, shook his head and made some stupid remark about road safety education.

She ran down Landsberger Strasse in the direction of Alexanderplatz, and heard her pursuer again, now shouting, 'Stop that girl!'

She glanced back to see him in his blue uniform, with his bloodied face. He seemed to have his anger under control, and surely wouldn't dare open fire here. People stared at him, but no one reacted. The man with the imperial beard made as if he hadn't seen a girl all day, let alone one trying to flee, and gazed studiously in the opposite direction.

She kept running down the street, further and further. The cop was still on the other side of the traffic. You haven't given him the slip yet, she told herself. Keep going!

Her strength started to leave her, but she ignored the pain, turning as she fled, and catching sight of him as he crossed the road. He had put his weapon away again.

Damn it! How could she shake him off? After endless terrace fronts, she came on a sidestreet and darted to the left where he couldn't see her. Where now? Breathless, looking around as she ran, she saw no courtyard, no open front door. KLEINE FRANKFURTER STRASSE, the sign said, and at the other end she saw the swathe of traffic on Frankfurter Strasse. Soon she reached the next street corner. There was still no sign of the cop. Now she darted to the right: ELISABETHSTRASSE, but no hiding place in sight here either. No matter, the main thing was that the shitface cop was nowhere to be seen. 'Slow down, girl,' someone said. 'You'll make that bus.'

On Frankfurter Strasse, on the other side of the road, she recognised the blue sign with the big, white 'U', shining like a promise. The U-Bahn!

First, though, she had to cross the motorway. This time she did it nice and easy to avoid attracting attention. Her breathing started to settle down, but her pain remained. She turned around discreetly, as if keeping an eye on the traffic—no sign of the cop. Had she shaken him off? When she reached the stairs leading down from the corner house, she cast a final glance over Frankfurter Strasse and saw him. Around a hundred metres to the east a blue uniform emerged from a side street.

She bent low and stumbled down the steps. The platforms were another floor down and, now she was here, there was no going back. Best to assume he had seen her. No time to make considered choices now, she had to take advantage of her head start. She rushed down the next set of stairs onto the platform. *Schillingstrasse* said the letters on the pink-tiled wall.

Any number of passengers stood here, but no one paid her any attention. She hesitated for a moment before continuing as calmly as possible along the platform to another set of steps and the second exit. This was where she had seen him, albeit above ground. If he took that route she'd run straight into his path. She strolled back along the platform, beginning to think she had walked into a trap.

There was a deep rumbling noise from the western tunnel. At the top of the platform she turned around. There was no one descending the eastern stairs, but a train roared out of the dark. The doors of a smoking carriage opened invitingly in front of her. A few people got off, a few got on, the door continued to stand open. With no police blue on the stairs she stepped into the nicotine haze of a car populated exclusively by men, at least half of whom had interpreted the *Smoking* sign as an order.

Waiting for the stationmaster to issue the all clear, she looked outside. The platform plotted a wide curve so that she could clearly make out the other end. The cop descended the stairs and stepped onto the platform in the same instant the stationmaster uttered his 'Keep back'.

All Alex could think of was: come on, come on, but the train didn't budge.

The cop sprinted forward, throwing himself into the car at the last moment; someone must have opened the doors for him. Shit, she still hadn't shaken him off, but at least he was in the front car, which meant he couldn't catch her on the train, only in a station. And that was where she would have to give him the slip, this stubborn cop, this killer, this pig, this fucking arsehole!

She felt her rage swell, an impotent rage that made her beat the steel bars of the train in frustration. Outside the windows it grew dark as the train entered the tunnel. She had the feeling that people were watching her, but pulled herself together, battling against her rage and despair, and prepared for the next stop.

STRAUSBERGER PLATZ. Now or never. The train stopped, the doors opened and a number of passengers got out. Alex stepped onto the platform with the crowd of smokers, but remained by the door, so that those boarding had to push past her as she looked towards the front of the train.

Damn it! The cop had got off too, and he'd seen her. He was pointing towards her and shouting, 'Stop that girl, she's a thief!'

Most passengers didn't react, or pretended not to have heard, but a fat man with a walrus moustache decided to intervene. 'Calm down now, lass,' he said. 'You won't be slipping through my fingers.'

'Don't touch me, fat ass!'

The fat ass grinned. 'Would you look at that. You're a cheeky one, aren't you. Claws and all.'

'Keep back!'

The stationmaster's voice crackled over the loudspeaker. The fat man stuck out a chubby finger and blocked her path, while the cop approached from the other side of the platform. She had to do something, and she knew what.

'Didn't you hear? *Keep back!*' she said, kicking the man as hard as she could between the legs. He doubled in pain, turned dark violet and sat on the platform facing backwards.

Someone tried to shut the door but she jammed it with her foot, squeezing her body into the sliding door and prising it open. No sooner was she on board with the door closed behind her, than the train began to move. This time the cop hadn't managed to follow.

All around her, passengers smoked as if what had happened was none of their concern. She pushed her way into a corner where no one could have witnessed the incident, feeling relieved but furious at the same time. The arsehole had tried to gun her down.

At least the train was heading east. She could get out at Petersburger Strasse and walk back to Flat A, where perhaps she'd run into Vicky or Kotze. She needed to feel as though she still had some friends in this city.

When the man in uniform spoke to her, a kindly sort with a white moustache, at first she merely shrugged her shoulders. She was so lost in thought that she didn't understand what he wanted until he repeated his request.

'Tickets please!'

19

It had worked, Goldstein had given them the slip. For a moment he thought he was being followed, but the man who emerged from a telephone booth on Kochstrasse and took the same route to the U-Bahn remained on the platform when he boarded. Through the whole journey he studied his fellow passengers to make sure there were no police among them. Only now, climbing the steps at Schönhauser Tor and stepping back into the light, was he certain the coast was clear. He took a deep breath, as if savouring a gentle sea breeze, when all he could smell was the city air with its lime-tree blossom, petrol and fresh asphalt.

How he enjoyed moving without that stubborn detective breathing down his neck. Rath was still sitting by the hotel lifts, convinced that Abraham Goldstein was inside reading the papers and twiddling his thumbs. All you had to do to shake off the cops was let them think they had everything under control.

He glanced at the piece of paper in his hand: GRENADIERSTRASSE. If he had understood her correctly, it had to be here somewhere. He looked around at workers laying steaming asphalt on a patch of road, newspaper boys shouting headlines outside a corner bar, a horse and cart turning the corner, carrying vegetables under a dirty-grey canopy. He crossed the motorway and followed. This had to be the way. He knew he was in the right place when he read the sign.

The street was busy, but a little run-down, the stucco on the fronts dirty-brown and starting to crumble. Washing hung from some of the windows. Almost everywhere, goods were being sold, even on pavements. Some traders sold directly from their carts. Everywhere he looked, he saw Hebrew letters and Stars of David, either on shop signs or painted on the display windows themselves. Apart from on the Lower East Side, he'd never seen so many Jewish shops in one place, not even in Williamsburg, or so many caftan wearers.

He wasn't sure whether he felt contempt or revulsion, he only knew that he didn't want anything to do with these men in their sombre, black uniforms, and that he liked the young men with dark sidelocks even less than their white-bearded elders. Their world seemed to embody everything he had left behind: the cramp of his parents' two-room flat, his sickly mother and his eternally praying, yammering father. He had hated all of it. Abe, Fat Moe had once said, you're a goddamn anti-Semite, a Jewish anti-Semite, and laughed his cackling laugh. Neither part was true of course, he wasn't an anti-Semite, but neither was he a real Jew. At least not the kind his father would have wished for.

The doubts had started after his Bar Mitzvah, when he ought to have felt a sense of belonging but instead turned his back more and more on the God of his fathers. Perhaps it was his mother's illness that drove him under the bridge to Moe? Or perhaps it was only her death? He could no longer say. All he knew was that, since that day he felt only revulsion for his father's world, and for those devout self-righteous men with whom Nathan Goldstein spent more and more time now that his wife was gone. The old man and his yammering . . . He called it praying but it was really no more than self-pity—and at some point Abe had no longer been able to stand it. Shunning the family home more and more, one day shortly after he turned fourteen he stopped going back. Better to live an unsettled life than to be sent to Aunt Esther, who wasn't even his aunt, or indeed to a home, for that was what his father wanted when he realised he could no longer issue orders to his son.

Back then Abraham Goldstein didn't know much about life, but he did know one thing: that he never wanted to be like his father.

He wanted to be an American, not a Yid who bemoaned his fate every day and railed at Yahweh; who knew nothing, and didn't want to know anything but his Mishnah and Gemara; who couldn't speak English properly and was afraid of Americans, as though every Goy was a Russian cossack, even in the middle of Williamsburg. No, Abraham Goldstein, whom everyone in the neighbourhood called Abe—another grievance of his father's—had decided not to be afraid of the Goyim, of the Jewish people or of God.

He had already been hanging around with Fat Moe's boys before he left his father and their claustrophobic little flat. In time, Moe's boys would become the family he never had, American through and through. Every one of them was Jewish, but they were American Jews, the sort who didn't bemoan their fate, but bent it to their will when it took an expected turn.

Even if he and his father walked the same streets, in the same Williamsburg, under the same grey American skies, they inhabited different worlds. So different, in fact, that they never saw one another anymore, even though Nathan Goldstein walked over Williamsburg Bridge every day on his way to work at Greenberg's clothes factory on the Lower East Side, every day there and back, too tight or too poor for the journey on the Jamaica Line. Abe wouldn't see him again until the day his mortal remains were installed in their last resting place at Linden Hill Cemetery. Abe was so drunk he could scarcely remember it, only that his father's bearded caftan-wearing friends were already saying Kaddish when the drunken, beardless son of the deceased descended upon the ceremony. Since Abraham Goldstein was no longer capable of praying alongside them, indeed, could scarcely stand on his own two feet, the men in black had bundled him into a taxi and sent him away.

That was the last time he'd had anything to do with the black hats, but here he was among them again, in Berlin of all places.

The man whose stairs he descended didn't look like a Jew. At least, he wasn't wearing a black hat. He was a craftsman in grey overalls, a scrawny man with a receding hairline and a braid of thick locks around his bald skull. When Goldstein entered the shop, which was more of a studio, the man ceased filing an unidentified tool and peered over his wire-rimmed spectacles. He didn't say anything, no 'What can I do for you?', no 'Good morning'; he just looked up, before going back to his filing.

RICHARD EISENSCHMIDT, WERKZEUGE, a discreet wooden sign over the entrance said, and Goldstein suspected that the taciturn man was the owner. If so, he was appropriately named. Goldstein continued into the dark room, observing the items on the shelves around him. He saw greasy metal parts as well as various drills and cutter heads, but had no idea about most of the tools. Eisenschmidt watched him the whole time over his file and workpiece. Only when the long shadow of his customer fell upon the lathe did he finally look up. Goldstein gazed into fearless eyes.

'You come highly recommended,' he said.

20

The operation commander sat across from him. Just like yesterday, Police Lieutenant Sebastian Tornow's uniform was immaculate, and, just like yesterday, they were in Interview Room B drinking coffee Lange had had brought up specially. Everything else was different. The uniformed officer made no secret of his impatience, bobbing up and down on his chair and constantly looking at his watch. Even the stenographer, whose pencil stood at the ready, was infected with his restlessness.

Lange knew he wouldn't be making any friends by recommencing interrogations instead of passing the file onto the public prosecutor, but Gennat had given him this assignment and he wanted to treat it as he would any other. He went through the notes he had made after his conversation with the superintendent that morning.

'It's a serious accusation you're making,' Buddha had said. 'Sergeant Major Kuschke has discharged his duties with the Prussian Police for a number of years. It is imperative that you rule out all other possibilities before accusing him of anything. You have my full support, but proceed with care.'

Lange snapped the file shut and lit a Muratti. Sometimes they helped with his nerves.

'You didn't smoke yesterday, Detective,' said Tornow. 'Can you refrain from it today? I can't stand the fumes.'

'Assistant detective,' Lange corrected, going red. 'If you insist,' he said and stubbed the cigarette out, without taking another drag. The stenographer, evidently a non-smoker too, looked gratefully at the uniformed officer.

'What are we waiting for?' Tornow asked.

'For the officer present at the time of death. I did request that you inform the man his presence is . . .'

'You won't be able to speak to Sergeant Major Kuschke until tomorrow. He's taking part in an operation.'

'And why are you telling me this now?'

'Because you didn't ask before.'

Lange cleared his throat. Although only a few years older, the man was several ranks higher than him.

'Where, if I might ask?'

'On the streets. Where people like me risk our necks every day so that you paper-pushers from CID can sit around on your fat arses.'

The stenographer blushed and gave an embarrassed little cough. Christel Temme, who normally sat in on Lange's interrogations, would have noted that last sentence stoically, without batting an eyelash, but her temporary replacement, Hilda Steffens, was obviously too busy listening. Only now did she appear to be considering whether she should commit the shorthand for *arses* to paper.

Tornow seemed to be enjoying himself. Flash fucking Harry, Lange thought! You don't look as if you'd risk your neck for anyone. 'You can spare yourself the rude remarks, Lieutenant,' he said, realising that his tone was sharper than intended. 'A police officer ought to remain objective.'

His words had the desired effect. Tornow yielded. 'Please excuse my ill temper,' he said, 'but you'll understand if I have more pressing things to do than appear before *you* every day. I thought you had asked all your questions yesterday. So, let's keep this as brief as possible.'

'That will depend entirely on you.'

'And on you—if you don't ask any questions, I can't give any answers.'

Lange ignored this fresh dig, and cast Steffens a glance as if to say: now you can start.

'The operation in KaDeWe,' he said, and listened as the pencil scratched across the page. 'There are a few . . . discrepancies.' Tornow said nothing, waiting for a definite question. 'Which officers,' Lange continued, 'were on the fourth floor at the time of the fatal incident?'

'You asked me that yesterday.'

'It's an extremely important question. Now, please answer.'

'As I said yesterday, I positioned two officers on each floor after the intruders sought refuge in the lift. Sergeants Kuschke and Hansen were on the fourth floor.'

'Where, exactly?'

'Hansen was monitoring the lifts and stairwell. Kuschke was combing the floor. In the process he discovered one of the intruders outside on the railings. The boy made a foolhardy attempt to escape down the front and plunged to his death. End of story.'

'You haven't answered my question. Where exactly was Kuschke when the boy fell?'

'You'll have to ask him yourself.'

'I will, but you were in charge of the operation and wrote the report, so I'd like to hear your assessment.'

'Kuschke was outside on the balcony when the boy fell. You know that already. He tried to help him, but . . . Well, he arrived too late.'

'How would you describe Sergeant Major Kuschke? The officer and the man?'

'For me, those categories are inseparable,' Tornow said. 'Sergeant Kuschke is an experienced officer. A man who keeps his nerve, even when things get dicey.'

'You'd say he had strong nerves?'

'What do you think? Kuschke has courage. Balls, if you like.'

Hilda Steffens stifled a giggle.

'Not the sort of man who disappears when the going gets tough?'

'No.'

'And the other possibility?'

'How do you mean?'

'In the face of danger, there are two possible reactions: fight or flight.'

'I don't know what you're getting at.'

'Does Sergeant Major Kuschke have a tendency to lose his temper and—how shall I put it?—act in an unnecessarily violent way?'

'Not in the least. Kuschke is one of the most level-headed members of my team.'

Lange opened a file. 'Then you don't know anything about . . .' he began reading from it. 'Ah, I see that was long before your time.'

'What was?'

'Doesn't matter. Back to our current case.' Lange snapped the file shut. 'Did anyone witness the boy's fall aside from the sergeant major?'

If Tornow was unsettled by Lange's manoeuvre, he showed no sign of it. 'I've mentioned that already, too,' he said. 'No one else from my team witnessed the fall. The same goes for the pedestrians we interviewed on Passauer Strasse.'

'And the other intruder?'

'Pardon me?'

'Several officers have stated that the other boy was crouched by the corpse of his friend before taking flight. Perhaps he saw something.'

'Perhaps, but you'll have to catch him first.'

Lange nodded. 'The balcony again. You said Kuschke climbed over the railings to help the boy. Did the boy refuse?'

'I don't understand.'

'Could the boy have tried to fend off the sergeant major? Might he even have punched him?'

Tornow was silent for a moment, a good sign. 'Not that I'm aware of,' he said. 'But you'll have to ask him yourself. I'm not sure how it'd be possible to hit someone when you're hanging from the edge of a precipice. What made you think of it?'

Lange pretended to make a note in the file. In fact he was doodling underneath one of yesterday's statements, but the scratch of his pencil achieved its effect. Suddenly the police lieutenant didn't seem quite so sure of himself.

It was only natural for a superior officer to back his men when something went wrong—and there was no doubt something had happened up there that didn't tally with the officers' statements, perhaps even a murder. Did Tornow know, or at least suspect? Was he trying to cover for one of his men, the indispensable Sergeant Major Kuschke? The main thing was Lange had unsettled the man, and that, for the moment, was enough.

He put his pencil to one side and stood up. 'So, that's it,' he said.

'That's it? That's the reason you summoned me here?'

'You requested that I keep it brief.' Lange stretched out a hand. 'If you would please tell Sergeant Major Kuschke to come and see me at eleven o'clock tomorrow.'

Tornow looked him in the eye, as if he could read the assistant detective's thoughts, and nodded. 'Of course. Tomorrow at eleven.'

No sooner was the man outside than Lange relit the stubbed-out Muratti.

'Should I type up the statement now?' the stenographer asked as she stood up.

'Not necessary, Fräulein Steffens. As you'll have no doubt heard, we already have the statements on file. Throw your notes away and finish there for the day. It's such lovely weather outside.'

Hilda Steffens looked at the assistant detective as if he wasn't quite right in the head before packing her things and leaving the room. Lange drew deeply on his cigarette and leaned back. Perhaps he was imagining things, or simply reading too much into the operation commander's behaviour, but he was certain that Lieutenant Tornow suspected something untoward had happened on his watch. Tornow was on the verge of starting a career in CID, and it would be most unfortunate if a black mark appearing so soon against his name were to compromise his future. Lange just had to convince the lieutenant that cooperating would be more beneficial to his career than stalling. Once he had the operation commander on side, he'd have Kuschke on a plate.

21

By the time he escaped the darkness and returned to Grenadierstrasse, Abraham Goldstein was a good pound heavier and felt like a different person. His fingers searched for the cold metal under the cover of his coat pocket, played with the weight, clasped the ribbed handle. It felt good in his hand. Though he hadn't been able to test the weapon in the shop, he was certain he had made the right choice. A Remington Model 51: small, easy to use, effective.

He hadn't thought he'd be able to get one in this country, so far from home. The taciturn toolmaker had surveyed him briefly when Abe asked for a firearm, then continued with his filing, before making for a cupboard in a dark corner of the studio. From its depths he had taken three pistols, a German model, a Belgian model, and the Remington. Even if the other pistols had been in better condition—the Belgian model was rusted, the German model had a slightly warped barrel—he'd still have gone for this. The Remington 51 felt as if it had been made for him, and the price was good. The toolmaker hadn't been able to give him much ammunition, but it would be enough for his purposes. It wasn't as if he was planning a session at the range.

He could still remember how it felt the first time he had fired a gun, when he was twelve or thirteen. It had been under Williamsburg Bridge, just before his Bar Mitzvah, at a time when he was anxious to shake off the God of his fathers.

He remembered the weight of the pistol in his hand, a Browning-Colt, almost twice as heavy as the Remington, with Moe's boys looking on expectantly. They told him how he should breathe, how he should aim over his outstretched arm, but the feeling of the weapon in his hand overrode all else. The Browning-Colt gave him more power and strength than a gaunt twelve-year-old boy had any right to possess. It fit his hand perfectly, and made him feel big and strong, like one of them. The trigger was so light; he just had to move his fingertips gently back until he located the slack. The elevated train approached the bridge and, just as it thundered directly above him, Abe squeezed. He knew how loud a shot was, but was still surprised at how it rang in his ears, and even more surprised by the recoil which almost took his hand off. The laughter of the others drowned out the iron thunder of the Jamaica Line. He hadn't even hit the car, a rusty old Ford which somebody had left under the bridge and on whose door they had drawn the target. It was said that one of O'Flannagan's men had been shot in it, but it was so riddled with bullet holes from shooting practice that it was impossible to know.

The train hadn't yet crossed the bridge and the laughter was still ringing in his ears when Abe took aim again. This time he was ready for the recoil, this time he was ready for anything. Imposing his will on the heavy pistol, he subjugated it to his desires. Then, calmly, he aimed, felt himself becoming one with the Browning. It was just like an extension of his arm, and he fired, again and again. Twice he struck the inner part of the target circle, once the outer part. Every shot hit home.

Nobody laughed now, just gazed at him in astonishment. Later they would let him shoot at rats on the bank of the East River, his first live targets. Red clouds of blood spattered everywhere, accompanied by hoots of delight. He had never understood their glee at seeing creatures suffer. When it came to killing a person for the first time, he was surprised at his own cold-bloodedness. He had screwed up a delivery (later he believed they had set him up to fail) and Moe had given him the chance to make good on a quivering wretch of a man they took from the boot of the car and threw onto the asphalt in the middle of the night. Moe looked at Abe and, without saying anything, pressed a Remington into his hand. Abe saw the shackled form in front of him, his ravaged face, and knew that one way or another this man was going to die. He also knew that he would win the respect of the entire gang if he took care of this whimpering fool as casually as possible.

He fired so quickly that even Moe was taken aback, a single shot to the back of the head, and returned the Remington to his boss. Moe couldn't help breaking out into a grin, and then roared with laughter. 'You're a handsome son of a bitch,' he said, and that had been Abe's nickname ever since. He was just sixteen.

That night he had realised, to his surprise, that he had no fear of death, neither of his own nor other people's. As soon as you accepted death, it lost its terror, simple as that. Perhaps that was what had estranged him from the religion of his forebears. If you didn't fear death, how could you fear God?

What was death anyway? It could catch you at any moment: your heart, a car, a bullet. If you wanted to live, you had to accept it, and Abe had understood that death was a necessary condition of life. The fact that we're alive is pure chance, he had once heard Moe say, the only certainty is death. And he was right. Most people saw it the other way around. They regarded their miserable existences as preordained and their *death* as chance, and that was their mistake.

Fat Moe's rise in the last few years was due, not least, to the sure hand and discretion of Abe Goldstein. If it became inevitable that someone must die, then Handsome Abe was the man you called. Goldstein had never known any of the people on his list; most of the time he was over in Manhattan, rarely in Brooklyn, and never in Williamsburg. He never knew *why* they had to die, only that their death was a necessity. He took care of his work scrupulously, quickly and without emotion, using a different Remington 51 for each new contract, which he got rid of as soon as the job was complete. The police would never find a weapon on him, nor could they prove anything against him.

He walked back to the U-Bahn station, slower than on the way out, an oasis of calm in the midst of the busy throng. Reaching a wagon he came to a halt and tasted the sour cherries, spitting the stones onto the pavement before nodding contentedly and buying a bag from the trader. People hurrying by couldn't realise, but the man crossing Grenadierstrasse was different from the one who had passed half an hour before. Only now did Abraham Goldstein feel complete, armed and ready to visit the address he had come to this city to find. Hopefully he wasn't too late.

The money he had spent on Rath's car had been worth it. The same went for Marion's dress. He mustn't forget their arrangement. Kurfürstendamm sounded like an expensive neighbourhood, but she had earned it. Without her he'd still be sitting trapped in that lousy hotel. It was only thanks to her help, thanks to her keys, that he could move about as freely as back home. No, more freely. He could do anything he wished here, absolutely anything. The police themselves would testify that Abraham Goldstein had spent the whole day inside his hotel room. The only thing he couldn't leave was fingerprints.

22

Leafing through the papers on his desk, it was clear that Special Counsel Weber thought the whole thing a damned nuisance. 'There's nothing we can use here,' he said finally. 'Not a single statement from the accused, not even her personal particulars.'

'If she doesn't say anything, how am I supposed to take down her personal particulars?' the officer facing him said. He had a strong Berlin accent. The girl handcuffed to him stared vacantly into space.

Had Charly imagined it, or was the poor creature shivering?

A representative from the Friedrichshain Youth Welfare Office stood like a lost soul. 'Perhaps she's deaf-mute, Officer.'

'No, I can guarantee you that. She knows how to curse, this one, but she buttoned it as soon as we tried to interview her.'

Weber looked at his watch. 'Fräulein Ritter, would you take care of the girl? I'll return for the warrant after my appointment with Dr Keller. Getting her name and address shouldn't be too difficult. The rest is just routine.'

While he was still speaking he reached for his coat and disappeared with a brief tip of the hat, leaving an embarrassed silence behind him.

So there she was: this taciturn girl who seemed rather shy to Charly, and who was alleged to have attacked a group of police officers on the underground. Routine. Nothing in this job was ever routine.

'Let's get started,' she said, sitting on Weber's chair, behind Weber's desk. Judging by the look on the stenographer's face she was already complicit in the fraudulent exercise of public office. The cop, the girl and the woman from Welfare waited expectantly. 'Please, take a seat,' Charly said, gesturing towards the row of chairs.

She skimmed the statement from the 81st precinct, which Weber had criticised moments before. According to it, the girl became violent after the conductor caught her riding the U-Bahn without a ticket. With the help

of several passengers he overpowered her and transferred her to police custody at Petersburger Strasse U-Bahn station where, after some resistance,
officers had placed her in handcuffs. They had found a knife on her person, a switchblade with traces of blood on it. At the same time they found
a cut on her left hand, bandaged in makeshift fashion. These facts were
enough to justify her temporary arrest, but witnesses also described a police
officer with a bloodied face who had chased the girl in Strausberger Platz
U-Bahn station. So far, this was unconfirmed. No wounded officer had
come forward to make a statement, nor had the girl made any comment. If
the statement was to be believed, apart from cursing and swearing wildly,
the unidentified girl hadn't uttered a word, at least not to the police. The
whole thing was a mystery, but the fact that the assailant had punched
and kicked officers repeatedly was enough for both a detention order and
a charge. In Prussia, resisting law enforcement officers was no petty offence.

Charly looked up from the file. The stenographer waited with sharp-
ened pencil. The lady from Welfare and the cop had sat down, but the girl
remained standing.

'You can take a seat too,' Charly said.

She didn't move, but her eyes flickered restlessly.

'It would be good if I knew your first name. How old are you? Don't
you want to sit down?'

The girl stared out of the window at the building fronts on Magdalenenstrasse.

'Spare yourself the effort,' the cop said. 'You can talk until you're blue
in the face, she won't say a word.'

Charly ignored him. 'The very least we need is your name,' she repeated.
'And where you live.'

Silence.

'Should I be taking this down?' the stenographer asked.

Charly shook her head.

'If you want my opinion,' the cop said, 'she's one of those brats who
hangs around the old axle factory, over by the slaughterhouse. I don't have
to question her to know that.'

'You're well informed, Officer.'

'I know my patch, and I recognise a runaway when I see one.'

'But you can't give me a name either.'

'Scum like that, who cares about her name?'

The woman from Welfare gave a start, but said nothing. Still unsure whether she should be writing anything down, the stenographer looked indecisively from one person to the next.

'With that sort of attitude it doesn't surprise me that you were unable to supply the accused's personal particulars. As an officer of the Prussian Police, you should display greater objectivity.'

'I'd like to see how objective *you* are, when you're trying to question a brat like that.'

'Perhaps you didn't go gently enough. The way you're acting now . . .'

'The way I'm acting now? Who is it who has to put up with these anti-social brats abusing him day in day out? Who is it they might gang up on and beat to a pulp? Who is it who's putting his life on the line every day, you or me?'

Charly's tone became sharper. 'Remove her handcuffs, Officer.'

'Pardon me?'

'You are to remove the girl's handcuffs before I begin the interrogation. We're not dealing with a hardened criminal here.'

The officer shrugged and rummaged around for the key. 'You're the boss.'

It didn't sound much like he meant it, but he unfastened the handcuffs without complaint. Nothing happened.

'You see,' Charly said.

'You weren't there this afternoon.'

The officer clipped the handcuffs back onto his belt.

'I'd like to question the girl in your absence,' Charly said.

'Pardon me?'

'I think she's afraid of you. You, or your uniform. If you would be so kind . . .'

The officer shrugged again and stood up. 'If you think so. You're the boss.'

Charly looked at the stenographer, who had made no move to get up. 'I think it's better if this stays off the record for now,' she said.

The woman from Welfare also stood up and moved towards the door. 'You're right. She doesn't trust any of us. She probably thinks I want to stick her in a home. Why not try your luck alone?'

'But you need at least one witness,' the cop said.

'This isn't to conduct an official interview. It's about regaining trust, so that an interview is possible. I'll call you back in when we're ready.'

Charly waited a moment for the door to close.

'Now, take a seat,' she said, 'or do you really want to stand the whole time?' The girl hesitated but sat in the chair. Charly pushed a carton of Juno across the table. 'Do you smoke?' she asked. Another hesitation, but she took a cigarette.

'Don't like talking much, do you?' Charly said, after she had given her a light. 'Afraid of saying the wrong thing . . .' Charly lit a Juno for herself too. 'You don't have to talk if you don't want to. You can just nod or shake your head. No one's writing down anything you say, anyway. It's between us.'

The girl drew greedily on the cigarette, avoiding Charly's gaze.

'Does it hurt?' Charly gestured towards the fresh bandage. According to the statement, several officers had to hold the girl still to inspect and re-bandage the wound. The panic in those eyes! No wonder. 'How did it happen?'

The girl tensed on her chair, and Charly realised she had asked the wrong question.

'There's no need to be scared. No one's going to be angry with you for defending yourself. We want to help you.'

The girl looked out of the window in silence.

'You didn't have money for a ticket, is that it?'

Silence.

'You know, I got caught by a conductor once too. I must have been about the same age as you. My parents weren't too pleased, but it wasn't the end of the world.'

The girl remained silent, and it didn't look as if that were about to change. Charly could imagine a simple cop losing his patience when confronted with this sort of obstinate behaviour.

'We can't help you if you don't help us,' she said. 'If you tell us your name and where you live we can send you home. Otherwise we'll have to keep you locked up until we find out.'

This was the first time she had issued a threat, but it had just as little effect as everything else. 'I don't want to lock you up, and I'm sure you don't want that either. But you have to give us something.'

The girl seemed to be thinking. That was progress at least. Just when Charly hoped she might say something, there was a commotion in the corridor outside. A babble of voices, a loud cry, worse than a band of hooligans being brought before the magistrate. She tried to ignore the din, but it wouldn't let up.

Finally she placed the Juno in the ashtray and stood up. 'Just a moment,' she said, opening the door to the corridor and total chaos. Most of the offices stood wide open, and everyone had gathered in little groups in the corridor. Handcuffed figures were being led in by uniformed officers. Their clothes were ragged and most of them had scratches to their faces or arms. One held a gauze bandage to a gash on his forehead. Everyone was talking and shouting. The boorish sergeant from the 81st precinct whom Charly had just scolded sat hunched on a wooden bench normally reserved for felons, face buried in his hands, with the woman from Welfare trying in vain to comfort him.

'What's going on?' Charly asked.

The woman shrugged. 'A group of unemployed who banded together on Frankfurter Allee. They shot a police officer, someone just said.' She looked towards the distraught officer. 'I didn't catch his name, but he seems to have been a friend of the sergeant here.'

'They killed Emil, the bastards!' The cop screamed, his face a deep shade of red. 'They should kill 'em all, Communist swine!'

He sprang to his feet and tried to collar a gaunt-looking man who was being led through in handcuffs. Two colleagues had to wrestle him to the floor.

What in God's name is happening here today, Charly thought.

Whether or not the sergeant was fit for duty was something she could decide upon later. First, she had to take care of the runaway, but when she returned to the room she found the chair the girl had been sitting on empty; two cigarettes burned in the ashtray, and the window to Magdalenenstrasse stood open. She rushed to the windowsill and looked onto the street, feeling her knees give way. The girl had disappeared.

23

Alex gripped her ankle. Only now did she feel the throbbing pain.

When the woman from the court or whatever she was, had stood up and gone to the door, she had sniffed her chance. With all the noise outside, no one heard her climb onto the windowsill and lower herself onto the wide ledge above the ground floor window. It was still a good two metres down to the pavement, but she had to move quickly before they noticed she was missing.

The drop was too great, but what choice had there been? She had dangled from the ledge, legs frozen for a moment in mid-air, before letting go. An intense pain shot through her left leg upon impact, but she got straight back to her feet and limped behind a car parked a few metres away. A little boy on a scooter gazed curiously at her. She put a finger to her lips, and the little boy nodded.

She looked up at the window as the court lady gazed out and then was gone. Someone else could look out at any moment, but she couldn't stay here forever. She had to move before the cops gave chase. It didn't matter if every step hurt like hell. She put as little weight as possible on her left leg, but a piercing pain shot up from her ankle. It felt as if it were about to snap. She gritted her teeth and limped onwards, keeping her eyes ahead. Making it to the U-Bahn station was her only chance. As long as there wasn't some idiot conductor . . . but don't think about that now!

Almost at Frankfurter Allee she turned around again. There was no one behind her, neither in uniform nor in plainclothes. Was she actually going to get out of this in one piece? Traffic noise spurred her on, the staccato, stabbing pain becoming more and more rapid, her breathing too. Damn it, first her injured hand and now her ankle.

At the steps to the U-Bahn, she looked back again. There was some commotion taking place further down Frankfurter Allee, probably the unemployed taking their anger out on the cops; the furious cries of the proletariat could be heard from almost a kilometre away. Police uniforms were like blue dots in the milling mass. From somewhere she heard the wail of police sirens and began to realise why her escape had been so easy. The cops had more pressing concerns than an eighteen-year-old guttersnipe who had done a runner.

She made her way down the steps unnoticed. No one on the platform paid her the slightest bit of attention. A girl with a limp—so what? She hauled herself a few metres along the platform, leaned her head against a cool steel beam, closed her eyes and yielded to exhaustion. Someone pressed something cold into her uninjured right hand. She opened her eyes and looked at a one-mark coin.

She wasn't a beggar. Her first thought was to return the money, but to whom? There was no sign of her benefactor, and people here seemed as distracted as ever, focused on their own concerns. Not knowing who to thank, she pocketed the coin. At least she'd have some money if she ran into a conductor again. They had taken her knife along with everything else in her bag, even the six-pack of Juno she had just opened.

A train arrived through the eastern tunnel. Where should she go? Flat B was too risky, Flat A too dangerous. Benny was dead, Kalli was dead. There was no one in this vast city who could help her, not a single place where she felt safe.

But wait, there was one. She hadn't been there in over a year and it wouldn't be easy to turn up and ask for help. There was no way of knowing how he'd react when he saw her. He wouldn't call the cops, but he might chase her away. She had to be prepared for that but, if he didn't help, everything would be over anyway. Exhausted by pain and stress, she flopped onto a seat.

The hopelessness of her situation, the fact of having no other choice, almost calmed her until, suddenly, she was overcome by a strange feeling of happiness. A smile crept onto her face. She was so tired, so at the end of her tether, that things could scarcely get any worse. Her mind was made up. She would throw herself on his mercy and hope he didn't let her down. In spite of everything that had happened.

24

Glass crunched beneath her feet, each step echoing in the empty room. Charly stopped and listened. The rush of traffic noise from Landsberger Allee was interrupted only by the rhythmical clatter of the nearby Ringbahn station. Every little scrape sounded louder and harsher than the muffled noise from outside.

The old axle factory, the cop had said, but there was no sign of the youths. A deserted ruin, perhaps they only came here to sleep?

There was a loud crash, as if something in the hall had been knocked to the floor. A jerky, scuttling noise followed in the chamber of echoes and a rat paused in the middle of the room, gazing insolently at the human intruder. There were people living in this hovel? Children even? Sharing a roof with rats? She shook involuntarily.

At the end of the workshop she found a stairwell and climbed upwards.

The rooms on the second floor were in better condition. Some of the windowpanes were still intact and there wasn't nearly as much broken glass on the floor. It was conceivable that the odd person slept here at night—even with rats present.

Did she really expect to find the girl and, if she didn't, why was she here? It wasn't as if Weber had asked her to spend the evening searching, quite the opposite. 'That's for the police,' he had said. 'Don't make things any worse by getting involved.'

Any worse. As if that were possible! She couldn't stop thinking about the empty chair, the cigarettes in the ashtray, then staring out of the window and onto the street; how she had sounded the alarm but no one was interested. No one paid much attention to a street urchin on a day when shots had been fired on Frankfurter Allee, and a police officer had lost his life. Even the woman from Welfare had shrugged, as if the girl's escape gave her one thing less to worry about. Charly had dashed out onto Wagnerplatz herself, and continued down Magdalenenstrasse. In vain; the girl was long gone.

Now, Weber, he *had* been interested, at least enough to shout at her on his return from the public prosecutor. *Must be out of your mind, flouted basic security precautions, completely unsuitable for this job* were some of the milder accusations. Imagine giving an arsehole like Weber such an easy platform! He had sent her home and told her to take the rest of the week off.

'This incident will be subject to an investigation,' he said, 'and the result will find its way into your personal file.' Still, by far the most hurtful thing was his hypocritical attempt to comfort her after he had raged for a full quarter of an hour. 'If I could give you one piece of advice,' he had said, his voice dripping with paternal sympathy. 'Don't torture yourself. You're a woman! Find a nice man and get married!'

Suddenly Charly found herself transported back to a Cologne cafe, listening to another sympathetic voice. *Once you're married you won't have to work anymore.* Now as then, she had been unable to speak.

She could still act though, and she wasn't about to follow Weber's instructions. She had climbed aboard the tram and made her way to Frankfurter Allee, travelling another two stops with the Ringbahn train. Reaching Roederstrasse she headed towards the old axle factory and climbed into the abandoned site through a gap in the rusty fence. She had to try, even if she could scarcely believe the girl would have fled here of all places.

She combed the first floor and the second, making a few discoveries along the way: wax residue, empty bottles, a battered old spoon, traces of trodden-out cigarettes. Search complete, she returned to the concrete stairs with the worn steel edges and descended them one by one. She felt a little uneasy alone in a place like this. The afternoon was simply the wrong time. Perhaps she should come back at dawn with Gereon.

Out of nowhere a boy appeared at the base of the steps, a broad-shouldered type with an angular skull and blackened fingernails, who couldn't have been more than seventeen. At first he seemed as surprised as she was, gawking idiotically before bringing his expression under control. He did at least seem aware of how terrifying he looked. He puffed out his chest and crossed his arms to make them look even more muscular.

'Can't you read?' he said. 'Entry's forbidden.'

'I was just going.'

Charly tried to remain unfazed but was surprised at how wispy her voice sounded. C'mon now, she thought, can't you think of anything better than that?

'Shame. I prefer my women to come.' His grin left her in no doubt that he was being deliberately suggestive.

Damn it, she thought, why did you have to go traipsing around here all by yourself?

'I'm looking for someone,' she said. 'A girl. About five foot seven, dark-blonde, slim, bandage on her . . .'

'What the hell is this, are you a dyke?' The boy planted himself in front of her. 'Or is it your daughter who's run away? Give me a better description. Maybe I've fucked her.'

Charly wanted to punch his ugly face. You don't scare me, she thought, you're still just a kid, a cheeky brat with no manners. 'Looks like someone forgot to bring you up properly.'

'You can always start now. Shall I show you where I'd like to be *brought up*?'

This potty-mouthed chatter was too much. Charly tried to push her way past, but the boy took her by the arm and flung her backwards. She stumbled but managed to grab hold of the rail before landing on the steel edge of the concrete steps, earning herself a few bruises.

She was wrong. This was no child she was dealing with, and no one knew she was here, not even Weber. She picked herself up and was about to say something when she heard a voice, sharp as a knife. 'Leave the woman alone, Kralle!'

She looked around at a girl in a thin coat, her black hair covered by a beret. Although her snub nose and massive brown eyes made her look sweet, Kralle seemed to respect her—or maybe it was the large knife in her hand.

'If it isn't little Vicky,' he said. 'What's this, have you founded a new club? Women helping women?'

'I don't want the cops breathing down our neck because you can't keep it in your pants. So apologise and let her go.' She pointed towards the exit with the tip of the blade.

'Naughty little Vicky has a knife. I'm so scared.'

'I would be too in your shoes, arsehole, or have you forgotten what girls with knives can do? I'm just as handy as Alex.'

'Alex, the stupid dyke.'

Vicky had touched a nerve.

'Alex,' Charly asked, 'is a girl?'

She could see Vicky thinking quickly. She had said more than she intended.

'Is she the one you're looking for?' Kralle said, almost politely now. 'Alexandra Reinhold? The description fits. Well, I'm afraid our Alex isn't home at the moment, otherwise I'd be only too glad to introduce the little tramp . . .' Stupid as he looked, he had an instinct for hurting people.

'Kralle, shut up!'

'The fuck I will! Who brought you up? When grown-ups ask you something, you answer.'

Charly tried to allay Vicky's fears. 'You needn't be afraid,' she said. 'I want to help your friend.'

'If you're from Welfare, you can piss off,' Vicky hissed. 'We know your kind of help!'

'Maybe the cops sent her on ahead,' Kralle said. 'Is Alex involved in this KaDeWe business? I thought she and her little Jewish friend had something to do with it.'

The girl with the knife suddenly lost her temper. 'Do you have any idea what you're saying,' she shouted. 'Do you have any idea what happened, you stupid, fat bastard? Now piss off before I cut you a second arsehole!'

Kralle hunched his shoulders and left.

'You'd better go too,' Vicky said to Charly, 'and forget what that idiot just said.'

'I want to help Alexandra. Do you know where I can find her? She's injured her hand and I think . . .'

'Didn't you hear me? Piss off!'

The knife in Vicky's hand shook, and she looked as if she could lose control at any moment. Charly decided not to take that chance. The knife looked sharp.

'OK,' she said, 'but if you change your mind, call me. Like I said, I want to help. I know that Alexandra is afraid of something; perhaps she should talk to me about it. I'm not from the police or Welfare.' From her handbag she produced the notebook she had carried since her time in Homicide, wrote down her Moabit number and tore out the page. She placed the paper on the stairs and picked her way across the shards of glass, back into the open air.

Her heart was pounding as she emerged onto the street. Walking quickly towards Landsberger Allee, she opened her handbag and counted her change as she went. At the Ringbahn station she made straight for the nearest telephone booth.

25

Dressed in a dark suit with a bouquet of flowers in his hand, Goldstein stood outside the door, stared at the brass number, and withdrew the hand that was about to knock. Seized by a sudden nervousness, he paced back and forth like a tiger in a cage. No one paid him any attention; only a child being dragged through the ward in his parents' wake looked at him for any length of time. He decided to go in, despite his reservations, just as the door unexpectedly opened. A man wearing a black hat came out, looked at him and his bouquet with a serious expression and walked past.

Beard and sidelocks made him seem older than he was, possibly about thirty, more likely mid-twenties. The brief moment the door was open had been enough for Goldstein to see the numerous visitors inside the room. It looked as if the entire family was gathered round the sickbed, including a second man in a black caftan. Everyone else was dressed in normal clothes.

He took a deep breath when the door closed again and the young man had disappeared inside the stairwell at the end of the corridor.

Arriving during visiting hours had been a bad idea. He couldn't go in, not with all those people there, and suddenly felt out of place with his bouquet of flowers.

Yet, until that point everything had gone so smoothly. No one had asked any questions, and the porter had provided the room number without hesitation. Dressed in his plain, dark, single-breasted suit and carrying his bouquet of flowers, Abraham Goldstein looked like an ordinary visitor, blending in with the many others moving about with flowers during visiting hours.

Everything had seemed so easy, except that it wasn't.

Goldstein paced up and down outside the door, unsure what to do. No one in there would recognise him, but he wondered whether he shouldn't wait until the family had gone. With that, he made up his mind. Pressing the flowers into the hands of a puzzled nurse, he exited the ward the same way he had come.

26

At the public entrance, Charly had said, but she wasn't there when Rath turned the corner past Alexanderhaus. The entrance to police headquarters on Grunerstrasse, right by the arches of the suburban railway, might have been the only one with an eye-catching perron, but that didn't stop the rest of the colossal brick structure from inspiring awe. Purpose-built and bigger, even, than the City Palace, Berliners referred to it as *Red Castle*. Most police officers, however, simply called their workplace *Castle*; others, somewhat less awe-struck, dubbed it *Factory*.

He was to wait on the steps outside, rather than at the porter's lodge or in his office. She hadn't said why, but he sensed she would have no great desire to run into her former colleagues. Well, there was little chance of that happening here. Although a great many people used the public entrance, those who worked at police headquarters tended to avoid it. She hadn't said a great deal on the telephone, only that they should meet at Alex and that she needed his help.

Kirie was sniffing at every corner and gazing at strange dogs as they passed. Already Rath had been forced to ward off the attentions of a pushy male pug during their lunchtime stroll, but that was as exciting as it got. His shift in the Excelsior had passed without event. Evidently Goldstein had given up trying to escape his minders and disappeared into his suite. He hadn't shown himself since, even choosing to have his lunch *brought* to the room.

Rath was so preoccupied with Kirie that only now did he register the eye-catching vehicle parked beside the railway arches. A slender man climbed out of the driver's door, and his appearance caused something of a stir, partly on account of his straight, black hair, which was bound in a long ponytail, and partly on account of his high cheekbones and impenetrable, dark, narrow eyes. Rath recognised him instantly . . . Liang Kuen-Yao, Johann Marlow's shadow, in a tailored suit as always.

What the hell was Marlow's Chinaman doing at police headquarters? Liang strode purposefully to the entrance, but only when he tipped his hat in greeting did Rath realise that he himself was the target.

'Inspector,' Liang said. 'Please come with me. Your presence is requested.' Without waiting for an answer, he turned and headed back to the car.

Rath looked around. When he was certain there was no one here who knew him, he followed. The freshly washed car was parked between a dusty Opel and a new Ford. The colour of a fine red wine, it looked as if it had arrived straight from Hollywood. Not even Hindenburg's Mercedes could have attracted more attention. Several youths gazed in wonder while maintaining a respectful distance. They were discussing what make it was.

'It's a Chevy.'—'Nonsense, a Buick Master Six.'—'American at any rate.'

It was indeed an American vehicle, but a Duesenberg, as uncommon on Berlin's roads as penguins in the Sahara. Liang opened the door and, to Rath's great surprise, Kirie sprang into the back. Before following, he took one last look to check Charly wasn't coming around the corner. Kirie crouched in the spacious footwell in front of the backseat, and allowed herself to be stroked by a man inside.

'Good dog,' said Johann Marlow.

'That must be a Boulette from Aschinger,' Rath said. 'Kirie would eat one of those out of the devil's hand.'

'I hope that's not a reference to me.' Marlow looked just as Rath remembered him: a little stocky but powerfully built, his linen summer suit tailored to perfection. 'Good to see you again, Inspector,' he said.

'I didn't know I had a choice?'

'I'm pleased to see you're as realistic as ever.'

Rath felt as if he'd stepped into his own nightmare. He had been expecting Marlow to show up again, but had pushed the knowledge aside, almost daring to hope that his dealings with the man were over.

Johann Marlow was known as Dr Mabuse or simply Dr M. At the start of his time in Berlin, Rath had become involved with him in the course of a case. Its resolution had brought a series of consequences.

At first everything had been fine. Rath had his killer, and Marlow had the gold he was after. Then a few months later an envelope containing five thousand marks appeared in Rath's mailbox. No letter, no sender, not even Rath's address—but he knew straightaway who it was from.

He hadn't asked for the money, but neither had he given it back. Several months later, he ignored the fact that it was dirty and bought a car. Perhaps to this day he wouldn't have touched it if his friend, Weinert, hadn't needed to sell his old Buick when he was in a financial jam. The money meant that Rath could help him, though the stubbornness with which the Free State of Prussia refused him promotion and, with it, a decent salary, were contributory factors too. What was left had lain untouched in an account ever since.

Among all this he had neglected one crucial detail: the five thousand marks weren't just a thank you and reward for his part in locating the Sorokin gold, they sealed a bond which Rath would sooner have dissolved—only, he didn't know how.

He looked at Marlow. What did the man want from him? 'I'm realistic enough to know that heading me off outside police headquarters is lunacy, especially in a flashy crate like that.'

'If you don't like it, then make sure you can be reached by telephone in future. Or, at the very least, that you spend your nights at home.'

'You were at Luisenufer?'

'If you had been there at four this morning we'd have had this conversation long ago. Poor Kuen-Yao had to wait in your flat for nothing. As for the *flashy crate*, the vehicle is a present from a girlfriend overseas, which I'm currently test driving.'

'There was I thinking it was *you* who sent your girlfriends cars.'

Marlow laughed. 'In this case, it concerns a female business associate, whom I helped gain a foothold in the States. She's doing rather well now, as you can see.'

'It's still a typical American show-off machine,' Rath said. Right now anything American could go hang. Except for their music.

'I must say I'm surprised. I thought you drove American vehicles too?'

'Singular,' Rath said. 'I drive an American vehicle, a used one at that. It's no match for your fleet.'

'You should work with me more often. You'd be able to afford something better.'

'Who says I want to?'

'Have I been misinformed about Prussian Police pay grades? Weren't your salaries cut again?'

Rath was tired of the subject. 'What's so important that you need to interrupt your test drive to speak to me?'

'I need your help.' Marlow made it sound like a request. 'Hugo Lenz,' he continued. 'Does the name mean anything to you?'

Rath shook his head. 'Not that I'm aware of.'

'Head of the Berolina Ringverein . . .'

'Red Hugo!'

Marlow nodded. 'You've come across him then?'

'No, but I know the name.'

Operating under his nickname, Hugo Lenz was a known figure in the Berlin underworld. Red Hugo, an experienced safebreaker, was head of Berolina, the Ringverein Marlow used for his shady deals—without ever having been a member himself. It was a profitable collaboration for both sides. Berolina did the best business out of all the Berlin underworld syndicates, and Marlow always had enough men at his disposal—and not just when there was work to be carried out. The men from Berolina were Marlow's muscle, a small army loyal to his illegitimate business empire. Nevertheless, he was careful to avoid anything that gave the impression he might have links with the Ringverein. He didn't even go to their receptions—in contrast to a number of police officers, who maintained good relationships with Berlin's criminal organisations. Even Superintendent Gennat had been known to attend the odd founder's day celebration.

'You're aware that Lapke and Höller were released from Tegel two weeks ago?'

Rath nodded. The heads of the Nordpiraten had been caught red-handed two years ago breaking into a vault at Reichskanzlerplatz. Their temporary incarceration in Tegel had decisively weakened the Pirates, with Berolina the main beneficiaries. With Lapke and Höller back on the streets they seemed determined to re-establish the old status quo, and incidents were stacking up. A week ago, unidentified men had thrown one of Marlow's drug-dealers through the closed window of a dance hall along with his goods, the victim sustaining not only cuts but paralysis to his legs and lower body. Shortly afterwards, a newly established Pirate betting office had been raided and destroyed. A gangland war seemed to be in the offing, a development many police officers observed with satisfaction, content to let the city's criminal elements take care of one another.

'I've heard about your trouble,' Rath said.

'Trouble's the wrong word. We have our first fatality. A . . . how shall I put it? Business associate of Berolina was found murdered in his shop.'

Rath was surprised. Murder was against the Ringverein code of honour. That said, the Nordpiraten weren't thought to take matters such as honour and tradition particularly seriously. 'You believe the Pirates are behind it?'

Marlow shrugged. 'Let's just say I no longer believe in coincidence.'

'Meaning?'

'Hugo Lenz has been missing since yesterday.'

Rath pricked up his ears. 'And you think the Pirates are behind that too?'

'That's what I want you to find out.'

Rath thought he saw a familiar face in the polished rear mirror of the Duesenberg. He turned his head to make sure. It was her! She was coming down Dircksenstrasse, gazing searchingly at police headquarters. Rath ducked.

'What is it?' Marlow asked. 'Are you playing hide-and-seek?'

'There's someone outside,' Rath whispered, 'who must not see me in your car under any circumstances.'

'Oh, let's not be coy now. You're talking about a woman. The cute dark-haired thing with the green hat?' Marlow laughed and signalled to Liang. The engine gave off a low, steady rumble and started. 'The same woman you took to *Plaza* back in the day, am I right?'

Rath didn't respond. Slowly he lifted his head over the seat and looked through the rear windscreen. Charly was still gazing at the public entrance, looking at her wristwatch.

'I like monogamous men,' Marlow said. 'It shows loyalty.'

'I'm a bachelor,' Rath said. He had no intention of speaking to Johann Marlow about Charly; it was bad enough the man recognised her.

Marlow laughed. 'But a loyal bachelor, evidently. Got a date, have you? Well, don't worry. We'll take a turn around the block and deliver you on time.'

Where on earth was Gereon? Charly took a crumpled packet out of her handbag and lit a Juno. In the same instant a bus came down Grunerstrasse, its upper deck plastered with images of the brand. She inhaled hurriedly and took another look at her watch. He was already more than ten minutes late. True, she had been running five minutes behind schedule herself, but what was the world coming to when even the men no longer appeared on time.

She was furious with him, even though she had no real reason to be; furious with his lateness, and with the fact that he hadn't even asked what it was about. She was furious with herself, too, furious with the passing time, as she stood there helplessly, driven almost to the brink of madness. Each minute she had to wait she felt her fury rise, and the last five went on Gereon Rath's account. She drew deeply on her cigarette, inhaling the smoke with the full force of her wrath. It helped a little, but didn't really calm her down, until there he was at last, standing on the other side of Grunerstrasse in front of the construction hoardings.

He didn't seem to have noticed her yet, but Kirie wagged her tail and pulled on the lead, as her master looked right and left before crossing the motorway behind a flashy American sedan. Finally, he saw her and smiled, and immediately she felt better. No longer alone, she stubbed out her cigarette, rage expunged.

Kirie was the first to reach her, jumping up to lick her face. She defended herself as best she could, and stroked the dog's black fur. 'Kirie, settle down,' she said.

'I should have taken a taxi,' he said.

She attempted to smile in return, but made a complete hash of it.

Gereon's smile vanished as he drew a step nearer and took her in his arms. Gratefully she allowed her head to sink onto his shoulders, felt his warm hands stroking the nape of her neck. She had to be careful she didn't start bawling her eyes out, like a child expelled from school.

'What is it, my love?' he asked, and she forgave him for every minute he had been late. She felt a lump in her throat, and it was a moment before she could speak.

'Oh Gereon,' she said. 'I've made such a mess of things. You have to help me.'

'You're shaking, what on earth's the matter?'

She hadn't realised, but he was right, she was shaking all over. She started to cry, which had never happened before in his presence, then turned her face away, but he only held her tighter. She could picture his face filled with consternation, but couldn't make it out through her tears.

Ten minutes later they were in Aschinger. Charly had wanted to go straight to the Castle, to Records; not to waste a second, but Gereon had insisted that she tell him what happened first, and give her tears a chance to dry. When she saw her face in the mirror of the ladies toilet, she realised it was a good idea. She needed a few minutes to redo her make-up, and when she returned their drinks were on the table: tea with lemon for her, coffee, black as always, for him. Gereon drank coffee at all times of day, even in the evening. For Kirie there were two Bouletten. No sooner had her master set the plate down than she pounced, demolishing the meatballs in record time and devoting herself all the more intensely to licking the plate clean. At least the greedy dog succeeded in coaxing a smile out of her.

Charly took a sip of tea and told Gereon the whole story: the frightened girl in her office, Weber's assignment, the boor of a sergeant, the commotion in the corridor on account of the dead policeman—and, finally, her catastrophic error.

His reaction wasn't quite what she had expected. 'You left a guttersnipe unattended in your office?'

'I couldn't know what would happen. I just went to the door . . .'

'You didn't even have her in sight. What if she'd taken a paper knife from the desk and attacked you . . .'

'Weber doesn't have a paper knife on his desk.'

'You know what I mean.'

'Gereon, don't you start. I know I've messed up. But this girl . . . there was something about her. She was scared stiff. Of the cop, I thought, but maybe it was just the uniform.'

'No wonder! Attacking a police officer is no petty offence. Even if it sometimes feels like it in this city.'

'I don't believe she really attacked him. The witness could have invented it. No cop's come forward to report it.'

'Charly, open your eyes! She's dangerous. When I think about what the little brute could have done to you . . .'

'She's not a brute. Who knows what she's been through? She's got a gash on her hand herself. When I think of those kids in that old factory . . .'

'Charly, Charly!' Gereon sighed. 'You can't afford to have compassion in our job. Even less as a judge or public prosecutor.'

Instinctively she reached for her cigarettes. 'Define compassion. I just want to know what happened. Now, are you going to help me look for her or not?'

Charly lit a Juno and took a deep drag, feeling her fury rise again. Gereon made a conciliatory gesture with his hands.

'Of course I'll help you.' He took a notebook and pencil from his jacket. 'So, her last name is Reinhold . . .'

'Alexandra Reinhold. I don't think they were trying to trick me in the factory. The guy seemed to get a kick out of annoying this girl, Vicky, by snitching on Alex. He seems to really hate the pair of them.'

'It must be possible to find out where she's from.'

'That's why I asked you to help. Let's go to Records and get the addresses of all Reinholds in Berlin.'

'We don't even know that she's from Berlin . . .'

'Gereon, I'm already at my wits' end. I don't know if I'm ever going to track this girl down. So, please, do me a favour and stop quibbling. Let's just try. I might not get another chance.'

'You're right, but do you really think you can impress Weber by delivering this Alex?'

'At least I'll have made good on my mistake. Besides, the girl needs help.'

'An arsehole like Weber is just waiting for you to mess up so he can write something negative in your file. He wants to destroy your career, that's been his aim from the start.'

'There are lawyers who hold me in higher regard.'

'But they're not the ones making decisions about your career.'

Perhaps they are, Charly thought. She stubbed out her cigarette.

'Let's see what happens,' Gereon continued. 'The way I see it, Weber won't want to make too much of a scene. He should never have left you alone like that. You're a judicial clerk. You can't be playing magistrate in your preparatory year!'

'I wasn't. Weber just didn't want his meeting with the public prosecutor to fall through. I was meant to get the girl's personal particulars, that's all.'

'He must have a guilty conscience.'

'He didn't appear to just now.'

'Maybe,' Gereon said, 'but have you thought about everything that's happened? The dead policeman, the shoot-out on Frankfurter Allee. Who's going to care about some tramp jumping out of the court window? I can't imagine Weber's going to be shouting his mouth off about this. He's trying to scare you because he wants to hound you out of his court, and the profession too. Don't let him intimidate you.'

'Maybe you're right.' She took a sip of tea and attempted a smile.

'Of course I'm right,' Gereon said, looking at her encouragingly. 'Now drink up, we've got work to do.'

27

The corridor lay empty ahead, with only the dim light of dusk reflecting from the polished floor. So far, no one. Most people had gone home long ago, and the patients were asleep. Goldstein had to wait for a moment outside, until two ambulances arrived one after the other, delivering the victims of a fight. At the same time a flood of relatives, friends, and others affected by the incident had rolled up and, within seconds, created an almighty stir in Accident and Emergency. Evidently, a wedding party had gone wrong.

He slipped onto the premises as the quarrelling started again, then through a door into a dim corridor, locating the stairwell and taking his bearings. This afternoon had been worthwhile after all.

The hospital wasn't especially big, not in comparison with the Jewish Hospital on Prospect Place where they had removed his appendix, but there were many wards, doors and long corridors. It was better to know your way around.

He stood before the brass-numbered door again, and though aware that all he would encounter was an old man wandering through dreams, he hesitated as before. This time he hadn't brought flowers, only the Remington in his inside pocket.

His hand pressed down on the handle and the door moved without a sound. He gazed once more across the corridor—the door to the nurses' office was still closed—and crept into the unlit room. The curtains were drawn, but a glimmer of light outlined its contours. The bed stood against the end wall, and in it lay an old man with a wrinkled face. The sign at the foot of the bed confirmed what Goldstein knew already. The only sound was the rattling in his chest, but his eyes sparkled. He was awake. He sat up as Goldstein drew closer.

He hadn't expected recognition, but the eyes in that lined face were alert.

The old man opened his mouth and his lips moved. His voice was scarcely audible, but each of the three syllables was plain to hear in the silence of the room. *Abraham.* They had never met, but the old man recognised him. The eyes that looked at him were already awaiting death.

28

Rath and Charly entered the Castle through the public entrance and made straight for Records. It reminded him of class trips where he and school-friends had roved the girls' dormitories of youth hostels. Charly was a civilian now, and here he was helping her procure information that ought to have been off-limits. It was easier than he thought.

When he showed his identification, nobody was interested in the woman at his side except the clerk with responsibility for the letters L to R. 'I know you, don't I?' he asked. 'Are you working in Homicide again?'

Charly had to think on her feet. 'Temporarily! I have to help the inspector here track down an address. Reinhold is the name.'

The clerk nodded and made for an enormous card index cabinet. 'D or dt?'

'Both.'

The man took a huge drawer out of the cupboard and hauled it onto the table. 'They should all be in here, both 'd' and 'dt'. What's the good fellow's name?'

'We're looking for a woman,' Rath said. 'More precisely: a girl.'

'A minor? That makes things trickier. Do you see? At the top of the cards you have the names of the heads of household. Wives and children aren't shown separately, and I'd be willing to bet some of them aren't registered.'

Rath sighed. Charly, on the other hand, got straight to work.

There were ninety-seven Reinhold families in Berlin. If you counted those that spelled their name with a 'dt', over a hundred.

'And we're supposed to find a girl called Alex among that lot,' Rath said, but Charly was already looking through the first card.

They found five Reinholds and one Reinholdt who had registered either an Alexa, an Alexandra or an Alexia. 'There's no way you can be sure that's all of them,' Rath said. 'Do you want to visit every Reinhold family in Berlin?'

Charly was now leafing through index cards, and beginning to sort them in piles.

'What are you doing?' Rath asked.

'I think she's from the East, Friedrichshain or Lichtenberg. We should start with those addresses.'

There were still around a dozen. Rath thought she was joking when Charly suggested visiting them all today. 'It's already half past six,' he protested. 'People are eating their dinner, and in a few hours they'll be in their beds.'

Charly's frosty gaze nipped his opposition in the bud. Rath sighed, pulled out his pencil and began transferring the first addresses from the card to his notebook. 'OK,' he said, 'but let's split up. We'll be quicker that way.'

Charly smiled at him, and Rath realised, not for the first time, that he'd do anything for that smile. Canvassing addresses was a cinch.

29

Outside the hospital Goldstein faced an unexpectedly fierce wind that cut through to his core, but decided against a taxi. Too restless to let himself flop onto the cushion of a vehicle, he walked. Walking always helped. He took out a Camel and lit it from behind his upturned collar.

The old man had the eyes of someone who knew he was about to die, but refused to let it affect him. How many people failed to recognise when their time had come and, if they did, couldn't accept it, clinging to their lives until the end? Most people simply didn't bargain on death, and when, inevitably, it came, their only response was surprise at the shocking revelation that it was all over.

At Badstrasse, behind the restaurant he had sat in earlier, the road led down to a perfectly straight little stream. He paused on the bridge, took a few drags on his cigarette and flung it into the dirty water. There was still a lot of activity on the street. He put his hands in his pockets and followed the flow of pedestrians.

A welcoming white 'U' shone in the night, above an elegant, modern brick building. Looking at the route map he saw that the next train was heading south. There was no queue and an escalator led below the ground. He allowed it to carry him down before checking behind. A figure in a black hat stepped on at the top and, for a moment, he thought his mind was playing tricks. The man stood on the stairs, gliding down at the same, monotonous pace as everyone else, an old Jew who reminded him of his father, whose hair was also white by the end. It wasn't so unusual a sight, what with a Jewish hospital nearby, but the man looked like a spectre, a dybbuk, the ghost of Nathan Goldstein returned to haunt his son.

On the platform, he lost sight of him and was tempted to put the experience down to his imagination, when the figure appeared again, floating down the escalator to fall into a short, mincing tread that bore an eerie resemblance to Nathan Goldstein's gait. His father had walked just like that over Williamsburg Bridge to Greenberg's clothing factory on the Lower East Side. The old man was reminiscent of his dead father in many ways except one: Nathan Goldstein would never have taken the train. He was too tight, or simply too poor.

In the middle of the platform the black hat came to a halt and to Goldstein he seemed like a man out of time among the advertising signs, electric lights and people waiting for their trains.

Four men in brown were laughing and talking far too loudly, their faces reddened with alcohol. They had followed the old man down the escalator. A passenger with a bandage on his face who must also have come from the hospital pointedly turned his back on them.

They wore uniform shirts the colour of an unhealthy bout of diarrhoea, military style caps, also in brown, with red brassards on their left arms. At first Goldstein thought they were Communists, until he saw the black cross against the white circle, a cross with hooks, a symbol Goldstein had seen a few times in Berlin without remembering where. The old man seemed to recognise the symbol and the uniforms. Discreetly he distanced himself from the four men, moving slowly and inconspicuously—no mincing now—to the opposite end of the platform. Others waiting had also registered the newcomers, but no one wanted to let it show. Instead they remained as unobtrusive and indifferent as possible.

The brownshirts, oblivious to the change in atmosphere, pushed their way past. You could smell the drink on them even in the stale underground air. 'Well now, what have we here?'

Their laughter trickled out like the last drop of rainwater in a gully; as did all conversation on the platform. 'Is someone lost? I thought this was an Aryan platform!'

The rest of the passengers stared either at their newspapers or their feet. The old man gave up trying to be invisible.

'Should we show the poor man the way?'

It didn't sound like the brownshirt was being a good Boy Scout. The old man lapsed into his mincing walk, back towards the escalator at the other end of the platform.

'Hey, old timer! We mean you, stay where you are!' He didn't turn around. 'Hey Jew! Stand still when Germans speak to you.'

The old man reached the escalator, climbing the moving steps one by one until he disappeared from Goldstein's field of vision. The brownshirts followed.

He seemed to be the only one who had seen the incident; everyone else continued looking at their newspapers or staring at the ground. Only when the train arrived did they raise their eyes. The doors opened, and they climbed aboard. No one got out. The train wouldn't depart for another few minutes. He looked at the open doors and then at the escalator, which continued to roll upwards.

30

Rath had taken the east. While Charly spoke to the five families who had registered girls called Alex, he would work his way through the list of Reinholds based in Friedrichshain. He strode to the top of the escalator and lit a cigarette. Before emerging from the U-Bahn station at Strausberger Platz, he took another look in his notebook. The first address was in Andreasstrasse, not far from here.

In her determination to make amends, Charly had reminded him of the year before, when she had flunked her exam. Clearly, failure was not a concept that existed in her world. Her only source of comfort was to act, which she had done by tackling the exam for a second time. She's a tough one, my girl, he had thought, as she started over again, studying long into the night. He felt an immense love for Charly in those hours he observed her unnoticed. At the same time her dogged grimness almost scared him.

He walked down Andreasstrasse, looking at the house numbers. The neighbourhood didn't bring back good memories. Not far from here, at a construction site on Koppenstrasse, which had long since been replaced by a new building, Rath had clashed fatally with Josef Wilczek, a small-time crook, and then disposed of the corpse. Later he had consigned the man's file to the Wet Fish, the Castle's store of unsolved cases, after sabotaging the investigation. At least that's what he thought, until Johann Marlow quite casually dropped the name Wilczek into a conversation. It was one of the reasons he couldn't refuse any of the gangster's requests, and that included searching for Red Hugo. At least—and this was to the man's credit—it was the first time in almost two and a half years that Marlow had tried to use him. Until now it had been the other way around, which only exacerbated Rath's debt.

He looked around. The pub where Dr M. had waited in vain for Hugo Lenz on Monday evening must be close. Not the sort of neighbourhood Charly should be walking around in at night.

On Langen Strasse, a flickering neon sign was engaged in battle with the oncoming dusk. Amor-Diele. That was the place. For an underworld meeting point it looked pretty respectable. Perhaps it had to be for Johann Marlow to frequent it.

Rath came to a halt. He looked at his list of addresses and then the sign outside the pub. Damn it, he thought as he pocketed his notebook. Charly's Reinholds could wait. He flicked his cigarette into the gutter and went over.

31

The old man didn't make it out of the station building. The brownshirts caught up with him and pushed him into a corner. Two or three passersby looked across, and suddenly rushed to get down to the platform. The man at the ticket counter leaned over his till to count his change. Goldstein entered the foyer from the top of the escalator and saw the lips under the white beard moving as if in prayer. 'Could you please to step aside so that I go back down the underground?' he asked politely.

'It's for Germans only,' said the red-faced man who had started the whole thing off. He tapped the old man's chest with his fingers. 'Who said you could take the train?'

'But I have ticket.'

'Didn't you hear? For Germans only, you'll have to walk!' One of the brownshirts struck the old man a hefty blow so that he stumbled into the arms of the ringleader.

'Hey, Jew, watch where you're going!'

'Well,' said a third, giving the old man, who was still holding his ticket, a sharp rap on the arm. 'Aren't you going to apologise to the Scharführer?'

The old man's eyes flitted this way and that, from one man to the next. Enough was enough.

'Why don't you just let the man go home?' Goldstein said.

Four pairs of eyes turned to face him.

As calmly as possible, Goldstein lit a Camel, and, for a moment, they were speechless, looking at each other before returning to the man with the cigarette. 'What do we have here?'

Goldstein would have liked to lay into them, but he didn't want to start a fight. He just wanted them to leave the old man in peace.

While the eyes of his tormentors were on Goldstein, the old man lunged to the right, darting sideways and out of the building with surprising speed. The four men gazed after him in confusion.

'We haven't finished with you yet!' the Scharführer waved his fist at Goldstein, a gesture that seemed laughable, and followed his three cronies outside.

'You're welcome, asshole,' Goldstein snarled in English. He was part of this now. By the time he stepped onto the street the old man had crossed the motorway. His pursuers waited for their Scharführer to catch up, then bore down on the old man from both sides. He looked to the left and right, before turning towards the park, which rose dark and threatening in the night sky, a wall of leaves illuminated by streetlights.

They had forced him into a corner.

Goldstein who, as a child, had been told never to walk through McCarren Park after dark, had no idea what the man was thinking. Perhaps the trees reminded him of the Galician forests, or he hoped simply to hide among the bushes. He disappeared between two box trees and, for a brief moment, the brownshirts looked around idiotically, before stalking after him.

Goldstein had to let three or four cars pass before he could cross too. The old man had struck out for the undergrowth, and his pursuers had followed. He decided on a gravel path. At least the way here was lit.

32

The man was smoking behind the wheel of his car.

Rath hadn't learned much in the pub, but at least they gave him a beer on the house. The landlord, obviously briefed by Marlow, showed him to a spacious room behind the lounge and toilets, with three tables that could be pushed together for conferences or large dinners, but would better suit games of skat. The most noticeable thing was the desk with the telephone, by which Rath knew straightaway that he was in one of Johann Marlow's many offices. This was where Red Hugo Lenz should have appeared yesterday evening, having last been seen at lunchtime. According to the landlord Lenz didn't have any quirks, only a passion for the horses, and regularly visited the racetrack at Karlshorst. Rath's theory that the Nordpiraten had taken him from outside Amor-Diele was rejected out of hand. The landlord claimed the Pirates were too cowardly to set foot in Friedrichshain, but it looked like he might be mistaken there.

Rath crossed the street, opened the passenger door and sat inside. The man stared at him wide-eyed. 'Hey,' he said. 'This isn't a taxi.'

Rath pulled out his identification. The man made to open the door but froze when he felt the barrel of Rath's Walther against his temple.

'Stay where you are, and close the door.' The man obeyed. 'Back on the streets, Johnny?'

'Do we know each other?'

'It was a long time ago. Vice squad. Bruno Wolter.' A light came on in Johnny's head. 'You were a doorman, weren't you? You've risen in the world.'

'Is this allowed?'

'Does it matter?' Rath pressed the Walther a little harder against the man's temple. 'You're from the Nordpiraten, if I'm not mistaken.'

'And you're a cop coming out of a Berolina dive. What am I supposed to make of that?'

'Nothing. You're here to answer questions, not me. Hugo Lenz has disappeared, and the majority of people in there think the Nordpiraten had something to do with it. How many evenings have you been sitting here now? Was it you who kept an eye on Red Hugo before giving him up?'

'Why would I do that?'

'Why break a drug-dealer's spine? Why make a bonfire out of a newspaper kiosk?'

'We're taking back what's rightfully ours.'

'No matter how many people are killed in the process?'

'That's rich. Do you know why I'm sitting here, Inspector? It's because Rudi Höller has disappeared. Lapke thinks Berolina bumped him off.'

'Rudi the Rat?'

'We deal with these things ourselves. No cops.'

'What makes you think Berolina are behind it? They don't go about killing people. They stick to the code of honour.'

'Well, maybe Red Hugo and his men don't get their own hands dirty, but if you knew who just landed in Berlin . . .'

'Explain!'

'Don't you know anything? You haven't heard there's an American killer in town? Now, who has the money to send for someone like that? Not the Pirates! You should spend some time probing the good men of Berolina.'

'What do you think I've been doing?' Rath gestured towards the pub. 'The things they're saying about your lot, you'd want to be careful hanging around like this.' He opened the door. 'Tell your boss that we don't want a gangland war here in Berlin. Tell him to keep the peace, or he'll be straight back in the can.'

33

Away from the streetlamps it was pitch black. Wind rattled the trees and gravel crunched underfoot. Goldstein had started to believe he was the only person in this nocturnal wilderness when he heard a cry, but the noise of a passing train drowned all other sound, even the rustle of leaves in the trees.

He moved in the direction of the cry until he saw the four brownshirts gathered in a little clearing around the old man. Silhouetted by the light of a streetlamp, their long shadows were thrown across the grass. The black hat was pulling himself up from the ground. 'You Shkotzim, why don't you let an old man go about his business in peace?'

'Speak German. This is Germany!'

One of the brownshirts launched a kick at the old man's solar plexus, and he fell to his knees, gasping for breath. A second kick struck him under the chin and he toppled forward, his hat rolling across the grass.

Goldstein stepped silently onto the soft grass, but they were too preoccupied to notice. The fat one fumbled around with his fly. 'Make a bit of room. I'm desperate here.'

The others laughed and stepped aside. The old man groaned but didn't move. The fat man had his dick in his hands when Goldstein shouted. 'Who shat on your uniforms?'

All four turned, and the one holding his dick said: 'I don't believe it. Someone must have a death wish.'

'It's the big mouth from just now!'

'Must be a foreigner who doesn't know who he's dealing with. Needs teaching a lesson.'

'I'll tell you who I'm dealing with,' said Goldstein. 'A group of cowardly mamzerim going at an old man, one with a fat belly and a tiny schmock. Put that thing away before it drops off. You won't find it in the dark.'

The fat brownshirt stuffed his penis back in his fly and fumbled frantically at the buttons. The other three turned their attentions to Abraham Goldstein.

'The way you're talking you must be a Jew too?'

'It doesn't fucking matter what he is, Stefan,' the ringleader said, still buttoning his fly, 'either way he needs a good slap.'

Stefan planted himself in front of Goldstein and looked him over. 'You don't look Jewish to me, so don't butt in. You'll regret it.'

Goldstein flung his cigarette onto the grass. 'Fuck *you*,' he said in English, putting his hands in his coat pocket.

'We're in Germany,' Stefan said, 'and in Germany we speak German. Time for your first lesson.'

He lifted his right hand but Goldstein rammed his forehead against the bridge of his nose before he could move. Stefan's eyes rolled and he fell to the floor, blood streaming from his nose. One down, three to go.

'Did you understand that?' Goldstein asked. 'Or do you need me to translate?'

The fat ringleader found his voice. 'Now you're talking,' he said. 'Show him, Gerd!'

Gerd put on his brass knuckles. 'You won't get *me* like that,' he said. 'Not so much as a warning, you cowardly piece of shit.'

'Consider yourself forewarned.' Goldstein pulled the Remington out of his coat pocket. 'One more step, and there'll be a hole in that nice uniform.'

Gerd stared uncertainly into the barrel and looked to his leader. 'He's got a piece, Günter. He must think we haven't seen it all before.'

'Put that away,' said Günter. 'You think the SA would venture into a Communist area unarmed?'

'I repeat. Reach for a pocket and you'll find yourself with a hole in your shirt.'

Abe must have been concentrating too hard on the ringleader and Gerd's brass knuckles. He lost sight of the third man. By the time he registered movement, his arms were gripped from behind. He lost his balance and, together with his attacker, fell to the ground. A shot went off and someone screamed.

'Aargh, my foot!'

His attacker loosened his grip for a moment and Goldstein slammed the Remington against his temple, knocking him out. He wasn't the only one rendered out of commission. Gerd was sitting on the lawn next to the unconscious Stefan, clasping his right foot with both hands. On his right hand he still wore the brass knuckles. Dark, shiny lines of blood seeped through his fingers and dripped on the floor.

'Damn it, my foot!' he yelled. 'What have you done, you arsehole?'

Goldstein looked over at the fat man, who stood off, making no move to approach. He picked himself up, ready for the next attack, but the man stayed where he was. 'So,' the man said, 'things look a little different now, don't they. Drop your weapon!'

At first Goldstein thought he must have misheard, but then he saw the Luger cocked in the man's hand.

'I'm warning you,' Günter said. 'I'm a good marksman. Pistol on the floor.'

Goldstein shrugged. 'You know, in situations like this, it doesn't really come down to who's the best shot.'

'Oh?'

'It comes down to who can hold their nerve.'

'Drop your weapon!'

'That's what I'm talking about. You're too nervy. Your voice is too loud. Any moment now your hand will start shaking.'

'An arsehole like you, I'd hit every time.'

'The problem is you don't *want* to shoot me. You can't. You're not capable. Otherwise you'd have done it already.'

The Luger began to shake.

'Shoot him!' cried Gerd. 'Do him! The bastard shot my foot! It's self-defence!'

Günter was already moving backwards.

'I think it's about time I issued another warning,' Goldstein said, nodding towards the Luger. 'Drop your weapon before I shoot it out of your hand. Have you ever thought how awkward life can be without a right hand?'

The panic in the fat man's eyes grew. Fight or flight? He dropped the Luger, turned on his heels and ran.

'Some Scharführer,' Goldstein said to the whimpering Gerd, who was still mourning the loss of his toes. 'Leaving you in the lurch.'

Stefan groaned and put his hands to his bloody nose. Reaching it, he gave a yawp and immediately regained consciousness. The third man was also coming round. All three looked at Goldstein. In the meantime Gerd had tears in his eyes, and was making an increasingly strained face.

'This isn't a picnic, you know,' Goldstein said. 'So far, you've managed to escape with a few bruises . . .'

'Bruises?' Gerd wailed. 'My foot!'

'. . . but I warn you. It's time to get the hell out of here before I change my mind.'

Stefan and the other man cast a final glance at their lame colleague, before taking flight in different directions.

Goldstein planted himself in front of Gerd.

'Stop dragging your feet, that means you too.'

'How am I supposed to walk?'

'Try hopping or crawling. Your whining is getting on my nerves.'

Moments ago, Little Gerd here had been prepared to smash his face in with brass knuckles. Now he was behaving like he'd just realised that life was unfair. He pointed the Remington at him. 'I'd get out of here, unless you want to lose the other foot.'

Gerd gave a cry of pain as he tried putting weight on his left foot for the first time. When he shifted the load to his heel it appeared to work. Slowly he limped towards the beam of light and the gravel path, and hobbled out of sight.

Goldstein went over to the old man and handed him his black hat. He was a little worse for wear, and there was a bruise under his white beard. All in all, though, he wasn't doing too badly. 'Up you get, old timer,' he said, helping the astonishingly light man onto his feet. The Jew dusted the dirt and blades of grass from his caftan, and looked at him as if he were the Messiah.

'Just so we understand each other,' Goldstein said. 'I don't exist. You never saw me!'

'But I do see you. You stand here now.'

'But really, I am somewhere else.'

'I don't understand. Who are you?'

'I could be the Archangel Michael for all it matters. Just to be clear again: this never happened. I'll take you home to your family, and then you'll forget about the whole thing, yes?'

'Many times, thank you,' the old man said. 'But you shouldn't have fired shot.' He shook his head. 'Shooting is wrong.'

Arguing with pig-headed old Jews of this kind was a waste of time, as Goldstein knew from experience. He gave the man his arm and led him towards the gravel path.

'Let me tell you the story of old Rabbi Zanowitsch from Lubowitz,' the old man said. Goldstein rolled his eyes. He had heard it many, many years before.

34

The new month began in a crush as Weiss summoned all senior CID officers, from inspector upwards, to the large meeting room.

For once Rath didn't mind. He pressed Kirie's lead into Gräf's hands, dispatched the detective to the Excelsior and treated himself to a coffee. In the cluster of people that formed outside the room were a few familiar faces from A Division, among them Wilhelm Böhm sporting a holiday tan. Rath wouldn't have begrudged Bulldog Böhm a few more days off, or, indeed, early retirement on full pay. He kept his distance, shuffling forward beside Narcotics, who were bitching about Nebe, their former boss, whom Weiss had made head of Robbery Division a few weeks before. Nebe was ambitious, unpopular, and seen as Bernhard Weiss's protégé. Those who enjoyed the protection of superiors at the Castle didn't have an easy time, as Rath knew from experience, having been seen as the darling of the former commissioner, Zörgiebel, when he started in Berlin.

The crowd pushed through the double leaf doors and into the room. Rath found a space at the back and sat down. The air was already sticky. Most officers were smoking, and no one thought to open a window. He yielded to the herd mentality and opened a packet of Overstolz, sniffing the fresh tobacco before lighting up.

Yesterday evening had ended with him and Charly smoking in his flat on Luisenufer, exhausted and resigned after many hours of fruitless door-to-door canvassing. Rath had waited over an hour for her, and was starting to worry when he heard the key turn. Moments later, her disappointed face appeared in the door. She hadn't found the girl, of course, although she had worked through her entire list. He consoled her with the prospect of tomorrow, and received a tired, battle-weary nod in return.

His telephone call to the Welfare Office had done nothing to assuage his guilty conscience, and the fact that Charly, tired and resigned as she was, had actually believed his threadbare excuses, almost shamed him more than the excuses themselves. He had visited only one Reinhold family and was met by an indignant woman who said she had no daughter by the name of Alex or Alexandra. At the other four addresses, he had claimed—and Charly believed him—no one had been home.

This morning, that same abandoned list had morphed into her final hope. She tore the evidence of his neglect from the notebook almost gratefully, and he said nothing more on the subject. Certainly not his true opinion, which was that the situation was hopeless.

The whispering that filled the large meeting room grew quieter and finally stopped. Rath looked up as the deputy commissioner stepped onto the podium with a grave expression. He threw his cigarette on the stone floor and trod it out with the tip of his shoe. Dr Weiss gripped the lectern and waited. Only when all was quiet in the room did he speak.

'I have gathered you here today,' he began, looking around, 'in light of recent, tragic events. I am sure most of you have heard already.'

His account of the clash on Frankfurter Allee sounded altogether more grave than it had coming from Charly. As expected, the deputy didn't mention anything about a guttersnipe who had escaped from Lichtenberg District Court. He simply listed the facts: a workers' demonstration in the middle of a Communist area; sudden escalation, and advancing police officers find themselves in a hail of bullets; a sergeant who storms demonstrators on the front line is hit in the chest, collapses, and dies shortly afterwards.

'You are no doubt aware, gentlemen,' Weiss said solemnly, 'that Sergeant Emil Kuhfeld is not the first police officer to lose his life in the line of duty. Nor, I fear, will he be the last. I know I speak for us all when I say that *we*, his colleagues, will not forget him.' He gazed around the room. 'Gentlemen,' he continued, 'Please rise and observe a minute's silence for our dead colleague.'

Hundreds of chair legs scraped across the floor and the room became eerily quiet. Everybody knew this minute's silence was no hollow, meaningless gesture, but affected each one of them personally. The much-invoked superiority of CID over Uniform had no place in this room. When it was a question of the mood outside, of the increasingly brutal hostility officers faced every day on the streets, they were all in the same boat, whether in uniform or plainclothes. The only difference was that Uniform had to risk their necks far more often. Out there were people who looked on police officers as fair game.

Rath had never felt drawn to life on the beat; now it seemed less attractive than ever.

'Thank you, gentlemen.' Weiss drew the minute's silence to a close, and the room filled with noise again.

Only now did he mention the state of the investigation. Initial enquiries from Section 1A, the political police, had revealed that the shooting was coordinated by Communist headquarters, and, for this reason, Weiss had ordered a series of searches. The ban on the Spartakiad was now to be implemented in all its force. Weiss had already forbidden the Communist sports event a few days ago, as well as an SA event scheduled for the same day. In his campaign against the violent, so-called politicians who had brought Germany to the brink of civil war, Bernhard Weiss, himself a former chief of the political police, was consistent like no other Prussian officer.

'Now let us move on to something altogether more agreeable,' he said, smiling for the first time. 'There is another reason I have gathered you here. In fact there are several reasons; specifically, the men sitting directly in front of me today.'

Weiss paused, and the atmosphere grew restless as everyone tried to see who was in the front row. Rath craned his neck, but couldn't see past the bulky Ernst Gennat, who was sitting in the third or fourth row.

'These are your new colleagues,' Weiss continued. 'CID is being supplemented by a number of cadets. Despite the compulsory saving measures imposed by the government, we are doing everything in our power to avoid police numbers being cut.'

'And what are you doing to avoid police salaries being cut?' a heckler shouted. Everyone turned, but the man was nowhere to be seen. No one dared laugh and Weiss remained calm.

'I see many well-nourished faces before me. To my knowledge, no CID officer has died of starvation this year. Should you genuinely be living in want and find yourself unable to afford the canteen, come and see me in my office. Just make sure you don't go nosing about Superintendent Gennat's cake selection.' A few colleagues laughed, but not many. 'Back to our cadets,' Weiss said. 'Allow me to invite the men onto the stage.'

Rath heard chairs shifting as half a dozen young men lined up in front of them.

'Messrs Start, Tornow, Schütz, Weisshaupt, Marx and Kluge begin their service as cadets today. Initially, they are assigned to J Division, as Warrants are currently suffering the greatest shortages. However, they can be assigned to other divisions on a case-by-case basis, at the discretion of Chief Scholz.'

Second from the left was the police lieutenant Rath had encountered outside Weiss's office. He cut an immaculate figure in a suit. Tornow, the deputy said his name was.

'I ask that you remain on hand with help and advice for these men,' Weiss continued. 'Most of you were in Uniform not so long ago, exposing yourselves to great danger in the service of our democratic state. If you are teamed with one of our cadets, please exercise patience as you show them the ropes. Remember, in time, one of these gentlemen could be your superior.' He paused until the laughter died. 'All joking aside, yesterday's events remind us how important it is to work together, *with* rather than *against* one another.'

Rath couldn't be sure through Weiss's thick reading glasses, but he felt as if the deputy had his eyes trained on him. It was probably just his imagination, an inherent sense of guilt exacerbated by his rigorous Catholic upbringing. Appeal over, Weiss brought the meeting to an end. The officers stood up and gradually filtered out of the room. In their midst moved a man whose vast frame made him impossible to overlook.

Rath considered whether he should speak to Gennat. Perhaps the chief of Homicide could exert a little pressure, even if it was clear that Bernhard Weiss had no intention of withdrawing Rath and his men from the Goldstein operation. Why the whole thing couldn't be transferred to Warrants, Rath didn't know, especially now that they had a few extra hands. After all, what better job was there for a cadet than a stake-out? Rath headed towards Buddha, before hesitating. Wilhelm Böhm stood alongside the superintendent. It would have to be Böhm! Approaching the two detectives he overheard the Bulldog mention something about a robbery homicide that wasn't.

'Good morning, Superintendent.' Rath tipped his hat. 'Detective Chief Inspector.'

'Ah, Inspector Rath,' Gennat said. Böhm broke off mid-sentence and cast the troublemaker an angry glance. 'I see you're back,' Gennat continued. 'How is everything going?'

'Fine, thank you for asking. I just wanted to check what was happening in A Division. We don't hear much out in the field. Looks like the number of cases is on the rise again.'

'Yes, a real tragedy, this business with our colleague. We'll touch on it in briefing later.'

'And DCI Böhm is investigating a death as well, I hear?'

Böhm shot him a second, angrier glance, which Rath chalked up as a minor victory.

'We found a corpse yesterday in Friedrichshain,' Gennat said. 'A second-hand dealer in a pretty bad way at the back of his shop. Everything points towards robbery homicide, except the man was a known fence with links to the Berolina Ringverein.'

'Which is why I suspect a different motive,' Böhm butted in. 'Berolina and the Nordpiraten are at loggerheads and it wouldn't surprise me if the robbery homicide was staged. There are, at any rate, a few discrepancies.'

Rath's ears pricked up. 'You think there's someone out there settling underworld scores? What do you think?' he asked Gennat. 'Would it be possible for me to take part in today's Homicide briefing? Just to keep up to date, in case my men report back for duty in the next few days.'

Gennat looked at him as if trying to establish the real reasons for Rath's interest. Buddha might appear a little sleepy, but his eyes were so alert and his gaze so intense that Rath couldn't help but blink. 'Any time,' he said. 'As long as you can make it work with your other commitments.'

That didn't sound as if Gennat was about to ask Weiss for his men back. Rath hid his disappointment and nodded.

A short time later, he sat with his old colleagues in the small meeting room, with everything just as before, except that Gräf was missing. Henning and Czerwinski were catching up on sleep after finishing the night-shift. Rath half listened as Assistant Detective Lange spoke blandly about the dead boy from KaDeWe, whom they had now identified, and Assistant Detective Mertens recapped yesterday's shooting in the east. The investigation was being headed by Section 1A, with Homicide operating in a purely ancillary capacity.

For a CID detective, there was nothing worse than acting as a grunt to the political police. Even so, Mertens couldn't hide his satisfaction that 1A had been unable to trace the gunman. Reading between the lines, it was clear he considered it wishful thinking not only that the shot had been intentionally fired, but that it had come from a Communist source.

Next up was Böhm, who received Rath's undivided attention. Evidently he still hadn't heard anything about Red Hugo's disappearance, mentioning only that Hugo Lenz, who was on his list of interviewees, was to be found neither at home nor at his regular haunt. Apparently that wasn't Mulackritze, as Rath had always assumed, but Amor-Diele in Friedrichshain, where he had been only last night. To think he could have run into one of Böhm's men!

Whether he was a victim of the Nordpiraten or not, Böhm's dead fence, whose name was Eberhard Kallweit, had been found in his shop yesterday, and probably been there for several days. The till was empty, but the perpetrators had left a surprising number of valuable items, high-quality wristwatches among them. That was one of the reasons Böhm thought the robbery homicide was staged, especially since the victim had been brutally tortured before death. So brutally, in fact, that it was all too much for one of his tormentors. Next to the dead man, Forensics had found a pool of vomit that definitely hadn't issued from Kallweit, a fact confirmed in Dr Schwartz's post autopsy report. Aside from the vomit, the pathologist had found numerous breaks and lacerations, as well as the source of the internal bleeding that was responsible for the victim's death.

Böhm then reported on the background to the current gangland feud. It wasn't open warfare, he said, and there still hadn't been any fatalities, or, at least, no *obvious* executions, but, in the past two weeks clashes between the Nordpiraten and members of Berolina had grown more frequent.

'We believe it to be connected to the release of Rudolf Höller and Hermann Lapke, both of whom have just served two years in Tegel for attempted bank robbery. Clearly they hope to restore the Nordpiraten to their former glory.'

The incidents were stacking up. Berolina drug-dealers had been beaten in broad daylight; bars that stood under the official protection of the Ringverein had been destroyed, their guests insulted. The attacks had culminated with the unfortunate drug-dealer who landed spine first on a set of basement steps. The torching of a new Pirate betting office on Greifswalder Strasse was seen as Berolina's response, even if neither police nor the Pirates could prove it. Had the fence been killed in retaliation?

'If Kallweit should prove to be the first victim in a gangland war,' Böhm said, 'things will soon escalate.'

'Lock 'em up,' someone cried. 'That's how you avoid your escalation right there.' The heckler received a murmur of approval. 'That's right,' said another. 'We know almost all the members of these Ringvereine. Why can't we just put them all behind bars?'

'Why not do the same with the Communists,' a third cried. 'Wouldn't be able to gun our men down from inside.'

'Quiet, gentlemen!' Gennat, who had been silent until now, stood and made a conciliatory gesture with his hands. 'Quiet, please!' The superintendent could be astonishingly loud.

The murmuring subsided.

'You are well aware why we can't do that. Locking people up just because we think they *might* commit a crime. In Prussia only those found guilty and convicted can be put in jail. There is no preventative custody, and rightly so. Otherwise the way is paved for misuse and despotism. Gentlemen, we live in a constitutional state . . .' He paused, seeming to look every single officer in the eye. '. . . and you are a part of its executive power, no more, but equally—and I stress this—no less.'

He had the room back under control. 'If it is as Böhm here suspects and we are dealing with the first casualty of a gangland war, then we will do everything in our power to prevent further loss of life. Using the means afforded to us by our constitutional state.'

'As far as I'm concerned, a single casualty isn't enough,' the officer next to Rath hissed. He didn't dare say it out loud; that much at least Gennat's sermon had achieved. 'Let the bastards take care of each other.'

There was a knock on the door and Assistant Detective Grabowski poked his head inside.

'Superintendent,' he said. 'Please excuse the interruption, but we've found a corpse, in Humboldthain.'

35

The murder wagon pulled up on Brunnenstrasse, outside the Himmelfahrt-kirche, whose pointed spire towered in the sky, drawing a crowd of rubber-neckers. Wilhelm Böhm shouted at the first cop he saw to clear the path in front of the church. 'Kindly ask people to use the other side of the road!'

'But . . . the corpse is behind the church . . .'

An angry glance was enough. The officer did as bidden, rounding up a few other cops and cordoning off the path. Böhm emitted a satisfied growl and waved Christel Temme, the stenographer, over. Together they proceeded around the back of the church. ED, the police identification service, was already in action, looking like a group of grown men hunting for Easter eggs, the biggest of which was apparently lying hidden behind a bush, with two ED officers and a cop standing by.

The cop gave a smart salute. 'First Sergeant Rometsch, 50th precinct, at your service, Sir.'

Böhm nodded and looked at the shrubs that had been planted in front of the chancel to denote the beginning of the park. Behind a thick gorse bush lay the dead man, wearing a uniform with a swastika brassard. Another victim of what too many people confused with politics.

'Who found the corpse?' he asked, and Christel Temme, who had already pulled out her notepad, started scribbling. The stenographer wrote down absolutely everything, even when someone asked the time.

The cop shrugged his heavy shoulders. 'Someone called in anonymously.'

'What precinct are you again?'

'I beg to report, Sir: the 50th precinct, Detective Chief Inspector, Sir.'

Böhm looked at the corpse. 'So. What do you think?'

Sergeant Rometsch was visibly thrown by the question. 'Well,' he said. 'I would say the Red Front's a possibility.'

Böhm nodded. 'Even though it's banned.'

'Yes, Sir, even though it's banned. We know that hasn't stopped them.'

'Cut out the constant standing to attention. You're not on the parade ground here.'

'Yes, Sir!' First Sergeant Rometsch from the 50th precinct stood with his back even straighter.

Böhm shook his head.

Assistant Detective Grabowski came around the corner, carrying the camera from the murder wagon. He unfolded the tripod. 'Tricky perspective,' he said. 'Couldn't the killer have left him by the church?'

Only now did Böhm see the pool of blood by the church wall, in the dark corner where the nave met the transept. The assistant detective was observant, he thought, and gave a grunt of appreciation. It didn't pay to praise these young men too much, or they took on airs and graces. He gestured towards the dead man's right foot. The shoe was split open by a gunshot, and out of the bullet hole swelled an unseemly, red-brown mass. The blood had spread to his gaiters. 'Don't forget to take a few close-ups of the foot.'

Grabowski got down to work.

'Ah, Böhm, there you are!' Kronberg approached, waving identification with a swastika on the front. An SA membership card, whose passport photo displayed the face of the deceased. 'The man's name was Gerhard Kubicki.'

'And he was a brownshirt?'

The Forensics chief nodded. 'To be exact: an SA-Rottenführer.'

'I can never get my head around these Nazi ranks—does that make him a big fish?'

'Relatively.'

'So, a mid-ranking Nazi.' Böhm gestured towards the pool of blood in the shadow of the church. 'Seems to have been dragged here, wouldn't you say?'

Kronberg nodded. 'Possibly to hide the body, but that's not the only stretch the man covered. Come with me!'

Böhm followed Kronberg to a footprint that a forensics technician was filling in with freshly mixed plaster.

'Footprints,' Kronberg said superfluously, 'one of which we have matched to the victim. He dragged his leg behind him.'

'No wonder, with an injury like that.'

'It looks like he made it to the church by himself. We found a trail which we were able to trace back to a meadow in the park.' Kronberg pulled a tin from his overalls and opened it. 'And this . . .' he said, 'is what we discovered there.'

In the police evidence tin was a bullet smeared with blood and dirt.

Böhm gave a nod of acknowledgement. 'Before you give it to Ballistics, you should take it to Pathology and have the blood group checked. We have to be sure it's from the murder weapon.'

Kronberg shook his head. 'The murder weapon wasn't a pistol,' he said, enjoying keeping Homicide on tenterhooks. He paused again, for slightly longer this time, and Böhm almost lost patience. He must have shot him an angry glance; Kronberg at any rate gave an apologetic shrug. 'I don't want to anticipate your pathologist, but if I've assessed his injuries correctly, we're looking for a knife or a dagger. A stabbing weapon at least.'

'Did you find one?'

'We're still looking. Most likely the perpetrator took it with them. Or threw it somewhere in the Panke or wherever else. But . . .' Again he made his clever-clever face.

Böhm rolled his eyes. 'What? Get to the point!'

'I can tell you what kind of stabbing weapon it was,' Kronberg said, looking triumphant. 'In all probability it was a trench dagger from the War.'

'How do you know that?'

'Come with me and I'll show you.'

They returned to the bushes where the corpse lay. Böhm took a closer look at the blood-soaked shirtfront. It did indeed display stab and slash wounds. Kronberg gestured towards the dead man's belt, and an empty knife sheath dangling from it. 'More or less every front soldier had one,' he said. 'Normally a trench dagger goes inside. Lots of SA men still carry their weapons from the War.'

'This man's too young to have served.'

'Perhaps he inherited it from his father. At any rate this sheath goes with a trench dagger, I'm one hundred percent positive.'

'Which means . . .'

'In all probability, the man was stabbed to death with his own weapon.'

'So, I'd say it was a fight that spiralled out of control,' Grabowski said. He was just about to photograph the man's injured foot. 'Did you see?' He pointed towards the deceased's right hand, which was clasping brass knuckles.

Böhm gave another grunt of appreciation.

'But if I've understood correctly,' he said, 'the fight didn't take place here.'

Kronberg nodded and led the DCI to the meadow where they had found the bullet. Here, too, forensics officers were looking everywhere for clues. Early walkers strolling through the park watched them curiously, but at least stayed on the path.

'We should cordon this area off too,' Böhm said. Moments later two uniformed officers were forcing passersby to make a detour.

Most of the clues were to be found in the middle of a clearing surrounded by bushes and trees. The gravel path only passed directly by the meadow on one side.

'A struggle seems to have taken place here.' Kronberg pointed towards the spot in question. 'There are a number of footprints and a few people also seem to have fallen. We found blood in the grass. A trail of blood leading from here to the church.'

'Sir!'

Kronberg looked around. One of his men had found something. Böhm and Kronberg went over to see what.

A cigarette butt, in a pair of tweezers, still damp from the morning dew. CAMEL the stub said in big letters.

'Who smokes those?' Böhm asked.

'Not too many people, I hope. I wouldn't have called you over if it was a Juno.'

They went back to the church where Böhm checked his watch. Barely a minute was needed to cover the distance. With a shot-up foot, perhaps a little longer.

In the meantime Dr Schwartz, the pathologist, appeared.

'Finished taking photographs?' Böhm asked Grabowski, who had already folded away the tripod.

'Making way for the doctor.'

'Good, then I have something else for you. Could you check which tobacconists in Berlin sell the brand . . . Camel, was it?'

'It's pronounced Cämmel,' Grabowski said. 'It's American.'

'Spare me the linguistics lecture and get down to work. Put the camera back in the car and take the next train to Alex. I don't need you here for the time being.'

Grabowski swallowed whatever he was about to say and turned back to the camera. Böhm left him and went over to Dr Schwartz, for whom they had already pulled the corpse a little out from the bushes.

'They cut him like a wild sow,' Schwartz said, displaying his customary empathy. 'Must have damaged a few internal organs in the process.'

'How long has he been dead?'

Schwartz shrugged.

'I'm not going to hold you to it.'

'Less than ten hours, I would say.' The doctor looked at the corpse unwaveringly, as if trying to bring it back to life. 'Though that isn't to say he didn't sustain his injuries much earlier. It probably took him a while to bleed to death. Judging by the amount of blood he lost, his heart must have kept beating for some time.'

'And the shot to the foot?'

'Harmless.' Schwartz sounded as if he were talking about a sniffle. 'Would hurt a bit, and there's a good chance you'd walk with a limp for the rest of your life, but otherwise . . . the man could have hobbled to the nearest hospital and got treatment. However . . .'

'What do you mean, however?'

'I don't know that they'd have been happy to take him in.'

'What are you saying?'

Schwartz gestured towards the swastika. 'The nearest hospital,' he said, 'is the Jewish Hospital.'

Böhm nodded. Just then it started to rain. The doctor gave the undertakers, who were waiting impatiently, a wave, and the mortal remains of Gerhard Kubicki disappeared inside a zinc coffin.

36

The garage was somewhere in the north, but the thought of being able to drive again made the long train journey more bearable. Second-class wasn't especially full; most people travelling on this line were content with third.

Rath took his cigarette case from his coat, lit an Overstolz and thought about Böhm's report at briefing. So, Kallweit was tortured before his death. Did Berolina have a secret the Nordpiraten were trying to extract? If so, it could mean that Hugo Lenz was sitting in a cellar in north Berlin being strong-armed by the Pirates. He was suddenly grateful to Johann Marlow for giving him a little investigative work. At least with Red Hugo's mysterious disappearance he had something to think about while he twiddled his thumbs in the Excelsior.

For a moment he actually thought Gennat would give him the corpse in Humboldthain, but Böhm got it after all, in addition to his dead fence. Weiss seemed to have issued Buddha with a clear brief: on no account is Inspector Rath to be handed a homicide case. This, despite all the deaths A Division was currently investigating. Charly was probably right: the Goldstein operation was a punishment Weiss had meted out personally.

He displayed his police identification to the conductor instead of a ticket. He was already at Wedding, and would continue to the final stop at Seestrasse. From there it was another two kilometres by tram. *Jotwede*, as the Berliners said. Bloody miles.

Rath didn't reach his destination for another half hour. In the light of day, the garage looked dirtier than he remembered. He crossed the courtyard and entered through a wide-open steel door. No one paid any notice. A Mercedes stood on the hoist. Below was a mechanic with a screwdriver. Another four men were gathered around an engine block discussing some technical problem. Rath gave a polite cough but, again, no one paid any attention. He took a large wrench from an oil-smeared table and tossed it on the concrete floor. Now the men turned around.

'What do you want? Orders are next door in the office.'

'I don't want to put in an order, I want to pick up my car.'

'Next door for that too.'

The office was deserted. Rath looked at his watch. Time was getting on and he couldn't leave Gräf in the Excelsior forever. He rang the bell on the desk and, after what felt like an eternity, heard a toilet flushing. A bored-looking man with a car magazine in his hand emerged from the back. 'Steady on,' he said.

'I'm here to pick up my car.'

'Order number?'

'No idea. The Buick I brought to you the night before last. An emergency. It was supposed to be ready this morning, your colleague said.'

'What colleague?'

'Blond type. Clean-shaven. It doesn't matter.'

'A Buick, you say?'

'Model 26 ES, sand-coloured.'

The man leafed leisurely through the mound of papers on the desk. 'No Buick here.'

'The car's outside. I saw it myself.'

'Then it hasn't been repaired.' The man reached for the telephone. 'Heinz, can you come here?' he said into the mouthpiece.

'This can't be right,' Rath said. 'The car was supposed to be ready by today. Your colleague promised. I need it professionally.'

The man shrugged his shoulders and Rath had to fight the urge to give him the hurry-up with his Walther. The same boiler-suited man who had hounded him out of the shop appeared, chewing a sausage sandwich.

'The Buick?' Heinz asked himself, looking through a second mound of papers. 'That's right,' he said, as if only now had it occurred to him. 'The carburettor!'

'What do you mean, the carburettor? I needed four new tyres, new headlights and a few spots of paint. Nothing more!'

'We had your car on the hoist. The carburettor needs replacing, nothing we can do there. Didn't you notice anything while you were driving?'

Rath shook his head. The carburettor! Bloody hell. Well, the Free State of Prussia could foot the bill. 'When will you have it fixed?'

'We'll need to order replacement parts,' said Heinz, taking another bite from his sandwich and scratching his head. 'That'll take time as it's an American model.'

'I'm glad you've noticed. So, when can I have my car back?'

'Thursday could work.'

'Woe betide you if I come out here tomorrow and . . .'

'Tomorrow? Heinz put on his most idiotic face. 'Not tomorrow, Thursday week.'

'You're pulling my leg? I need my car professionally!'

'We can offer you a replacement vehicle,' the man at the desk said. 'Heinz, will you provide the customer with a car please.'

Heinz shoved the rest of his sandwich into his mouth and led Rath into the courtyard, past the damaged Buick. All four tyres were still flat.

'Did you really have the car on the hoist?' Rath asked, but Heinz wasn't listening. He moved past all the vehicles Rath could have pictured driving away in, took a sharp turn by the shop floor and came to a halt. 'Here she is, the Hanomag,' he said.

Rath thought he was dreaming. A cyclops was staring back at him, a cyclops that had been shrunk to the size of dwarf. 'What on earth is that?'

'A lick of paint and she'll be good to go.'

The one-eyed car standing in the corner, all shy and reserved, was the polar opposite of Marlow's Duesenberg. It wasn't just the paltry ten horsepower, but the fact that its designer had only given it one headlight and a single door.

'You're not serious!'

'It's a reliable car,' Heinz replied indignantly. 'German craftsmanship.'

'Do you have any others?'

'It's this one or the BVG. Your choice.'

With a heavy heart Rath opted against making the return journey by public transport.

37

The uniformed officer was barely recognisable. A bandage ran across his face from below his eyes, held in place by sticking plasters. Lange calmly arranged his files, scribbling notes and making ticks in the margin. He and the man hadn't exchanged a word after a brief greeting. Hilda Steffens looked forlorn with her notepad and pencil.

None of his colleagues were interested in the case, making his presentation at morning briefing a resounding success. He had reeled off a series of platitudes, agreed in advance with Gennat, and no one had asked any questions. No one in the Castle could guess that Assistant Detective Andreas Lange suspected a police officer of murder. Before any information leaked out, the public prosecutor had to have all the evidence, and it needed to be watertight.

First he had to be sure he was on the right track. It wouldn't do any harm to keep the man in suspense. He was already on edge, that much was clear from his face, even if he was making every effort to hide it.

'Looks pretty nasty, that injury of yours,' Lange began finally, out of the blue, gaze still directed on his files. 'How did it come about?'

Kuschke started as if he had been awoken, and Hilda Steffens' pencil began scratching across the page. Kuschke looked at her in irritation. 'Is this an interrogation?' he asked.

'Witness examination,' Lange said, fixing the man with a stare.

This observation seemed to displease Kuschke, who was here for the second time. Recovering himself he decided to fight back.

'In the line of duty.' He leaned back provocatively. 'The sort of thing that wouldn't happen to you. Unless little Miss here's ever pricked you with her pencil?'

The scratch of the pencil ceased for a moment. Lange ignored the attempt to provoke him. 'What duty, exactly?' he asked.

'I thought this was about KaDeWe.'

'Don't think, just answer.'

Lange had found the right tone. Evidently a man like Jochen Kuschke needed to be treated with the arrogance of a Prussian officer.

'Some coked-up little fag boy from Nolle who got a little edgy when I tried to ID him. I couldn't know he was packing a knife.'

'Then I'll be able to read all about it in your report.'

'There isn't one yet.'

'Then please submit it,' Lange said, making a little note to himself. 'What did you do with the assailant?'

'Nothing! He was long gone, but if I see him again, he's finished.'

'Meaning?'

'That he needs to be held to account. Can't go around stabbing officers.'

'But you won't be overseeing the punishment personally . . .'

'Pardon me?'

'Well.' Lange opened the folder and looked through the file. 'There are colleagues among us who occasionally . . . anticipate judicial proceedings.'

'How do you mean?'

Lange read from the file: 'April 14th 1927, violent infringement whilst on duty. Grievous bodily harm proceedings discontinued in September of the same year, but internal warning, noted in your personal file.'

'As you say: proceedings discontinued.'

Lange read the next entry: 'May 3rd 1929.' He paused and checked to see that Hilda Steffens was noting everything down. 'On that day you beat a passerby, later identified as a journalist, unconscious with your baton . . .'

'I'm not someone who shirks his duty when things get hot,' Kuschke said. 'There are no prizes in this job. Either you're shot by the fucking Commies—like we've just seen—or some arsehole turns you in.'

'The complaint in '29 came from one of your colleagues. You had to be restrained in order to prevent further injury.'

'I didn't say that some of my colleagues weren't arseholes. They wanted to land me in the shit.'

The man had a gift for provocation, that much was clear.

'What I'm trying to say, Sergeant Major,' Lange said, 'is that you have a tendency towards violence. I'm starting to wonder what really happened on that balcony in KaDeWe.'

Kuschke jumped to his feet, his face under the snow-white bandage somewhere between bright red and violet. Hilda Steffens' grip tensed, the notepad sagged under the weight and became scored.

'What are you trying to say?'

Lange looked at the sergeant as an entomologist might regard a newly discovered species. Kuschke sat down again.

'Do you know how it feels to put your arse on the line for this system, and then be treated like this?'

'What system are you talking about? Do you mean our state? Our democracy?'

'Draw your own conclusions.'

'We've established the identity of the dead boy,' Lange said. 'He was just fifteen.'

There was no trace of remorse, guilt or sadness in Kuschke's face, not even consternation.

'Benjamin Singer. Does the name mean anything to you?' Kuschke shook his head. 'He ran away from the Maria Schutz orphanage about a year ago to live on the streets. A difficult boy, apparently, but he wasn't known to police.'

No reaction from Kuschke.

'We were only able to identify the deceased thanks to an anonymous telephone call. A girl gave us the name and demanded a proper burial. That's how we stumbled on the orphanage. One of the nuns came to the morgue. Sister Agathe identified him straightaway.'

Lange paused and gazed at Kuschke as he sat on the condemned man's chair. It made him look like a hardened criminal.

'This girl who telephoned could have been the second KaDeWe intruder, don't you think?' Kuschke didn't think anything. 'I've spoken to our colleagues in Robbery. They now assume the deceased's accomplice was female.'

Kuschke feigned indifference. 'Looked like a boy though.'

'You saw the second intruder? You've never mentioned this before.'

'You only asked me what happened on the balcony. The little brat was on the street below.'

Lange made a further note in the folder, realising how much it unsettled

Kuschke. It looked like there really was a female witness to the incident at KaDeWe. The anonymous caller hadn't been lying.

'This girl said something else,' Lange continued, paying close attention to Kuschke's reaction. '"*It was murder*," she said, "*you cops killed Benny*."'

38

'Gereon, here you are at last!' Gräf vacated the desk. 'I've been sitting here like a cat on a hot tin roof. Can you imagine the fuss Kirie's been making? Fortunately, a boy took him out. In exchange for a hefty tip.'

'Lucky for the dog.'

'But not for me.' Gräf's voice was unexpectedly strained. 'Sorry, no time for a proper handover. I have to pee!'

With these words, Gräf made his exit. Rath shook his head and looked at Kirie, who had made herself comfortable under the desk again. 'Can you understand it?' he asked the dog. 'How can anyone be so frantic?'

Rath sat at the table and opened the notebook he had filled with abstract patterns the day before. Gräf, who suppressed even the urge to pee while on duty, had been more conscientious. Judging by the date and times, he had made notes yesterday afternoon and this morning. He had written down everything that happened in the vicinity of room 301, even timing the appearances of the chambermaid and floor waiter down to the last minute. According to Gräf, Goldstein had only left his suite once since yesterday morning. It looked as if they had managed to spoil the Yank's stay in Berlin.

Gräf returned from the toilet. 'I needed that,' he said. *'Just going to pick up the car*, were you?'

Rath nodded. The Hanomag hadn't even managed the journey from Reinickendorf to Kreuzberg without incident. When the lights on Invalidenstrasse switched to green, the engine flooded and resisted all attempts to restart. Cursing, Rath left the crate by the side of the road, walked the few metres to Stettiner Bahnhof and telephoned the garage. It took a while to get hold of the right man.

'Ah, the fuel line,' Heinz said. Even on the telephone it sounded like he was eating a sandwich. 'I thought I'd explained it to you?' He hadn't, so only now did Rath learn the whole truth. The Hanomag had a tendency to take on too much fuel and stall, but the driver could reduce the diameter of the fuel line with a clamp stored in the glove compartment. Rath did as bidden, and, after a moment or two of stubbornness, the car sprang back into life. Not that it was any more fun to drive. In neutral, the clunker shook from side to side to such an extent that Rath came to fear every red light.

'Goldstein doesn't seem to be enjoying his time here,' he said, gesturing towards the notebook. 'A real stay-at-home, it looks like.'

Gräf nodded. 'Probably spends the whole day telephoning overseas, homesick.'

'Or looking for a crafty lawyer to get him out of this. To be honest, I'm not sure what else we can do. On paper, he's a respectable American citizen.'

'I've kept less dangerous men under surveillance,' Gräf said. 'I think he's just fed up. I bet we'll see a boy wheeling his luggage trolley out of suite 301 before the week is out.'

'You really want to bet?'

'A crate of Engelhardt. He'll be gone by the weekend. At the latest.'

Rath considered a moment before shaking on it.

At that moment, the chambermaid emerged from suite 301 and cast the two officers a curious glance before disappearing down the corridor. 'Somehow that girl seems familiar,' Rath said.

'Of course she does. It's the same one as yesterday and the day before.'

'No, I've seen her somewhere else, I think. I just don't know where. How long was she in with him?'

'No idea.' Gräf looked in the notebook. 'I didn't see her go in. Was it when I was in the toilet?'

Rath shook his head. 'I didn't see anything. She must have spent the night with him.'

'Come off it! Your imagination's running wild.'

'You said it yesterday yourself. He had the chambermaid for breakfast.'

'That was a joke.' Gräf was outraged. 'She'll be out on her ear if this gets out!'

Rath shrugged.

Gräf took his hat and coat. 'So,' he said, 'I'm off to stretch my legs. See you later.'

'No you won't. I've got an assignment for you—from Gennat himself. You're to head back to the Castle and report to Böhm. They've got a new case. A corpse has been found in Humboldthain.'

He said it as casually as possible, but Gräf froze in mid-motion, his coat only half on.

'What about you?' Gräf looked like a scarecrow with his dangling coat sleeves.

'I'm staying put. Someone's got to look after the important jobs.'

39

Charly had already visited three of the Reinhold families in Friedrichshain. At the first door no one opened; the second family, the Reinholds in Romintener Strasse, had only been blessed with sons; and at the third address a woman of at least seventy answered. It transpired that she was unmarried and took the very question of a daughter or granddaughter named Alexandra as an insult.

Here in Grünberger Strasse, the fourth address on the list, Charly was having difficulties even finding the name Reinhold. She compared Gereon's note with the house number again: Grünberger Strasse 64. The address was right, but there were no Reinholds here, either with a 'd' or a 'dt'.

A man in grey overalls was sweeping the yard, shouting at a few boys playing football. He kept on until they finally picked up their homemade ball and pushed off. Charly went across.

'The Reinholds haven't lived here for a long time. They were given the boot around Christmas.' He had a Berlin accent.

'The Reinhold family is on the streets?'

Charly was so excited she didn't realise she was thinking out loud. She had a good feeling about this: family on the streets, daughter neglected. Everything seemed to fit.

'Don't look at me like that,' the man said. 'I didn't kick them out! I just keep things tidy, but that's how it goes when you don't pay your rent.'

'But a family . . . with children?'

'Are you from Welfare or something?' Charly looked at him steadily as the words sputtered out. 'You couldn't call them a family anymore. They do have *one* respectable son, Helmut, but he won't have anything to do with them. If he's sensible, that is. The younger brother, Karl, is almost certainly in Moscow by now, or wherever it is the Reds are hiding him. He's a wanted man. Didn't you know? The Beckmann murder.'

The name didn't mean anything to Charly, but she hadn't worked in Homicide for a long time. She shook her head as the man continued.

'Heinrich Beckmann was the buildings manager here. It was in all the papers. Karl Reinhold's meant to have shot him dead, that's what people say. About the rent, maybe, but maybe also because Beckmann was in the SA, and little Kalle was in the RFB, the Red Front. Like father like son and, well . . . since the murder he's vanished. His sister as well, maybe she's involved too, a right little devil, she was. The cops were asking after both of them anyway. And now they're gone. Strange wouldn't you say?'

Charly was overwhelmed by the torrent of words, but remembered the story. It had made the headlines around Christmas. The Nazis had made a meal of it at the time but decided that SA-Führer Heinrich Beckmann didn't have it in him to be a second Horst Wessel. At some point the matter had ceased to interest people. 'You're well informed,' she said.

'You've got to keep a close eye on those Reds, best to know who's living in your building.'

'I take it you're not a Communist then . . .'

'Do I look like one?'

'The sister, you don't happen to know what she's called?'

'Alex. Well, Alexandra, actually. You must have that in your files.'

He still thought she was from Welfare. 'Of course,' she said, and smiled, 'but do I look as if I've brought my filing cabinet?'

Kopernikusstrasse was lined with tenements, and the mouldings were crumbling on the fronts. The building where Helmut Reinhold lived was the only one to have been given a lick of paint since the war. Charly had come by a few hours ago but no one had been home; now the door opened first time. A woman looked at her out of tired eyes amid the smell of fried onions.

'Good afternoon, I'd like to see Helmut Reinhold, please. Am I in the right place?'

The woman nodded. 'My husband's eating at the moment. What do you want from him?'

'Just a few questions about his sister. It won't take long.'

The caretaker didn't know where the rest of the Reinhold family were staying, but he'd given her the older brother's address, so Charly had returned to the flat where she'd stood in vain that morning. Beforehand she had sat in a little cafe at Boxhagener Platz and treated herself to a cup of tea and a read of the papers. The headlines of the regional section were dominated by the fatal shooting on Frankfurter Allee. There was no mention of a girl who had escaped from Lichtenberg District Court.

'You wanted to speak to me?'

A powerfully built man in his mid-twenties stood at the door. Helmut Reinhold was just as reluctant to ask her in as his wife.

'You're Alexandra Reinhold's brother?'

The man nodded. 'That's the reason you're here, Martha says.' He eyed Charly suspiciously. 'From the Welfare Office, are you? Well, you could have saved yourself the bother. I haven't seen Alex in almost a year.'

'Apparently she's living on the streets . . .'

'Then why are you here?'

'Could she be staying with your parents?'

'Typical Welfare, no idea about anything!' Helmut Reinhold was another who associated a woman asking questions at his doorstep with the Welfare Office. He shook his head. 'Do you know why Alex has been living on the streets all this time? Because my dear old father kicked her out a few days before Christmas.'

'Then why don't you take her in?'

'If only I knew where she was. But she won't come to me, she's too proud for that.'

'You sound as if you don't care much for your parents.'

'I can't see how that's any of your concern.'

'In as much as it concerns your sister.'

'My father hasn't spoken a single word to me since my wedding. I invited my parents but they didn't come. Mother sent a card, that was all. *His* signature wasn't on it.'

'Your parents are homeless. Isn't it time to bury the hatchet?'

'I went out to see them,' he said bitterly, 'to this camp on the Müggelsee, and was about to offer them a bed with me and Martha, but . . .' He fell silent. 'He can go hang for all I care.'

'Is it possible that Alexandra is there?'

'What do I know? Listen, I thought this was supposed to be a brief chat.

I'd like to finish eating. I need to go back on shift soon.' He slammed the door in her face.

There were many more questions Charly could have asked, about the missing brother, the Beckmann murder, about Alex's friends and acquaintances, places where she might have found shelter, but the closing of the front door left her in no doubt that it would be pointless coming back. At least she knew where to find Alex's parents.

She took the U-Bahn to Magdalenenstrasse. The way to Wagnerplatz seemed steeper than usual, the walk more arduous. Everything had changed since yesterday. The District Court building appeared strange and forbidding. The window on the first floor was open, and, for a moment, she thought it hadn't been closed since yesterday.

It felt almost as if she was entering for the first time. Like that day six months ago when, heart pounding, she had stepped through the doors and her gaze had fallen on the marble slab in the lobby that had survived even the revolution: WIPE YOUR FEET/NO SMOKING/USE A SPITTOON. Three commands, etched in stone, that told visitors in no uncertain terms what was expected of them in this building. Charly had never felt comfortable here thanks to Weber, who was the living embodiment of those expectations.

She jostled past a few people and climbed the stairs, needing to get the news off her chest, to rehabilitate herself in front of her boss. Now that she was back on Alex Reinhold's tail, she felt hope again.

Weber looked surprised as she entered. 'Fräulein Ritter? I thought I had relieved you of your duties.'

'Some good news, Sir. I wanted to let you know.'

He eyed her suspiciously, none too pleased that she was back just one day after the incident. '*You* have something to tell *me*? When I've been trying to contact *you* for hours.'

'I was out the whole morning.'

'Yes, I noticed.'

'That doesn't matter now.' Charly pulled herself together, trying not to sound too euphoric. 'I've managed to identify the girl; I think it's only a matter of time before I . . . before we track her down. Her name is Alexandra Reinhold and . . .'

Weber interrupted her. 'Great news. So, you know the girl's name.' Charly's euphoria disintegrated like a dry leaf. 'Since you've taken the trouble to come here, allow me to confide something in you: I know what she's been up to.'

'Pardon me?'

Weber shook his head, as if unable to comprehend her dim-wittedness. 'My dear Fräulein Ritter . . .' she hated it when he spoke to her like this, mixing false sympathy and contempt. He shook his head as he spoke, and repeated his opening line in the tone of a psychiatrist dealing with a patient. 'My dear Fräulein Ritter . . . It seems the girl who escaped your custody yesterday is the second member of the KaDeWe duo. You remember, of course? Sonnabend. The dead boy.'

Charly felt the blood rising to her face as Weber continued. Though it had since been replaced by a new dressing, it was now apparent that the girl's bandage was in fact a rag torn from the dead intruder's shirt. The original had been retrieved from the 81st precinct's ash can, where suspicions had subsequently been confirmed. CID had launched a further investigation and discovered that the girl's blood group matched that of the sample left by the KaDeWe duo at the display cases. Everything pointed to the fact that an unidentified girl who was being sought citywide had fallen into police hands by chance. This same girl had then managed to escape from the Lichtenberg District Court, of all places, which, of course, hardly showed the authority in a positive light. Charly listened, but felt all at sea, as if Weber were speaking to another person.

'At any rate,' he concluded, 'Inspector Nebe from Robbery Division wishes to speak with you urgently. After which you are to contact Homicide . . .'

'Homicide?' It was the first word Charly managed to get out. What did her old colleagues in A Division want?

'An Assistant Detective . . . Lange,' Weber continued. 'I'd advise you to be on your way as soon as possible. Best *before* they finish for the day.'

He no longer attempted to conceal his grin.

40

Reinhold Gräf brooded over the file Böhm had left him. It was from Section 1A, the political police: the politicals hadn't kept a file on Gerhard Kubicki, but had been monitoring the storm unit he had joined several months ago, detailing a few fights with Communists, but nothing more serious until now.

He snapped the file shut, pushed it away and gazed at Gereon Rath's abandoned desk. Was this really more exciting than surveillance work at the Excelsior? At least over there he breathed fresh air once in a while. It appeared Wilhelm Böhm didn't want him to leave the office. New files kept arriving as the DCI was driven around town. It seemed to Gräf that he was suffering Böhm's mood swings on Gereon's behalf. To think, they had been a good team when he was still an assistant detective, but that was a distant memory now.

There was a knock. Erika Voss entered and placed another file on Gräf's desk. 'Just in on the Kubicki case,' she said. 'From E Division this time.'

He looked at it curiously. 'An SA man who's attracted the attention of Vice? Was he a pimp?'

'No idea. I didn't look inside.'

Gräf opened the file and whistled through his teeth. 'A 175er. He was caught in a fairly notorious establishment.'

'A gay Nazi? I thought they were against that sort of thing.'

'They are in theory. In practice, things are a little different. Haven't you heard? Apparently, the new SA chief of staff is a homosexual.'

'If only the Führer knew,' Erika Voss said, and disappeared back inside the outer office.

Gräf gazed after her. Was she being ironic? He worked his way through the file in astonishment. The kind of places Kubicki frequented were exactly the sort the Nazis would close down, given half the chance. When he had finished reading the file he asked to be put through to the political

police. 'Detective Gräf, Homicide. Could you send me everything connected with the Berlin SA and homosexuality?'

Half an hour later there was a mountain of files on his desk. He opened
the first just as the telephone rang.

'Gräf, Homicide.'

'I read your appeal in the *B.Z.*. You're seeking witnesses?'

The lunchtime papers had run the article. 'That's right. Did you see
something?'

'I know exactly what happened in Humboldthain.'

Gräf took out a pencil. 'Go on.'

'A brown arsehole got what was coming to him. That's what happened!'

'Who am I speaking to, please?'

'My name has fuck all to do with you. You pigs are in cahoots with the
Nazis. Social fascists!'

Gräf was speechless. He tried to think of an appropriate response, but
nothing came.

The caller hung up.

41

Charly knew Arthur Nebe from her time in A Division. The head of Robbery was in Narcotics then, but had been brought in by Gennat to help Homicide on a number of occasions. Recently, he had solved the sensational murder of a chauffeur and been showered with praise by the press. He was an experienced, if slightly aloof, criminal investigator with a distinctive nose, whose eyes sparkled with thwarted ambition.

Although he was pushing forty, he hadn't progressed beyond the rank of inspector, despite being seen as one of Bernhard Weiss's favourites. In this he was in good company. The Castle's moratorium on promotions applied to everyone, whether top brass liked you or not. Gereon, whose special relationship with Zörgiebel had brought him little more than envy, had learned that the hard way.

Nebe seemed surprised when he saw Charly. 'It's *you*?' he said.

'You know me?'

'Charlotte Ritter, Gennat's stenographer.'

He had a good memory for people, she thought. 'I haven't worked for Gennat in a long time. State examination. Nine months ago now. I'm currently completing my legal preparatory service . . .'

'. . . and evidently at Lichtenberg District Court.'

Charly nodded. 'Of course, you know already. It's me you have to thank for all this.'

'Let's not go blaming ourselves. This sort of thing can happen to anyone.'

'If I'd known what she'd done . . . I just thought she was some full-of-herself fare dodger who'd bust out of reform.'

'You couldn't have guessed who you were dealing with. We only made the connection ourselves this morning.' He was trying to comfort her, and doing a better job than Gereon yesterday.

'Well, at least I've been able to discover her name,' Charly said.

'You have?' Nebe raised his eyebrows in surprise.

'Alexandra Reinhold: no fixed abode, from Friedrichshain.'

'Reinhold with a 'd' or 'dt'?'

'With a 'd'.'

Nebe's pencil scratched across the page as he noted the name. Charly felt like a traitor, but it was the least she could do to atone.

'That's more than I dared hope for, Fräulein Ritter. It's something your superior at Lichtenberg was unable to provide.' Nebe snapped his notebook shut. 'But that's not why I summoned you here. We need a personal description.'

'Wasn't Special Counsel Weber able to do that?'

'If I understood him correctly, he has absolutely nothing to do with the case.'

Weber, you coward, Charly thought, trying to wash your hands of this, are you? Perhaps Gereon was right, perhaps she shouldn't conceal Weber's complicity. That the man was trying to sweep the matter under the carpet was testament to his guilty conscience.

'Be that as it may,' Nebe continued. 'You, at least, saw the girl . . . Alexandra Reinhold . . . yesterday, and can provide a description. I've called for a sketch artist.'

A short time later Charly sat in front of a man with a sketch pad, describing Alexandra Reinhold. When the sketch was finished the face that stared out from the pad was exactly as she remembered it. Only the gaze was different; not quite as anxious. On paper Alex looked defiant and provocative, almost intimidating.

She didn't want to nitpick, perhaps that's how wanted posters had to look. The sketch artist tore off the page and passed it to Nebe.

'Many thanks, Fräulein Ritter,' he said. 'You've been a great help. At last, something we can give to Warrants.' He handed the sheet to a colleague. 'Have duplicates made right away and pass it onto J Division along with our appeal. And here . . .' He tore a page from his notebook. '. . . is the girl's name. That ought to make things easier.'

Warrants. Once the department's machinery was set in motion, it would be tricky for Alexandra Reinhold to go underground. For some reason the thought of Alex falling into the hands of Warrant Officers made Charly uncomfortable. She couldn't help thinking of the distraught girl sitting in her office with fear in her eyes, and then of the merciless apparatus of the Prussian Police's Warrants Department.

As she paced the corridors of Homicide shortly afterwards, breathing in that strange but familiar smell of sweat and dusty files, ink and paper, she briefly considered paying Gennat a visit or, at least, Wilhelm Böhm. In the end she simply knocked on the door she had been assigned, not far from Gereon's little office at the end of the corridor. Today wasn't a day for chatting with ex-colleagues.

She had never worked directly with Andreas Lange, although she had met him before. Most of what she knew came from Gereon. A conscientious type, he had moved to Berlin from Hannover.

Charly knocked on the door and entered to a reedy 'Come in', to find Lange on his own, seated behind his desk, making notes in a file. He wore a serious expression. When he looked up he recognised her straightaway.

'Fräulein Ritter!' he said, and promptly turned red. That didn't seem to have changed.

'You asked to speak to me?' Charly gave him a helping hand. 'Lichtenberg District Court.'

'You're working for the District Court?'

'Legal preparatory service.'

His colour slowly returned to normal. 'Special Counsel Weber told me he could send someone over who had seen the KaDeWe fugitive.'

'I've spoken with Nebe already. No doubt I'm being passed around the whole Castle.'

'Inspector Nebe and I are working closely on this. I'm investigating the death in connection with the KaDeWe break-in.' He sounded almost apologetic.

The boy who had plunged to his death while fleeing police. The headlines from a few days ago. Charly suddenly realised where the fear and horror in Alexandra's eyes came from. 'Could it be that the girl was a witness?' she asked.

'Just what I was about to ask you, Fräulein Ritter. You spoke to her after all. Before she escaped, I mean.' There was a hint of red in his face again. He seemed embarrassed to mention her error.

'That's true, but she was totally distraught.'

'Based on my findings, she did, indeed, see the boy fall. He had just turned fifteen.'

'Dear God,' Charly said.

'The girl . . .'

'Alexandra,' Charly interrupted, and this time it didn't feel like a betrayal. 'Her name is Alexandra.'

'. . . Alexandra is an important witness. She . . .'

There was a knock so loud it felt as if someone was trying to kick the door down. Wilhelm Böhm stepped into the room. He looked at her in surprise. 'Charly, what are you doing here?' He sounded a little offended. As if reproaching her for calling on the assistant detective rather than him.

'Fräulein Ritter is here on duty, so to speak,' Lange explained, turning red again. 'The KaDeWe case. In her role at Lichtenberg District Court she questioned a wit . . .'

'The KaDeWe case . . .' Böhm blustered, incapable of speaking quietly, '. . . is the reason I'm here. I have an important . . .'

'Could you please wait outside, Fräulein Ritter?' Lange asked.

Wilhelm Böhm looked at him in irritation. He wasn't used to being interrupted.

Charly stood up.

'Stay where you are, Charly,' Böhm said. 'You're involved in this case?'

'If you say so, Sir.'

'Lichtenberg District Court. Preparatory service, is it? You'll have to tell me sometime over coffee.'

'How about I buy you one afterwards in the canteen, and you tell me what you know about the Beckmann case. It was you who dealt with it at the time, wasn't it?'

Böhm nodded. 'It's a cold case. We have a suspect, but he's probably slipped off to Moscow—still a minor, but already a staunch Communist. Why are you interested?'

'From a purely legal point of view.'

Böhm turned back to Lange. 'I have a piece of news that will surprise you,' he said. 'As you know, I'm working on the murdered fence from Friedrichshain: Kallweit, Eberhard. The robbery homicide that wasn't.'

Lange nodded. 'I'm familiar with it, Sir. I was at briefing this morning.'

'It looks as if we ought to coordinate our investigations—amalgamate them, even. It concerns the stolen goods found in the deceased's stockroom.' Böhm looked pleased with himself. 'Among other things, our colleagues found a load of high-quality wristwatches. They're from the KaDeWe break-in at the weekend.'

42

Gräf slammed the phone into the cradle. He'd had enough, sitting here with this crap! Böhm was gadding about with Grabowski, God knows where, while he, Reinhold Gräf, was left to do the dirty work. Fighting running battles with idiots who called the station at minute intervals. Since the abusive Communist almost an hour ago, he hadn't had a moment's peace.

The appeal in the lunchtime papers had yielded the same dubious results as ever. Until now, the only calls had been from busybodies: masochists who'd confess to any crime so long as it brought them attention; or whistleblowers pointing the finger at their own neighbours. Worst was the third group: the self-appointed world saviours who, in the absence of a world that would listen, had resolved to make their opinions known to the Prussian Police. On the one hand they were Communists who wished *death on all Nazi bastards*; on the other, Party members, or at least Nazi sympathisers, who asked why police weren't in a position to protect *respectable citizens* (evidently referring to the SA man with brass knuckles) from these *red hooligans*.

The telephone kept ringing, almost without pause. Gräf looked at the black device, picked up, dialled 1 and placed the receiver next to the cradle.

Peace at last!

The important calls would land somewhere. The main thing was that he could devote himself to the files. He sensed that Kubicki's homosexuality could be a lead.

Erika Voss poked her head around the door. 'Sorry,' she said, stealing a glance at the telephone. 'But the porter just called. A woman downstairs says she wants to make a statement about the death in Humboldthain.'

'A woman?' At least it wouldn't be one of the masochists, Gräf thought. They were all men. 'Send her up.'

'She's on her way.'

The detective nodded. 'Fine.'

Erika Voss remained at the door.

'Was there something else?'

'Well . . . it's almost six, and Inspector Rath usually . . .'

'Of course, finish there for the evening. As soon as you've shown the witness in.'

Moments later, a slim, prematurely grey woman in her mid-forties stood in her place. She was a little uncertain, but in no way shy, and introduced herself as Renate Schobeck. Gräf motioned for her to sit in the visitor's chair in front of Rath's desk.

'This business in Humboldthain,' she said. 'I'm not here to report anyone. But . . . my lodger . . . Leo Fleming his name is.'

One of the whistleblowers, then. Gräf sighed inwardly, but noted down the name and looked at her. 'Yes?'

Renate Schobeck seemed a little helpless. 'I don't know if it means anything, but he came home very early this morning. He's unemployed, if you must know, but leaves the house at half past five every morning and stays out until the afternoon. Looking for work, he says, though he's never missed a rental payment.'

Gräf gave a little cough, making a point of not writing anything down. Instead he looked at his wristwatch. 'Please get to the point. It's already late.'

She looked mildly peeved. 'I know that he waits at the Himmelfahrt-kirche every morning for his bride-to-be. I've seen them there together. A lovely couple if you ask me, and he's never tried to bring her back to his room. He knows what's right and proper.'

Gräf rolled his eyes. 'What exactly are you trying to tell me?'

She looked around, as if afraid someone might be listening. 'Yesterday I didn't hear Herr Fleming leave the house, but I did hear him come back. Just after six. I asked if he was sick, if I should make him a cup of tea, but he said he just wanted to be left in peace. Well . . .' there was a pregnant pause '. . . that was when I saw it.'

'What, Frau Schobeck?'

She leaned in closer and lowered her voice.

'Blood,' she said. 'His jacket was smeared with blood. Not much, but I saw it. He was so strange; wanted to go straight up to his room. I didn't think anything of it, but then I read the appeal in the *B.Z.* . . .'

Gräf pricked up his ears. 'You're certain it was blood?'

'Of course! I used to work in a butcher's, and . . .'

He cut her off. 'Many thanks, Frau Schobeck, this could be very help-ful. Now, where can we find this Herr Fleming?'

'At mine, of course,' she said. 'Putbusser Strasse 28, rear building, third floor.'

43

Lange had spoken more in the last few days to Superintendent Gennat than ever before. He wasn't sure if that was good or bad, but clearly Buddha was keeping an eye on him. He couldn't afford any mistakes.

Trudchen Steiner, Gennat's secretary, placed the cake tray on the table and Gennat served his guest. Discussions like this were more akin to a coffee morning than an official briefing. Lange thanked him for the slice of poppy seed cake that had landed on his plate, and took a bite.

'How long have you been with us now, Assistant Detective?'

Lange replied with his mouth full, feeling ambushed. 'Almothst two yearsth,' he said. 'Thinthe Dethember thwenty nine.'

'Before that you did two years at Robbery Division in Hannover?' Lange was glad that a nod of the head would suffice. His mouth was still full of poppy seed cake. Buddha seemed to have studied his personal file. 'We've just taken on a number of cadets.'

'Dr Weiss has introduced them already, Sir.'

'Have you thought about applying?'

'With respect, Sir, it seemed a little premature. I haven't been at the Cas . . . ah, in Berlin, two years yet.'

Lange realised he had turned red, and felt annoyed, but Gennat didn't seem to have noticed.

'You've made a very good job of the KaDeWe case so far. Officers Nebe and Böhm are full of praise.' Gennat shovelled a slice of gooseberry tart into his mouth, his favourite. 'At the same time, you were disciplined enough not to mention our own suspicions.'

'Well, Sir, I thought . . .'

'And you thought right.' Gennat leaned a little closer. 'You're aware that without a witness statement, you can't give the public prosecutor anything.'

'Yes, unfortunately. I still don't know how I'm going to get hold of her. I suppose it'll come down to Warrants.'

Gennat nodded. 'I'd like you to take over the Kallweit case from Böhm. You've been working together on it anyway.'

'DCI Böhm mentioned that this might happen. Does it mean I can close the KaDeWe file?'

'For Goodness sake, no! Don't be so hasty. Keep it simmering. Let's bide our time for this witness.'

'But the Commissioner is pushing for a swift resolution.'

'He always does, but don't let him bring you to heel. You can't close the file until you've heard what the witness has to say.' Lange nodded. 'And this dead fence,' Gennat continued. 'There are enough links to the KaDeWe case. It might yield the odd insight.'

'It could do, Sir. I just hope the KaDeWe witness doesn't have the dead fence on her conscience. That would be a link I could do without.'

'You'll get support from Officer Mertens. But . . . as far as our suspicions go: not a word to anybody!'

Lange took another bite of poppy seed cake.

'And,' Gennat said, 'if I don't see an application for inspector on my desk during the next round of recruitments, there'll be trouble.'

44

They were late. Dusk was already falling. Kirie pulled hard on her lead. Some scent or other was enticing her onwards, and it was all Rath could do to hold on.

'To heel,' he scolded for the umpteenth time. Kirie kept pulling. Rath wasn't in the best of moods after his nerve-shredding journey home with the Hanomag. He had been looking forward to a quiet evening but, instead, was traipsing around the banks of the Müggelsee.

'For God's sake, Kirie, to heel!' He pulled furiously on the lead. The dog gave a brief yelp and looked back in surprise, but at least she stopped. Charly too.

'What on earth's the matter with you?' she said. 'Pull yourself together.'

'We should have left the dog at home.'

'So she can keep the whole building awake? You know she doesn't like being on her own.'

'Maybe all three of us should have stayed at home.'

'If it's too much for you then you should have said.'

'It's fine. I just had a lousy day, that's all. Sorry.'

Rath was still annoyed that he'd let himself be talked into it. God knows, he could imagine better things than searching for a homeless camp on the Müggelsee. If he was right, then this business with Charly's fugitive had come to a head, and Alex Reinhold was no mere fare dodger. She was also involved in one of the most spectacular break-ins of recent times, as well as two possible murders.

First Beckmann, one of Böhm's cold cases. Heinrich Beckmann was shot dead in his flat on the evening of December 20th. There was no sign of the killer, but witnesses attested that they had seen Karl Reinhold emerge from the house. Others claimed to have seen his sister Alexandra entering the building around ten minutes beforehand. Both had been missing until yesterday afternoon, when Alexandra had done a bunk from Lichtenberg

District Court. Her parents had been thrown out of the flat just two days after the murder, a forced eviction which Beckmann, the buildings manager, had set in motion on the morning of his death.

The second murder had to do with the KaDeWe break-in. Some of the spoils had been found with the dead Berolina fence. Whatever Alex's role in these cases, Charly's error had taken on a new significance, and could no longer be brushed aside.

Although needing to find the girl as quickly as possible, Rath still couldn't see the use in visiting her homeless parents, especially when questioning them had been a dead end six months before. 'You have her name, you've tracked down her family and you've even dug up an old case, so why don't you just leave the rest to Warrants,' he said once Charly had told him everything. It was meant to be comforting, but she had looked at him with that blank gaze he so hated, that ever so slightly contemptuous gaze which seemed to say: how can you still not understand me?

The settlement, a strange mix of campsite and shanty town, was clean and tidy, almost as if it were regularly swept. The smell of fried potatoes hung in the air. They reached a kind of square where wood was neatly stacked in the middle. A woman was hanging out washing and two children were playing tag, otherwise there was no one to be seen. The woman eyed the two well-dressed visitors suspiciously. The last rays of the setting sun made the scene appear almost idyllic.

The hairs on the back of Kirie's neck stood up and she growled.

The woman took the wash basket and disappeared inside one of the shacks and a dog started barking fiercely.

'Hold Kirie tight,' Charly said.

Rath had already wrapped the lead several times around his wrist, but Kirie made no attempt to break free. She stood stock-still, growling to herself and quivering like an electric motor with fur. She gazed at the lane which led into the middle of the settlement. The barking grew louder, and at last they saw a big dog the colour of a cockroach, an unhealthy mix of Dobermann, Rottweiler and Werewolf rolled into one.

Rath realised to his horror that the monster wasn't on a lead. For a moment it stayed where it was and looked at the newcomers curiously, before breaking into a trot and making straight for them. Now Kirie started barking too, yapping at the onrushing jumble of muscles, hide and teeth, but she sounded like she always did: harmless. She certainly didn't scare the charging brute. Rath stood stiff as a board, feeling as if his heart had stopped. The dog was only a few metres away when there was a shrill whistle and it threw itself to the ground.

A man of perhaps thirty was sitting in the shadow of a corrugated iron wall. He stood and went over to the dog. 'Good boy,' he said, patting the dog on the back of the head. 'Good boy, Stalin.'

The dog looked at Rath and Charly as if he wasn't finished with them yet.

Rath stood close to Charly, whose face was slowly regaining its colour. Stalin's master left the dog where it was and approached.

'If you're from the public order office, I advise you not to show up here without the police.'

Rath was about to pull out his identification when Charly nudged him in the side.

'We're looking for Emil Reinhold,' she said. 'Apparently he lives here with his wife.'

'What do you want from him?'

'We're friends of Helmut's,' Charly said. 'The son of . . .'

'I know who Helmut Reinhold is, but I don't know if Emil will have much time for him. Or his Social Democrat friends.'

'That's why he sent us.' Charly lied. Rath was astonished at how convincing she was. 'He knows his father resents him, and he'd like to make peace.'

'So you're his envoys, are you?' The man laughed. 'There I was thinking you were cops.' He ran both hands over the dog's neck fur. 'Stalin has an allergic reaction to cops. But . . .' He lifted his hat towards Charly, 'then I saw there was a lady present.'

'So where can we find Herr Reinhold?' the lady asked.

The man pointed in the direction of the shore. 'Down there by the lake. See the trail of smoke?'

Charly nodded and pulled Rath away. Stalin followed them with his eyes, but stayed where he was even when Kirie issued a brief, spirited bark. Rath pulled the lead and she followed obediently.

Emil Reinhold's hut was a former Christmas market stall. Rath had difficulty imagining it had ever been so badly put together as here on the banks of the Müggelsee. The roof looked as if it were built solely for the purpose of gathering rainwater, before transmitting it inside, drop by drop. The side wall didn't appear to have a single right angle. Clearly, Emil Reinhold was no carpenter. In front of the entrance he had constructed a little lean-to, which was covered with what might have been a grey flysheet, or perhaps a discarded lorry tarpaulin.

Rath gave Charly a nod, positioned himself by the fitted door and knocked. An ill-tempered man of about fifty appeared. 'Emil Reinhold?' The man nodded. 'My name is Ritter, and this is Herr Rath. We're looking for your daughter Alexandra.'

'Well, you're in the wrong place.' Reinhold tried to shut the door, but Charly had wedged her foot in the crack.

'Perhaps you have some idea where we might find her. Your son, Helmut . . .'

The mention of his son acted like a trigger on him. 'So, that's the way the wind is blowing. Is Helmut sending his Sozi friends, because he no longer dares come here himself?' He gestured towards the settlement. 'Take a look around. This is the mess you Social Democrats have landed us in. Class traitors!' He spat, and Charly had to move her feet to avoid being hit.

'Herr Reinhold, we're not Social Democrats; this isn't about Helmut, it's about your daughter!'

'I don't know where she is, and I don't want to know. Maybe she's started at Wertheim again. If he's so keen to see her he can go looking for her himself.'

'*We're* looking,' Charly said. 'Because we're afraid something bad has happened. We want to help her.'

'And who is *we?*' Charly gave Rath a nudge and he pulled out his identification. Reinhold stared at the metal badge. 'I thought you wanted to help her?'

'We do,' said Rath.

'Always nice to hear from your local police department.' The man gave a jerky laugh. 'Go on, you have my blessing. Give that brat what for. If you find her that is!'

Charly struggled to keep cool. 'We don't want to give her what for. We want to help her,' she said, 'even if that's hard for you to understand. Alexandra is suspected of having broken into a department store . . .'

'Do what you want. Just leave me in peace.'

Finally, Charly's patience ended. 'You need to learn how to listen! Is this how you treated your son? I'm not surprised your family wants nothing more to do with you.'

'We proles don't need help, especially not from Social Democrats. We look after our own!'

'You're too proud to accept the help of your son, just because he's a Social Democrat?'

'A social Fascist! Complicit in the exploitation of labour by capital!' Reinhold's face turned red. 'It won't be long before the hour strikes and the proletariat rises in arms!'

Rath understood why the Reinhold family had fallen apart. 'I think the hour has struck already,' he said. 'Many thanks for the information, Herr Reinhold.'

He linked arms with Charly and pulled her away from the hut. Emil Reinhold closed the door as soon as their backs were turned.

'Why did you do that?' she asked. 'I had more questions.'

'That he wouldn't have answered. You heard the nonsense he was spouting!'

'Perhaps he'd have given us something.'

'Perhaps if you'd been a little friendlier. And besides . . .' Rath gazed skywards. 'Take a look up there. It's getting dark, and I don't know how old the batteries in my torch are. We need to make sure we get back to the car. It was hard enough in the light.'

Charly said nothing, but Rath could see she was angry. They reached the square in silence, where Stalin's master was sparking the bonfire. 'Is the Sozi-delegation leaving our workers' paradise so soon?' he asked.

The dog lay dutifully next to the blazing fire, which had already started to crackle. Kirie began to growl once more, cautiously this time, so that no one could hear, especially not the other dog.

'I don't know what everyone here has against the SPD,' Rath said.

'Well, take a look around: unemployed, homeless people everywhere. Families with barely anything to eat thanks to Social Democrat policies. At the expense of us workers!'

'Looks rather idyllic to me,' Rath gestured towards the bonfire, which had drawn the first people from the settlement. 'Almost like a gypsy camp. All you need now is a guitar.'

'Why don't you come back in February when the lake's frozen over and you can barely get any water; when the cold saps all the warmth from your body. Then you'll rethink your gypsy romanticism. This is no operetta. This is real life.'

They left the camp, returning through the wood, and with every step visibility grew poorer. Rath switched on his torch. The beam of light flashed along the tree stems, making anything it didn't illuminate seem darker. The torch was no use here. They couldn't find the trail.

'Maybe we should let Kirie go on ahead,' Charly said. 'She relies more on her nose than her eyes.'

Rath nodded and, unable to think of anything better, gave the dog the car key to sniff. It seemed to work. She fixed her nose to the ground and took up the scent. Rath loosened the lead and followed through undergrowth that became thicker and thicker.

'Are you sure this is the way we came?' Charly asked after a while.

'No idea. At least the dog has a scent.'

'Yes, but what?'

Five minutes later Kirie accelerated when they reached the edge of the wood. She pounced on something that lay on the ground, taking it in her mouth and swinging it back and forth.

'Drop!' cried Rath who, despite the torchlight, wasn't sure what she had picked up. Only at the third 'drop' did Kirie let her prey fall to the ground. Rath shone the light on a bundle of fur that had been ripped to pieces, a soggy red sludge pouring out of it like a burst plush cushion.

A dead squirrel.

Kirie looked guilty. Charly couldn't help but laugh.

'Don't laugh,' Rath said. 'We have to be strict with her.'

She pulled herself together, but when Rath said 'Bad dog' in all seriousness, she burst out laughing again.

'We're never going to be able to train her,' he sighed.

'Now that both your torch and your dog have come up short, how about we rely on *my* sense of direction.'

Rath switched off the torch, and Charly gazed into the night sky. She seemed to go by the moon, or perhaps the stars. Either way they were soon on the right path, though it still took them half an hour to reach the car. They found themselves in marshy terrain along the way, a detour that left

Rath with only one shoe. All their searching with the torch, temporarily switched back on, proved futile; the marsh had swallowed the shoe and wasn't about to give it back.

Rath sat with the car door open and wrung out his socks. Charly's feet didn't look much better, but at least she still had both shoes. They couldn't wring out Kirie's wet paws. The dog made a huge mess of the car and Charly's coat when she placed her head on her lap. Rath stuffed his socks and shoe into the footwell and started the engine.

'Can you drive without shoes?' Charly asked.

'Mit bläcke Fööß jeht alles. You can do anything barefoot.'

They jolted slowly across Köpenicker Landstrasse back into town. Naturally the Hanomag didn't make the journey without letting them down, this time at Schlesisicher Tor, right in the heart of the city. Passersby looked on with a mixture of interest and amusement as a barefooted but otherwise impeccably dressed man climbed out of the car, opened the hood, fixed something, closed the hood, got back inside and started the engine.

Charly grinned when he reclaimed his place alongside her.

'Sorry,' he growled, putting the car in gear. 'Normally I'd have a replacement pair of shoes.'

Charly's grin disappeared. 'What's the matter with you?'

'What's the matter? Only that we haven't made any progress. Unless you count wet feet, dirty clothes and a missing shoe. Oh, and a few hours' less sleep.'

'So what? I'll sleep at the end of the month. Isn't that what you always say?'

'We could have had a nice evening at home with a bottle of red wine, instead of wasting our time out here.'

'Wasting our time?' Charly feigned indignation. 'Please! I've never been more emphatically warned about the dangers of social democracy.'

'True. The rubbish that Reinhold and his comrades were spouting makes more sense than anything else this evening!' He looked at her. 'Now, won't you please admit that this was a crackpot idea.'

Charly said nothing, as he observed her out of the corner of his eye. When her features became hard like that, it was better to seek cover. She needed almost a minute to compose herself.

'What is this?' she said, her voice as chilly as it had been in a long time.

'Are you really just upset about your stupid shoe? Or do you regret helping me with my *crackpot* idea?'

'That's not how I meant it!'

'Then how did you mean it?'

'You have to admit I'm right: we should have given this to Warrants right away.'

'But that's exactly what I *don't* want. Can't you understand that? I want to find Alex before Warrants do!'

'Why? It's no longer your concern. You've made good on your error, now let other people take care of the rest.'

'Why don't you understand? She saw her friend plunge to his *death*. She's terrified of blue uniforms. Something happened up there.'

'It'll all come out when Warrants bring her in.'

'I can't shake the feeling that's exactly when something terrible will happen.'

Rath looked at her in disbelief. 'Have you been reading tea leaves again?'

'You're such an ignoramus!'

'I'm just realistic. I'm starting to feel you're getting carried away by all this. You're not her mother. Believe me, she's a shrewd customer. She doesn't need your help.'

Charly fell silent, but it was a baleful silence.

The lights of night-time Berlin flitted past. Only when they were labouring through the construction site bottleneck on Jannowitz Bridge did she open her mouth again.

'Pull over there,' she said.

'Pardon me?'

'Let me out past the bridge.'

'What's the matter?' Rath switched on the indicator and did as bidden. He turned the engine off.

'Nothing's the matter. I just can't talk to you about this. You're not taking me seriously, and I can't stomach it right now. I want to be alone!'

Rath sighed. 'Charly, of course I'm taking you seriously. But you're a lawyer, not a Samaritan.'

'If you don't want to help, I'll do it myself. Now, please let me out.'

Rath could see from her face that she meant it. She had put her wet shoes back on. He opened the door and climbed out of her way. Kirie was surprised to find herself placed on the wooden seat, only to watch both master and mistress exit the vehicle.

'If that's really what you want,' Rath said, suddenly realising how furious he was. 'Then it's the perfect end to a lousy evening!'

'Just what I was thinking,' she said, buttoning her coat. 'At last we agree on something.'

'Can I at least drive you to Spenerstrasse?'

'No, thank you. I'll take the S-Bahn.'

She hesitated a moment before heading to the station, and he didn't know whether to give her a goodbye kiss or not. While he was still umming and ahhing, she made up her mind. 'Good night, Gereon,' she said.

That was something, at least, but her back was already turned by the time she said it. She pressed her handbag in front of her chest and moved quickly towards the S-Bahn station. It, too, was a massive construction site, like so much in this city.

Rath stayed where he was but gazed after her. It all seemed unreal. He wanted to chase after her, but pride paralysed him. Let her go! Hopefully she'd miss her train. Someone as pig-headed as Charlotte Ritter had to suffer the consequences.

Kirie gave a bark. The dog didn't seem to understand what was happening either.

Rath slid across the wooden seat towards her. 'Looks like we're back in Luisenufer for the time being. Alone.'

It wasn't far to his flat from Jannowitz Bridge, and the Hanomag made it without breaking down again. He couldn't help thinking of Charly as he drove, the way she disappeared inside the train station and how he had stared after her, unable to move. He should have shouted something: 'Please don't go!' or 'Piss off then!'

Either would have been honest.

What was wrong with her? What was wrong with them? It wasn't just tonight that had been ruined; it was the last few weeks, ever since Cologne. Yes, things had gone badly there, but not badly enough to poison the atmosphere for weeks on end.

At Luisenufer he stayed in the car, staring through the windscreen into the night. That stubborn, fucking woman! He slammed his fist against the steering wheel, so hard that Kirie, who was crouched quietly on the passenger seat, gave a start.

He got out and took the dog by the lead, getting rid of his solitary, wet shoe in one of the metal rubbish bins. The clatter of the lid echoed in the inner courtyard. He climbed the steps quietly, bare feet sticking to the wood. In the rear building all was still; he didn't seem to have wakened anyone. He was all the more startled, therefore, when the telephone rang as he opened the door.

Could it be Charly hoping to make peace? Admitting what a stupid quarrel it had been? His mood brightened immediately. Leaving Kirie in the kitchen he hung up his coat, pitter-pattered over the cold floor to the telephone, and took up position on the warm living room carpet. He let it ring one more time before picking up.

'OK, you're right. It wasn't a crackpot idea,' he said, charmingly. 'Can I still come over?'

'That won't be necessary.' It was Johann Marlow.

'Do you realise what time it is? Most people are asleep.'

'If you had got in touch, I wouldn't feel obliged to disturb you.'

'I've only just got home. I was on the job until now.'

'You were in Amor-Diele yesterday, Krehmann said.'

'That's right. I learned a few interesting things there too. I'm surprised you didn't tell me.'

'You were in a rush to leave my car.'

'You already knew that Rudi the Rat had disappeared . . .'

'He's probably sleeping it off somewhere with one of his girls.'

'And who's to say Hugo Lenz isn't doing exactly the same thing?'

'I know he isn't.'

'Did you send for Goldstein?'

'Who?'

'An American contract killer. The Pirates seem to think he was engaged by Berolina. And that Rudi Höller was his first victim.'

'Inspector, if that was the case I'd have told you long ago. I don't know this Goldstein of yours.'

'I wish I could believe you.'

'Why shouldn't I play with an open hand? I'd only be hindering you in your work. You do work for me after all.'

'Supposing someone else hired the Yank? Someone out for Berolina and the Pirates at the same time?'

'I can't think who that might be. Who would be delusional enough to take on two Ringvereine at once?'

'Perhaps you should have a little think about that,' Rath said. 'One more thing: Krehmann said Hugo Lenz had a girl.'

'Come to Venuskeller, and I'll introduce you to Hugo's little friend myself.'

'Now?'

'The evening's only just begun.'

'It's a little tricky. My Buick's in the garage.'

'Which garage?'

'In Reinickendorf, the arse-end of nowhere. Arse-end's about right for its employees too.'

'Then come tomorrow, let's say at twelve. Leave the car to me.'

Marlow hung up. That was no suggestion. It was an order.

45

She was still furious. For half the night she had lain awake wishing him to hell, while at the same time longing for his presence beside her. She went to the window and looked out at the day's first dismal rays of sunlight as they groped their way timidly towards Spenerstrasse.

It was quarter past seven according to Gereon's alarm clock on the bedside table. She swept it aside, and it landed with a clatter on the wooden floor. That was no good either.

Her rage had surfaced again in the S-Bahn, gnawing away at her on the journey home, and continuing into the night.

The worst thing was that she didn't even know why she was so angry, or at whom. Gereon, possibly, but just as likely herself. Ultimately, it was the silence of the last few weeks that had fuelled it, and this silence wasn't just Gereon's, but her own.

She no longer trusted him, no longer knew what he thought about her and her work. Did he take her seriously, or acquiesce just to keep her onside? What did he want from her, damn it?

Once you're married, you won't have to work anymore. Those were his mother's words, but Gereon had said nothing in response. Was it because he felt the same way?

Charly had only wanted to tell Erika Rath about her work at Lichtenberg District Court, to get their faltering conversation in that stuffy cafe off the ground. Then came the offending sentence, and an even more embarrassed silence. Gereon looked at his shoes and sipped his coffee; Mother Rath didn't seem to realise what she had done.

In all the months they had been together, they had never once spoken about marriage, not even jokingly, but that hadn't stopped him from brazenly introducing her as *my fiancée* when they ran into Mother Rath by chance outside a large department store. *For simplicity's sake*, he had whispered in her ear.

Cologne had been a total disaster, yet she had been so looking forward to getting out of Berlin, to seeing Gereon's old friend Paul, and visiting his home city for the first time. Things had started so promisingly too.

It was the football that had sealed the deal. She had seen Hertha Berlin play a few times at the Plumpe, their home stadium, but never away, and certainly not in a final to decide the German championship. What a game it was! At halftime, Hertha were unlucky to be behind München, but had turned the game thanks to Hanne Sobek. When the winning goal was struck, shortly before the final whistle, she flung her arms around Gereon, then around Paul, and the two men joked that she was the *only woman to be interested in football*. They celebrated the win in Cologne's old town, together with the visiting Hertha fans and a few sympathetic Rhineland Prussians until, at some point, Paul discreetly took his leave. Gereon had booked a room with a Rhine view, and later, as she stood by the window in her nightshirt and gazed onto the lights reflected in the river, he had taken her in his arms and kissed her on the nape of the neck. She felt as happy as she had done in a long time.

She wouldn't discover how illusory this feeling was until the next day when, wandering through Cologne's shopping district, they were caught unawares by a woman whom Gereon introduced as *my mother*, before gesturing towards Charly and saying: 'Fräulein Ritter. My . . . fiancée.'

Erika Rath's eyes widened in a mixture of curiosity and suspicion as she dragged them into the nearest cafe. 'I'd have invited you to our home, of course,' she said to Charly. 'But Gereon never tells me anything.'

She had never seen him so subdued. 'I . . . we were going to visit you, of course,' he said. 'But it was meant to be a surprise. We only arrived yesterday.'

Mother and son looked at each other in silence. Charly spoke a little about the District Court, until Erika Rath voiced her opinion about work and marriage, whereupon they lapsed back into a suddenly icy silence.

'We'll be round tomorrow,' Gereon said. 'Don't tell Father, it's meant to be a surprise.'

In the evening, Gereon took her to an exclusive restaurant on the banks of the Rhine, a modern building with windows all around, which offered a spellbinding view of the cathedral and river, but the evening was ruined before it began. Erika Rath was still present. It would have been better to talk about it, but Gereon preferred to remain silent.

The next day they paid the Raths a formal visit as promised. Charly was still his *fiancée, for simplicity's sake*, and it became clear that Gereon had never breathed a word about her to his parents. The Raths felt ambushed by their presence and, for Charly, that second afternoon was even worse than the first.

Afterwards they left, as planned, by overnight train for a week on the Baltic Sea. The holiday flat in a captain's cottage was tiny and wonderfully pretty, the weather in Prerow superb, but the atmosphere between them was soured. The blue skies over the Darss couldn't salvage things, and their first holiday together was a disaster. Even if they had never spoken about it.

In fact they hadn't spoken about anything, had simply returned to their daily lives upon arriving back in Berlin. Of course, she could have made the first move, but she didn't see why she should. It was his silence that had got them into this situation, and so it was up to him now to break it.

She just didn't know where she was with him anymore, and the more she thought about it, the more she realised she never had. What did Gereon Rath want? To marry her? Then he should damn well go ahead and ask! But if he thought she would abandon her career, he'd better think again.

Charly went into the kitchen and put on water for coffee. The place still smelled of dog. Kirie's guest basket stood outside in the hall under the coat stand. She gazed at the rims of her eyes in the bathroom mirror and decided for once to follow Weber's orders and stay home.

She had a slice of bread with honey and two cups of coffee, and gradually her mind felt clear enough to reach for the telephone. She knew the number by heart. A secretary answered.

'Good morning, Ritter here,' she said. 'Could I speak to Assessor Scherer please?'

46

Rath had a strange dream. Dancing with Charly through the lobby of the Excelsior, she kept standing on his bare toes with her pointed high heels. The music was bizarre and out of time. Behind reception, he thought he could make out the face of Johann Marlow above a gold-embroidered Excelsior uniform. Abe Goldstein sat at the bar, drinking one enormous glass of whisky after another and, with each new glass, toasting Rath and smiling cynically. Suddenly, he slid from the barstool, pulled a pistol from his jacket and pointed it at Rath, at Charly, at Marlow. Three times he pulled the trigger and the barrel spewed fire, but there was no bang, just an ear-splitting DRRRRRNNNG, DRRRRRNNNG, DRRRRRNNNG.

Rath sat up with a start. His hands groped for Charly, but couldn't find her. Gradually he recovered his bearings, but only when the fourth DRRRRRNNNG sounded did he realise it was the doorbell. Damn, what time was it? Where was his wristwatch? His alarm clock was still in Moabit. He must have overslept.

It rang for a fifth time. Whoever it was they were damn stubborn. Rath got up and looked for his dressing gown, but it was in Spenerstrasse too. He fished fresh underwear and socks out of the wardrobe, threw on yesterday evening's suit, which hung damp and mud-splattered over the chair, and went to the door. Kirie gazed at the door as curiously as her master. It couldn't be Charly; the dog would have greeted her differently.

When Rath opened the door, a man in dirty blue overalls was crouched on the floor, trying to slip something through the letterbox. There were dark circles under his eyes, suggesting a lack of sleep. He gave a start and sprang to his feet. In his hand he held a familiar-looking key.

'Sorry,' he mumbled, 'I didn't think there was anyone home, so I . . .' He held the key under Rath's nose. A car key. 'Your vehicle. You're a busy man, and we thought why don't we drop the car round, seeing as it's ready.'

Rath was speechless. He took the car key and nodded thanks.

The man marked time for a moment, then gave a little cough. 'Ehm, the replacement—could I take it back with me?'

Rath needed a moment to work out that the *replacement* was the Hanomag. He nodded, still not sure if he was really awake. 'Of course,' he muttered, searching in his coat pocket for the Hanomag key. The man took it and disappeared with a tip of his oil-stained cap.

'The bill?' he called after the mechanic, who had already reached the bottom of the stairs.

'We'll send it on,' it echoed from below.

Rath went back inside. The kitchen clock showed just after half past eight. No need to panic, he wasn't that late. Through the window he saw the mechanic crossing the courtyard with quick steps. He seemed to be in a hurry. Rath looked at the car key, then at Kirie.

'Bark, so I know I'm awake,' he said. 'Or talk, so that I know I'm still asleep.'

He went into the bathroom, switched on the stove, gave the dog something to eat and returned to a lukewarm shower, washing away the previous evening's disappointment. Only one suit hung in the wardrobe. He had to get the grey one to the dry-cleaner's. He bagged it up, deciding against a coffee in his rush to leave the house. Kirie looked bewildered. Usually they didn't set off in such a hurry, but usually they didn't sleep so long either.

A sand-coloured Buick was parked outside the house, its paint so shiny that at first Rath didn't recognise his old car. It wasn't until he saw the little scratch on the steering wheel that he was sure. He checked the paintwork, couldn't find a scrape, and then the wheels: four new tyres fitted. At least three people must have pulled a nightshift to get this done.

Rath was continually astonished at how much influence Johann Marlow wielded. Anyone who could give a garage the hurry-up—literally overnight—must really have a lot of power. Nothing had impressed him more than the remoulded Buick standing outside his front door: not the luxury Marlow could afford, nor the private army, nor even the many connections to the police and municipal authorities.

'Well, Kirie,' he said to the dog. 'Perhaps it was no bad thing Charly didn't spend the night.'

If anything it was better. She'd have smelled a rat. Charly didn't know anything about the five thousand marks, or the mutual favours linking him to Dr M., nor could she ever find out.

Rath put the key in the lock and turned—a perfect fit. 'Looks like we're all here now,' he said as he opened the door. 'You, me and the car.' Kirie sprang onto the passenger seat, panting expectantly.

47

The man cut a forlorn and hostile figure, sitting uncomfortably on the wooden chair in Interview Room B. Gräf knew they had scored a bullseye yesterday when he oversaw Leo Fleming's arrest with a troop of uniformed officers. Renate Schobeck's lodger had briefly eyed potential escape routes when Gräf pulled his badge but, in the end, come peaceably.

In the absence of Böhm and Grabowski, Gräf had taken matters into his own hands. There was no doubting it was the correct decision, but the Bulldog had still given him an earful this morning, before downgrading him to the role of spectator. The DCI wanted to lead the interview himself.

Böhm said nothing initially, a trick he must have learned from Gennat. Cheap as it was, it seemed to work. Fleming grew visibly nervous, and began polishing the chair with the seat of his trousers.

'So, tell us what you were doing the night before last in Humboldthain,' Böhm said.

Fleming gave a start. 'In Humboldthain? What makes you think I was doing anything there?'

Böhm opened the file in front of him. 'You were a member of the RFB,' he read. 'Got into a few scrapes with the Nazis down the years, haven't you?'

'What if I have?'

'After the RFB was banned too. In theory, anyway.'

'The SA hasn't been banned. They're allowed to fight with impunity.'

'No one in this country is allowed to fight with impunity.'

'There's the odd knuckle sandwich when the brownshirts take things too far. Have you seen how they carry on? You shouldn't go thinking it's always us Reds who start it.'

'You don't go out of your way to avoid it.'

'We're not cowards.'

Böhm nodded sympathetically. 'In the small hours of Wednesday morning one of these fights spiralled out of control, isn't that so?'

'I don't know what you're talking about. I cut myself peeling potatoes. Didn't Frau Schobeck tell you? Ask her!'

'We've already spoken to Frau Schobeck,' Gräf said.

Fleming looked at him in confusion. 'Didn't she confirm it? I gave her my things to wash.'

'In the meantime we've run a blood test on them,' Böhm said. 'Blood type B.'

'So what?'

'You're blood type O, Herr Fleming.' He turned white as a sheet. 'Take a guess who else has blood type B.' Fleming was silent; no doubt he could imagine. 'Exactly. Gerhard Kubicki, the dead man from Humboldthain.'

'That's a coincidence.'

'Don't talk nonsense!' Böhm shouted. 'Why are you feeding me this crap about peeling potatoes? Do you really expect me to believe you've never seen Kubicki in your life?'

Fleming sat ramrod straight on his chair and fell silent.

Böhm tossed a pin onto the table. A hand held a weapon, upon which flew a flag bearing the inscription 4. REICHSTREFFEN BERLIN PFINGSTEN 1928. Underneath were the letters R.F.B.

Fleming stared at the pin. 'You have no right to go rummaging through my flat,' he said. 'You need a search warrant for that.'

Böhm leaned back. 'We didn't search your flat. It was the coroner who found it, underneath Gerhard Kubicki's corpse. It's safe to say he wasn't in the Red Front.'

Fleming flung his head this way and that, before positively screaming his response. 'Alright, for God's sake. Yes, I dragged the dead Nazi into the bushes.'

'So you admit it.'

'Only that I hid him! I didn't kill him.'

'You really expect me to believe that?'

'It's the truth.'

'If you didn't kill him, then why did you hide the corpse?'

Leo Fleming calmed down a little. 'I meet my girl by the church there every morning. I didn't want either of us to get in trouble.'

'Well I must commend you there.'

'Should I tell you what happened or not?'

'Go on.'

48

Dark patches on the paving slabs were all that remained of the morning's rain. Sitting here drinking coffee and cognac definitely had something. The drinks warmed from inside, the sun from outside, and a waiter appeared at regular intervals with fresh coffee, fresh cognac, and anything else you might wish for, even a copy of the *Evening Post*. Café Reimann had an international flavour.

Goldstein had heard English, French and Russian spoken in the hour and a half he had been here. He liked the European custom of placing tables and chairs outside, and here on the Kurfürstendamm the pavements were especially wide. Meanwhile, the passersby, who were mostly elegantly dressed and counted many pretty women among them, made for a spectacle he never grew tired of.

There was no news from Brooklyn in the *Evening Post*, or at least none that interested him. Not a single line about Fat Moe, and nothing about the war of the New York Gangs. The paper was six days old, but it was impossible to get a more recent edition. Nevertheless, he was glad to read anything that kept him up to date on events at home, and might inform him of Moe's untimely demise.

The fat man's days were numbered, that much was certain. Moe Berkowicz had rubbed too many people up the wrong way, starting with the Italians. He had an inkling he was on the way out, of course, which was why he had grown more suspicious in the last few months, eliminating more and more people, enemies both real and imagined, and weakening his position with every corpse. By now, his bloodlust had accounted for a number of his closest confidants. When even Skinny Sally, Moe's old companion Salomon Epstein, the walking adding machine, whose precision brain had contributed more to the fat man's rise than all his gang's guns and muscle put together, stood on the blacklist, nobody was safe. For the first time in his life Abe Goldstein had failed to complete a contract.

Skinny Sally's heart jumped when he saw the lights on in his flat and his boss's killer sitting inside on the sofa. His gaze said simply: make it quick.

Abe had reassured him. 'Don't worry, Sally. If I wanted to kill you, you'd be dead already.'

Salomon Epstein understood Goldstein's visit meant it would be wise to disappear for a few weeks, as far away as possible from Moe Berkowicz and his men. He packed a suitcase and, ever since that evening, Abe Goldstein had a new friend.

On that momentous day, when he let Skinny Sally go free, Goldstein's passage was already booked. The letter from Berlin a few days before had made the decision easy. He spent the four days prior to his departure in a cheap hotel with his suitcases packed, venturing outside only to buy papers and cigarettes. The day before leaving he read that there had been a gunfight in the Congo Club on Amsterdam Avenue, a bloodbath, in which five people had lost their lives. The Congo was one of Moses Berkowicz's speakeasies. Fat Moe ought to have been dead, but had broken his routine and left the club at ten. After that he had gone underground. The incident finally brought home to Abe how important it was that he skip town. A wounded Moses Berkowicz was more dangerous than ever.

A day later, Goldstein stood on the upper deck of the *Europa*. Leaning against the rail he saw two young men in light-grey summer coats on the pier below. He had never seen them before, but was in no doubt they were sharing board and lodging with Fat Moe in some lice-ridden apartment out in the Bronx. The fat man's last reserves: two amateurs picked off the street, who looked as though they had never worn suits before in their lives. When one of them spotted him and pointed up, he gave them a friendly wave, knowing he was safe. The steamer had already cast off, and the foghorn issued its deafening farewell to Manhattan. Nevertheless, one of the two—perhaps thinking no one would be able to hear over the noise—drew his weapon and took aim. His partner stopped him pulling the trigger. A cop had seen them, and Moe's kindergarten killers made themselves scarce.

After searching in vain for Moses Berkowicz's obituary notice, Goldstein leafed through the sports section. The Dodgers had lost again.

'Anything else, Sir?' the waiter said in English. His tone was polite and worldly, in anticipation of a hefty dollar tip.

'Schwarzwälder Kirsch, please.'

The waiter gave a nod of acknowledgement hearing Goldstein's impeccable pronunciation. He had probably never taken an order like that from an American tourist before.

Goldstein leaned back, lit a Camel and surveyed a girl in a light summer dress. She seemed to notice; at any rate, she gave him an enchanting smile. He smiled back and crumpled the empty cigarette packet. He only had one pack of twenty left in his suite, and still hadn't located an alternative source. Despite an otherwise excellent selection, the hotel tobacconist's didn't have any Camel, nor, surprisingly, did the big train station opposite. Maybe he should write to the American embassy. Or try here in this neighbourhood. The rich west was where most American tourists seemed to spend their time.

Someone had left a Berlin paper on the neighbouring table. Goldstein's gaze fixed on a familiar portrait. He reached over and grabbed it. *B.Z. am Mittag* the title page said, and on the first page of the regional section stood the headline: SA MAN MURDERED. Below it was the photo. The man wore a neat parting, but aside from that bore a fatal resemblance to Brass knuckles Gerd from Humboldthain. The caption also carried his name: VICTIM OF A POLITICAL BRAWL? GERHARD KUBICKI (27).

'One Schwarzwälder Kirsch. Would the gentleman like anything else?'

The waiter placed a plate containing a large slice of cake on the table and discreetly removed the crumpled cigarette packet. Goldstein continued reading the paper.

BERLIN—*The bloody corpse of a 27-year-old man was discovered by police yesterday morning in Volkspark Humboldthain, near the Himmelfahrtkirche. The victim suffered cuts and stab wounds. The man, who later succumbed to his injuries, has been identified as SA-Rottenführer Gerhard Kubicki, resident at Berlin Gesundbrunnen, currently unemployed. Police suspect that Kubicki was the victim of a politically motivated brawl, and have requested the assistance of B.Z. readers. Did you notice anything suspicious in Volkspark Humboldthain on Tuesday night? Witnesses are asked to contact their nearest police precinct, or get*

in touch directly with CID at police headquarters, Alexanderplatz.
Telephone: Berolina 0023.

Goldstein pushed the cake plate aside. His appetite was gone. The police were making a real fuss over this. Damn it! He stubbed out the Camel and pushed five dollars under the saucer. Instinctively he smelled trouble. He had to do something.

49

Dull as it might be playing Abraham Goldstein's minder, Rath was satisfied with his working day as he got into the Buick at Anhalter Bahnhof. Soon they'd have the Yank worn down. How must it feel to spend the whole day trapped in your hotel room? Lunch was the only meal Goldstein had left his suite for. Breakfast had been taken to his room, likewise dinner the night before. As Czerwinski had painstakingly noted: a platter of cold roast beef and a bottle of chilled champagne. The man had to console himself somehow.

The garage had done a good job; the Buick felt good as new. Marlow would expect a favour in return, but Rath would supply. His investigation for Dr M. was a hundred times more interesting than being on shift at the Excelsior. Or searching for Charly's guttersnipe, a task that was as ridiculous as it was futile.

Those endless hours in the hotel had given him too much time to think about his quarrel with Charly. Again and again, he saw the image of her green hat as it disappeared between the S-Bahn scaffolding poles. A few times he had been on the verge of calling her; the telephone he had brought up to the desk kept urging him on. Once he even dialled the operator, only to hang up before he could give Charly's number.

He was furious at her pig-headedness, but couldn't stop thinking about her. At the same time he would have liked nothing more than to take her in his arms, and not just because they usually landed in bed when they made up after quarrelling. But yesterday was different, he could feel it.

He should have proposed like he planned, but the timing in the last few months had never been right. He wanted it to be special, which was why he had organised the trip to Cologne, even got hold of football tickets. Everything had been planned down to the final detail, including booking a table in the *Bastei* for the day after the game. After that he'd have performed his filial duty by officially introducing Charly as his fiancée, making it clear once and for all that he was determined to marry a Protestant. Then he'd have disappeared back to Berlin and finally been rid of his parents and their advice.

The *Bastei* was one of the classiest restaurants in the city, a generously proportioned, modern build with spectacular views of the cathedral and the Rhine. The waiter had been in on it: rings in the champagne. But then they had run into his mother. How could he forget that she shopped at Leonhard Tietz every Monday?

They had gone out to eat that night as planned. The table was booked, but the timing wasn't right. He managed to catch the waiter at the last moment, and had the rings taken out of the glasses. They were now hidden in his living room cabinet, waiting to be deployed again.

He cursed his indecision. He should have asked her long ago, or left it once and for all.

Should he really propose to a woman whose career was evidently more important to her than marriage and children? Rath no longer knew what was right and what was wrong. Sometimes he wished he belonged to his parents' generation; things were easier for them. Or, at least, so he thought.

He had been engaged before, but Doris had dropped him after he hit the headlines following the shoot-out in Cologne's Agnesviertel. At best, their marriage would have resembled that of his parents, and that was something he could do without.

He wanted Charly and no one else. So, why hadn't he told her that long ago?

'Damn it!' he shouted, and Kirie, who had been dozing peacefully on the passenger seat, woke with a start and stared at him.

He wanted *her*, damn it! Why shouldn't he just tell her, right now? Then she could decide one way or another. There was no other way, no more waiting, no more half measures. He needed to know! He would accept her answer, whichever way it came out. He couldn't bear the uncertainty anymore. It was now or never.

He felt a sudden surge of optimism, like a suicide candidate who, at long last, had summoned the courage to enter the lift at the Funkturm in preparation for one final jump.

Taking a U-turn under the steel bars of the elevated train, he drove the

Buick back up Stresemannstrasse, past the Excelsior, heading further and further north until finally he reached Moabit.

Arriving at Spenerstrasse, he sat in the car for a moment. Should he get out or not? Give in to impulse or come to his senses? He tapped a cigarette out of the case, and Kirie looked on in surprise. Why was no one getting out of the car?

She hadn't expected his advice to be so clear, but his clarity did her good; the whole conversation did her good. She should have called him ages ago; the only reason she hadn't was Gereon's stupid jealousy. Guido's presence was like a red rag to a bull. Well, so what? Whose problem was that? Not hers anyway.

Now Guido, with whom she had studied—and suffered—together for most of her university years, was back in her kitchen, and it was just like old times, like when he advised her to resit the state examination. She couldn't have wished for a better guide when it came to her dilemma. Court Assessor Guido Scherer was a man who knew a thing or two about making a career in law.

'You have to take up Heymann's offer,' he said. 'Do you know what an honour that is?'

'Of course I do, but what good is it?'

'You'd have a name in the academic world.'

'I don't want a name in the *academic* world. I want more justice in this one.'

Guido smiled. He smiled often. That was another thing Gereon hated about him, but he had never been able to stand her old classmate anyway. She had explained to him countless times that he had no cause for jealousy, but he never seemed to believe her.

'He's still pursuing you, you realise that?'

'Don't exaggerate. He knows he won't get anywhere with me, and he's fine with that.'

'But the way he looks at you, like . . . like . . . And that stupid grin!'

'Oh, cut it out with your jealousy, and stop trying to dictate who I see!'

Gereon had eased back on his criticism, but somehow she met Guido less often.

Suddenly Charly was furious again. Gereon had succeeded in putting her off one of her best friends. It was only now, more than a year since she last saw him, as they spoke about the law and everything else under the sun, that she realised how much she had missed these conversations. Conversations that weren't possible with Gereon Rath were exactly what she needed now, after her trouble at Lichtenberg. It did her good to speak with someone who knew about these things; who valued her ability when it came to questions of the law. Despite everything, with Gereon, she still wasn't sure.

'Another drop?'

Guido nodded and Charly poured a little more of the red wine she had intended to share with Gereon. So that they could discuss the same subject: Heymann's offer.

She stood up. 'If you'll excuse me. I have to go to the little girls' room.'

Charly disappeared and, just as her guest raised the glass to his mouth, the doorbell rang.

Rath unwrapped the flowers nervously. His brio on the journey, his determination, his certainty that he was doing the right thing, all shrivelled as he stood in front of the door. On the street he had needed to take a little walk to calm himself down, and had bought a bunch of roses before returning to her flat. Kirie, who was used to going straight into the drawing room from the car, looked at her master patiently, knowing that humans are fickle.

She wagged her tail; she must be able to smell Charly already. Even so, there was nothing doing in her flat. Rath rang a second time. He was starting to think he had made the trip for nothing, that she must be back in Friedrichshain, at the Müggelsee or somewhere else looking for the escaped girl, when he heard steps. His heart pounded, they were going to make up, he knew it, but whether she would accept his proposal . . . he wasn't at all sure. He'd need more than simple charm. Damn it, he thought, you have to see this through. Do it right, or not at all!

The door opened and Rath's boyishly cheeky smile froze.

'Herr Rath!' said Guido, grinning.

It couldn't be! He had been through this exact situation once before, managing, on that occasion, to vent his fury elsewhere. This time he stood rooted to the spot. Rage consumed him. The knowledge that he had nothing to counter it with seemed, finally, to release him. He drew back and, just as Guido was saying something like 'Won't you come in?', slashed the roses to the left and right across his face, long-stemmed flowers, with big, sharp thorns.

Kirie barked, because she barked at anyone her master fought, and it was this barking that returned Rath to his senses, and prevented him from wiping the stupid grin off the man's face with a straight left. For the grinning man was, of course, still grinning, even though his face was streaked with blood. Flinging the shredded roses at the man's feet, Rath took Kirie by the lead and returned to the car.

50

The landlord placed two beers on the table, with two schnapps glasses alongside. Rath and Gräf clinked glasses, downed the schnapps and cleansed their palates with beer.

'So?' Rath asked. 'How's it going?'

'I arrested a suspect yesterday evening, but Böhm's the one conducting the interview.'

'What are you going to do? He's leading the investigation. Just be glad if your name turns up somewhere in the file.'

'Well, I suppose it's better than hanging around the Excelsior. Goldstein still hasn't left town?'

Rath shook his head. 'Looks like you're going to lose your bet.'

'It isn't the weekend yet. Where's your dog by the way?'

'In bed.' Rath fumbled an Overstolz out of his case and lit it. 'What case are you investigating? The dead fence?'

Gräf shook his head. 'Böhm passed that one to Lange. It's connected with the KaDeWe break-in somehow. No,' he said. 'I get to deal with gay Nazis.'

'I'm sorry?'

'Gerhard Kubicki. The dead SA man from Humboldthain. He was a fairy.'

Rath couldn't help but laugh. 'So that's why Goebbels hasn't made him into a second Wessel.'

'You wouldn't believe how many homosexuals there are in the SA. Especially in the new SA. The gay clique heading them are like a red rag to Stennes' old guard.'

The SA war had kept Berlin on tenterhooks for months. Oberführer Walther Stennes, the highest-ranking SA chief in Berlin, Brandenburg, East Prussia and Pommern, had rebelled against Hitler and Gauleiter Goebbels, on one occasion occupying Berlin party headquarters in Hedemannstrasse.

With Hitler's backing, Goebbels had managed to apply the brakes: Stennes was relieved of office, over five hundred of his supporters were expelled from the SA, and a clean sweep was made of Berlin members. Rival SA factions had clashed with increasing frequency ever since.

'Do you have any leads?' Rath asked.

'We picked up a Communist with Kubicki's blood on his clothes.'

'There you are then. Business as usual. Red on Brown.'

Gräf looked sceptical. 'The man admitted to hiding the corpse, but denies killing the SA man. He says he was propped against the church wall, dead as a doornail. He just hid the corpse to avoid getting into trouble.'

'When does he say he found the body?'

'In the early hours. He meets his girl in front of the Himmelfahrtkirche every day before work. Before her work, that is. He's unemployed.'

'Handy. Is she providing his alibi?'

'No, that's just it. She didn't see him at all on the morning in question. He says he noticed the blood on his jacket and went straight home.'

'Strange story.'

'Which is why I'm inclined to believe it.'

'Who killed the dead Nazi then?'

'I don't know.'

Gräf lifted his empty beer glass, which caught Schorsch's attention. The *Nasse Dreieck* landlord brought a fresh beer, exchanging it for Gräf's empty glass and glancing disapprovingly at Rath's, which was still half full.

'It could be,' Gräf said, 'that the victim's homosexuality is relevant somehow.'

'A gay Nazi the victim of a homophobic murderer? Doesn't sound right to me. Always leaves a funny taste when these Nazis or Commies style themselves as victims.'

'The man isn't styling himself. He is a victim. He was killed after all.'

'You're right. It's just that since Goebbels made a hero out of that pimp Wessel . . .'

'Wessel was no pimp. That's Communist propaganda!'

'Well, he was no martyr either. I know the case pretty well.'

Rath decided to back down. He had no desire to quarrel with his friend over politics. They usually avoided such topics, just as they avoided talking about Charlotte Ritter. 'You're saying this Kubicki died because he was a homosexual.'

'It's a possibility. I found something interesting in the files. About a week ago Stennes' men threatened one of the leaders of the new Berlin SA. Karl Ernst, the local Gau's aide-de-camp, was sitting with a few fellow officers in a bar in Halensee when a group of Stennes' supporters tried to lay into them. Before it could go too far a riot squad took them in.'

'So?'

'One of Stennes' men said some pretty nasty things to Ernst and his pal Paul Röhrbein. It's the first time I've ever read the phrase *arse-fuckers* in a police statement. There was talk of *gay boys* and *faggy bastards* too.'

'Sounds pretty homophobic.'

'Right. Ernst and Röhrbein are both homosexual.'

Rath nodded pensively.

'But the most interesting thing about the file was something else,' Gräf said. 'Among the brownshirts in the bar was a certain Gerhard Kubicki.'

'Let me guess: he was one of the arse-fuckers.'

'Got it in one.' Gräf took a few more sips of beer and drained his glass. 'I've suggested to Böhm that we canvass the names on the Halensee list, but he won't have it. Thinks we'd be better off softening up a few Communists.'

'I never knew Böhm was such a Commie-basher.'

'He doesn't care if they're Communists, Nazis or small children.'

'But he saves his best for CID officers.'

Gräf laughed. 'At least I have permission to question our dead Rotten-führer's superior officer tomorrow. Let's see what comes of that.' His gaze fell on the two glasses again. 'What's up with you?' he asked. 'You're a beer down already.'

The detective made a move to order a fresh round, but Rath waved him away. 'Not tonight,' he said, stubbing out his cigarette and reaching for his hat. 'I've made other plans.'

Gräf looked at his watch. 'At quarter past eleven?'

'Sorry,' he said and placed five marks on the counter. 'Let me take care of this.'

The detective grinned. 'So, what's her name?'

Rath shrugged. 'Not sure,' he said, pleased at the look of bafflement on Gräf's face.

51

Rath parked the Buick a walking distance from the door. If his former colleagues at Vice were on surveillance and took down his number plate, he could have a lot of explaining to do. He left the car by the Weberwiese and walked down Memeler Strasse. The fresh air did him good. He had packed his Walther, as he didn't fancy his chances here unarmed, especially at night. When he reached the junction at Posener Strasse a dim memory surfaced.

Venuskeller was an illegal cellar bar near the former Ostbahnhof, concealed in the rear courtyard of an unprepossessing tenement house. Dim was the word. This was where his first meeting with Johann Marlow had been contrived during a visit more than two years before. Marlow's men had led Rath, the coked-up policeman, to a warehouse on the site of the Ostbahnhof, where the gangster received him. The evening had marked the start of their fateful relationship. Well, Rath thought, at least this time he was invited.

Guards stood watch on the street, but let him approach the building and the stairs that led down to the cellar bar. A man stepped out of the shadows.

'Herr Rath, I presume,' he said. Rath nodded. The man tipped his hat. 'You're expected. Please follow me.'

The guard didn't take him to the entrance at the foot of the stairs, but further towards the back where a staircase led directly to the office and back rooms. He would be spared the noise and scandal of Venuskeller. He wasn't in the mood for an illegal nightclub, not after Charly and the grinning man had ruined his evening. In fact, he was just happy to have something to do, even sleuthing for an underworld heavyweight. The guard gave two brief knocks and Liang opened.

Marlow's Chinaman frisked him, fishing the Walther out of its holster and taking his coat. Johann Marlow sat behind Sebald's desk. There was no sign of the bar's owner, however. Apart from Marlow, Rath and Liang, there wasn't a soul in the room. Sebald's office appeared to be one of the many Marlow had dotted across the city, to be used as and when required. Through the door came the muffled sound of music aimed at getting patrons in the mood. Marlow offered a friendly greeting as usual, even standing to proffer a hand.

'Do take a seat,' he said, pointing to a leather chair that Liang was already straightening. The silent Chinese always seemed to be in several places at once. Rath sank onto the cushion, and Liang set down a whisky glass and poured.

'I thought I remembered you having a taste for my malt,' Marlow said, and raised his glass.

Rath lit an Overstolz. His supplies were dwindling again. He was smoking more than was good for him, especially in the five hours since the grinning man had opened Charly's door.

'You were going to introduce me to Red Hugo's girl,' he said, realising he sounded a little unfriendly.

'Later.' Marlow said. 'I've been asking around. You have this Goldstein under surveillance?'

'Since Monday.'

'Why didn't you tell me?'

'Because I don't think he has anything to do with the disappearance of some Berlin gangster. He hasn't left his hotel in days.'

'So he couldn't have killed anybody . . .'

'That's why we have him under surveillance.'

'As if it makes any difference to you if a man like Red Hugo is taken out of circulation . . .'

'Or Rudi the Rat . . .'

'Leave that idiot out of this. Now, what have you found?'

Rath told Marlow what he knew. As far as possible, he had pieced together Red Hugo's movements on the day of his disappearance. It appeared that after leaving his house, Hugo Lenz had eaten lunch in Amor-Diele, where he had received a number of fresh complaints about the Nordpiraten. They had destroyed a kiosk whose owner paid protection to Berolina since time immemorial; thrown a cocaine dealer out of a nightclub on Berolina's patch; and put two bookkeepers in hospital. Rath had made contact with all four men. Apparently Red Hugo had assured each one in turn that the

Pirates would soon be eating humble pie, and that all wrongs would be set right in a matter of days. Then he had given his driver and bodyguard the rest of the day off and headed to a meeting alone. Marlow's people had found Lenz's red-black Horch on Stralauer Allee, just by the Osthafen.

'Do you have any idea what he might have been doing there?' Rath asked. Marlow shook his head. 'When did you last see him yourself?'

Marlow took a cigar from a case on his desk and snipped off its end, a gesture that appeared threatening somehow. 'Last week,' he said, exhaling little clouds of cigar smoke into the room. 'At the hospital. We were visiting one of our men. Kettler. You know, the one the Pirates crippled.'

'You visited a minor drug-dealer in person?'

'People need to know they're being looked after. Otherwise they succumb to the promises of the Prussian Police.'

'Which hospital and when?'

'Last Friday. In Friedrichshain. We don't see each other too often. Mostly we talk on the telephone.'

'So when was the last time you spoke to him?'

'Monday morning. Before he left.'

'Did you know of his plans for the day?'

'Only that we were due to meet in Amor-Diele that evening. Krehmann's back room is Hugo's study, so to speak. Mine too sometimes.'

'What was the meeting about?'

'Is that relevant?'

Rath shrugged. 'I won't know until I find him.'

'It was about the Nordpiraten. Countermeasures we could take without triggering all-out war. To regain respect for Berolina, and yours truly as well.' Marlow balanced the ash of his cigar, and let it drop into the tray. 'Lenz was optimistic that morning. He seemed to have a plan. Unfortunately he vanished before he could tell me what it was.'

'Could this plan have something to do with Rudi Höller's disappearance? Could Lenz have eliminated him before going underground?'

Marlow shook his head. 'I'd know about that. I'm afraid Hugo's plan had something to do with his *own* disappearance.'

'Because the Pirates got wind of it, and got to him first . . .'

'That would be the most obvious explanation, but I don't buy it. It would mean the Pirates declaring war on Berolina.'

'Is that so unlikely?'

'It would suggest that either the Pirates are unbelievably stupid or . . .' Marlow paused thoughtfully, '. . . that they have an ace up their sleeve which I know nothing about.'

'What kind of ace?'

'It's your job to find out. Perhaps it's this American gangster, or someone in uniform.'

'A police officer? What makes you think that?'

Marlow pushed a button under the desk and a door opened, granting Rath a fleeting glimpse into the artists' dressing room—or whatever it was called in Venuskeller. At any rate it was the room where the girls got changed, which, in most cases, meant getting *un*dressed. The blonde who emerged wore only a white bathrobe and glittering tiara. She seemed to have been waiting for this moment, and made quite an entrance, her light bathrobe fluttering elegantly to reveal tantalising glimpses of her body. Rath was stunned into silence.

'Christine, this is the inspector I was telling you about.' He gestured towards the leather chair.

Christine's cheeky Berlin-girl face gazed at Rath so provocatively that he felt a tingling sensation between his legs. Perhaps it was also because leaning over to stretch out her hand, she just happened to display her breasts. Rath tried to think of something else, before finally alighting on the flabby arms of Frau Lennartz, the caretaker's wife at Luisenufer, as she wrung out a cleaning rag over a metal bucket filled with dirty water.

'A pleasure,' he said, standing up and taking her hand.

'So I see,' Christine replied.

Rath sank back in his chair.

The girl sat on the desk and crossed her legs so that the bathrobe no longer concealed any part of them. Without asking she fiddled a cigarette out of the case on the desk and lit up.

'You haven't been here for a long time, Inspector,' Marlow said, clearly amused. 'Christine has been our main attraction for half a year now.'

Rath reached for his whisky. Liang had topped him up again. 'How well do you know Hugo Lenz?' he asked.

The main attraction drew on her cigarette and blew a cloud of smoke into the room. 'Better than you could stand, believe me.'

'Oh, I do. When did you last see him?'

'Sunday evening. In Amor-Diele. In his office.'

'You mean the back room . . .'

'His office.'

'What did you do there?'

'Any number of things. Stay for a moment and I'll give you a taste on stage.'

'No need to go into detail.' Rath cleared his throat. Christine seemed to enjoy discovering how Catholic he was. 'What I would like to know is, did you notice anything about him? Did you talk about anything that could be linked to his disappearance?'

'He always talked a blue streak. Afterwards.' She cast him a glance that ought to have been made illegal. 'There is something that might interest you—he didn't talk about it explicitly, but he was pretty euphoric. He thought he'd found a way of outwitting the Pirates.'

'Go on.'

'That was all he was prepared to say while he still hadn't discussed it with his boss.' She glanced at Marlow.

'Do you have any idea what it could have been?'

'Maybe what I've already told the boss: that Hugo had met a police officer of whom he expected certain things.'

Marlow shook his head gruffly. 'I always told the idiot to leave that sort of thing to me.'

'Was Lenz planning to meet this police officer on Monday?' Rath asked.

'I've no idea what he had planned that day.'

Rath turned back to Marlow, a move Christine met with an insulted expression. 'Have you already been to his flat?' he asked.

'Of course, but if we'd found him, you wouldn't be here.'

'Clearly you didn't find *him*, but perhaps some leads, a few clues . . .'

'Inspector, we're not police officers.' Marlow's gaze was almost reproachful. He gave the girl a nod and she disappeared back into the dressing room. Marlow waited until the door was closed. 'I can give you the keys. As long as you promise to forget that you're a policeman.'

'I can be very forgetful.'

'You seem tired,' Marlow said.

'I have a lot on my plate.'

Dr M. must have given Liang a sign. The Chinese stood next to Rath's chair, and opened a silver jar containing white powder.

'Might I offer your something?' Marlow asked. 'Guaranteed to perk you up.'

Rath shook his head.

'I've never known you so reticent.'

'Never between meals.' It was meant to be an offhand remark, casual, indifferent, but the sight of the cocaine gave him cravings. He hadn't taken any for a long time, above all for Charly's sake, but he had liked it, back then. He stood up. 'I just need a little sleep and I'll be fine.'

'I hope you're right,' Marlow said. He opened a drawer and pulled out a set of keys, which he handed to Rath. 'A few men from Berolina are keeping watch on the building. Show them your identification. I'll let them know you're coming.'

Hugo Lenz's house was better guarded than Venuskeller, and more discreetly. Rath locked the car and crossed the street feeling watched, but there was no one to be seen. A man stepped from behind a tree.

'What are you doing here?'

Rath showed his identification, remembering him as one of those guarding the Sorokin gold two years before. The man returned the papers.

Hugo Lenz had moved into a nice little house in the Prinzenviertel of Karlshorst, close to his beloved racetrack. You had to be more than just a head of a Ringverein to afford a place like this. Working with Marlow had clearly paid for the former safebreaker.

Three men playing cards spun around as he entered the kitchen. One drew his gun. Rath showed his identification and they relaxed.

'Take as long as you need,' the man with the weapon said.

Rath's heart was pounding. It was a good thing Marlow had warned them in advance.

'What were you about to play?' another asked. No one paid the late-night visitor any more attention.

'Grand Hand.' The man placed his gun on the table. 'Woe betide any of you shitbags if you've looked at my cards!'

Rath exited the kitchen. Why was Marlow guarding the flat so closely if Hugo Lenz wasn't here? Perhaps they were guarding something else, or just preventing the Nordpiraten from torching the property?

The drawing room was conservatively furnished to the petit bourgeois tastes of a safebreaker who had come into money. Everywhere you looked, the carpets were plush and plump. Hugo Lenz was still trapped in 1890. Missing was the portrait of the Kaiser above the piano, although the obligatory Beethoven bust glowered from its rightful place on the piano. Rath doubted that Hugo Lenz could play, but its shiny black presence would correspond to his ideas of refinement. Likewise the books on the shelves were sorted according to colour. None appeared as though it had been read. Rath looked around, finding nothing valuable or noteworthy in the cupboards. He didn't know what he was looking for, though that wasn't always important; often it was precisely when you weren't looking that you hit upon something of value.

It didn't seem as if Hugo Lenz spent much time here; no doubt his real living room was the Amor-Diele. Things were different in the bedroom, however, a room of formidable size. The bed wasn't made and worn trousers were draped across a chair, with old socks and underwear strewn across the floor. Hugo Lenz hadn't planned on disappearing. A quick glance inside his wardrobe confirmed no empty hangers, and apparently nothing was missing. If Lenz had made a run for it, for whatever reason, then he hadn't had time to pack. Rath was starting to rule out the possibility that Red Hugo was a turncoat, gone over to either the police or the Pirates to sound the death knell for Johann Marlow.

He even had a kind of study—or at least a room that was dominated by a large desk. Rath rummaged through the drawers, finding neither an appointments diary nor a notebook, nor, indeed, any papers. Only a dozen sachets of cocaine. He did as Marlow asked and forgot he was a police officer.

The lower drawer also contained a number of forbidden items: pornographic photos. Not for sale, it appeared, but private use. They weren't staged, like the ones Rath knew from his time in Vice, but snapshots, albeit of rare quality. Some gifted photographer had taken pictures of the Venuskeller sets down the years, and the results were for adults only. Right at the top of the pile Rath recognised Christine, only this time sans bathrobe and cavorting with a muscular gymnast. The picture left him strangely cold.

He leafed through the pile of photos and Venuskeller bills from previous years, at length finding one he had marvelled at two years before. The photographs showed a fake Indian working over a white woman tied to a stake—and not in the way old Karl May would have it.

He looked through the pictures, trying to recognise himself in the audience, but saw only unfamiliar faces. He couldn't help thinking back to that night, when all *this* had started. Then, suddenly, he hesitated when he saw the face of the woman at the stake, a face he had long since forgotten, but which now seemed very familiar. Feverishly he searched for a better photograph. The photographer had fixed the lens on his subjects' body parts, rarely their faces. Nevertheless, Rath managed to find a picture of such portrait-like quality it could have been used for a passport—at least, if you edited out the sexual characteristics. Suddenly he was wide awake. It took a moment for the penny to drop, but now he knew where he had last seen her, and it wasn't all that long ago.

52

The 50th precinct was on Zingster Strasse, a stone's throw from the Ring-bahnhof and the new U-Bahn station at Gesundbrunnen. First Sergeant Rometsch hadn't exaggerated. The station was mobbed. He received the visitors from Alex at the gate and led them into his office.

'I place my office at your disposal, Detective.' The sergeant stood up straight, as solemn as an army soldier about to lay down his life for the Fatherland. Gräf managed not to laugh.

'Thank you,' he said. 'How many witnesses is it?'

'Around a dozen.'

'And they're all here?'

'Yes, Sir. I didn't let anyone go before giving a statement.'

'What about those who made their reports by telephone?'

'I've summoned them too. They should be here by now.'

Gräf was no longer surprised by the crush in the corridor. 'Send the most important witnesses in first.'

Rometsch saluted and disappeared.

While Böhm had another word with the unfortunate Leo Fleming at Alex, Gräf had been dispatched to the 50th precinct. 'You wanted to pay that SA type a visit,' Böhm had said. 'Well, you can take care of this at the same time.'

Gräf made himself comfortable behind a desk that was so tidy it must belong to First Sergeant Rometsch himself. Christel Temme stood with her pad, unsure where to sit. Gräf pointed to a second desk in the office, which was far less tidy. She sat down, pushing a file, a half-eaten apple and some greaseproof paper to one side and, with a disgusted expression, placed her notepad on the newly cleared surface.

After a minute Rometsch sent in the first witness, a small man with a pointed nose. The man held a hat in his hands and was clearly very proud at being called first. He let fly before Gräf could ask him anything.

'It wasn't a fight with Communists, I can tell you that much. You're barking up the wrong tree.'

The witness's brazen manner, the way he sat complacently, straddle-legged on the chair, drove Gräf up the wall. 'I see,' he said. 'And how do you know? Did you see the killer?'

'No.'

'Then perhaps it was you?'

The man gave a visible start. 'For God's sake, of course not!'

'Then just tell me what you actually saw before you draw any hasty con-clusions. From the beginning.'

'It wasn't a Communist the Nazis picked a fight with that night. It was a Jew.'

'A Jew?' Gräf looked up. 'Are you sure?'

'Who else goes around in black with a beard and sidelocks? It isn't Car-nival yet.'

'From the beginning, I said. What exactly did you see?'

'I was in the U-Bahn station, and . . .'

'Which U-Bahn station?'

'The one here, of course. Gesundbrunnen. Where else? I was waiting for my train.'

The comforting scratch of Christel Temme's pencil made Gräf feel as if he were sitting behind his own desk at the Castle. 'OK, go on.'

'Well, a Jew was waiting there too. Then the Nazis came. The man from the paper was there, the murder victim. I recognised him straightaway from the photo.'

'What happened on the platform?' This might be the first witness they could take seriously.

'Not much. At some point the Jew went up the stairs. And the SA fol-lowed.'

'Just like that?'

'They made fun of him a little first. Nothing serious.'

'Nothing serious . . .'

'I don't know why he ran away. The train had just arrived.'

'What did you do?'

'I got on the train.'

'See anything else?'

The man shook his head. 'I was already on the train. They all went up-stairs.'

'How many were there?'

'Four or five.'

Gräf took out the photo of Scharführer Günter Sieger he had found in the political files, and pushed it across the table. 'Was this man one of them?' he asked.

The witness only needed a brief glance. He looked at Gräf and nodded.

53

Rath fought against sleep by sketching meaningless patterns in his note-book. He had already had five cups of coffee with no discernible effect. Last night had been late, but he still hadn't got any sleep when he finally crept into bed. He began to miss the cognac in Moabit. He could have done with it at Luisenufer, and urgently needed to get hold of a bottle today. Three more nights without sleep and he'd be on his last legs.

It would have to be the grinning man! Rath had wished that idiot to hell the moment he first clapped eyes on him. He clearly had designs on Charly, even if she always denied it. Rath had actually thought he was rid of him, but old perma-smile had just been waiting for his chance. Well, now it had arrived. The widow chaser! He should have socked him one on the nose, damn it!

The lift opened and a boy placed a cup of coffee on the antique desk, clearing away the empty cup at the same time. Rath could no longer stand the table surface with its intarsia-decorated top, the lift, even the doors. He was sick of the whole hotel, except, perhaps, for the service.

He had been glad to see Goldstein crawl into his suite like a bear enter-ing hibernation, chalking up a victory in their little contest, which had be-gun with the car chase on the first day. Now, he longed for their next encounter. Rath couldn't understand why the Yank didn't just skip town. What business did he still have here? Was he lulling his minders into a false sense of security, all the better to strike? Or perhaps he was taking care of his affairs from the comfort of his hotel room, and they had been watching him in vain the whole time?

Well, Rath thought, so long as he isn't out on the streets spraying bul-lets and creating anti-Semitic headlines, we're doing our job.

Someone appeared in the corridor and all of a sudden he sprung awake. She hadn't come out of room 301, but was pushing a laundry cart down the corridor. He intercepted her before she could disappear.

'Don't I know you from somewhere?' he asked.

'Assuming you're not blind. You've been here a few days now, haven't you? In front of the lifts?' She pointed with her chin towards the desk.

'I don't mean from here.' She shot him a questioning look. 'Two words. Venus. And Keller.'

'I don't know what you're talking about.'

'The Venuskeller? You've never heard of it? It's a nightclub, an illegal nightclub.'

'Do I look like the sort of person who hangs around illegal nightclubs?'

'I'd be willing to bet I've seen you onstage at the Venuskeller.'

She eyed him suspiciously. 'And if you had? Are you trying to black-mail me?'

'I just think it's strange I should see you here again, of all places.'

She looked him up and down. 'I wouldn't have thought you were the type.'

'I used to work in Vice.'

She raised her eyebrows. 'So, you *are* a police officer!'

'Word's got around then.'

'Do you really think anyone believes that author rubbish Teubner's been putting about?' She looked at him with contempt. 'A bit strange for an author to have four different faces, don't you think?'

'Your hotel detective insisted on the story in order not to unsettle the guests. I hope I can count on your discretion.'

She tried to push the cart onwards, past the lifts and into the next corridor. Rath blocked her path.

'What is this? Let me get on with my work!'

'Just a few words on the guest in three-o-one.'

'The American?'

'The very same. Have you noticed anything suspicious in the past few days?'

'Depends on what you mean by suspicious. That he rarely goes out, perhaps. He seems to have a lot to do, anyway. He's almost always in his room when I bring in fresh towels or make up the bed.'

'What makes you think he has a lot to do?'

'The fact that he spends the whole day in his room, on the telephone.'

'Have you managed to listen in on any of his conversations?'

'I don't speak English.'

Rath gave her his card. 'If you should think of anything, let me know. What was your name again?'

'Marion.' She put the card in her pocket. 'I'm sorry,' she said, 'but I really have to be getting on.'

There was a *pling* and the left-hand lift opened. Rath gave an imaginary tip of the hat and returned to his desk. Marion wheeled the laundry cart on past.

54

In his day-to-day life Günter Sieger, who occupied the rank of SA-Scharführer, was caretaker of a run-down tenement on Bernauer Strasse. Gräf caught him eating lunch. The smell of sauerkraut and smoked pork loins reminded him how empty his own stomach was. Apart from half a bread roll and a cup of coffee, he hadn't eaten anything all day.

The interviews in the 50th precinct had dragged. A further four witnesses had confirmed the story that, led by Scharführer Sieger and dressed in full regalia in spite of the uniform ban, Kubicki's SA troop had abused an old Jew at Gesundbrunnen U-Bahn station. A witness reported that the abuse had continued upstairs until the man fled the station building. 'That was when the other man became involved,' he said. 'He can count his lucky stars the Nazis went after the Jew, otherwise they'd have given him a good thrashing.'

Gräf had sent Christel Temme back to Alex. He had no need of a stenographer out here. His joint operations with Charly had been very different. More than just a stenographer, Charly thought like a CID officer. Christel Temme, on the other hand, didn't think at all, she just took notes. Her reward was to sit down for lunch at the same time each day in the canteen while Gräf stared hungrily at the other man's food.

'You don't have anything against me eating?' Sieger said. No sign of a wife, perhaps the Scharführer was gay too. No hasty conclusions now, Gräf thought. You eat alone too. If you eat at all.

He sat at the table. 'Looks delicious,' he said, but Sieger didn't think to offer him any.

'Frau Ruland from number two cooks for me,' he said, hacking off a large slice of pork. 'In exchange I take care of whatever repairs need doing.'

Gräf waited with rumbling stomach until Sieger finished.

'So what can I do for you, Detective Inspector?' Sieger asked, wiping his mouth with a white napkin. Probably Frau Ruland did his washing too.

'It's just detective,' Gräf corrected. 'As I said, it's about Gerhard Kubicki.'

'I read about it in the paper. Poor Gerd.'

'You're his direct superior in the SA?'

Sieger nodded.

'When did you last see him?'

'What's that supposed to mean? Am I a suspect?'

'You were seen with Kubicki on the evening of 30th June. Apparently you were in uniform.'

'Says who?'

'Kubicki's corpse was still in uniform when they found it.'

'A man has been murdered, and the Prussian Police have nothing better to do than accuse the victim of wearing a banned uniform?'

'I'm not accusing anyone, I'm just trying to find out what happened. Is the uniform ban the reason you haven't made a witness statement until now?'

'You never know how the police'll treat you. When old Isidor Weiss releases his bloodhounds, a man of my political beliefs is easily cast as villain.'

'You should choose your words more carefully. Before I charge you with insulting a public official.' Sieger fell silent. 'I'm not interested in the uniform ban,' Gräf went on. 'I want you to tell me what happened on Tuesday night. I already know that you and your comrades hounded an old man out of the U-Bahn station after harassing him on the platform.'

'But, Inspector!'

'Detective.'

'Detective, then. It was nothing serious. An old Yid. We just made a little fun of him.'

Scharführer Sieger looked as innocent as a young boy trying to justify concealing his sister's doll. 'It can hardly come as a surprise when someone goes around dressed like that.'

'Why did you pursue the man? You could have let him go. Wasn't it enough to drive him out of the station?'

'What do you mean "drive him out"? The lads went upstairs, and I followed. They can be a little over-exuberant at times.'

'How *exuberant* were they on Tuesday night?'

'Nothing would've happened if he hadn't been there.'

'Who are you talking about?'

'Gerd's killer, of course. It's a disgrace you still haven't caught him. He accosted us upstairs in the station building, and we walked away. We weren't looking for a fight, but he wouldn't let go.'

'You weren't looking for a fight? Is that why you marched through a workers' district in your banned uniforms?'

'I thought this wasn't about the uniforms.'

'So tell me what happened.'

'He insulted us. Said someone had shat on our uniforms, and worse. I don't want to repeat it here. We went to the park to be rid of him.'

'But he came after you.'

'We couldn't have known he had a pistol.'

'Otherwise you'd just have beaten him up, four on one. That was your plan?'

Sieger looked outraged. 'I won't have the SA's honour being insulted in this way.'

'The SA's honour! No doubt your mysterious pursuer besmirched it too?'

'What are you trying to say?'

'That I'm surprised four SA men should raise the white flag as soon as someone insults them.'

'Well, the man seemed a little off his head. Drink, drugs, what do I know? Someone like that, you try to avoid.'

'But he followed you anyway.'

'Caught up with us by some meadow. Then started abusing us again. We thought this guy must be off his hinges. Until he pulled the gun.'

'So, who was he? A Communist?'

'He was too well dressed.'

'A drawing room Communist then.'

'A foreigner, I'd say. Spoke good German, but used some strange words.'

'Russian?'

'A Bolshevik in a suit like that? Come off it. He was a Yank.'

Gräf remembered the American cigarette butt, whose origin Grabowski was trying to trace. An SA troop that's insulted before beating a peaceful retreat . . . arcane as it might sound, there was a grain of truth in Sieger's tale somewhere. 'A Yank, and he charged you on his own, did he?'

'That's not how I'd put it.' Sieger was offended. 'He broke Comrade

Schlüter's nose, and sent Comrade Mohnert to the floor. As for Comrade Kubicki . . .' the Scharführer broke off, apparently overcome with grief.

'That's what I'd be most interested in hearing.'

'But you've seen for yourself.'

'Tell me!'

'He shot him, the bastard.'

'I need a little more detail.'

'He shot him in the foot. Said if we didn't scram right away, he'd finish us all off.'

'So you scrammed.'

Sieger nodded.

'And left your injured . . . comrade where he was?'

'Gerd ran too. How were we to know the bastard would follow him and stab him to death?'

Gräf looked in Sieger's eyes, as if the truth were to be found there. 'Would you be able to describe the man? So he can be sketched by a police artist, I mean?'

Sieger nodded and Gräf handed him his card. 'Come to Alex tomorrow morning, A Division. Ten o'clock. I'll have a sketch artist by then.'

55

Rath leafed through one of the Tom Shark crime novels Czerwinski had left for him. They were idiotic, but still beat the hell out of boredom. *Das Hotelgespenst*. The Hotel Ghost. The title was apt. Sometimes Rath thought they really were keeping tabs on a ghost, so seldom had Abraham Goldstein been seen in these last few days. He yawned. Only an hour to go, and Czerwinski would take over for the nightshift.

There was nothing doing in suite 301. The man hadn't even had breakfast taken up. Rath leafed back through the notebook. Czerwinski had last seen him about seven yesterday evening. Goldstein had greeted him politely, gone down to the lobby, drunk a whisky at the bar, smoked a cigarette and returned to his suite. An excursion totalling half an hour, the detective had painstakingly noted.

It looked like Marion had finished for the day. A different chambermaid approached from the corridor. She was noticeably older and less attractive than her pretty colleague, if not to say profoundly ugly. Rath couldn't help but grin. Served the Yank right! He had almost envied him Marion's presence, even if he didn't think Goldstein had actually started anything with her. But the sight of her alone . . . Rath pictured Marion making the bed; she would definitely make it easier to stay in your room.

The chambermaid who was about to knock on Goldstein's door, however . . . well, perhaps she'd scare him to death. Or manage to achieve what the Berlin Police had singularly failed to do and hound him out of town.

Rath watched out of the corner of his eye while he leafed through Czerwinski's penny dreadful. What a sour face. So, she was ugly *and* ill-tempered. Rath couldn't have been happier for the Yank.

Only, he didn't open.

The chambermaid knocked again, and Rath began to wonder. Was the man asleep, or had he sensed what awaited him? The woman jangled a set of keys, opened the door and went inside. Rath put the novel down. Tom Shark had lost his attention once and for all.

What followed was an interesting insight into the hotel's hierarchy. First it was a slightly older boy who emerged from the lift and headed for 301, knocking and entering as soon as the door opened. Not a minute later came Teubner, the porter, stepping hurriedly into the corridor and following suit, without so much as a glance at Rath.

Then, suddenly, all hell was loose; people swarming this way and that across the floor. Among all the official and important-seeming people, Rath recognised Grunert, the hotel detective.

'What's going on?' he asked.

'I'd never have thought something like this could happen,' Grunert said. 'Not with the police themselves watching him.'

'What do you mean?'

'Come and see for yourself.'

Rath feared the worst when he stepped inside. Could Goldstein be lying dead? Of boredom? Or had he taken his own life? Perhaps some rival gangster had managed to kill him? Someone who had scaled the hotel front? Or a sniper who had lain in wait on the roof of Anhalter Bahnhof?

No one was lying dead, neither on the bed nor in the bathtub. Any number of people stood inside the luxurious suite and yet it seemed lifeless. Sterile. Even if the bed wasn't made, and the bins hadn't been emptied. Rath followed Grunert into the bedroom. The hotel detective moved over to the wardrobe and opened the doors, where he was confronted by the clatter of empty rails, and a void of empty shelves.

'Gone,' Grunert said. 'Your guest's done a runner.'

It took Rath a moment to realise that he had a problem. A missing Goldstein was worse than a dead Goldstein.

Now you know how Charly must have felt, he thought, and sank into the nearest chair.

PART II

PUNISHMENT

Sunday 5th July to Saturday 18th July 1931

56

The wound was healing well. A scar stretched across the back of Alex's hand, a keepsake, but there was nothing she could do about that. Too bad, she thought, but you were never the prettiest anyway. She gave her reflection a wry smile, threw the blood-soaked bandage in the rubbish and bound her hand with a fresh dressing. At the window she looked outside. She'd sooner be splashing through puddles like the kids downstairs than sitting up here holding her breath at footsteps on the stairs.

She was alone in the flat. Martha and Helmut were out; her sister-in-law had insisted on heading to the country with her husband. Helmut had suggested staying home to play cards, but saw the look on Martha's face and yielded. Alex sympathised with her sister-in-law. It wasn't just the sultry, warm weather that made her insist on the journey to Köpenick; a trip to the countryside meant a day without Alex.

Yesterday evening they had huddled together in the cramped flat and played cards, just like old times, when Alex and Helmut still lived with their parents and occasionally managed to persuade Mother to join in a hand of skat. It was Helmut's idea and the game had lasted the whole evening. Alex would rather Helmut had taken Martha to the cinema or out dancing, but he wouldn't be dissuaded. Martha dutifully fetched beer from the cellar and said nothing, even if her eyes told a different story.

It was too much. Alex had imposed upon her brother's hospitality for long enough. She had enjoyed a roof over her head, eaten as much as she liked and licked her wounds. Now it was time to move on.

That woman, the court assistant or whatever she was, hadn't come back. Alex couldn't believe that she had appeared outside the door to ask her stupid questions. At the last moment she had hidden in the cubbyhole by the sink alongside scrubbers, brushes and preserves, and tried to breathe as quietly as possible. In the end the woman stayed outside in the stairwell. When she asked, in all seriousness, if *Alexandra*—Alex had almost forgotten that was her real name—might be staying with her parents, she almost laughed out loud. With her *olds*! Emil Reinhold, who let his own daughter fend for herself on the streets? Who had disowned his son? The woman had no idea.

Yet she couldn't be completely stupid either. She had managed to find out Alex's name, as well as Helmut's address. This, despite the fact that Alex hadn't said a word while she was in custody, or indeed afterwards. She had been scared stiff by all those blue uniforms, more frightened, even, than at KaDeWe when they chased her, or later when that cop opened fire.

Benny's killer.

The whole time she had been in custody, she was afraid he might appear to finish the job. Each night she dreamed of him, his mug against hers, close enough to see every pore of the face she had marked for life. And then of Benny plunging silently to his death, every night plunging headlong to the ground. High above, the same face stared over the balustrade, grinning, sweating.

She'd recognise it twenty years from now, but she didn't intend to wait that long.

She felt a kind of longing for the old factory. Not for the draughty corridors where she tried to sleep, but for the people, for Vicky and Fanny, Kotze and Felix. She'd have to accept that Kralle and his band of rats came with the package. There are two sides to everything.

Another of Benny's phrases. God, she missed him!

If he was right, and everything good had its bad side, then didn't everything *bad* have its good side too? Try as she might, she couldn't find anything good about her situation, but perhaps all she needed was a few more days. At least she had seen Helmut again. Without all the shit that had happened to her, she'd never have dared to turn up at his door. She was too ashamed of what she had done, of what Karl had done, but her big brother had taken her in his arms, and, suddenly, she didn't feel the least ashamed of anything that had happened before Christmas. It was the first time she hadn't celebrated the day. How many more Christmases would go uncelebrated? She couldn't picture it happening in the old axle factory, anyway.

Beckmann's death was such a joke. She didn't mourn the Nazi, but hadn't wanted him dead. Still, it was her fault; without her stupid idea it would never have happened. Without Alexandra Reinhold, Heinrich Beckmann would still be alive, damn it.

What a crackpot idea, paying the rent with stolen money. No one understood that she was trying to help, not her father who had thrown her out, nor her brother who thought she needed protection. It was Karl who had pulled the trigger, the idiot. How she missed him!

Helmut was the only one who'd been able to get on with his life, because he had cut ties and gone his own way. That was why she felt so ashamed about Beckmann. Only now, with her despair outweighing her shame, had she confided in him, and soon realised that all her worries were for nothing.

Without her brother she wouldn't have survived the past few days.

She rummaged in the kitchen table drawer for the paper and pencil Martha used to write her shopping lists. She sat down to think, and suddenly knew what she was going to write. The pencil scratched across the page. Somewhere outside a car beeped its horn.

57

Bernhard Weiss spent most weekends at his private home in Dahlem, away from his official residence in Charlottenburg. As he turned into the tree-lined Bachstelzenweg, Rath could see why. No problem finding a parking spot here. Most people had their own garages. The only sound he heard when he cut the engine was the twittering of birds.

He had made the journey with mixed feelings. Weiss was his sole principal in the Goldstein affair, but, since he was at a summit in Breslau on Saturday, Rath had spent the day with Hotel Detective Grunert reconstructing the man's disappearance. They had done a reasonable job, but Rath's hopes of picking up the gangster's trail before reporting to Weiss had been shattered. The Yank had disappeared and could be anywhere in this four-million-strong city. Why had he gone underground? What had he done or, worse, what was he about to do?

This morning Weiss had invited Rath to submit a report. He opened the garden gate and entered an oasis of green. A walnut tree stood by the fence, with apple and pear trees in the middle of the lawn.

'Are you looking for Papa?' a child's voice asked from above.

He looked up and saw a kind of treehouse in an old beech. A girl of eight or nine was gazing down curiously.

He nodded.

'Are you a criminal?' she asked, deadly serious.

Rath couldn't help but laugh. 'I don't think so. I work for your father.'

'Then you're a policeman?'

He nodded again.

'You can see how well guarded I am,' a deep voice said. 'No one gets by my Hilde unseen.'

Dr Bernhard Weiss stood outside the house, his hands buried in light canvas trousers. Over his shirt he wore a thin knitted waistcoat. 'Please come in, Inspector,' he said. 'We have matters to discuss.'

'I fear we do, Sir.'

Inside, a maid took his hat and coat.

'We don't want any disruptions,' Weiss said, leading Rath into a spacious office that was far more impressive than his room at Alex.

At an upholstered suite, a pot of coffee and two cups stood on the table, along with fresh pastries. Rath interpreted that as a good sign. 'Have you heard anything from Warrants?' he asked.

'Nor did I expect to,' said Weiss. 'We don't even have a photo. In a city this large, all a description will get you is the wrong man. Or no man at all.' Weiss poured coffee for his guest. 'What have you found out, Inspector?'

'According to what we know so far, the fugitive must have had help. What with our surveillance, he could only have made it outside using a pass key. He must have used an adjoining room, then taken the staff staircase.'

'We should have thought of that.'

'If we'd wanted to guard all exits, we'd have needed seven or eight men, but . . .'

'I'm not making accusations. You did your best.' For some reason, Weiss spoke momentarily in Berlin dialect before switching back.

'I hope you're right, Sir.'

'You asked for reinforcements that I was unable to provide. Given the circumstances, keeping his room under surveillance made most sense. We couldn't expect the man to get his hands on a pass key.'

Rath nodded.

'You don't have any leads?' Weiss asked.

'We have a statement from the laundry driver, who was surprised to see an elegantly dressed man with two suitcases at the staff exit. We asked him to describe the man, and it's as close to a match as we're likely to get. The driver says he left the hotel on Friday morning around six.'

'Almost twelve hours before his disappearance was uncovered.'

'We've been trying to trace him through the Taxi Drivers' Guild. So far to no avail. It's possible he took the U-Bahn. He did that a week ago when trying to give me the slip.'

'Do you know how he got hold of the pass key?'

'The hotel detective's looking into it.'

'Well,' Weiss said. 'That's not a priority. First we have to see how we can get out of this shemozzle, before the press get wind that there's an American gangster at large.'

'Meaning?'

'Meaning: find Goldstein. As quickly as possible.'

Rath had to cross the city to reach his next destination. Niederschönhausen, another neighbourhood of villas. This time, however, he wasn't seeing a police commissioner but an underworld boss. He got out of the car and looked around.

Where was he going wrong? He'd never be able to afford houses like these, either as a police officer, or as a gangster. Perhaps it was because he was neither one thing nor the other.

Johann Marlow lived in an impressive villa on Victoriastrasse. One of the reasons it was so impressive was that it didn't need to try. There were no gun-toting thugs circling the property; Liang's presence provided ample protection. The Chinese himself opened the door to modern decor decidedly more tasteful than Red Hugo's *nouveau riche* apartment.

They traversed the house before stepping back into the open air on the rear terrace. Dr M. stood bare-torsoed, pointing a bow and arrow towards a large target at the opposite end of the garden. More muscular than Rath had thought, he took aim calmly, not letting himself be put off. The arrow struck right in the target's centre.

'Respect,' Rath said.

Marlow lowered the bow and turned around. 'Have you ever tried archery, Inspector?'

Rath shook his head.

'It's amazingly relaxing, and the perfect way to effect a silent kill.'

'Like the Native Americans. Did you learn that in the States?'

'They use different weapons these days. Above all, Thompson machine guns.'

'You know your stuff.'

'I've been to the States a couple of times. Once to Chicago and twice to New York. What are you trying to say?'

'You really don't know Abraham Goldstein? You've never had anything to do with him?'

'No, what's this about?'

'I'm wondering why you helped him escape from his hotel.'

'Pardon me?'

'*You* smuggled the chambermaid into the Excelsior, didn't you?'

'Stop speaking in riddles. Tell me what's happened and what you want to know. Then maybe I can help you.'

'Isn't it strange that one of your employees should begin as a chambermaid in Goldstein's hotel just days before his arrival? Was she there to keep an eye on him, or was it about evading police surveillance?'

'One of my employees? What are you talking about?'

'Bosetzky. Marion Bosetzky. A dancer in Venuskeller.'

'Marion? She hasn't worked for us in ages. Sebald kicked her out.'

'Why?'

'A minor loyalty issue. She was working for someone else on the side, which we couldn't tolerate. Maybe you should have a word with him. Maybe he's the one who smuggled her in.'

'Gladly. If you would be so kind as to tell me who *he* is.'

'Not *he*, so much as *they*, Inspector,' Marlow burst out laughing. 'Your colleagues. That is to say: your former colleagues, you know, in E Division.'

58

Rath hadn't been down this way in a long time, certainly not this early in the morning. He didn't encounter many colleagues, but the officers he had worked most closely with in Vice were both dead, and he hadn't had much to do with the rest. He had been with the squad only two months but, even so, seemed to have made a lasting impression on the division chief.

'Inspector Rath,' Werner Lanke said, offering a hand. 'What a surprise! You were never this early back in the day.' He gestured towards Kirie. 'You must be working like a dog.'

Werner Lanke laughed at his own joke and Kirie wagged her tail, realising they were speaking about her. Rath managed a friendly grin. He had to remain civil, even if he and Lanke were linked only in mutual antipathy.

Krumme Lanke, after the lake, was an accurate nickname. The man had such a pronounced stoop that, over time, his official six foot three had become more like five foot eleven. There was something vulture-like about him, an impression intensified by his prominent nose and piercing eyes that peered over reading glasses.

'A good thing I've caught you, Sir.'

'I don't know that it is. I'm in a hurry.'

'Just two minutes?'

'Alright then.' Lanke sat down again. 'To what do I owe this honour?'

'I'm looking for a female witness . . .'

'If you're referring to Fräulein Lübbe, she isn't here yet.'

Jutta Lübbe was Lanke's secretary. Rath's stock of dutiful smiles was dwindling. 'The woman's name is Marion Bosetzky,' he said. 'She became a Vice informant two years ago.'

'I see.'

'She was a nude dancer in an illegal nightclub until her employers learned of her sideline.'

'You're well informed.'

'The alpha and omega of police work.'

'What would you like me to do about it?'

'I need as much information as possible on her, and I'd like to speak with her go-between. Who recruited her, is she still deployed? That sort of thing.'

Rath realised that it was a mistake to ask someone like Werner Lanke for help. The superintendent savoured his power even more in view of Rath's helplessness.

'You're talking about things that are subject to strict confidentiality. E Division internal affairs, and I . . .'

'I'm talking about an investigation in which Fräulein Bosetzky could be an important witness.'

'If it's so important Superintendent Gennat will put in a request to examine the files, as one division chief to another.' Lanke stood and reached for his coat. 'Now, please excuse me. I don't want to keep Prosecutor Rosanski waiting.'

Lanke threw on his hat and black coat, looking even more like a vulture. A vulture with a hat. Rath followed him into the corridor, where Lanke made a point of locking the door, as if to show Rath how little he trusted him. He briefly tipped his hat and stooped down the corridor towards the atrium and his car.

Erika Voss was already there by the time Rath entered his office. She gazed in surprise, first at him then at Kirie. The dog wagged her tail. 'Inspector,' she said, replacing the receiver she had just lifted back on the cradle. 'You're working in the office again?'

'Yes,' Rath said, hanging his hat and coat on the hook. 'The Goldstein affair is resolved for the time being.'

'Goldstein?'

'The man we've been keeping under surveillance.' Rath hadn't mentioned the assignment to his secretary, not even that they were stationed in the Excelsior.

Erika Voss was so surprised she forgot to stroke Kirie, who was standing expectantly before her. She fetched a well-thumbed newspaper from her handbag. *Der Tag*, a scandal sheet published by the Scherl Verlag, which underlined its headlines in red.

'I read it every morning on the train.' She pointed to an article. 'Do you mean this Goldstein?'

Rath felt like he was in a bad dream. It was exactly the headline Dr Weiss had been seeking to avoid.

JEWISH GANGSTER RESPONSIBLE FOR COWARDLY HUMBOLDTHAIN MURDER?

Below, the paper had printed a sketch that bore an unmistakable likeness to Abraham Goldstein. Rath recognised the work of a police artist whose services he had used in the past. He skimmed the article. An SA man, found on Wednesday morning with fatal stab and gunshot wounds in Humboldthain; witnesses unanimously described the man identified as Abraham Goldstein, a Jewish-American gangster striking terror in Berlin, as police apparently stood idly by.

59

Gereon still hadn't been in touch. No word of apology, nothing. He hadn't even come to collect his things. What a stupid man! She wouldn't have thought it could come to this. In fact, she had sworn to *never* let things get this far again.

What on earth was wrong with him?

True, she had left him in the lurch on Wednesday night, and that wasn't nice. Ditched him and headed home because she couldn't take either the silence, that was like a wall between them, or his insensitivity about her search for the missing girl. Not that it justified treating him like that, and no doubt at some point she'd have apologised, but it didn't give him the right to beat Guido to a pulp either! Did he think the whole world was just waiting for Gereon Rath's next show of jealousy?

Seeing the roses on the hall floor, she had figured out what must have happened and, for a moment, the flowers mollified her. Until she saw what he had done to her friend. Since then, Gereon had been avoiding her. How would she have reacted if he'd appeared at her door with a second bunch of roses? Perhaps she'd have hit *him*, just to even things up!

Heymann was making her wait.

All was quiet in the corridors; not a trace of the bloody noses and worse of last week. She hadn't thought scenes like that possible at the university.

She stared at Heymann's door, knowing that time was on her side. She felt completely free now that she was relieved of her court duties. After Guido's visit she had no desire to return to Weber's stuffy office anyway, to these men who called themselves colleagues, but had never accepted her as one of their own.

She was learning that it was almost impossible for women to prevail in the service of Lady Justice, at least not without the presence of a strong male mentor. Even then there was the suspicion that you were providing services of a different nature.

She had never had that problem at the Castle. Böhm did everything in his power to encourage her. Gennat also valued her work, and she set great store by their judgement. She didn't care what her other colleagues thought, Gereon included. Let him think she was fixating on matters that weren't important. That she showed too much compassion. That she wasn't suited to the job. Wasn't that what he had meant? Pah!

How was it she was thinking about *him* again! Weren't there other men in her life?

The door opened, and a student emerged. He was a few years younger than her, and still wet behind the ears, but already he wore a duelling scar with pride. He gave her such an arrogant look that she forgot to say hello. Goodnight, Germany, she thought, as she watched him swagger down the corridor: a skinny boy who thought he was creation's crowning glory. Goodnight, if these were the people who stood to inherit the constitutional state. Last week, he'd have been one of those hiding behind friends as he swung at Communists and Jews, as well as classmates he thought were Communists or Jews. Now, here he was at the Professor's office, hair neatly parted, wilfully ignoring the fact that Heymann was of Mosaic faith so long as it served his career. She knocked on the door and went inside. Heymann sat at his desk.

'Good day, Fräulein Ritter. Apologies that my previous meeting overran. Take a seat.'

'Thank you.'

Heymann made a few notes while Charly surveyed the Hindenburg portrait above his desk. It reminded her of police headquarters, where a likeness of the German President hung in every office. It wasn't so common at the university, however: Heymann must have hung it himself. The professor was a highly decorated war veteran and admirer of the general field marshal, but otherwise a genuinely nice man as well as a real authority in his field. Not a straight-out democrat, perhaps, but still a tireless propagandist for the constitutional state.

Heymann snapped shut his notebook. 'I know I haven't given you long to consider,' he said. 'A week isn't much time when you've got your day-to-day work to think about, but the matter is urgent. Have you decided?'

Charly nodded. 'Yes, Professor, I have.'

60

The headline in *Tag* caused a stir at the Castle, and made a meeting with Bernhard Weiss inevitable. This time he asked for Rath and Böhm together, but Rath had gone in feeling the more composed. It was Böhm who looked stupid, since the press were better informed about the Humboldthain murder than the officer in charge. For Böhm, the questions were not just who provided the paper with the police sketch but also, more worryingly, who identified it as Abraham Goldstein.

Until that point, no one who had seen the likeness had been able to put a name to the face, neither Böhm nor Warrants. But someone at Alex must have recognised Goldstein, and this same person hadn't told Böhm, but Stefan Fink, a journalist who craved sensation as a morphine addict craves his next phial.

So, where was the leak? The police sketch had gone to Warrants and police stations citywide on Saturday evening. That meant someone must have passed it to Fink during the night.

Gereon Rath and his men were among the few who knew who Goldstein was, and Rath vouched for them all, even if he was a little unsure of Czerwinski. Weiss dismissed them with clearly defined tasks: Böhm was to step up investigations in the Kubicki case, while Rath was to continue searching for the missing gangster with the help of J Division, for whom the search was now priority number one. They couldn't keep the fact that there was a known American gangster in the city under wraps any longer.

Rath's men were already in position. Henning and Czerwinski had been in the Excelsior since eight o'clock continuing their interviews with hotel staff. Plisch and Plum were to question all employees who had been on duty in the relevant section of the hotel. If Goldstein had used the staff staircase, then perhaps someone had seen something.

It should have been Gräf conducting the interviews, but Böhm had pinched him again. He was in Interview Room B working his way through the list of witnesses. The number of people who claimed to have seen something, but really just wanted attention, had risen further since the article in *Tag*. More often than not it was anti-Semites taking advantage of the opportunity to remind police of their failure; there was an American gangster roaming the streets, a Jewish killer who clearly had it in for the SA!

Rath was especially tickled by the prospect of brownshirts up and down the city huddled indoors in fear of venturing out. If that were true, Goldstein's escape had actually made the streets safer, but Rath didn't envy Gräf the task of dealing with such idiots, knowing he lacked the patience for it himself.

By now it was lunchtime and he was at his desk. He had telephoned Czerwinski and spoken with Warrants but, so far, DCI Kilian had no leads. The paper's unauthorised printing of the sketch had brought a number of innocent people to the department's attention. None bore any resemblance to Abraham Goldstein. The one thing they had in common was that they were Jews, denounced by resentful neighbours or colleagues.

Needing fresh air, Rath attached Kirie to her lead. After stopping at Aschinger for a few Bouletten, he made for the telephone booths at the train station. Luckily, one was free. While the dog busied herself with the meatballs, her master pressed a ten-pfennig piece into the slot.

'Herr Weinert isn't in the office,' said the voice on the line. 'Didn't you know? He's with Dr Eckener.'

'In the Zeppelin?'

'That's right. Didn't he tell you? He's covering the Iceland flight.'

Rath hung up. Berthold Weinert might have given him something on Fink's informer, but he was hovering somewhere above the Arctic Ocean. He took Kirie's lead and stepped back into the fresh air, heading for Monbijou Park to think things through.

When he returned to the office an hour later he had to use his key. Erika Voss had gone for lunch. He sat at his desk, with Kirie underneath.

He thought back to Lanke's office that morning, before all the fuss about Goldstein had started. Rath could tell by the superintendent's face that he knew exactly who Marion Bosetzky was. Since the division chief, a pencil-pusher *par excellence*, couldn't have recruited the nude dancer himself, another suspicion presented itself. Rath decided to look into it before asking Gennat's permission to access the files. The bureaucracy involved there, he'd be drawing his pension by the time it was approved. He couldn't wait that long.

He had left the door to the outer office open and, while he was still thinking, there was a timid knock. Who the hell could that be? Another knock.

'Enter!'

A short time later, there was a third knock. Whoever it was, they were as stubborn as they were deaf. He stood up and went to the outer office. Kirie pitter-pattered after as he threw the door open. 'What in God's name do you want?' he asked, staring at the figure outside.

An old man, dressed in black, with a grey beard and sidelocks; an orthodox Jew who looked as if he had just arrived in Berlin from his shtetl in Galicia.

'Detective Gräf, please,' the man said, looking now at Rath, now at the dog.

'I'm sorry, he isn't here.' Rath hated giving answers that were Erika Voss's responsibility. 'If you're a witness, Interview Room B is down the corridor, then the second or third door on the right. There'll be a sign outside.'

'I already was, the room is closed. I ask but am sent here.'

'Detective Gräf must be at lunch.' Rath gave a pointed look at his watch. 'If you come back in an h . . .'

'Please, I do not have much time. I need to make statement.'

'Then please take a seat.' Rath pointed down the corridor. 'There are benches outside.'

'Please, I do not have much time.'

Rath bade the man enter, Gräf's witness or no. At least he wasn't an anti-Semite here to insult the police. 'Please sit down, and I'll take your statement,' he said.

There was no stenographer, but that wouldn't matter. He showed the old man to a chair and sat behind Erika Voss's desk, opened his notebook and pulled out a pencil.

'So, let's get started,' he said. 'Your name, please.'

'Please, I just want to make statement.'

'I understand that, but I still need your name.'

'I can't give you name, I just want to make statement.'

'To make a statement we need your name and address.'

'Please, I just want to make statement.'

'Which is why I need your name.' Rath rolled his eyes. 'Tell me what you saw, and we'll take care of the formalities later.'

'Not tell. I met man you are searching for.'

There was a pile of newspapers in Erika Voss's filing tray. Rath took one and passed it across. 'You mean this man?'

The old man nodded, and Rath sat forward.

'Where and when did you see him?'

The old man pointed at the photograph. 'Didn't have knife. Had pistol.'

Rath cleared his throat. 'Can we agree on something? I ask the questions and you answer them.' The man nodded. 'So, where and when did you meet him?'

'Helped me, this man.'

'Where and when?' Rath felt like a broken record.

'Under the ground. They were bad men.'

'You mean the underground?'

The man nodded. 'Men insulted and cursed me.'

Rath thought of the witness statements made by several passengers at Gesundbrunnen. He drew a swastika in his notebook. 'These men?'

Again the man nodded. 'I wanted go. Didn't want no trouble. Better dog in peace than man at war.'

'But they didn't leave you in peace?'

'They chase me, into woods.'

'Four men, is that right?'

The old man nodded.

'One more time for the record: four men in SA uniform abused you at Gesundbrunnen U-Bahn station; you tried to avoid a confrontation, but the men followed you to Volkspark Humboldthain . . .'

The old man nodded.

'What happened in the park? Is that where they met *him*?' Rath tapped the Goldstein picture.

'Not there. Was before. Already in station.'

'He followed them?'

'I don't know. I only know he reappear when men attack me.'

'Then what happened? Tell me exactly.'

'Well . . . He hit them and drive them away.'

'Who did he hit?'

'Two men he knock to ground. The third he shoot in foot, the other he just make scared. But all run away.'

'He pursued one of them, am I right? The man whose foot had been shot?'

The old man shook his head. 'He do nothing. He just bring me back to station. A good man. But he shouldn't have shoot. Shooting is sin.'

'Hang on. He brought you back to the station? He didn't chase any of them? None of the men?'

'Men were all gone.'

'He brought you to the station. Then he went back to the park?'

'The man sit with me on train. Get out with me, too, at Rosenthaler Platz.'

Rath was astonished. Goldstein had an alibi for the murder of Gerhard Kubicki. Or had the gangster bought the old man as a defence witness? Rath looked at him, his bearded face, and saw in his eyes an indelible faith in God. No, he didn't look like someone who could be bought, not even with Abe Goldstein's American dollars.

'Can you show us the place where you were attacked?' The old man nodded. 'Did you sustain any injuries?' The old man waved the question away, although there was a bruise under his beard. Rath made a renewed attempt. 'Your statement is very important. If you set any store by our investigation, then we need your name and address.'

'No name. I just want to make statement.'

Even Charly's stubbornness paled in comparison. 'Your address then. So we know how to reach you, in case . . .' The telephone on his desk rang. Rath glanced over his shoulder towards his office, then back at the old man. 'Would you excuse me a moment?'

The man nodded.

He went into the adjoining room and lifted the receiver. Kirie followed, almost as if she knew who was on the line.

'Hello, Gereon.'

She didn't even sound unfriendly. He had to sit down. 'Charly! I wasn't expecting you to call.'

'We should talk, don't you think?'

Damn it, she was good at catching him off guard. He stretched out an arm and closed the door to the outer office. 'What is there to talk about?'

'What do you want? For me to send your toothbrush in the post?'

Of course he didn't want that.

'I'm sorry,' he said, 'but these last few days . . . I had the feeling you were trying to get rid of me. And then this guy . . .'

'If you mean Guido, he's not some "guy", but a friend. Someone you should be apologising to. He didn't deserve to be treated like that.'

'I'm sorry. The roses were meant for you. A peace offering.'

'I wouldn't like to see a declaration of war.'

Rath couldn't see her, but could tell from her voice that Charly was grinning broadly, or at least trying her best not to. His heart skipped a beat. He hadn't lost her yet! 'I'm really, truly sorry.'

'Don't apologise to me, apologise to him.'

Did she have to keep mentioning that idiot? 'You're right,' he said. 'We need to talk. Your place or mine?' The possibility of reconciliation turned him on. It didn't matter if it was in his bed or hers.

'Neutral ground. That's what you do during a ceasefire, isn't it?'

'No idea.'

'I was thinking Café Uhlandeck, you can . . .'

'Not Uhlandeck.'

'Then make another suggestion.'

'How about I invite you to dinner? Tonight. Kempinski on the Ku'damm.' The restaurant had a lovely terrace, and Rath was hoping for a balmy summer's night.

'Agreed.'

He could have jumped for joy, but despite the closed door decided against it. He replaced the receiver carefully in the cradle and let out a yelp of delight. Hell, he might just get out of this! He had overreacted with the grinning man; of course there was nothing going on with Charly. Still, the bloody nose served him right. Even if there *was* nothing going on, Rath was certain old perma-smile would jump at the opportunity. If Charly insisted he apologised, he would, but he'd also make it clear that it was time grin-face found himself someone else to comfort.

He stood up and moved towards the door. 'My apologies,' he said, pausing when he reached the outer office.

The old man's chair was empty.

Rath ran out of the office and looked down the corridor, but there was no chance of catching him. He shook his head. He was a strange bird, but what he had said was entirely plausible.

It looked as if Abraham Goldstein hadn't manifested himself as a killer, but as some kind of Boy Scout. At any rate a man of civic courage.

61

Charly felt strange as she stepped out of the telephone booth at Alexander-platz. She had telephoned him within view of the station. Couldn't she just have gone in? No, of course not, but the call had been smoother than expected. He didn't realise how serious it was. Now she just had to see it through.

Crossing the enormous construction site, which was beginning to hint at how Alexanderplatz would soon look, she headed for Tietz. The department store's restaurant was a good choice. Close to the station, but a place few police officers visited of their own accord. Who wanted to spend their lunch break among whining children and ill-tempered mothers?

It took a moment to see him. Lange had found a secluded table where they could talk uninterrupted.

'Fräulein Ritter,' he said, straightening her chair like a gentleman of the old school. 'I'm glad you found the time to speak to me.'

He must be glowing red, she thought, taking her place opposite.

'No doubt you're wondering why I asked to meet here, rather than my office.'

'I'm perfectly happy here,' she said.

'I have my reasons. The matters I'd like to discuss with you are strictly confidential.'

'Aha.' She lit a Juno. It seemed to make him nervous, or was he nervous already?

'Superintendent Gennat thinks very highly of you. Did you know that?' She found praise a little embarrassing, but it was good to hear. 'Can I count on your discretion?' he continued. 'Only Superintendent Gennat, Dr Schwartz and I know about this.'

'Not even Böhm?'

'Not even Böhm.'

'I thought you were working together.'

'Not on this.'

'Is it about Alexandra Reinhold?'

'Indirectly. When we spoke recently we were interrupted by DCI Böhm.'

'Don't keep me in suspense.'

'It concerns the death of Benjamin Singer. Alexandra's accomplice, who died attempting to escape.'

'The case you're investigating, but that's no secret.'

Lange cleared his throat, finding it very hard to utter the decisive sentence. 'We have reason to believe,' he said finally, taking a sip of Selters, 'that Benjamin Singer was sent to his death by a police officer.'

He said it very softly, but still looked around as if someone might be listening. All of a sudden, Charly realised what he was after, and where the fear in Alex's eyes had come from. 'You need Alexandra Reinhold as a witness?' she asked.

'We received an anonymous call. Probably from this Alexandra. *You cops killed Benny*, the caller said.'

Charly was contrite. 'All the more infuriating that she gave me the slip.'

'No, no,' Lange appeased her.

'If Alex really did witness the murder, the killer might have seen her too.' Lange nodded. 'Then she's in danger.' Lange nodded again. 'Do you have a suspect?'

'A sergeant from the 127th precinct, but I fear we won't get him without a witness statement. It's a difficult thing, accusing a colleague of murder.'

'You think they'd believe Alex in court?'

'We have other evidence,' Lange said, 'but it's no use without a witness.' The waiter arrived with the menus. 'It's on me. Homicide will pick up the tab.'

Charly ordered a mineral water before the waiter disappeared. They looked at the menu.

'I saw her,' she said after a while. 'She was scared stiff. Do you think it's possible he's the officer who chased her?'

'Absolutely,' Lange said, and couldn't help but smile. 'For all the good it did him. This Alex must have claws, or at the very least a knife.'

'Is the man still on active duty?'

Lange nodded. 'Didn't even want to take sick leave.'

'Why have you summoned me here, Herr Lange? I'd like to know before I order anything.'

'Two things. I know you're looking for the girl. Keep going. Try to find Alexandra.'

'Why should I?'

'Because Superintendent Gennat was hoping you'd still be interested.'

'OK,' she said. 'I'll help you, but under one condition.'

'Which would be?'

'You have to promise to protect Alex.'

'Her cooperation will mitigate her sentence.'

'I'm not talking about that. I can't just hand her over to you, that won't work. If she comes in, it will be of her own accord. And if she decides to go, then you have to let her.'

'What am I supposed to say to the public prosecutor? I *did* question a witness, but unfortunately she gave me the slip?'

'It's that or not at all. I don't want to be responsible for anything that happens. If she's killed, for instance.'

'Do you really think she's in that much danger?'

Charly nodded. 'Yes, I do.'

Lange took a sip of mineral water and appeared to consider. 'OK,' he said finally. 'You have my word. I'll protect the girl.'

Charly stubbed out her cigarette. 'Two things, you said. What's the second?'

Lange pushed a copy of a personal file across the table. 'Keep an eye on this man, as best you can.'

Charly opened the file and stared into the face of Sergeant Major Jochen Kuschke. 'That's him. That's our suspect.'

'I can't tail him around the clock,' she said.

'You don't have to. So long as he's on duty, we'll have him in our sights; he isn't walking the beat alone. We want you to look out for him in the evening. If you can manage, that is—the search for Alex takes priority.'

'Why me? What about J Division?'

'He doesn't know your face. With Warrants he might suspect something; perhaps he knows the odd officer there. We don't want to take any risks.'

The waiter arrived to take their order. She decided not to worry about the cost.

As she stepped out of the U-Bahn on Frankfurter Allee an hour later, Charly was still thinking about her meeting with Andreas Lange. Superintendent Gennat had put the young assistant detective onto her because he needed allies in his bid to prosecute a Prussian police officer for murder. Ernst Gennat was Charly's great hero, perhaps even her role model; so naturally she had agreed. Especially since, through Lange, he had offered her something in return. A position as police cadet, to be taken up in summer 1932, before the conclusion of her legal preparatory service, with the prospect of a senior role at the Castle.

For that, she'd gladly call it quits with Weber; it was better than making a timid request for half a year's unpaid leave which he would most likely refuse, if only to torpedo her joint project with Heymann. He wouldn't be able to reject her resignation.

Charly wasn't sure that she hadn't been bought. Still, she was only carrying on what she had already started: looking for Alexandra Reinhold. So why did the offer make her feel so uneasy when, a year from now, she'd be a CID cadet?

Because somehow it didn't feel right.

There was too much secrecy. Although, at least she could be sure that nothing would happen to Alex. Lange had promised. She just had to make sure she found the girl before Warrants did.

In Kopernikusstrasse she stood for a moment before entering the stairwell. This time, she knew, she'd make it inside.

As she hoped, Martha Reinhold was home alone and recognised her straightaway.

'It's you,' she said. 'My husband isn't here. I'm sorry you've made the trip for nothing.' She tried to shut the door of the flat but Charly wedged her foot in the crack.

'No matter, Frau Reinhold,' she said politely, pushing the door open and stepping into the narrow corridor. 'I just wanted to have a quick look around.'

Martha Reinhold didn't protest. Charly went to the kitchen-cum-living-room, where a wooden door led to a little cubbyhole next to the stove and sink.

'What is it you're after? Martha Reinhold had followed her, but her resistance was broken. When Charly sat at the kitchen table, she sat too. 'Didn't my husband tell you that he's cut all ties with his family? That he no longer has anything to do with those Communists?'

'Alex isn't a Communist, is she? Has he cut ties with her too?'

Martha Reinhold was silent. She seemed to be one of those people capable of withholding the truth, but incapable of telling a lie.

'When did you last see Alexandra, Frau Reinhold?' Charly asked. 'She was here, wasn't she? Maybe she still is?'

'No!'

'But she was here! The last time I called she was in the flat, am I right? Your husband deliberately laid a false trail with that business about his parents?'

'How am I supposed to know?'

'Was Alexandra here or not?'

Martha Reinhold began nodding. First slowly, then quicker.

'So she was here.'

'I told Helmut it's no good, while police were out looking for her.'

'I'm not from the police, Frau Reinhold. I know Alex is afraid of the police. I want to help her. There are some dangerous people looking for her.'

'Helmut can never know I betrayed his sister.'

'Don't worry, he won't. I wasn't even here. All I want is for you to tell me where I can find Alex. Where is she hiding?'

'If only I knew. She's been with us the whole time, since Tuesday. But . . .' She fetched a crinkled piece of paper from her apron pocket and unfolded it. 'I found this on the kitchen table when I got back from shopping today. Helmut still doesn't know; he's away on a job and won't be back until tomorrow.'

I'M SORRY, the note said in scrawled but legible handwriting. YOU'VE BOTH HELPED ME A LOT. THANK YOU FOR EVERYTHING. I WON'T FORGET IT. BUT I HAVE TO KEEP MOVING, THERE'S STILL SOMETHING I HAVE TO TAKE CARE OF. DON'T WORRY ABOUT ME, I'LL BE OK. SOME DAY I'LL RETURN THE FAVOUR, I PROMISE. ALEX.

'You don't have any idea where she went?'

Martha Reinhold shook her head, and Charly believed her. She thought there was a touch of relief there, and not just on account of her confession. Martha Reinhold was glad to be rid of her criminal sister-in-law.

'I don't think it's her style to fit in with other people,' she said. 'I knew she'd be gone soon, but Helmut . . .' She looked at Charly. 'I think he wished she could stay forever. It was almost like having his family back. And now . . . now they're scattered to the four winds just like before.'

62

Rath hadn't told anyone about the old man, who now seemed more like an apparition, with nothing tangible left but a few notes in his black book. Not even a name or address.

Erika Voss was surprised by the note with the swastika she found on her desk. She had returned quarter of an hour after the old man vanished, looking round in confusion before throwing the crumpled paper in the bin. Perhaps there was a Nazi in the office.

Reinhold Gräf also popped his head in after the lunch break before returning to his interview marathon. Rath briefly considered closing the door and telling his colleague about the old man, but decided against. He couldn't face admitting to a junior officer that yet another witness had slipped through his fingers.

Especially not after Gräf had told him about the trader from the Scheunenviertel, who recognised Goldstein from the sketch. He had promised to protect him from criminal proceedings and received a valuable statement in return. A man fitting Goldstein's description had bought a pistol from the trader's shop the week before. He had paid with dollars for a Remington 51, a gun seldom used in Berlin.

'It could be a direct hit,' Gräf said, before returning to the interview room. 'If the Kubicki bullet was fired from a Remington.'

Rath agreed, fetched a Pharus map from the drawer and unfolded it on his desk. Walking with Kirie it had occurred to him that they should be looking for Goldstein in Wedding, and Wedding alone. At first Rath had suspected it was Goldstein's taxi driver who had advised shaking him off in Kösliner Strasse. But then: Goldstein's second excursion: Humboldthain, Gesundbrunnen U-Bahn station—the same neighbourhood, a kilometre or two away from Kösliner Strasse at most.

That couldn't be coincidence.

During that first, seemingly random, taxi journey across Berlin, Goldstein must have been up to something, but Rath got in the way. Something in this neighbourhood exerted a magical pull on Abraham Goldstein.

Studying the map, Rath took out a soft pencil and marked, first, Kösliner Strasse, then, Gesundbrunnen U-Bahn station. After staring for a while he drew a large circle around the area between the Ringbahn line and Christiania Strasse. Folding and pocketing the map he left Kirie in the devoted care of Erika Voss, and set off.

The longer he sat in his car, the better he felt. Something to do at last! He drove north via Rosenthaler Strasse until, at Humboldthain, he throttled back to look across at the Himmelfahrtkirche where they had found the dead SA man. Driving at a leisurely tempo past the southern entrance of the U-Bahn, where Goldstein must have emerged in pursuit of the old Jew and the brownshirts, he crossed the tracks of the Ringbahn.

His plan was simply to drive around the area he had circled. If there was something here that could help them pick up Abraham Goldstein's trail, he'd find it. He usually did his best thinking while driving anyway.

From Badstrasse he turned left onto Pankstrasse, the road linking Kösliner Strasse with Gesundbrunnen, the two most prominent markings on his map. The road opened onto a large square on the right-hand side, above which stood the forbidding stone structure of the Wedding District Court.

He pulled over and surveyed the stern neo-Gothic façade as if it had something to tell him, trying to picture Goldstein here. What business could an American gangster have in a German court? Did he mean to kill a German criminal, a judge even? He made a few notes, drawing three large question marks underneath.

At Kösliner Strasse he stopped to glance at the Rote Laterne, which was already open, leaving the engine running. No, that wasn't it either. Goldstein had gone into the pub to shake off Rath's tail and recruit a few volunteers to smash up his Buick. A few curious faces peered through the vehicle's windows. This, after all, was a red stronghold where two years ago Communists had taken to the barricades. Park an overly expensive car here, or even use a car, and you made yourself suspicious. He engaged first gear, turned right at the corner and continued along the banks of the Panke, which was concealed by thick trees and shrubs, until the rear façade of the District Court reappeared overhead. At length he reached the long wall of an S-Bahn depot, to re-emerge onto the busy Badstrasse.

As he was considering his next move, he realised he had found what he was looking for. A large sign at the junction at Exerzierstrasse said: JEWISH HOSPITAL.

He took a sharp left onto Exerzierstrasse, a quiet residential street with next to no traffic. A lone tram rumbled over the road surface. Rath kept behind it until a three-storey building appeared on his right. More reminiscent of a school than a hospital, its carved lettering left him in no doubt. KRANKENHAUS DER JÜDISCHEN GEMEINDE, it said. JEWISH COMMUNITY HOSPITAL.

He parked the Buick under a tree and searched for the police sketch in the glove compartment. Before pocketing it, he unfolded it and looked again at the face: a good likeness. If Abraham Goldstein had been here in the last few days, he could be recognised from this.

He walked the few steps back to the hospital. The building on Exerzierstrasse was only one part of the complex; the much larger ward block rose behind it, with its entrance on Schulstrasse. Rath paused outside, unsure for a moment whether he should go in. Wasn't he just making a fool of himself?

He had just decided to enter the grounds when a surprised cry prevented him.

'Inspector?'

On the other side of the road, Sebastian Tornow, the police lieutenant training as a CID inspector, stood in the shadow of a tree. Rath almost didn't recognise him in plainclothes. He went over.

Tornow surveyed him curiously. 'What are you doing here?'

'I could ask you the same question.' Rath sounded more caustic than he intended, but somehow felt caught out. Stupid: apart from being on his own, he had done nothing wrong. 'This is a coincidence.'

'I'm working for Warrants. We received a tip-off.' Tornow gestured towards the hospital. 'Abraham Goldstein. Apparently he's been seen here.'

The cadet didn't seem particularly excited. In fact, he gave a disengaged impression overall. No wonder, with all the false sightings, but could this be the one? Suddenly, Rath was seized by the fever, that tingling in his veins he felt whenever things started to come together.

'Well, perhaps you're right this time,' he said. 'I've also received information which suggests Goldstein might have been here.'

Tornow brightened. 'Perhaps we could go in together? Although it would be the fifth false lead for me today.'

'Not quite as exciting as you thought then, CID work?'

'What are you going to do?' Tornow asked. 'An apprentice is not his own master.'

'Let me guess—Kilian said that?'

'Respect! I see you know our colleagues well. You'll have to tell me more about them sometime.' He looked in the direction of Badstrasse. 'There are a few nice cafes over there. What do you say?'

'Business before pleasure. DCI Kilian must have taught you that too, or hasn't he had the chance?'

'Lack of business or lack of pleasure?'

Rath pointed to the hospital complex. 'Come on. Let's go inside and ask our questions, then the coffee's on me. How about that?'

'Your wish is my command, Sir.'

They crossed the street, Rath surveying the cadet out of the corner of his eye. They could use a man like him in Homicide, he thought, he'd be a good addition to his team. He'd be only too happy to part with Paul Czerwinski in exchange. He wondered why someone like Sebastian Tornow was assigned to DCI Kilian, of all people.

Although expecting to uncover a lead, Rath was still surprised to see the porter nodding through the glass after one look at the sketch.

'He was here,' the porter said. 'A few days ago. With a bouquet.'

'Was he visiting someone?'

'I'd say so. Asked for someone anyways.'

'Do you remember who?'

'A Herr Goldstein, I think.'

'Goldstein?' Rath said, trying to stay cool. He gave Tornow a discreet nod. 'That's the name of a patient?'

'Yes,' the porter looked at a long list. 'Jakob Goldstein. First floor, room 102.'

'Do you remember when he visited?'

'I'd reckon Wednesday or Thursday. During afternoon visiting hours, anyway. I can't tell you any more than that. Only that he wasn't the only one with a bouquet of flowers.'

'Did he come a second time?' Rath asked.

'Not that I'm aware of. At least not while I've been on shift.'

'We'd like to visit Herr Goldstein in room 102. Is that possible? Now, I mean.'

63

The old man was clearly in pain. The skin in his face seemed thinner, more transparent somehow. On the table stood fresh flowers, another bunch that was beginning to wilt, just like him. Everything in the room smelled of death and departure.

Abraham Goldstein had pictured his grandfather, whom he knew only from his father's stories, with a long, white beard like all the old men in Williamsburg. And, of course, sidelocks—an older edition, so to speak, of his father Nathan. But Jakob Goldstein was about as much of a black hat as his grandson, Abraham, or he'd never have asked for such a favour.

Looking at his grandfather was like staring into a mirror: Abraham Goldstein fifty years older. No beard, no sidelocks, the same facial characteristics, only more prominent, the skin more wrinkled, the eyes deeper, the nose bigger, and the ears. Since arriving in Berlin he had realised that he looked more like Jakob than Nathan; and that Jakob looked more like him than his son.

Having only wanted to come once, he was now a daily visitor, and entering the hospital by the rear door had become almost routine. He moved through the corridors with the confidence of a young chief physician and, so far, no one had smelled a rat. A little bit of chutzpah made things easier, he'd known that for a long time. Even dying.

'Abraham, there you are,' the man smiled into his pillow. He barely had any strength left. Each word caused him pain, but it was clear from his face that he wanted to speak for as long as he still could. 'Have you been to see your aunts?'

'I don't know if they really want to see me. You haven't mentioned anything?'

'You have to go and see them! They're your father's sisters. The mishpocha is important, even when it gets on your nerves.' He laughed softly before the pain became too much. Abe nodded vaguely.

The old man gripped his hand. 'Did you get it?'

This time Abe's nod was more decisive. This would be his final visit. 'Yes.' He squeezed the old hand in return.

His grandfather's face relaxed. 'Show it to me,' he said.

Abe took the syringe out of the bag. He had already filled it, prepared everything in the hotel—a nasty little flophouse that bore no comparison with the Excelsior. Still, they didn't want to know his name or see his passport, and the porter had a few useful tips up his sleeve, like where you could get hold of cheap morphine.

He showed his grandfather the syringe, and the old man gazed at the liquid shimmering through the glass bulb. He nodded contentedly, gave a soft groan and grimaced. His hand clenched around Abe's and held tight.

The flash of pain was over; his grandfather looked at him. 'Now,' he said. 'I want it now.'

'Right this minute? What's the big hurry?'

'Before dinner.'

'It must be goddamn awful . . .'

The laughter lines around his grandfather's eyes tightened. 'It is,' he said and nodded. 'I'd rather die than eat that slop again.' He laughed at his own joke, but it only hurt more. 'Now,' he said, serious this time.

Abe nodded. He took the syringe out of the case and pressed lightly, until the first drop of morphine appeared. He exposed his grandfather's right arm and searched for a vein. The arm was shockingly thin, the skin pale and covered in age spots, the skin of a dead man. Abe squeezed the entire contents of the bulb into the vein, before dabbing the injection site with a cotton wool ball. There was no going back.

When Abe set the syringe aside, his grandfather gripped his hand once more, holding it tight, as if he never wanted to let go. 'Thank you,' he said quietly. 'How long?'

'A few minutes. You'll fall asleep. There'll be no more pain.'

The old man sank back into the pillow, feeling the effects of the morphine already.

'Broadway,' he said, and his tired eyes sparkled at the word. 'Tell me about Broadway.'

For all his visits to the hospital, Abe still hadn't been able to reveal the truth: that there was a big difference between the Broadway in Manhattan, which everybody knew, and the one in Williamsburg, where Nathan Goldstein and his family eked out their existence. So, Abe maintained the same cock and bull story his father had begun all those years ago. Nathan Goldstein had written regularly to Jakob, who had remained behind in Berlin, but Abe never knew how the pious old fool had littered his correspondence with lies: how he had made his fortune in America after starting his own clothing factory and moved into a flat on Broadway. What else could he write?

Only now, in Berlin, did Abe realise what hopes the Goldsteins had invested in Nathan, the eldest son. They had only been able to cobble together enough for one passage, and sent him on their behalf, expecting him to bring them over when he was able. But Nathan's sisters found happiness in Berlin, persuaded Jakob to stay, and no one learned what a pig's ear Nathan Goldstein had made of things in the States. The only person who knew was his son, Abraham, and he kept his father's secret.

Aunt Lea had married a scrap metal dealer, a black hat who devoted his life to God but was no less successful in business for that. Aunt Margot, meanwhile, became a lawyer's wife, a liberal, secularly minded man, which regularly led to huge family arguments and amused Abe's grandfather no end.

With each visit Abe embellished his father's fantastical tales, taking delight in the sparkling eyes of the sick, old man. Even now he told his grandfather about the day Nathan Goldstein hit upon the idea of combining the production and sale of off-the-rack clothing within a single company, although he sadly did not live to see its success. Abe recounted his father's funeral in such heart-rending terms that he felt almost moved himself, as if half of New York had been part of Nathan Goldstein's cortège, when in reality it had been a wretched affair, the appearance of a drunken son being its questionable highlight.

Abe had avoided his German relations because he didn't feel like serving up the same old lies. In fact he had only seen his aunts and their families on one more occasion, yesterday, as he waited in the shadow of the trees on Schulstrasse for visiting hours to end. The young black hat was there again, Joseph Flegenheimer, going by his grandfather's description. The oldest son of the scrap metal dealer was roughly his own age. His cousin had squinted across and hesitated for a moment, before turning to face the others. Since then, Abe, who had pulled his hat over his face, had been wondering whether Jossele, as his grandfather called him, had recognised him from their brief meeting in the hospital corridor. Or perhaps he had seen that blasted picture in the newspaper.

The old man was speaking so softly now, Abe had to lean over the bed to hear. 'It's almost time, Abraham. We must say our goodbyes.'

Abe squeezed his grandfather's hand, feeling an indefinable ache as he stared into the wrinkled face that would soon no longer stare back. Had Jakob Goldstein written to his grandson in America in order that he fulfil this wish? Did his grandfather have some inkling that he wasn't a harmless textile dealer who had taken on his father's flourishing business?

For some reason he felt much closer to this old man, whom he had met for the first time five days ago, than he ever had to his father. He felt almost ashamed of having loved his father so little, just as he felt ashamed of turning up drunk at his funeral.

'Promise me something!' The bony, old hand squeezed his palm with astonishing force, the eyes gazed at him, miraculous in their youth. Such intense eyes in such a weak, withered face, Abe thought, leaning over to hear what he had to say.

'You have to say Kaddish at my funeral. Promise me you will.'

Abe made a promise he wasn't sure he could keep. He hadn't said Kaddish for an eternity, but that wasn't the problem. The Kaddish was one of those things he'd never forget, that he'd carry with him for the rest of his life. That, at least, his father's upbringing had achieved. The problem was that he needed to get out of Berlin as soon as possible. He hadn't planned on attending his grandfather's funeral, but, still, he nodded, the old man saw him nod, and that was enough.

'That's good,' Jakob Goldstein said. '*Schma Jisrael, Adonaj Elohejnu, Adonaj Echad.*' His voice grew softer and softer.

Somewhere deep inside Abe recognised the words, even if he hadn't spoken them for years, and inwardly he prayed, despite no longer believing in the figure he was invoking.

His grandfather closed his eyes, as if recovering from a great exertion, though it wasn't clear if it was the exertion of speech, or the exertion of a life fully lived. His face was calm and contented, and his breathing grew steadier as the morphine took control of his emaciated body.

Abe held his grandfather's hand. 'Farewell, Seide,' he said, and the old man opened his eyes once more.

'Not farewell. Until we meet again,' Jakob Goldstein smiled. 'You'll visit me at my grave, say Kaddish. You promised.'

Abe nodded and his grandfather closed his eyes, the contented smile remaining on his face long after he had ceased to breath.

Goldstein didn't know how long he had sat at his dead grandfather's bed, but the old man's hands were still warm when he was startled by a loud noise in the corridor. The nurses usually took their break about now, before everything started again and dinner was brought to the rooms. He opened the door a crack and peered out.

Two men approached from the corridor, one of whom he recognised. Detective Rath, that stubborn mule! He should have known they'd pick up his tail. But now! Today!

Rath's companion must have bumped into one of the serving trolleys standing ready for delivery. A teapot had fallen to the floor, which he bent to pick up. The door to the nurses' room opened and a fury in white shot out and took the two officers to task.

Abe closed the door, and returned to his grandfather's bed. He pocketed the empty syringe, cast his grandfather a final glance and went to the window. A kind of pergola extended around the whole building. He swung onto it and looked down on the rear courtyard just as an ambulance arrived.

Driver and passenger climbed out and opened the rear door. For a moment he thought about jumping on top of the vehicle, but in the end climbed over the railings and clambered onto the rainwater pipe that led down from the roof. An elderly patient in a dressing gown, taking a stroll through the grounds, saw him but said nothing.

The metal buckled a little during his descent, and he ripped his coat but, after a few seconds, he was safely down. A quick upward glance told him the cops still didn't know he had escaped, but he couldn't afford to lose any time.

The ambulance puttered away on idle while two orderlies lifted out an unconscious man on a stretcher and carried him towards Accident and

Emergency. They hadn't noticed him. The man in the dressing gown was the only one watching.

Goldstein opened the driver's door, gave the elderly patient a friendly nod and sat behind the wheel. Releasing the handbrake he engaged first gear and accelerated. The rear door swung this way and that as the vehicle lurched forward, tyres spraying gravel.

64

This nurse was a tough customer. The combined persuasive power of two police officers could not appease her.

Tornow had overlooked a service trolley and knocked a teapot to the floor. They were picking up the pieces when she stormed across the corridor and had barely got a word in since. The greatest crime wasn't the destruction of the teapot, no, it was that two men, police officers or not, had dared to make such a racket—and outside of visiting hours at that!

How her own raised voice promoted the patients' afternoon rest was another matter. This time Tornow attempted to appease her.

'My good woman,' he said, 'we just want to take a quick peek inside room 102. It's possible your patient can help us trace an escaped criminal.'

'I'll give you my good woman . . . !' When the sister began another tirade, Rath lost patience.

'Now, listen here! You can complain to the police commissioner himself for all I care, but, if you detain us any longer, I'll charge you with obstructing a police investigation.'

She fell silent and, after a moment of paralysis, said meekly: 'Room 102.'

Rath gave a friendly smile.

'It's over there,' she said, 'but please don't get the patient too worked up. He's on his deathbed.'

'We'll proceed with caution,' Tornow said.

The sister followed them to the door at a respectful distance. Tornow knocked, but there was no response.

'Perhaps he's sleeping,' she said. 'He sleeps a lot, when he's not in pain.'

Rath opened the door quietly.

There was a lone patient, an old man whose gaunt face was nestled deep inside his pillows. On a handwritten sign at the foot of the bed was the name JAKOB GOLDSTEIN. The bedside table held an enormous bouquet of flowers.

Rath had seen enough dead bodies to know the man smiling peace-fully was no longer alive.

Loud cries came through the open window, and the sound of a roaring engine. An ambulance was heading towards Schulstrasse at full tilt, its rear door swinging this way and that. Two male orderlies gazed after it open-mouthed. A man in a dressing gown shuffled over the gravel path towards them.

'He just *left*,' Rath heard him say. 'Came down from up there and climbed into the ambulance!'

He explained what he meant by *up there* by pointing directly at Rath.

'What's wrong?' Tornow asked.

'Goldstein. He's escaped.'

'Damn it!'

They stormed past the sister, out of the room and into the corridor and, a minute later, were on the street. It was already too late. The ambulance was long gone.

Tornow kicked the nearest waste bin. 'It's my fault. That stupid service trolley must have warned him!'

'Not so much the service trolley as dear old Sister Rabiata,' Rath said. 'Don't blame yourself. We couldn't have known he was in the building. We came here to question a witness, not chase a fugitive.'

'A witness who's now dead. Must be our lucky day.'

Back at headquarters, Goldstein's reappearance caused quite a stir. Wilhelm Böhm summoned Rath and Tornow to his office. The Bulldog seemed to have a clearer take on the issue of culpability, blaming neither Tornow, the service trolley, nor the recalcitrant sister; least of all the fact that Goldstein just happened to be in the building at that precise moment. Instead, he laid the blame squarely on the shoulders of Gereon Rath.

'Am I right in thinking you've let a murder suspect give you the slip for the second time in a matter of days?' he yelled.

Rath knew it was pointless defending himself, but tried nevertheless. 'We couldn't have known the suspect was in the building. Officer Tornow and I received a tip-off that he had been seen at the Jewish Hospital. We then established that his grandfather . . .'

Böhm interrupted: 'What tip-off, and why do I know nothing about it?'

'We can't go bothering you with every anonymous call.'

'Not every one, no, but the important ones.'

'With respect, Sir,' Tornow said. 'It was me who took the call not Inspector Rath, and I'm assigned to Chief Inspector Kilian, J Division, not Homicide.'

Böhm wasn't used to subordinates interrupting. Rath was also astonished, but gave nothing away.

'Besides,' Tornow continued, 'it's only possible to judge the importance of a call like that with hindsight. In the last few days Warrants have had any number of tip-offs, and more or less every single one has come to nothing.'

It took a moment for Böhm to regain the power of speech.

'Then tell me how the whole thing went so belly-up,' he growled, which, for a man of his temperament, was akin to a peace offering.

'We knew from the porter that there was a Jakob Goldstein in room 102,' Rath said. 'As it turned out, Abraham Goldstein's grandfather.'

'He was the one you wanted to question?'

'Correct.'

'So did you see the Yank?'

'When we entered the room he had already escaped through the window onto the courtyard, then stole an ambulance.'

'How the hell did he get warning? Surely he wasn't *intending* to escape through the window!'

Tornow was about to say something, but Rath got there first. 'Chance. Perhaps Goldstein opened the door just as we entered the corridor. He knows my face; we've run into each other a few times at the Excelsior.'

'He recognised you,' Böhm mumbled and nodded. The answer appeared to satisfy him. 'In future you ought to remain in the background, so that Goldstein isn't warned again.'

Rath nodded demurely.

'Did you get anything out of the witness?'

'No, unfortunately. Jakob Goldstein is dead. We found him when we entered the room.'

Böhm hesitated. 'You're not trying to tell me that Goldstein killed his own grandfather?'

'It's a strange coincidence that he should die precisely at that moment, don't you think? After consulting with the public prosecutor, I've had the corpse sent to Pathology.'

'You're aware that an autopsy is forbidden by the Mosaic faith?'

Rath hadn't been aware until a few hours ago, but the ward doctor had told him in no uncertain terms. 'Dr Schwartz is Jewish,' he said. 'He'll know what to do.'

'Dr Schwartz is a goddamn agnostic. He'll cut anything he gets his hands on.'

'Then I'll ask him to proceed with caution. Maybe a blood examination will be enough. The man was terminally ill. He had pancreatic cancer.'

'You should mention that too. We don't want Schwartz examining a man who might have been dead for hours.'

'He can't have been. His family was with him until just before the end of visiting hours.'

'Goldstein has more relatives in Berlin?'

'Two aunts, if I'm not mistaken.'

'Damn it! Why are we only hearing about this now? Pay them a visit. Maybe they know something. You can show our cadet here how to tease information out of people.'

Tornow rose from his lethargy and looked at Böhm in disbelief. 'My apologies, Sir, but I'm assigned to Warrants, DCI Kilian, not DI Rath. I . . .'

'I'll speak to Kilian, everything will be fine. For the time being you'll work with Rath.' Böhm gazed sternly at him, trying to regain lost authority. 'You've made your bed, now you have to lie in it. Goldstein is the priority for both of you. Understood?'

Rath gave a dutiful nod. The audience with Böhm was over.

'It looks like you're my new partner then,' he said, when they were back outside. 'Here's to us.'

The cadet shook his hand. 'I know I made a mess of things in the hospital. But you didn't have to protect me like that. All the same, thank you.'

'You didn't make a mess of anything. But there's no reason for Böhm to know every last detail.'

'I'm here to learn,' Tornow grinned.

'That's right, you're my apprentice now. What I'm interested in, is why you became a policeman?'

'Why do you ask?'

'I ask every new colleague. You can give me several reasons if you're not sure.'

'There's only one reason.'

'And that would be?'

'My sister.'

Rath waited, but nothing followed, and Tornow was so serious he didn't probe further. 'Fetch your things,' he said, to end the silence, 'and I'll introduce you to your new colleagues.'

'There isn't much to fetch. Besides, I'd rather Böhm speaks to Kilian before I show up in Warrants again.'

'Right then. We're just around the corner.'

When Rath opened the door Kirie stood expectantly, wagging her tail.

'You bring your dog to the office?' Tornow asked.

'Only when it can't be avoided.' He gestured towards Erika Voss, who was sitting behind her desk on the telephone. 'Our secretary, Fräulein Voss.'

Erika Voss hung up and looked across curiously.

'A new colleague, Erika,' Rath said. 'Herr Tornow is a cadet who'll be working with us for the time being.'

The secretary returned Tornow's smile. She seemed to like her new colleague.

65

Charly had to resist a buying frenzy in this cathedral of consumption. Tables of clothing and scents, wrap-around galleries across four floors, the enormous skylight that crowned it all, it was hard to escape the magical appeal. Wertheim on Leipziger Platz had been her favourite department store since she was a little girl accompanying her mother. Today she wasn't here to shop, but even so caught herself browsing the summer offers. She could definitely use a new blouse . . .

'Does the young lady require assistance?'

A saleswoman had noticed her.

'I'm looking for Personnel.'

'I'm afraid we're not hiring.'

'That's not why I'm here. I just need some information.'

A little later, Charly sat in a small office overlooking the venerable row of houses on Vossstrasse.

'Alexandra Reinhold?' The man had introduced himself as *Herr Eick*, stressing the *Herr* as though it were his first name, and stood by a wall-high shelving unit of files. He fished one out. 'Let's take a look.'

Herr Eick made every effort to appear important, as well as being extremely helpful. He stole a glance at Charly's legs before sitting down to skim through the files. 'Might I ask why you are interested in Fräulein Reinhold?' he said, without looking up, but he was still squinting at her out of the corner of his eye.

'We're family,' she lied, crossing her legs, which threw Herr Eick for a moment. 'I'm in Berlin for a few days and wanted to surprise my cousin. I thought I'd pick her up after work.'

'Here we are! The delicatessen section.' The man gazed triumphantly, then regretfully. 'I'm afraid you won't be able to pick her up,' he said.

'Oh?'

'We had to let her go. In October '30.'

'I didn't know that. Why? I hope she didn't do anything wrong?'

Eick shook his head. 'No, no, don't worry. Purely a budgeting measure. Times are hard.'

Charly stood and stretched out a hand. 'Well, what can you do? Thank you for your efforts, Herr Eick.'

He seemed disappointed that she was leaving so soon. Before he could say anything—invite her to dinner, or maybe out dancing—she departed the office.

In the delicatessen, she could no longer resist temptation and bought a crab meat salad and a bottle of champagne to go. She might need consoling after meeting Gereon later, and wasn't sure if she should accept his invitation to dinner. It might be better to insist on just a glass of wine. She was afraid he might attempt to bribe her. In more ways than one.

Asking the saleswoman in neat white overalls to weigh out a hundred grams, she added casually: 'An Alexandra Reinhold is supposed to work here. You don't know where I can find her?' The woman hesitated. 'I'm her cousin.'

'From Jerichow?' She had a Berlin accent.

Charly nodded.

'Alex didn't tell you either! She hasn't worked here for ages. Almost a year now.'

Charly feigned surprise.

'I remember her da' standing here just a few weeks after it happened. He didn't say a word. He'd come to pick her up, just like you.'

'Do you know where I can find her?'

'You don't have an address?'

'The Reinholds have moved. There were strangers in the flat.'

The woman wrapped the packed crab meat salad in wax paper and passed the package across the glass counter.

'They're homeless, apparently, the Reinholds,' she said, quietly, as if ashamed to discuss it. 'I thought they'd moved out to you, in Jerichow. But they must be somewhere else.'

'Homeless? I don't believe it!' Charly feigned shock. 'There's no one here who might still be in touch? Who might know where she's living?'

'Maybe Erich. The butcher's apprentice, here at Wertheim. He had his eye on her. The way he looked at her when he brought up the stock.'

'Were they friends? I mean, together?'

'Not officially, anyway.' The saleswoman shook her head. 'It's strictly forbidden here. You carry on with a minor and you're out the door, but he certainly had a big crush on her. If you ask me, your cousin wasn't completely averse either . . .' She winked at Charly.

'You think he might be able to help?'

'If you're unlucky, she'll have told him just as little as she told everyone else. She hasn't been back since she got the boot. I think she was ashamed.'

'Erich, you say?'

'Erich Rambow. In the butcher's downstairs.'

Charly picked up a bottle of champagne and paid at the till. She had something to celebrate, after all: her future with the Berlin Criminal Police. Besides, she had skipped lunch so could afford this little luxury. Shopping bag in hand, she asked the way to the butcher's, but this time her luck was out. Erich Rambow had already left for the evening.

66

Rath arrived at Kempinski ten minutes early. He couldn't afford to be late, not tonight. He had thought about taking Kirie, who was always useful when he needed to appease Charly, but the poor dog wouldn't have been allowed in. Instead, he had fallen back on the services of Frau Lennartz and her husband, who enjoyed taking her overnight, especially as it meant money for them. If things continued like this, they'd soon be earning more from Kirie than their day jobs.

He handed the bouquet to the head waiter and slipped him a small note to ensure they sat on the terrace overlooking the Ku'damm, far enough from the action to talk in private. Everything had to be just right. He wanted her back; wanted, finally, to show her how he felt and put an end to the atmosphere between them. He was ready to go the whole hog again, but this time hoped for better luck. He hadn't simply showered and thrown on a new suit, but pocketed the rings that had waited in vain in champagne glasses all those weeks ago in Cologne.

He smoked while he waited. The waiter placed the flowers on the table in a pretty, modern vase with the Kempinski 'K', changing the ashtray with the same exaggerated attentiveness as the boy in the Excelsior, when she appeared. Rath held his breath.

She looked stunning in her red dress. He savoured the moment as she looked around and was approached by the head waiter. In that instant Rath knew he would do anything for this woman, but first he had to convince her that he, Gereon Rath, was the right man for her. The *only* man for her—in spite of everything.

His heart started beating faster as the waiter escorted her to the table and he thought he saw a smile flit across her face. He straightened her chair, but she kept her distance as she greeted him and sat down. No embrace, no sign of a kiss. Rath was just as cool, however difficult he found it.

She looked at the flowers, realising they hadn't been paid for out of Kempinski funds. The flower arrangements on the other tables were more modest. 'From you?' she asked.

'There was a complaint about the last batch. I hope these are up to scratch.'

Without smiling, she looked in her handbag, took out her cigarettes and a carton of matches, and placed both on the table. It looked as if she were preparing her weapons for a duel.

'How was your day?' he asked.

'So-so.' She lit a Juno and threw the match in the ashtray. 'Yours?'

'Our surveillance has gone belly-up. Goldstein gave us the slip.'

She pricked up her ears. A reaction, at last! 'The gangster?'

Rath nodded. 'Some time on Friday. A member of staff helped him.' He lit a cigarette too, even though he had stubbed out his last only three minutes before. 'Any progress with your Alex?'

Charly shook her head and blew smoke into the hedgerow that separated the terrace from the Ku'damm.

'I'm sorry about recently,' he continued. 'You mustn't think I'm not taking things seriously. You're right to look for this girl.'

'You understand what I'm going through now that you've got problems of your own?'

'I've had problems before. You know that. This isn't the first time.'

Charly nodded. He had never seen her draw so greedily on a cigarette, but perhaps he had just never noticed before?

'Did you try the brother again?' he asked, playing the experienced man. 'That's where I'd start, or at Wertheim. Her father said she used to work there.'

'Thanks for the tip, Inspector. Let's talk about something else.'

He drew quickly on his cigarette to avoid saying something he regretted. Last week she had picked a quarrel because he wasn't taking her concerns seriously enough; now she couldn't wait to get him off the subject. They'd barely been here two minutes, and already he was struggling to keep it together. He tried a different approach.

'I have a new colleague.' The waiter's arrival closed this line. Rath ordered a Gewürztraminer, Charly a Selters.

'Thank you for the invite,' she said.

'You can order something more expensive, you know. I've got plenty of cash. Or are you afraid I might get you drunk?'

Charly didn't respond to his tired joke. It seemed she hadn't even heard. He drummed his fingers quietly on the tablecloth, growing impatient. No more jokes. He wouldn't even try to lighten the atmosphere, if that's how she wanted it. 'You said we needed to talk,' he said. 'So, let's talk.'

'Yes, let's talk,' she said. 'But perhaps we could mention the elephant in the room. Are you going to apologise to Guido?'

Was that all they were here to talk about? The fucking grinning man? 'Yes, for God's sake,' he said, louder than intended. 'I told you I would on the telephone. Is that all you wanted to discuss?' He was taken aback by his own aggression, but she wasn't making things any easier.

She stubbed out her cigarette and fumbled around in the carton, almost pulling out a replacement before pushing it back inside. Her coldness was a mask, he realised. She was more nervous, even, than him. He wasn't sure if that was a good or a bad sign.

'Sorry,' he said. 'I know I messed up. Maybe that's why I'm acting so annoyed. It won't happen again.'

This time Charly did take another Juno from the carton, while Rath drew on his Overstolz. Let's have a smoking competition, shall we? he thought, but understood that whatever she wanted to discuss would not be good news. He was expecting the worst, but wouldn't just give up. That much he could promise already.

He gave her a light, and she looked at him with an expression that broke his heart: tentative, questioning, uncertain. What was wrong with her? Something was weighing heavily. Surely she didn't want to . . . ?

The waiter burst into the silence with the drinks. Even he seemed to realise something wasn't quite right. When he disappeared again Rath raised his glass in such a way that it wasn't clear if he was toasting her health or not. The wine was fine, the temperature just right. He took another sip. Charly smoked quickly, without touching her Selters.

'You're right,' she said. 'Let's not keep on about this Guido business. We have more important things to discuss.'

Rath watched his worst fears become reality. That was how he would have started if he'd wanted to draw a line, but that wasn't what he wanted, damn it! Not what he wanted at all.

He kept looking at her mouth, waiting for the next sentence, not daring to breath. She seemed to find it difficult to say what she had to say. The silence lasted an age, and Rath feared he might suffocate.

'You remember Professor Heymann,' she said at length. 'Criminal law. My supervisor if I ever do a doctorate.'

Rath only vaguely remembered, but nodded anyway. The legal world, all these academic circles, had always felt alien to him. He had picked Charly up from the odd meeting and run into a few professors or classmates in the process but, apart from the grinning man, he couldn't remember a single face. If Heymann was who he thought he was, then he must be pushing sixty, perhaps even seventy. Rath felt his mouth grow dry. What was this? Was she about to confess to a relationship with her former professor?

'Heymann made me an offer,' she continued. 'I wanted to discuss it with you before I decided, but after last week . . .' She lit a new Juno from the old one. 'Today I accepted.' She stubbed out the smoked cigarette. 'I'm accompanying him to Paris for six months. An international research project. Territorial jurisdictions of criminal law.'

Only now did she sip her mineral water.

Rath waited for more, but nothing came. That was her news. Charly wanted to go abroad with her professor for six months. Nothing more and nothing less, and harmless in comparison with what he had been expecting.

'Paris is nice,' he said simply. What a stupid comment, but it didn't matter anymore. He felt a weight lift from his shoulders, simply falling away from him.

'Is that all you have to say?'

He stubbed out his cigarette. 'When?' he asked, but he might just as well have asked 'how' or 'why' or 'how many?' It was pure chance that his response made sense. He could barely think.

'Next semester. I'd have to leave in September.'

Suddenly, even the wine tasted better. He had been expecting the worst and, against that, half a year didn't seem nearly so bad. He'd get through it.

Instinctively, he felt for the little package in his inside pocket. As good as her news was, now wasn't the right time for the rings. Could he really propose now, when she was about to disappear for half a year? How would that look? Celebrate their engagement, then pack his fiancée off to foreign parts? With another man! He could imagine the gossip, the well-meaning advice. His parents alone would . . .

'Say something!'

She was expecting an answer.

'Wonderful,' he said. 'That means Weber and the Lichtenberg District Court can go get knotted, right?'

Charly laughed uncertainly, and he realised that a weight had been lifted from her too. 'I'm not sure I'd put it quite like that, but you're right. A joint project with Heymann means I can kiss goodbye to preparatory service in Lichtenberg.'

'Then it's the best thing you can do.' Rath waved the waiter over and ordered a bottle of fizz. 'We have to make a toast,' he said. 'Why didn't you tell me before?'

'I . . . I didn't know what you would say. I didn't know what I wanted myself.'

'But now you do.' For once Rath felt comfortable in the role of sponsor.

Charly nodded.

'What about your old dream of joining CID? Are you giving that up in favour of an academic career?'

She grinned broadly. 'I could start in a year's time as a police cadet, without the preparatory service. I have Gennat's word.'

'When did this happen?'

'When I was with Nebe and Lange last week, in the Castle.'

'You didn't tell me about that either?' She shrugged. 'Congratulations,' he said. 'Buddha doesn't make that sort of promise to just anyone.'

'Thank you.' She stubbed out her cigarette, and, at last, didn't light a new one. The air was thick with smoke.

'Good news all round,' Rath said. 'That means in a year from now, you'll be back in the Castle.' He smiled, and he didn't even have to strain. 'I wonder who'll be showing you the ropes. I'm getting my first taste with a cadet right now. Maybe at some point Gennat will entrust me with the more problematic cases.'

'Pardon me?'

'You'd have to show a little more respect for authority . . .'

'*You* show *me* the ropes?' She feigned indignation. 'You should be so lucky! Besides, I wouldn't be a cadet in Homicide, but G Division. Might I remind you that I'm a woman.'

'So I'll apply for a transfer.'

Charly laughed in that unbridled way he adored. She was so loud other people looked across at them. 'Sorry,' she said. 'I was just picturing it.' G Division was the women's CID.

'What will we do while you're away,' he asked. 'Will we see each other for the occasional weekend?'

'Paris is a long way away. I won't get back to Berlin very often.'

'What about Cologne? That's half way.'

He said it without thinking. His home city didn't evoke good memories in Charly. Or, for that matter, in him. They were silent for a moment. Fortunately the waiter came with the bottle of champagne and took their order at the same time. Charly, who had been sipping like a canary on a diet, had brought her appetite. They clinked glasses.

'To us,' Rath said, hoping he hadn't taken things too far. He was pretty good at misreading situations, above all situations that involved Charly, but she raised her glass and gave him a blissful smile.

'To us,' she said.

At that moment the first drops of rain fell on the awning. The balmy summer's night on the terrace had come to nothing. They would have to move inside, not that it mattered now.

67

The address of the 127th police precinct was Bayreuther Strasse 13, but the station building itself was on Wittenbergplatz, close to the U-Bahn, bus and tram stations which thousands of Berliners used on their journeys to and from work. Thus the big letters painted in reddish brown across its front were seen by a great number of people that morning. Huge letters, smeared crudely across the wall.

In Communist areas, slogans scrawled overnight were usually political and might be normal, but here in the west they were anything but. The dirty-red graffiti, wet and running down the wall, had a deeply unsettling effect. Whether or not it was political was open to debate, but it certainly provided ample conversation material on an otherwise drab morning.

Not least for the three men in the Berlin Police Commissioner's office currently discussing what it could mean.

Commissioner Albert Grzesinski, back on duty only yesterday, skimmed through the black and white photographs on his desk, which were still damp from the lab, and shook his head. He wished he could change the words, but they stubbornly remained the same.

A MURDERER WORKS IN THIS PIG PRECINCT! REVENGE FOR BENNY S.

'The 127th precinct?' Grzesinski asked, in his characteristically sober way.

Ernst Gennat nodded, his ample form spread across the visitor's chair.

'Why did the ward sergeant call in Homicide? I hope he isn't taking this nonsense seriously?'

'He didn't,' Gennat said. 'Homicide is here of its own accord. One of my officers changes at Wittenbergplatz on his way to work. He notified me and I sent Herr Lange to photograph the whole mess.' Andreas Lange sat in the second visitor's chair. 'I spoke to the ward sergeant over the telephone,' Gennat continued. 'He's putting it down to Communists, which is unusual enough in this area. But I . . .' he pointed towards Lange, '. . . that is, *we* don't agree.'

'Go on.' Grzesinski waved his hand impatiently.

Gennat explained that Homicide currently suspected one of the precinct's officers of murder, outlining the fatal incident at KaDeWe. When he mentioned the name of the dead boy, Benjamin Singer, Grzesinski shook his head. When Gennat finished, he shook it again. 'A uniformed officer, who causes a boy to fall to his death,' he said, more or less stunned. 'Are you certain?'

'Everything points that way. Above all the pathology report. Of course, that's not enough for the courts, which is why we've been handling the matter as discreetly as possible.'

'So discreetly that not even I knew about it.'

'Well, now you do,' Gennat shrugged.

Lange raised his hand as if he were in school.

'Not so formal, man,' Grzesinski said. 'You can speak freely here.'

Lange's face turned red. 'We're assuming that the graffiti comes from the dead boy's female accomplice, who almost certainly witnessed his fall. We received an anonymous telephone call.'

'And you think this witness will be able to help you. A juvenile department store thief—not exactly ideal.'

'She's the only witness we have,' Lange said.

'Then see to it that you bring her in as soon as possible.'

'Yes, Sir.'

He looked at Gennat. 'Who else knows about this?

'So far, only Officer Lange, who came to me with his suspicions right away, Dr Schwartz, and myself. I've deliberately involved as few people as possible.'

'Good, but with this . . .' Grzesinski pointed towards the photos on his desk, '. . . it could grow out of all proportion. We need to send someone to keep the press quiet.'

'With respect, Sir, I think that would be a mistake,' Gennat said. 'Best let sleeping dogs lie.'

'So, what should we do, in your opinion?'

'Nothing. The best thing would be to do nothing. If the press believe the story about Communist graffiti we won't have any trouble. As soon as we issue a denial, the problems will start.'

Unlike his predecessor, Karl Zörgiebel, Albert Grzesinski was capable of conceding mistakes in front of colleagues. 'You're right. So what do we do with this sergeant? If we stick him in custody, the press will have a field day. Even if we didn't leak anything about our suspicions, journalists would have plenty of reasons to start digging.'

'That's my view too,' said Gennat. 'We would only create unease among our fellow officers, and such evidence as we have might not be enough for the magistrate.'

'Nevertheless, you'll agree that I cannot simply allow an officer accused of such a heinous crime to carry on as if nothing has occurred.'

'Absolutely, Sir.'

'Then I'll suspend him from duty with immediate effect.'

'It's probably for the best,' Gennat said. 'But you'll need plausible grounds.'

'We have them already,' Grzesinski said. '*In the wake of the intense pressure he has faced since the tragic events at KaDeWe, Sergeant Major Kuschke has been temporarily excused from duty. The measure is taken to avoid placing further strain on his work, as well as that of his colleagues.*'

'There is something else,' Lange said, taking a brown envelope from his jacket and placing it on Grzesinski's desk. 'We should deal with this too, before the press get wind of it and start joining the dots.'

The commissioner opened the envelope. 'What is it?'

'After taking the photographs at Wittenbergplatz, I went out to Kuschke's home. It's nearby, in Schöneberg.'

Grzesinski held the envelope upside down and half a dozen photos came tumbling out.

'Kuschke hasn't reported this, which I find very surprising. It reinforces our suspicion that the man has something to hide.'

Grzesinski listened attentively, looking at the photos spread across his desk. They showed a Schöneberg tenement, on the front of which four words were hastily scrawled.

REVENGE FOR BENNY S.

68

Charly hadn't been up this early in a long time, especially not after such a late night, but business at Wertheim began with the lark. She wrenched herself out of bed, showered and took the U-Bahn to Kaiserhof. Alighting there she retraced her steps to Vossstrasse, past the Department of Justice and country embassies that filled one side of the street, with its relics of Berlin's Royal Prussian history. On the other side was an enormous building complex several hundred metres long, which, despite its ornamentations, appeared strangely industrial.

Wertheim's front looked onto Leipziger Strasse, leaving Vossstrasse a view of its rear. The once quiet street had become the department store's lifeline, feeding the hungry Moloch with an endless supply of goods to keep its thousands of daily customers happy. It was in Vossstrasse that the delivery vans arrived with fresh produce, in Vossstrasse the rubbish trucks picked up whatever wasn't sold, and in Vossstrasse the majority of Wertheim employees reported for duty. To gain access they passed through a huge wrought-iron gate, more like the entrance to a castle or villa than the delivery area of a department store.

Charly yawned. She hadn't had much sleep. The evening with Gereon had turned out differently than expected, and she hadn't drunk the champagne alone after all. They shared the crab meat salad too; enjoyed a little picnic in bed. After. And before.

That was yesterday, but this morning things were no clearer. Six months abroad with Heymann, a decision made over Gereon's head, and he had accepted it. Then, somehow, she had yielded to his charm again, his stupid jokes. When had the turning point come? Certainly by the time she switched from mineral water to champagne, and then later to white wine, leaving all her best-laid plans in the dust. They had wound up back at Spenerstrasse, in bed—the place where they had always understood each other best.

The alarm clock this morning had sounded brutally early. She let

Gereon sleep on and got up, sitting at the kitchen table with a coffee after her shower. She wanted to smoke but her Junos were finished, and so she reached inside Gereon's jacket for his Overstolz. Whereupon she discovered the rings.

She had a guilty conscience even now thinking about it. Two identical rings that looked damn expensive, and one of them fit her ring finger perfectly. The other was a little bigger.

Damn it! So many opposing thoughts ran through her mind that she had to sit down. In the process she even forgot about the cigarettes.

Engagement rings! He had engagement rings in his pocket!

Was he really planning to propose yesterday evening, on the same night she had summoned him to talk? With Gereon, anything was possible. She couldn't help thinking back to Cologne, to that awful evening in the restaurant, to the roses he had used to strike Guido. He could have been carrying these rings around for days, weeks, months, waiting for the right moment. It seemed hard to imagine that Gereon Rath, who could be pretty bold when dealing with superiors and criminals, was too cowardly, or too meek, or whatever, to ask for her hand in marriage. But, then again, was it really? Perhaps it wasn't.

She didn't know whether it was joy or despair, this feeling that was coursing through her veins, gnawing away at her insides and, even more than her jumbled thoughts, had her slumped on the nearest chair.

She always thought she knew what she wanted. But with Gereon she wasn't sure. He had disappointed her more than anyone in her life, but she had never given up on him and, if that was a mistake, it was one she savoured with every fibre of her being.

The six months they would have to spend apart suddenly seemed like a godsend. If after these six months she still didn't know what she wanted, whether she wanted to share her life with him or not, then perhaps she really was beyond help. Until then—well, why shouldn't she just enjoy being with him, and cast all reservations aside.

At the Wertheim gate a lorry halted directly beside her, smelling of blood and diesel. On the driver's door was the logo of the Central Stockyard and Slaughterhouse. The driver got out and showed the uniformed guard his papers, climbed back and drove into the courtyard. It proved trickier for Charly to enter. No papers, no right of access. Not even her feminine wiles, so effective on Herr Eick, could help. The man at the gate was unmoved.

'No entry for unauthorised persons!' seemed to be the only sentence he knew.

'I'm looking for an Erich Rambow.'

She might as well have been talking to the no parking sign. After two or three more attempts, the gatekeeper froze to a statue and simply ceased to react, not so much as flinching until the next truck appeared, likewise bearing the Central Stockyard and Slaughterhouse logo. The meat they handled at Wertheim must come from Friedrichshain.

For the first time in her life she found herself thinking a little queasily about the mountains of flesh Berlin must consume each day, and felt a sudden desire for a simple green salad. The smell of blood soon overwhelmed everything else, leaving no room for vegetarian thoughts. A cigarette helped.

She stood smoking in Vossstrasse, waiting for she didn't know who. Alex's erstwhile suitor must be in his early or mid-twenties, she thought, keeping an eye out for men who fitted this description. Someone approached now who looked like a butcher's apprentice. She intercepted him a few metres outside the gate.

'Are you Erich Rambow?'

The boy was twenty at most and looked her up and down unashamedly. 'What do I get if I am?' he asked.

Charly was speechless, but only for a moment, then she found an appropriate response. 'How about a boot between your legs?' She hadn't grown up in Moabit for nothing.

'Alright, alright!' The boy raised his hands in self-defence. 'I wouldn't like to be in Erich's shoes.' He shook his head, swung his bag over his shoulder and carried on to the gate, where he showed the gatekeeper his time card and went inside. Charly gazed after him. This could get interesting. Three more attempts, she told herself, and no more. She had better things to do than listen to little boys cracking wise.

The next candidate approached riding a bicycle. He braked furiously in front of the entrance. Charly went over and tried her luck again, this time armed with a proper comeback.

'Erich Rambow?'

'Who's asking?'

It sounded more suspicious than hostile. He looked a little spare for a butcher, but his flushed cheeks denoted the slightly raised blood pressure common among meat-eaters.

'I'm a friend of Alexandra Reinhold,' she said.

Rambow dismounted and pushed the old boneshaker in the direction of the gate. 'OK,' he said, still suspicious. He had a thick Berlin accent. 'What is it you want from me?'

'I'm looking for Alex. You're friends with her, aren't you?'

'I haven't seen her in ages. You're asking the wrong man. She ran away, didn't she? Now let me past. I'm running late already.'

Erich Rambow ditched her, waved his time card at the gatekeeper and entered. Countless bicycles gleamed in the sun next to the steps by the loading platform. He parked his alongside and bounded up. Standing at the door for a moment and gripping its metal handle, his eyes searched for Charly through the bars of the fence. He looked her up and down shamelessly, which she observed, back turned, from the safety of her make-up mirror, before disappearing inside the enormous building.

She waited for a moment before approaching the gatekeeper again.

'No entry for unauthorised persons,' he began, before she could speak.

'I don't want to go in,' she said, pleased at the look of bafflement on the man's face. 'When do staff in the butcher's usually finish for the evening?'

This time, the gatekeeper was more forthcoming. He was probably just glad to be rid of a nuisance like her.

69

Margot Kohn was flabbergasted. Her nephew Abraham was in Berlin, her brother's son? She didn't know anything about it. And that Nathan's boy was a gangster, a killer to boot, well, she just couldn't believe it.

'My brother founded a textile dealership in America, which Abraham's been running for years.' She looked outraged. 'A gangster, you say? He's a respectable textile trader!'

'Has your brother retired?' Rath asked, pouring oil on troubled waters.

'My brother is dead.'

'I'm sorry. I didn't know that.'

This was anything but a model interrogation. Rath glanced at Tornow, who seemed unmoved. At that moment a girl broke the embarrassed silence with a tray of tea and biscuits.

They sat in an elegant drawing room, a little old-fashioned perhaps, but impeccably furnished. Margot Kohn, née Goldstein, lived with her family in the shadow of the Siegessäule, barely a stone's throw away from the Reichstag and only a few doors from the Interior Ministry. From its beginnings as a pleasure quarter, over the decades In den Zelten had become a more exclusive address, especially where it bordered on the Alsenviertel, an area full of diplomats and politicians.

Rath looked out of the window at the stony bulk of the Kroll Opera House silhouetted by the grey-blue sky behind the trees. The girl handed out the tea things and, after a nod from her mistress, disappeared, leaving Margot Kohn to serve her unbidden visitors herself. Rath added a little sugar and glanced briefly at Tornow, who understood. Time for a change-up.

'When did you last see your father?' Tornow asked, and Rath was astonished by the sympathy in his voice.

Margot Kohn immediately opened up. 'Yesterday afternoon,' she said, skilfully balancing her teacup as she sat. 'We visited him as a family. We've been there almost every day these past few weeks.'

'And he was fighting fit yesterday afternoon?'

'We all knew he didn't have long, my father more than anyone, but he wasn't afraid of death. He never has been. He is . . . or was, very devout. The only thing that troubled him was the pain.'

'Didn't he mention anything about Abraham; he must have visited a few days ago?'

She shook her head indignantly. 'Even if he did, he didn't kill his own grandfather! You don't really think that, do you?'

Rath was about to respond when the door flew open and a man entered. There was no need for an introduction; this had to be Dr Hermann Kohn. The lawyer was surprised by their presence. 'Might I ask what you are doing here?'

'Just routine questioning,' Rath replied. 'Your wife is related to a fugitive murder suspect, and . . .'

'Pardon me?'

'Abraham Goldstein,' Rath said, before Margot Kohn interrupted.

'Nathan's son,' she said. 'From America. Apparently he's in Berlin.' She showed her husband Saturday's edition of *Der Tag*, which Rath had brought, containing, as it did, the essential information. Hermann Kohn skimmed the article, the details of which were clearly as unfamiliar to him as to his wife. Journalists at *Der Tag* weren't averse to anti-Semitic sentiment.

'This still doesn't explain why you're here. My brother-in-law emigrated to the United States many years ago. The last time Margot saw him she was fourteen . . .'

'Fifteen!' his wife sobbed. 'Nathan is long since dead, and here you are telling me his son is a gangster and murderer, who might even have killed his own grandfather.'

'We had your father's body sent to Pathology precisely to rule out that possibility,' Rath said, realising at the same moment how tactless he was being—and not just because Margot Kohn started heaving again.

'Without informing his next of kin,' the lawyer said.

'With respect, we did, of course . . .'

'You told Flegenheimer! Not me!'

'Then you must have heard it from your brother-in-law.'

'I heard it from the hospital. They said you had seized my father-in-law's corpse.'

'That's not how I'd put it. We . . .'

'How would you put it? We want to bury our father and, thanks to you, it isn't possible. You are aware that Jewish tradition dictates that the funeral take place on the day of death?'

'I wasn't aware of that, no . . .'

'Tell that to my brother-in-law. He's a good deal less sympathetic than me.'

So . . . Rath thought. Dr Hermann Kohn regards himself as sympathetic.

'As far as autopsies go, the Jewish faith is even clearer. They're forbidden, since they take away the deceased's dignity. Viewed from the perspective of an orthodox Jew, what you have done is so egregious that it led to my brother-in-law telephoning me for the first time in five years.'

'Our forensic pathologist Dr Schwartz is Jewish himself and is sure to know . . .'

Again Kohn interrupted. 'Magnus Schwartz is many things, but he is certainly not an orthodox Jew.'

'You know Dr Schwartz?'

'Magnus and I attended the same school.' Kohn looked Rath straight in the eye, an expression that made the inspector hope he'd never encounter him in his professional capacity, before shaking his head, as if to satisfy a judge of the prosecution's incompetence. 'My father-in-law was terminally ill, and you suspect he was murdered. It's utterly ridiculous.'

'As I said, we're having the corpse examined to *eliminate* the possibility that he was murdered.' It was clear that arguing with Kohn was pointless.

'Then off you go and get eliminating! So that the body can be released.' Hermann Kohn gestured unequivocally towards the door. 'And stop harassing me and my family. In case you hadn't noticed, we are trying to mourn the death of my wife's father.'

Their second visit was no more successful. Lea Flegenheimer lived with her family in a grand apartment in the Bayerische Viertel, where many other Jews resided, but where the Flegenheimers somehow didn't fit. Her husband, Ariel, might have been a successful businessman but, in his black clothing, he was all too reminiscent of the Shtetl Jews who had settled in the Scheunenviertel around Grenadierstrasse. His Jewish neighbours didn't approve, at least that was Rath's impression when they entered the building and asked for the Flegenheimer family. The disdain and incomprehension that the liberal Jew Hermann Kohn felt towards his orthodox brother-in-law were much in evidence here too.

Nevertheless, as different as the families that the Goldstein sisters had married into were, they were united in their outrage that their American nephew should be sought in a Berlin murder investigation.

'It must be a case of mistaken identity,' Lea Flegenheimer said. 'I said that to your colleagues at the morgue. My nephew isn't in Berlin; if he was, he'd have been in touch.' The woman must have shed a lot of tears in the last few hours. 'Even so, they refused to release Father.'

Rath was surprised. 'You've visited the morgue?'

'Of course!' Ariel Flegenheimer said. 'Yesterday evening, just after Dr Friedländer informed us that you had had our dead father removed from the hospital.'

Though he looked as if he had just arrived from Grodno, Flegenheimer spoke perfect German, without a trace of Yiddish accent. If his speech was modified by any dialect it was Berlin's. The beard, sidelocks and black caftan didn't bespeak his origins, but his religious faith. The mezuzah on the doorpost told visitors they were entering a Jewish apartment where religion played a decisive role. Everywhere Rath looked, there was evidence of their faith. He was reminded of his childhood. Aunt Lisbeth's house had a similar feel, though she was Catholic, of course, with crucifixes, sacred images and rosary beads everywhere. He had always hated visiting his aunt, and he felt as uncomfortable now. It didn't help that Ariel Flegenheimer made no effort to put him at his ease.

'The way you're treating my father-in-law: violating the dignity of his body. We should have buried him yesterday evening!'

'If you could just be patient for a little longer.'

'This isn't about *my* patience, but *your* lack of respect. The soul remains present until the body is buried. Only then does it leave this world.' He seemed, genuinely, to believe this. 'That's why Joseph is holding Shmira with him.'

'Pardon me?'

'My son. He's been keeping watch over his grandfather's body overnight.'

'In the morgue?'

'It was *you* who had our father sent there. If it was up to us, we'd have buried him by now. Or at least kept watch over him here. I don't understand why you did it in the first place.'

'That's exactly what we're here to talk about.' Rath no longer made any effort to conceal his impatience. 'We're hoping to rule out the possibility that Jakob Goldstein died an unnatural death. That's why we're having the corpse examined.'

Flegenheimer jumped to his feet. 'That is simply outrageous!'

'Take it easy. There will be no autopsy. I've spoken with Pathology to ensure that blood is taken only for the purposes of examination.'

'What makes you think he could have died an unnatural death? My father-in-law was terminally ill.'

'It's just surprising that he should die at precisely the moment your nephew, Abraham Goldstein, was in his room.'

'Stop talking nonsense! My nephew would have visited us long ago if he were in Berlin.'

Rath showed them the newspaper article. The Flegenheimers skimmed it and looked incensed.

Lea Flegenheimer shook her head. 'It can't be.'

'I thought you had never met him.'

'I know . . . knew my brother. I just . . .' she pounded the newspaper with her fists. 'I just can't believe that's his son.'

'But it is, Frau Flegenheimer,' Rath said. 'And I *have* met your son. We'll find out whether or not he's responsible for the death of this SA officer, but it is beyond question that Abraham Goldstein is under police surveillance in the USA as a multiple homicide suspect.'

'What does all this have to do with my father-in-law's corpse?'

'It's purely a matter of routine,' Rath said. 'This is the procedure the public prosecutor is obliged to follow should there be anything unusual about the circumstances of death. If I'm not mistaken, you've already spoken with your brother-in-law about the legal background.'

With nothing to be gained, Rath prepared to beat an orderly retreat. This visit had been just as pointless as the first. The Goldstein sisters clearly had no idea where their nephew was; they didn't even know *who* he was.

He stood up. Tornow, who until now hadn't uttered a single word save for 'Good morning', did likewise. Rath handed Lea Flegenheimer his card. 'If your nephew should get in touch, please let me know.'

The woman's mind seemed to be elsewhere.

'I hope you'll see to it that my father-in-law can be buried soon,' Ariel Flegenheimer said. 'The Aninut mustn't be extended any longer than is necessary.'

'The what?'

'The period of mourning between death and burial.'

'Ultimately, it's the public prosecutor who decides,' Rath said, 'but I promise to contact you as soon as I know more.'

He took his hat and, heading for the door, halted at the bookshelves and the books of the Torah. In front was a small metal tin with a coin slot, a kind of piggy bank.

'What's this?' he asked.

'It's our Tzedakah box,' Flegenheimer explained. 'If you like, you can put in a few coins. Give Tzedakah.'

'Give what?'

'A donation. Not for us. We're collecting for a charitable cause. Every day we set aside a little of the change encumbering our purses.'

The idea appealed to Rath. He took out his wallet and dropped in a few coins. Tornow kept hold of his money, but Rath couldn't blame him; a new lieutenant in CID was hardly going to be rolling in it.

'Strange people,' Tornow said after they left the flat. 'They could try and adapt a little, having moved to Germany.'

'There have been Flegenheimers here for generations. They're Prussian through and through. It's the Goldsteins who arrived from the East.'

'So why does he act as if he just got in from Poland?'

'*Jeder Jeck ist anders*,' Rath said.

'I'm sorry?'

'It's a saying in Cologne. It means something like: *Let every man seek heaven in his own fashion.*'

'That's Old Fritz, isn't it?'

'It was one of you Prussians, anyway.'

As a Prussian, Tornow didn't find being lumped together with Ariel

Flegenheimer amusing. He fell quiet, but kept a straight face, only breaking his silence in the Buick. 'Where are we going?' he asked. Rath drove north via Friedrich-Ebert-Strasse, rather than take the turn for Alex at Potsdamer Platz.

'Hannoversche Strasse,' Rath said. 'We'll have this done and dusted by lunchtime.'

Joseph Flegenheimer was recognisable from a long way off. Dressed like his father, he was especially conspicuous in Pathology where most workers wore white. The man wasn't thirty but wore a Methuselah-like full beard. He had placed a prayer shawl over his black caftan, and bobbed back and forth as though he were in a synagogue rather than the lobby of the morgue. He seemed to take his religion even more seriously than his father.

Thinking of Abraham Goldstein, Rath could scarcely believe the two men were related. Cousins! But then he recalled his own cousin Martin, Aunt Lisbeth's son, who had also spent the whole day praying, having built a little altar in his bedroom underneath a sombre crucifix. Martin had become a monk at eighteen, maybe even a priest. Rath could no longer say; he had avoided his aunt's family ever since he was able to decide who to visit for himself. He remembered not being able to play with Martin, or talk to him much either.

Dr Schwartz, a man who wasn't easily intimidated, seemed nervous when he greeted them, but perhaps he was just tired. Rath introduced his new colleague.

'A cadet,' said Schwartz, 'and straight into Homicide. Congratulations! I hope you have a strong stomach.'

'We'll see,' Tornow said, clearly unimpressed. He gestured towards the praying man. 'I see you have company?'

Schwartz forced a smile. 'We Jews can be a real nuisance, can't we? No one better when it comes to pig-headedness.' He led them into the autopsy room. 'He was here when I arrived this morning. The porter said he couldn't be dissuaded; wanted to be as close as possible to his grandfather. I tried to encourage him to visit the canteen at the Charité or one of the nice cafes nearby, but he insisted on staying here to pray.'

'Have you examined the corpse?' Rath asked. 'I'd like to release the body as soon as possible.'

'The examination is complete,' Schwartz said, leading them to the gurney on which the covered corpse lay. 'Here he is, but I'm afraid his release is up to the public prosecutor.'

'Perhaps we overreacted—because he had a visitor just before he died. It might have been better not to send him at all.'

'Don't say that. If you ask me, people don't arrange for autopsies as often as they should. Still, that would mean having more staff here, and that's something no one's willing to pay for. The reason most killers get away—and this is my avowed opinion—is that no one believes a murder has been committed in the first place.'

'And in this case?'

'Hard to say, but I wouldn't call it murder.' He paused thoughtfully. 'Death was a relief for this old man. The final stages of pancreatic cancer. The poor fellow must have been in terrible pain.'

'You didn't open him up, did you?' Rath asked, horrified. 'I telephoned here specifically and left a message with the por . . .'

'I know better than to open the corpse of an orthodox Jew. I'd need to have a very good reason for that. No, I had Dr Friedländer send his medical file.'

'So, he did die a natural death after all.'

'Like I said, it's hard to say. I didn't find any traces of external trauma on his body—apart from injection sites from various needles. But the blood examination revealed something interesting: a high concentration of morphine, over a thousand nanograms per millilitre.' Dr Schwartz looked over the rim of his glasses, first at Rath then at Tornow. 'Dr Friedländer assures me he only administered morphine in moderation, and I've no reason to disbelieve him.'

'What are you trying to tell me?' Rath asked.

Schwartz hunched his shoulders. 'That's for you to find out, but I wouldn't discount the possibility that someone tried to spare the man further suffering.' He nodded towards the frosted glass in the swing doors where the shadow of the praying Flegenheimer was still bobbing up and down.

'It's up to you whether you choose to pursue what is no more than a hunch. If it was a family member, then their conscience ought to be punishment enough. For an orthodox Jew, assisted suicide is forbidden under any circumstances, no matter how adverse.' He gazed over his spectacles. 'Don't forget it was we Jews who invented Job.'

70

At least there was a cafe, so Charly didn't have to loiter on the street.

What were they thinking? A surveillance job without a car? She stirred her coffee and looked across to the house front opposite: REVENGE FOR BENNY S.

Keeping Sergeant Major Jochen Kuschke under surveillance was a tedious chore, unlike the search for Alex, which dovetailed nicely with her own interests. She had only been shadowing Kuschke in the evenings as agreed, but the call from Lange at lunchtime had changed all that. He had surprising news. 'Kuschke is going on temporary leave from today. This alters our plans.'

Above all, it altered Charly's plans. She had intended to surprise Gereon and have lunch with him somewhere, since they hadn't been able to eat breakfast together. Instead, Lange had given her Kuschke's address in Winterfeldtstrasse, a solidly middle-class neighbourhood, and identified this cafe as an ideal observation post. She sat at a window seat behind a curtain, with an excellent view of the street outside. The view in the opposite direction was less good, however, owing to the reflection in the glass pane. As agreed, she had called Lange when she arrived.

'I'm here,' she had said quietly, so that the staff behind the counter couldn't hear. 'What happens if he isn't there?'

'He's there, believe me. I think you'll catch sight of him soon.'

Lange proved to be right. Charly had just added milk to her second cup of coffee, and lit her first cigarette, when he emerged. There was no mistaking the bandage across his face. In all likelihood, Kuschke had Alex to thank for that little keepsake. He carried a pail of water, a scrubbing brush and a wooden stepladder. After unfolding the ladder in front of the mural, he climbed up and began to scrub, starting with the word REVENGE.

Charly looked on calmly. She was starting to enjoy this. It was always nice watching other people work, but in this case it was particularly gratifying to know that the words most likely belonged to Alex, which reminded her of her plans for the afternoon. Another hour and she would have to go and collect her bicycle from Moabit.

From time to time people would speak to Kuschke, but he didn't seem to like it and answered with a few terse words. Most times he didn't even turn, just kept on scrubbing. The colour was coming off nicely; the word REVENGE was now scarcely legible. FOR would be next.

She glanced at her watch. Time was getting on if she didn't want to miss Erich Rambow. She drank the last of her coffee, placed a one-mark coin beside the cup and set off. The search for Alex took priority: Lange said so himself.

Half an hour later she stood in the Wertheim delivery area for the second time that day. On this occasion, however, she stayed in the background. She had taken Greta's Miele bicycle out of the cellar this morning after returning from Wertheim and pumped up the tyres. She hadn't ridden one like it for a long time but, for today's operation, it was essential.

He emerged punctually. Erich Rambow pushed his bicycle out with the first wave of Wertheim employees. To the carrier he attached a package dripping with blood, probably his supper or offcuts for the dog. He mounted on Vossstrasse and pedalled off. Charly swung herself onto Greta's rickety two-wheeler and followed.

Erich Rambow cycled mighty quick; she pedalled hard to keep up, taking care not to get too close. She had taken the precaution of changing her clothes, wearing completely different colours from this morning, a subdued mixture of brown and grey.

Rambow cycled right across town, via Werderscher Markt and Königstrasse, out towards the east. Passing Alexanderplatz he skilfully weaved his way through the maze of diversions created by the construction site; Charly prayed that no one from the Castle would see her cycling after a scrawny butcher's apprentice. Luckily no one did, and she was able to stay on him. She just hoped he didn't live too far out east, as she was beginning to run out of breath. Rambow turned uphill onto Greifswalder Strasse, before, finally, riding into a rear courtyard in Lippehner Strasse. The smell of the nearby brewery hung in the air: malt and mash.

Charly dismounted and peered carefully through the entrance to the courtyard to see Rambow carrying his bike down a set of basement steps.

She felt her heart pumping and her lungs gasping for air, but got her breath back before he returned with the blood-soaked package in his hand. He vanished inside the rear building. She waited a moment, then went over, leaning her bicycle against the wall and looking at the mailboxes until she found his name. FAM. GÜNTER RAMBOW. So, he lived with his parents. Good to know. She mounted the bicycle again, cycling at full speed through the entrance and back onto the road. She had to look like she was in a hurry, with a long journey still ahead. No one could suspect that she had no intention of leaving the neighbourhood.

71

They had found the stolen ambulance at last. Böhm left a message with Erika Voss while Rath was on his lunch break with Tornow and Gräf: Warrants had located the vehicle near the freight depot at Moabit. It was empty of course; of Goldstein, not a trace.

'DCI Böhm said you should head out there with your team, Inspector,' Erika Voss said.

'Reinhold, take our cadet with you,' Rath said. 'I have a meeting I can't afford to postpone.'

In the canteen Rath had the impression that the two young men got on well. Gräf was scarcely older than Tornow, but his career path had been very different, having never served in uniform. As far as Rath knew, Gräf had worked in Homicide almost from the start, which spoke volumes, as Buddha only took the best. There had been a few rotten eggs, such as Czerwinski or Brenner, but Czerwinski, at least, must have been good once upon a time. Over the years though, he had been passed over too often and subsequently lost all motivation and ambition. As for Brenner? The idiot had been put out to pasture. After last year's disciplinary proceedings they had transferred him to East Prussia, to the furthest reaches of the country, where he couldn't get up to any mischief. He was probably sitting in a stuffy office plotting his revenge on Gereon Rath. In reality, he had been responsible for his own downfall, but he wouldn't see it like that.

Even at lunchtime, conversation had centred around Goldstein.

'I don't know why they didn't just nab him at the border and send him straight back home,' Gräf said. Tornow agreed.

'It's a disgrace that a proven criminal should be allowed to do simply as he pleases.'

The two men had worked themselves into a rage, and Rath had no choice but to play the considered older colleague. He could understand where they were coming from but, ultimately, there was no alternative to the legal system that said you were innocent until proven guilty. It wasn't enough simply to be *thought of* as a criminal.

'Do you need the car for your meeting?' Gräf asked.

'You take it,' Rath said. It wouldn't hurt to make Gräf's task at the freight depot a little more appealing. Better to drive to Moabit in a Buick than a green Opel from the motor pool. He tossed him the keys.

'What kind of meeting is it then?' Gräf asked. He had always stood out for his healthy curiosity.

'An informant.' Rath took his coat and hat from the stand and grabbed Kirie's lead. 'Besides, the dog could use some exercise.'

He could see from their eyes that they wanted more, but he left it at that, tipping his hat as he went. Erika Voss would be the most put out by his secrecy.

Stefan Fink, the journalist, was waiting for him at Aschinger in Leipziger Strasse. He had suggested the meeting point himself, though probably not without an ulterior motive. This was where he and Rath had met for the first time. Fink, back then a reporter for *B.Z.*, had tried to recruit the inspector as a press informant. Rath politely declined and was hung out to dry.

Fink had a huge plate of Holsteiner Schnitzel in front of him.

'Bon appétit,' Rath said.

'Late lunch,' Fink replied, wiping his hands with a serviette. 'Inspector! I'm delighted that you've decided to work with me at last. You'll see that it's worth it.'

'I'm not so sure about that.' Rath tied Kirie's lead to the table leg, ordered a few Bouletten for the dog and a small beer for himself. He sat and waited for Fink to devour his schnitzel.

'Right,' he said finally, dabbing his mouth. 'I needed that. Five cups of coffee for breakfast.' He laughed and lit a cigarette.

Rath grinned. The man was a muckraker, which would make this easier. 'Good of you to find the time,' he said. 'You seem to be very busy.'

'Always. So, what is it you have for me? You made it sound very exciting on the telephone.'

'It's pretty explosive. A man with serious gambling debts could be in a lot of trouble.'

Fink hesitated as a light went on in his head. 'What am I supposed to do with that, and since when are you interested in illegal gambling?'

'I'm interested in anything worth pursuing.'

'Can't you just tell me what this is about? You're talking in riddles.'

Rath got out the by now very crumpled edition of *Der Tag* and unfolded it on the table. 'Here, this is what it's about.'

Fink forced a weary smile. 'That's yesterday's. You want to see the latest?' He placed his copy of *Der Tag* on top. It was hot off the press, the headline underlined in red.

JEWISH GANGSTER LEFT TO TERRORISE BERLIN.

'Why are you stirring things up?' Rath asked.

'Because it's what people want to read.'

'Why is the man's religion so important that it has to be included in the headline? It almost reads like *Der Angriff*.'

'Has Isidor Weiss sent you?' Fink laughed. 'What do you want, Herr Rath? I thought you had information. This is old hat.'

'I do have information.'

'You mean about the gambling debts? Who cares about that?'

Fink still had a big mouth, but Rath heard uncertainty behind the steady voice.

'No *dice*? Then how about something else?' He lit a cigarette. 'I can reveal, for example, that you personally will fare much better in the coming days and weeks if you tell me how you got hold of the police sketch and internal information which you used to cobble together your wretched article.'

Fink stubbed out his cigarette and sighed, as if Rath was worthy of his deepest sympathy. 'Inspector, I can't see what you hope to gain from this. How many times do you think your colleague Böhm has tried to pump me for information in the last few days? My answer remains the same.'

'Which is?'

'Shield law. A serious journalist doesn't name his sources. At any price.'

'Is that so?' Rath pulled an envelope from his pocket.

'A German journalist cannot be bribed!'

'All in all you have debts totalling fourteen thousand Reichsmark from illegal gambling.'

'I don't know what you're talking about,' Fink said, though it was plain he did. He just couldn't work out how the inspector had got hold of the information.

'I think you do, and, whether you believe it or not, I'm the man who can help you. If, that is, you are prepared to cooperate.'

Fink lit his next cigarette. The look he gave Rath contained a mixture of suspicion, fear and contempt.

'I can't release you from your debts, but I can ensure that your deadline is extended. Perhaps spare you a few broken fingers in the process.'

'What kind of cop are you? You're not only corrupt, you're trying to threaten me.'

'You play your dirty little games, and I'll play mine.'

Fink inhaled as if he needed nicotine like he needed oxygen. 'What makes you think I have gambling debts?'

'Sorry,' Rath said. 'Shield law.' He stubbed out his cigarette and stood up. 'I have to take the dog for a walk. She's getting restless.'

He leaned over and untied Kirie, who began wagging her tail as soon as she realised they were leaving. Rath was halfway to the door when he heard Fink's voice.

'Stop. Wait!'

Rath kept his back to Fink. That way he didn't have to hide his smile.

72

No, it was hardly the Adlon here. The brick walls were damp, the floor hard, and it stank of slurry and muck and salt and blood. To say nothing of chemicals; Alex didn't even want to know how poisonous they were. And the cries at night. True, she had heard them from the axle factory too, but here they were so loud that she was startled out of sleep on the first night, believing the doomed animals were crying next to her.

What a place! The old tannery, or whatever Erich Rambow had called it. A hellhole, at any rate. Was she supposed to be grateful? She was, of course, after a fashion.

It was just too bad he was full of false hope again. She hadn't seen him since she had been let go by Wertheim, and was glad to have closed that chapter in her life. Nevertheless, when she had waylaid him the day before yesterday, ready to run if he reacted strangely, she realised that nothing had changed. He still idolised her. She was using him, it was true, but it was a chance for him to get sex, so it all balanced out. As soon as this business with the murdering cop was over, she'd move with Vicky to another city, Breslau perhaps, where Vicky's family came from. So far away the Berlin Police couldn't lay a finger on her.

First, they had to finish things with the cop. Kuschke, the bastard's name was, Vicky had followed him to his flat. Last night had been a success. A bucket of pig's blood and a brush was all they needed. Vicky stood watch as Alex painted. It took barely five minutes. In Winterfeldtstrasse, even less.

Outside his flat they had screamed: 'We'll get you Kuschke!' before running off laughing, as if it were a game of ring and run.

All the same, this was serious. They wanted to give the dirtbag a fright, to land him in trouble, before Alex launched the decisive strike.

If that meant spending a few days in this hole, so be it. She glanced at her pocket watch. Vicky was late again. Hopefully she wouldn't burst in when she was busy with Erich. Still, maybe it would be OK. Alex could think of better things than 'making love', as Erich insisted on calling it, in this stench. At least he didn't talk much. She heard steps and pricked up her ears. It couldn't be Vicky or Erich; there were too many of them. Probably workers moving from one hall to the next. Fortunately, no one strayed into her dilapidated little hovel, which had been out of use so long it was beginning to rot. It still smelled like a slaughterhouse, however, the whole site did, a nauseating mix. It was what she had always hated about Erich, that the smell had seeped into his clothing by the end of the working day, but here she didn't notice it so much.

The steps drew closer. Something was different this time, and she needed a moment to work out what it was. There were steps but no voices.

While she was still thinking, the great metal door swung open up ahead. All manner of thoughts raced through her mind as she prepared to retreat. She could only head further back, into the rear rooms, where the stench was at its worst. Damn it, what a stupid hiding place, but what else could Erich have come up with at such short notice? He could hardly have smuggled her under the bed at his parents' house—or under his own bed, for that matter, which was a mattress in the kitchen—but he remembered the stockyard and slaughterhouse where he'd done his training, and the abandoned building there.

Alex stood with her back against the wall in the furthermost room, like a mouse caught in a trap. Hopefully the intruders would stay up at the front somewhere, otherwise her hideout would be blown, and she wasn't sure she could find a new one at short notice. She had to stay out of sight of the cops. Vicky wasn't much use at this sort of thing, having only ever stayed at the old axle factory. Unlike Benny and Alex, she, Fanny and Kotze hadn't assigned each of their flats a different letter of the alphabet.

Alex peered through the crack, saw them but couldn't make out their faces. It didn't seem to be people from the slaughter yard: no blood-spattered white clothing. Instead they wore normal outdoor clothes, nothing special, patched in places and full of holes. A few harmless bums looking for a roof over their heads, just like her.

Or so she thought, until she heard them, and knew they were anything but harmless.

'Where is she then, the whore? You're certain she's here?'

'Of course. This is where Vicky came out of.'

Alex froze. She had hoped never to hear their voices again. The first belonged to Ralf Krahl, the biggest scumbag in the factory; the second, to one of his crew, Felix Pirsig, nicknamed Peaches, a suitably incongruous moniker given his acne-ridden features. Only, right now, it was no laughing matter.

Damn it!

Peaches must have followed Vicky, even though Alex had warned her to be on her guard! Kralle and his crew had had it in for her since she rescued the court woman. A rat like Kralle had a long memory. He had never forgiven Alex for jamming a knife in his arse when he had groped her a while back, rubbing his hard dick up against her as he tried to stick his tongue down her throat. While he was busying himself, she pulled the knife and stabbed him through his trousers right in the middle of his fat arse. Since then he had left her in peace, even if she knew he was only biding his time.

Things were looking better for Kralle than for her. She didn't even have her knife since the cops had taken it off her. Her best chance was if they assumed she was gone and gave up.

They didn't oblige. Through the crack she watched them draw closer. There wasn't much here to defend herself with. She'd have had more choice in the axle factory. Fucking hell! She had deliberately avoided going back there, but these arseholes just had to come to the one place where she thought she was safe.

A wooden handle lay under a mountain of junk.

She pulled until realising what it was: a fleshing knife, an old, rusty fleshing knife which would have been used to scrape the hide from leftover meat. The warped blade was rusty and blunt and had wooden handles on both sides. She grabbed it and searched for a hiding place as the steps drew closer.

No luck, God damnit! There was only one possibility left . . .

The door opened and suddenly Kralle was so close she was afraid he might hear her pounding heart. 'Shit, Peaches. What kind of dump is this? Do you see that lezzie anywhere? Or are we supposed to fuck the rats?'

Alex was starting to believe in miracles, holding her breath behind the door, when she heard someone step past Kralle into the room. Felix Pirsig turned slowly around but, before he caught sight of her, she drew back and slammed the fleshing knife against his head. She only struck him with the handle, but it sounded like he had lost a few teeth as he tumbled to the floor. The momentum carried her along and out, so that she stood over Peaches as he bled, staring into the empty eyes of his friends.

73

Erika Voss was bursting with curiosity when Rath returned to the office, but his lips were sealed. Gräf and Tornow weren't back from Moabit, so he withdrew to his desk and closed the door, which told her that he didn't want to be disturbed. Kirie settled under the table, devouring a Boulette as a reward for covering so many kilometres. Rath took out a large brown envelope from between the newspapers he carried under his arm. He had good reason to conceal it from her curious gaze. He couldn't reveal to anyone at the Castle how he had got hold of it. No doubt Böhm would have given anything for its contents, which made keeping it from him all the more appealing. Knowledge is power, his father used to say, and Engelbert Rath had made it to Police Director.

He opened the envelope. The police sketch of Abraham Goldstein tumbled out, complete with a few composition notes, alongside six typewritten sides which packed a serious punch. There was a profile of Abraham Goldstein, at least as informative as the one the *Bureau of Investigation* had sent by teleprinter two weeks ago, only this time in German, and supplemented by the information that the same Abraham Goldstein, whose weapon of choice was known to be a Remington 51, had come to blows with a troop of SA men in Humboldthain on Tuesday night. Then came summaries of two ballistics reports, one dated from Friday concerning the bullet that had been recovered from Humboldthain; the second, dated yesterday, dealing with two bullets of the same calibre which had been discovered in an unidentified corpse, found at the dump at Schöneiche a few days ago. This was confidential police information, ready made for the press and augmented by certain theories, for instance that the unidentified corpse could have been the victim of a gangland shooting, and that the bullets most likely stemmed from a single weapon, an American Remington 51.

Rath skimmed yesterday's article. There was no mention of a Remington; Goldstein's weapon of choice wasn't mentioned until today's edition. JEWISH GANGSTER LEFT TO TERRORISE BERLIN. Fink had taken up the suggestions of his informant and posited the theory that Abraham Goldstein was operating on behalf of a Communist-infiltrated Berlin Ringverein; and that the dead SA man and landfill site corpse were simply the first of many expected victims in an orchestrated campaign of retaliation.

Rath couldn't help thinking of Hugo Lenz and Rudi Höller. Was it possible that this wasn't a struggle between Berolina and the Nordpiraten at all? Was a third underworld organisation involved? Or had he simply been taken in by the freewheeling imagination of Stefan Fink, who had let the discovery of confidential police information go to his head?

He put the paper aside.

Realising that Rath had him over a barrel, Fink had passed on everything he knew, which, unfortunately, wasn't quite as much as Rath hoped for. He still didn't know where the leak at Alex was. Fink had found the envelope with the sketch, Goldstein's profile and the first ballistics report, on Sunday in his pigeonhole at work. The second report he had discovered in the same place yesterday afternoon. There was no reason to doubt him. Following their meeting at Aschinger, Rath had accompanied him into the nearby editorial office and made off with the envelope.

He returned the papers and sketch to the envelope and placed it in the lower drawer of his desk, stowing a few files on top and weighing it all down with the Funkturm miniature that stood on his desk, a souvenir commemorating his status as the broadcasting tower's millionth visitor, and a prime example of the category *Gifts that no one needs*.

After that, he asked Erika Voss to keep an eye on Kirie, who was still lying under the desk, and stepped into the corridor.

Rath thanked God he had never had to work with Gregor Lanke. The head of Vice's nephew had been taken on as a replacement for Rath when he was transferred to Homicide. Lanke junior hadn't developed any ambition in the intervening years, and still hadn't made it past the rank of detective despite his family connections. That said, he had now managed two years in Vice without rebuke, which, by his standards, was quite an achievement.

Rath stood outside the door and considered for a moment, before deciding on a surprise attack. He threw the door open and entered without knocking. He was in luck: Gregor Lanke was alone in his office. Rath's successor hastily cleared a stack of photos into the top drawer of his desk.

'What do you want?' he asked, horrified, only to recognise Rath. 'Inspector?' he said. 'Well, this is a surprise! Pining for your old workplace?'

Rath came straight to the point. 'Good afternoon. I need to contact one of your informants. A Marion Bosetzky.'

Lanke stared at Rath. 'Why? You're a Homicide detective, aren't you?'

The surprise tactic had worked. Lanke didn't deny that he had an informant named Marion Bosetzky.

'It concerns a homicide investigation.'

'There are proper channels for this sort of thing,' Lanke said. It seemed he had spoken with his uncle. 'A request for inter-departmental cooperation, for example.'

'Come on, now,' Rath said. 'Our offices are on the same floor, two minutes apart at most.'

'Then why don't you head back to your desk and fill out that official request?'

'Why are you so keen to get rid of me? Is it so you can get back to looking at your smutty pictures?' Rath gestured towards Lanke's desk, which had once been his own.

'I think you should leave. Otherwise I'll be forced to ask Superintendent Gennat whether he isn't giving his men enough to do.' Lanke reached for the telephone.

Rath had got what he came for. 'No offence meant,' he said and smiled, knowing that was what would annoy Lanke most.

74

Erich Rambow parked his bicycle by a tree on Forckenbeckplatz. Charly dismounted in good time before she reached the square, and stood outside a medical supplies store. Reflected in the display window, she watched Rambow carefully lock his bicycle, shoulder his leather bag and set off at a determined march. She rested Greta's two-wheeler against a lamppost and followed him at a safe distance, using the square's many trees for cover.

She had had to wait around quarter of an hour by the shops in Lippehner Strasse before he emerged from the courtyard leading to his parents' house, a leather bag strapped to his bicycle carrier. Rambow had then cycled directly to Friedrichshain, and this time Charly found it easier to keep pace.

Even as a pedestrian he moved at a decent lick. Nevertheless, he didn't head for the main entrance to the stockyard and slaughterhouse as Charly expected, but ignored the gatehouse and sped down Eldenaer Strasse, keeping to the endless brick wall. She kept her distance on the other side of the street until he came to a halt so abruptly that she only just managed to jump into an entranceway. When she peered out, he had vanished. She checked that he wasn't still there before leaving her hideout to cross the street.

Examining the masonry discreetly she located a brick that had been dislodged. Only when she was certain that no one was looking did she pull herself up and swing her legs over the wall, lowering herself onto the other side immediately. She stood in the lane between two brick buildings. The smell here wasn't sweet, a mixture of blood and slurry, and other things that didn't bear thinking about.

There was no sign of Rambow. She moved to the end of the lane and looked around the corner. Nothing, not a living soul. The butcher and his leather bag had vanished.

75

If Peaches had been alone, she'd have been OK, perhaps even if it had just been him and Kralle, but there were five of them. Kralle, the coward, had sent his crew in first. Alex caught another of them with the knife handle, albeit not as cleanly as Peaches, but Theo, the strongest, landed a punch. She tumbled to the floor, clasping the fleshing knife tightly, but Theo and the others were on top of her straightaway. Theo kneeled on her upper arms, while the other two prised the blade out of her hand, before pressing her flailing, thrashing legs to the floor. She felt paralysed, utterly defenceless.

The only thing she could do now was spit but, when she did, Theo smacked her again, so hard she felt her lips swell and start to bleed.

Damn it, Vicky, Alex thought, as she tasted blood. You should have made sure no one was following you. What have you gone and done, girl?

Kralle's grinning face appeared over her.

'Let me go, you cowards!' She struggled in vain.

'Looks like we've got ourselves a wild horse,' Kralle said, 'that needs breaking in.'

Alex gave up trying to resist. 'What do you want from me, damn it?'

Kralle pulled a knife. 'I think you can guess that. This is the slaughter-house, after all.'

He flicked open the knife and the boys gave a muffled, spiteful laugh. Alex thought she had earned Kralle's respect after her exploits with the knife, and perhaps she had. Perhaps that was why he had brought four of his crew along. He might be out for revenge, but she didn't think he'd kill her. He wanted to give her a fright—and was doing a pretty good job of it too. There were a whole lot of nasty things he could do with a knife without killing her. Alex tried to counter her fear with her fury at the crew who had made her life and Benny's hell from the moment they first set foot in the axle factory.

'Before we make for the block,' Kralle said, putting his knife away, 'it's time to break this one in.' Again the boys laughed, with the exception of Peaches, who had just announced his return to the living with a groan. 'First *I'm* going to fuck you,' Kralle continued, fumbling with his fly. 'Then it'll be their turn. How often, is up to us.' He laughed. 'Oh, one more thing, and this'll be a novelty for you. This time there'll be no exchange of cash.'

Alex reared up in her futility. The three boys held her down with an iron grip. Theo, the one she had thought was the most intelligent, dealt her another blow before climbing off her arms, which were now devoid of feeling.

'So,' Kralle said, taking his dick out of his trousers. 'I think it's time this little whore got her just desserts.'

He had an erection. The sadistic little arsehole was turned on by the fact that she was defenceless and bleeding from her mouth.

Alex couldn't keep her trap shut, which had always been her undoing. 'What the hell is that? Is your dick still hard from your boys sucking on it?'

One of them gave another knuckleheaded laugh, breaking off as Kralle's grin froze to a grimace of rage and he kicked her in the guts. Pain went through her like a fist burrowing and tearing through her insides, and she almost blacked out.

They heaved her onto the rickety table that stood at the back of the room against the windowless rear wall. Although she felt she might throw up at any moment, she defended herself as best she could, but the two boys gripped her legs tight, using their entire body weight to prise them apart. Behind her, Theo held her arms at such an angle that every movement was painful, and Alex feared he might dislocate them. They laid her out ready for Kralle, their lord and master, who now approached with trousers pulled down.

It was useless. It was fucking useless.

She could only fight him with words now. He'd hit her again, but that was preferable to what he had in mind.

'If you arse-fuckers touch me, you'll regret it, I swear!'

'Ho ho,' Kralle grinned. 'Where did you learn that word? More! I like it, and the boys too, am I right?'

The boys laughed idiotically.

'Don't laugh. I'll stab you all!'

Kralle flicked his knife open again.

'If I were you I'd keep quiet, or I'll carve you a few extra holes to rent out.'

Theo twisted her arms painfully and forced her head back. She felt Kralle lifting her skirt with his stubby fingers, running the tip of his knife along the edge of her inner thigh.

'All quiet now?'

She heard him panting and gritted her teeth. If she got out of here alive, she'd see they paid for this!

She started as he suddenly jerked the knife, but felt no pain. He had merely cut her underwear. His crew roared. Even Peaches, on the mend after spitting out a few teeth, gave a tentative laugh.

'Keep her still,' Kralle said, 'so I can break her in.'

Alex closed her eyes. You'll regret this Kralle, damn it!

She felt his sweaty hands on her thighs and sensed her whole body cramping; her nausea was returning. Would he lose interest if she vomited over him? She felt a sharp pain as Kralle penetrated her brutally, accompanied by the howls of his crew.

Alex tried to imagine herself away: away from her body, away from this stinking room, away from this moment, into a future where she'd take revenge on this arsehole and his crew, where every one of them would regret what they were doing to her. She tried to escape her body, but couldn't; she felt his thrusts, heard his panting, felt her rage growing and growing, alongside a feeling of helplessness. Her despair almost brought her to tears, but she wouldn't let it, no, these idiots would not see her cry! Dear God, please let this be over soon, she prayed, if you really exist, then let me out of here alive, damn it, so that I can avenge these bastards.

As if He had heard her prayers, Kralle stopped. At the same time, Alex felt the boys' grip slacken, as though distracted by something.

'What are you doing here, friend? Take a wrong turn, did you?' said Kralle, as he pulled out of her.

'It'd be better if you lot disappeared,' said a familiar voice.

Kralle and his boys laughed.

'I don't believe it,' Kralle said. 'Feeling powerful, are you? After your night in the nuclear plant? Or do the pigs have us surrounded?'

'Who can say,' the voice said, and Alex suddenly realised who it belonged to. He was here much earlier than agreed, but she wasn't about to hold that against him. She opened her eyes and lifted her head. Erich Rambow stood in the door, leather bag over his shoulder and a steadfast expression on his face, as if it were no problem dealing with these five boys, one of whom had just pulled a knife from his pocket, the rest looking like they were no strangers to violence. Erich shot her a brief glance, which said something like: *Don't worry. I have this under control.*

'Now listen to me,' Kralle said, flicking his knife open. 'I'm not sure you quite understand what this is, but I think it's best if you make yourself scarce and leave us in peace.'

'I'll leave you in peace, when you leave the girl in peace.'

'Why would we do that?'

'Scram, and nothing happens to you.'

That brought another round of laughter. 'And if we stay?' Kralle asked. 'What are you going to do? You're not even armed.'

'Who says?' Erich opened his bag and pulled out a butcher's cleaver.

'What is this?' Kralle took a step towards him. 'It doesn't even look sharp.'

'It doesn't have to be,' Erich said. 'The key is how hard you strike. And how fast.'

While he was still speaking, he calmly slashed the cleaver across Kralle's stomach, double-quick so that he didn't have time to react. Kralle gazed at the weapon, whose blade was gleaming red, then at his stomach slick with blood and finally at his dick, from which the blood had now drained once and for all. Then he dropped the knife, because he needed both hands to prevent his insides from spilling out of his abdominal wall.

Erich Rambow stood impassively with his bloody cleaver.

'So,' he said. 'Who's next?'

76

Charly had no idea where Erich Rambow had got to: the dilapidated brick building up ahead? Perhaps he had disappeared to another part of the grounds. The site was almost a city in itself, built for the sole purpose of ushering animals to their deaths so that Berlin wouldn't go hungry.

She debated how long she should wait. Or whether it wouldn't be better to call Andreas Lange and have the grounds combed by a squadron of officers. That would be the easiest thing to do, but she'd feel like a traitor to Alex. Even if she hadn't made the girl any promises.

The rusty iron gate of the building flew open and four boys dashed out, pale-faced and eyes full of panic. One held a bloodied cheek. They ran past almost without noticing her, as if someone else were in pursuit.

For a moment she gazed after them, then turned towards the door, which was still squeaking quietly on its hinges, and went inside.

The building smelled even worse inside, the animal stench compounded by something more chemical. Charly listened, thinking she heard voices, but all was quiet again. She groped her way forwards, ears pricked, trying to make as little noise as possible. Now she checked her weapon, the little pocket pistol Lange had given her, an old Belgian Pieper Bayard. Strictly speaking it was there for Kuschke, if she ran into difficulties shadowing him. She released the safety catch and slowly worked her way forwards, moving from room to room. The stench increased, the voices grew louder. She thought she heard a whimper, someone blubbing behind the door that stood open a crack at the far end. What was going on?

She kicked the door open with her foot, pistol aimed into the half-dark ready to fire.

'This ends now!' she shouted into the room, without knowing what 'this' was, since only now could she see what was actually happening. She couldn't believe her eyes. Alexandra Reinhold sat on a table by the far wall of the room, her head resting on Erich Rambow's shoulders; from her left leg dangled the remains of shredded underwear. Rambow's left arm was draped comfortingly around her, while in his right hand he held a cleaver that glistened bloody red. A few metres from them on the floor crouched a boy holding his stomach, his trousers pulled down. It was that arsehole from the old factory, the burly youth who had intimidated her: Kralle, or whatever his nickname was. At any rate he sat blubbing and groaning in pain, a picture of misery.

All three stared at Charly wide-eyed, as her pistol flitted to and fro. Instinctively, Alex and Rambow raised their hands, but the boy on the floor only held his stomach. Blood gleamed between his fingers.

'I'm dying,' he whimpered over and over again. 'I'm dying.'

Charly dropped her pistol. 'What in God's name happened here?' she asked.

77

Kronberg knew straightaway which corpse Rath was referring to.

'The one from the dump? Nasty business, that,' he said down the line. 'Completely gnawed by rats. Dr Schwartz says the poor man's been dead a week, maximum, but there were only two fingers we could use for prints.'

'And now you're ploughing your way through the files . . .'

'Luckily, not me personally.'

'The ballistics report states he was killed by a Remington?'

'First I've heard of it.' For a moment there was silence. Kronberg seemed to be thinking. 'Interesting theory,' he said. 'Pretty exotic weapon, but it could fit.'

'It's in today's paper,' Rath said. 'Apparently it's the same weapon as the one used in Humboldthain.'

'I don't set much store by these press types but, in this case, they might be right.'

Rath was surprised. Fink's informant even seemed to be ahead of ED. 'Have you compared the prints with those of Hugo Lenz or Rudi Höller?' he asked. 'They're on file somewhere, I assume?'

'Rudi the Rat and Red Hugo? Of course they are, but my guy's only on F, as far as I know.'

'You're doing this alphabetically?'

'You have to have some kind of system.' Kronberg sounded a little offended. 'What makes you think of Lenz and Höller out of everyone?'

'A tip-off,' Rath lied. 'They're both missing.'

Kronberg burst out laughing. 'Wouldn't that be something. Rudi the Rat eaten by his own kind.' He lowered his voice. 'I'll look into it. Thanks for the tip.'

'Don't mention it.'

Rath hung up. He was the last in the office and it was time to leave. Looking forward to the evening, he grabbed Kirie's lead.

Charly's scent that morning on the pillow had stayed with him all day, and now he wanted more. What a change from the weekend when he had just been getting used to life on his own again.

First he drove to Luisenufer, where he showered and put on a clean suit, before going on his way. This time he gave the flowers a miss, picking up a bottle of champagne instead. True, they still weren't engaged, but there was reason enough to celebrate . . . He hadn't thought they'd make up so quickly, had even doubted for a moment they'd make up at all. Even Kirie seemed happy when she realised they were heading back to Spenerstrasse; no sooner had Rath opened the car door than she leapt onto the street and started wagging her tail.

'That's right, my friend,' Rath said. 'You'll be seeing mistress again soon.'

He checked himself and Kirie in the display window of the general store. They were looking good! He straightened his tie, made a minor adjustment to his hat, and went inside, whistling as he climbed the steps.

It took a long time for anyone to open, and a strange feeling came over him once more. But then: no grinning man, no nasty surprise. Charly opened it herself.

'Gereon!'

She looked a little flummoxed. More than he'd been expecting, anyway. He'd tried to reach her a few times at home, without success. No wonder, he thought, if he was on leave, he wouldn't spend the day at home either. But then he would have been looking forward to seeing her even more.

'Surprise,' he said, superfluously. Kirie waggled her tail.

'What are you two doing here?' Charly bent down and ran her fingers through Kirie's black fur. 'This really is a surprise.'

'Don't you say hello to people?'

She looked around, and, seeing no one, gave him a kiss, but remained in the door as if guarding a temple.

'Aren't you going to invite us in? That way you wouldn't have to worry about old Brettschneider having a heart attack seeing us out here.'

Charly appeared contrite. 'I'd love to but right now, I can't.'

'Why not?' Rath realised that, once again, his surprise tactic hadn't worked.

'I have a visitor.'

He must have pulled a pretty idiotic face. She laughed. 'Don't worry! It isn't Guido! It isn't a man at all.'

'So why all the secrecy?'

'It's—I'll explain some other time.'

'I wanted to surprise you. I've been trying to reach you all day.'

'I had a lot on my plate. Listen, I'll tell you everything tomorrow, OK? I really can't now.' She looked at him almost ruefully. 'I'm sorry, Gereon. We'll talk on the telephone, OK?'

The bathroom door opened and a girl emerged wrapped in Charly's red dressing gown, hair still wet. She turned around briefly and gazed at him through suspicious eyes before disappearing inside the kitchen. Rath put her at eighteen or nineteen, maximum. Her upper lip was swollen on the right-hand side.

He didn't need to ask who it was.

'Well, then,' he said, lifting the bottle. 'I suppose Kirie and I will just have to drink this alone.'

'Oh, Gereon,' she said, full of regret now. 'Don't be annoyed.'

He forced a smile and hoped it didn't look too contrived. 'I couldn't have stayed long anyway. I have to sleep at Luisenufer tonight. Tomorrow I'll need my black suit.'

'Do you have to go to a funeral?' She sounded horrified. There hadn't been much talk yesterday . . .

Rath nodded. 'Maybe even two.'

78

Alex was sitting in the kitchen, wrapped in a warm dressing gown and blowing on a cup of tea. 'Who was that?' she asked.

'Just a friend.' Charly sat down. 'Feeling better after your shower?'

'I don't know if I'll ever feel clean again.' The cup jangled as she returned it to the saucer. 'Kralle, the stupid arsehole! I hope he croaks.'

'Then your friend would have a human life on his conscience.'

Alex pulled the dressing gown tighter. She looked as if she wanted to crawl inside it. 'The man you were speaking to on the telephone just now,' she asked. 'Was he a cop?' She sounded tentative, uncertain, wondering whether she could really trust Charly.

'Yes, it was a cop, but a nice one.'

Alex gave a wry grin. 'I didn't know there was such a thing.'

Charly smiled back. She didn't want to say that the man at the door was also a cop. She didn't want to destroy Alex's already fragile trust. 'Don't worry. I promised you no police.'

She couldn't help remembering how anxious Alex had been when she mentioned the word *police* at the old tannery. 'No cops,' she had said, turning white as a sheet, 'please, no cops.'

'But . . . do you want that bastard to get away with this? He raped you.'

'Please, no cops . . .'

Ultimately, Charly contented herself with sending for an ambulance so that Ralf Krahl, nicknamed Kralle, could receive medical attention. Perhaps the injury would be a lesson to him, more than a court appearance on charges of rape and grievous bodily harm.

The fact that Charly had kept the police out of it, as well as letting Erich Rambow go, had helped. The only reason Alex had come back to the flat, along with her friend Vicky, whom they had met on Eldenaer Strasse, was that the two girls had nowhere else to go. Erich Rambow, who had recovered his bike from Forckenbeckplatz, was in no position to offer them a place to stay, so Vicky now lay in Greta's bed, asleep. Alex had dark circles under her eyes, but was holding out better than her friend.

'Why are you doing all this?' she had asked in the taxi.

'What do you mean, *all this*?'

'Helping us. Keeping the cops out of things. Why are you so stubborn? Is it because I got away from you?'

'I just wanted to find you.'

'Why?'

'Perhaps I can help you. I think you have problems with the police.'

'That's hardly news.'

Charly placed a finger to her lips and glanced over at the taxi driver, but he kept his eyes on the traffic ahead.

'That's not what I mean. You saw Benny plunge to his death. You saw a police officer *push* him.'

Alex looked at her wide-eyed. Disbelieving, yet relieved at the same time.

By the time they arrived in Moabit, Charly knew the whole story. They had to shake Vicky awake and bundle her upstairs into the flat, but Alex told her everything. She and Lange had figured most of it out long ago, but the information about Benny's fall was new.

'There was a man there,' Alex said.

'What man?'

'The one who called the ambulance. He saw everything.'

Alex hadn't been able to give a perfect description, only that he wore metal-rimmed spectacles, and looked a little like that American with the boater who was always in the cinema, just that he wore a bowler, not a boater.

'Harold Lloyd,' Andreas Lange said when Charly called, before requesting that Alex provide the police sketch artist with a description.

Charly looked at Alex and how she held her cup of tea. As if it were her only comfort. 'The policeman I just spoke to wants to send this Sergeant Kuschke to jail.'

'He belongs on the scaffold, not in the clink.'

Charly was constantly amazed by how many petty criminals advocated the death penalty.

'First, he belongs in a court that will convict him.'

'They'll acquit him! Birds of a feather flock together.'

'If we have sufficient evidence and witness statements, he'll be convicted, I promise. Our judicial system will see to it. Besides, a judge isn't a police officer; there's a big difference between the judiciary and the executive. They're completely different beasts.'

'Between what?'

'It's called the separation of powers. What I really mean, is that we need you to get to Kuschke. You saw everything, you can testify to it.'

'Who's we?'

'Myself and Assistant Detective Lange.'

'I thought the police and courts were separate. Isn't that what you just told me?'

The girl was hard work. 'They are, but I want to see this Kuschke convicted just as much as Herr Lange. I think that's where our interests align. Am I right?'

'I don't want to see him convicted. I want to see him whining and whimpering and begging for his life. That's what I want.'

'You're talking about vigilante justice.'

'I don't care what you call it. I call it revenge, and I'll get it. I owe it to Benny.'

'Please don't do anything rash.'

'Rash? You wouldn't believe how much thought I've given it.'

'It was you and Vicky who painted his house, the police station too, wasn't it?'

'What if it was?'

'If anything happened to Kuschke, suspicion would fall on you two pretty quickly, if not Vicky then you at least. So please, for your own sake.'

Alex fell silent, thinking.

'You've already slashed his face. Isn't that enough? Let the police take care of the rest. And the courts.'

'I'm not going to the cops. They'll only lock me away. As for my witness statement, do you really think any judge is going to take what I say in court seriously? It doesn't matter whether I'm the witness or the accused, they aren't going to believe me.'

Charly fell silent. Alex had touched a nerve. The girl wasn't the most trustworthy witness, even if they dressed her in new clothes for the court.

A suspected (and, by that stage, possibly even convicted) thief would hardly be the best weapon in the murder trial of a police officer.

'You could be right,' she said finally, 'but they might take your man with the metal-rimmed specs more seriously.'

'If he had anything to say, he'd have done it ages ago, wouldn't he?'

Charly shrugged. 'Maybe he has his reasons, who knows? If we issue an appeal and throw in a description, perhaps he'll come out of his hiding place.'

'Then why don't you? You don't need me for that.'

'Actually we do. You need to describe the man to a sketch artist. You don't have to come to the station. There's a cafe on the next street.' Charly looked at her watch. 'We're meeting there in exactly twelve minutes.'

Alex froze.

'Don't worry. He's not a police officer, just a sketch artist.'

79

Rath didn't crack the champagne, but placed it in the cupboard and reached for the cognac instead. Kirie lay asleep at his feet, the sun having long since disappeared below the clouds. He could see his reflection in the windowpane, sitting freshly showered and dressed in his Sunday best, a glass of cognac before him alongside an ashtray. Just smoking and drinking and listening to music; thinking. Rarely had he looked so good in the process.

He guessed Charly hadn't let him in to spare him a moral dilemma. She was housing a fugitive sought by the police, and the way things looked, she wasn't about to give her up. He couldn't help but smile: Charly of all people, who had always criticised him for failing to do things by the book. In some ways he was glad, but at the same time it hurt that she didn't trust him. As if he'd have squealed! He wouldn't even have tried to talk her out of it. He'd have let her go right ahead, only to make damn sure he reminded her of it next time she questioned the legality of his investigative techniques. Always a stickler for the rules, it seemed that Charly had finally realised the law wasn't the decisive factor.

The decisive factor was the result.

He felt pleasantly drunk, and, thinking about such things, reached a decision. He left Kirie where she was, the dog squinting briefly as he rose from his chair, and grabbed his hat, coat and car keys.

Quarter of an hour later, he stepped out of his car onto Dircksenstrasse. It was stormy outside. He hadn't parked in the atrium since he wanted to draw as little attention to himself as possible, something that the Buick, understandably, didn't allow. It was also why he used one of the southern stairwells, where the greatest risk would be encountering someone from the motor pool, or perhaps a guard from the detention wing.

The wind was cold enough to sober him in the few metres between the car and the southwest entrance. He checked his shoe soles in the stairwell, to make sure they were dry, before entering the long corridor of E Division. It was deserted. That was good. If anyone was doing overtime, or in Vice for any other reason, he'd have some explaining to do, especially now, as he crept into the dark office and closed the door behind him. This was definitely breaking and entering, even if he hadn't needed to force any doors. In the confusion surrounding his transfer to Homicide two years ago, no one had thought to ask for his key back, and even he had forgotten he still owned one, until it occurred to him again that evening.

It was eerily quiet, with only the rain drumming on the windowpane for company. Rath switched on Lanke's desk lamp, which cast its dim, green-yellow light into the room, and searched for the key to his old desk. Even that still worked.

The light was sufficient. He rummaged in the drawers, searching for something that looked like an address book or index file. Nothing doing. Greaseproof paper rustled between his fingers. He found pencils, empty cigarette cartons, a half-eaten apple, everything under the sun except what he was looking for. No sign of Marion Bosetzky. Not even an idiot like Gregor Lanke was daft enough to keep a file on an unofficial informant.

The lowest drawer contained nothing but pornographic photos. Lanke junior, like his uncle, worked for Vice squad, where this sort of thing was used as evidence, but there seemed to be an enormous amount of evidence gathered here. Some of it was worn, covered in fingerprints. Rath skimmed through the images. The collection was unbelievable!

It looked as if Lanke had picked out his favourites from each arrest and kept them for himself. Rath even came across the odd photo he had confiscated himself: a Hindenburg double engaged in close combat with Mata Hari. Nevertheless, it wasn't these images that grabbed his attention, but a different set entirely. A series of private snaps, taken by an amateur, showed the same naked woman in action, photographed from the perspective of a man whose erect penis was the only part of him visible, and even then not entirely, since it was mostly inside some bodily orifice or other. Though lacking intimate knowledge of Lanke junior's anatomy, Rath was certain that the detective had taken the pictures himself. This confirmed his hunches on two counts: one, that Gregor Lanke was the dirtbag he'd always taken him for, and, two, that Marion Bosetzky wasn't simply engaged as his informant, but also in an entirely different capacity—even if it looked like one she didn't always enjoy.

Rath leafed through the images, grinning when he found one of particular interest. He held it against the light and stowed it in his pocket. It wasn't as good a picture of Marion as the others, but in the background was a large wardrobe—with mirrored doors.

80

They were in Tietz again; it had proved to be a good meeting point. This time Lange had invited her for breakfast. Cutting an unhappy figure, he seemed to have slept badly. A copy of the *Berliner Tageblatt* lay before him on the table next to a cup of coffee.

'In case you haven't had breakfast, it's on me,' he said, and waved the waiter over. They had the restaurant almost to themselves.

'Thank you, that's not necessary.' Charly ordered tea with lemon and pointed towards the paper. 'Heard anything from our witness?'

Lange shook his head. 'Still no response to our appeal. Six papers carried the story this morning, with his picture.'

'It's a pretty generic face.'

'You're telling me.' Lange looked sceptical. 'Yesterday I tried to trace the person who took the emergency call. So far, no luck.'

'You think our witness called the ambulance?'

Lange nodded. 'Perhaps he gave his name. If he isn't just a ghost, that is.'

'That would mean Alex invented him. I don't believe that.'

'If she doesn't want to turn herself in, the obvious solution is to invent a witness.'

'She might be a criminal, but I think she's telling the truth.'

'Which leads us to our next topic,' Lange sighed. 'Alexandra Reinhold *is* a criminal. If it gets out that we're using her for information, only to turn her loose, it'll be curtains. For both of us. Your career will be over before it's even begun.'

Charly took a cigarette from the carton. 'May I?' she asked.

'Please do. A few weeks ago watches and jewellery worth several thousand Reichsmark were stolen from right here, from Tietz.' Lange gestured towards the floor. 'The thieves locked themselves in the department store overnight. The same as ten days later in Karstadt. Who do you think the principal suspect is?'

'I see you've got a hotline to Arthur Nebe.'

'If Nebe knew we were shielding his main suspect!' Lange spoke louder than he intended. He gazed around him, horrified.

'How's he going to find out? No one's allowed to know anything about our agreement.'

'So long as you realise you're covering for a felon. That *we're* covering for a felon.'

'Listen,' Charly said. 'I know what Alex has done, and that she's no angel, but she's given us important information.' She drew on her cigarette, almost defiantly. 'If I give her up now, she'll most likely be convicted and then her life really *will* be ruined.'

'It makes me uneasy,' Lange said. 'As a police officer, I always thought I'd automatically be on the right side, but with this case I just don't know.'

'Sergeant Major Kuschke is a police officer with a man on his conscience, a boy in fact; a murderer who tried to kill the girl who recognised him. He shot at Alex. Is that the right side?'

'Of course not.' Indignation hung in Lange's voice. 'If I thought that, I'd have filed this case away long ago. Do you think this is making me any friends in the Castle? As for when it all goes public . . .'

'I'm sorry,' Charly said. 'I know where you stand, but you can't lose sight of our goal of building a watertight case against Kuschke.'

'And turn a criminal loose in the process?'

'Look at Alex as an informant who's pointed you towards an important murder witness. Tip-offs like that come at a price.'

'Informants don't have free rein. All these department store break-ins—they're hardly petty crimes.'

'Forget about Alex. Use me as your informant. Pitch me as someone with links to the criminal underworld. That way it'll be me drawing the short straw.'

'What about Berlin's highest-grossing department store thief?'

'Alex is an intelligent girl who's been through a rough time. She just needs a little help getting back on the right track. I think she can make it, but not if we take her into custody. Besides, do you really want her sitting in a cell with someone like Kuschke still at large?'

'OK, OK, I know,' Lange said. 'First we need to get Kuschke so that she's no longer in danger. If this mysterious witness doesn't come through and we need Alex after all—will she turn herself in then?'

Charly shrugged. 'Not as long as Kuschke remains at large.'

'The whole thing's a vicious circle. We need Alex to get at Kuschke, but so long as he's still roaming free, we've no chance of getting Alex.'

'That's a knot for *you* to untie.' Charly stubbed out her cigarette. 'I'm not giving Alex up. I've given her my word.'

She'd never have thought herself capable of talking like this, she who had been raised to be conscientious and loyal to the state. Was Gereon's Rhine-Catholic nonchalance rubbing off on her?

Lange still cut an unhappy figure. 'It'll be curtains for both of us,' he said again, shaking his head.

'So what if it is,' Charly said. 'We'll open our own office.' She drew an imaginary sign with her hands. '*Private Detectives Lange and Ritter, enquiries of all kinds.* Now, doesn't that fill you with confidence?'

Her attempt to lighten the mood misfired. Lange turned red.

'Right,' Charly said, packing her cigarettes back in her handbag. 'I've fulfilled my side of the agreement. I've found Alex.' She made a move to get up.

'Wait a minute,' Lange said, with surprising sharpness, and Charly sat back down. 'Don't forget there's a second part. Sergeant Major Kuschke will have read the papers this morning. You still need to keep an eye on him.'

'How long do I have to keep the man under surveillance?' Charly sighed.

Lange smiled and tapped the paper. 'Until this witness turns up and we can take him into custody. Or until Alex changes her mind and turns herself in. In the meantime, I'll speak to Gennat about what concessions we can make, and see if we can't get her sentence commuted.'

Charly stood up. Lange might go red easily but he was tough. She had understood: so long as she couldn't persuade Alex to turn herself in, she'd have to continue her surveillance of Kuschke. A nice little incentive to see her on her way.

81

Rain drummed non-stop against the windowpane. The perfect weather for a funeral. Rath hadn't slept much and had a hangover, even though he hadn't touched a drop after his late-night visit to the Castle. Otherwise, he was in the best of spirits, despite the lousy weather and the fact that he hadn't got anywhere with Charly. She had fobbed him off, but then, if she hadn't, he wouldn't have drained half a bottle of cognac, nor, most likely, would he have hit on the crackpot idea of raiding Lanke's office.

He parted his hair with a wet comb and gazed at his reflection in the bedroom mirror, liking what he saw, dressed in black with an elegant top hat set on his head at a slight angle. It lent him a touch of gravity that he didn't otherwise possess. Just a shame he could only dress like this on unhappy occasions.

Rath hated funerals, and police funerals above all. The last time he'd decked himself out like this was for his colleague Stephan Jänicke. He didn't know the policeman being laid to rest this morning, but Weiss had requested that senior CID officers attend to show that the death of a uniform cop mattered.

The caretaker was cleaning out a blocked drain, but paused when he saw his tenant approach dressed all in black, with a black dog and black umbrella, and tipped his cap by way of greeting. Rath responded by briefly raising his umbrella before entering the front building to ring the ground floor flat. Annemarie Lennartz looked surprised as she surveyed him from head to toe.

'I'm here to drop the dog off,' Rath said. 'I hope that's OK.'

The caretaker's wife gazed at Kirie's fur, which was still halfway dry. 'Of course,' she said, taking the lead. Kirie understood, and pitter-pattered into the flat as if it were her second home.

'Can I ask who died?'

'A colleague,' Rath replied.

'My condolences.'

'Not necessary. I didn't know the man.'

Rath said goodbye to Kirie, who had forgotten about him already, and went on his way.

Erika Voss gave him a nod of acknowledgement as he entered. 'Well, I never,' she said. 'If it wasn't such a sad occasion, I'd say you looked like a new man.'

'Thank you.' Rath almost hung the top hat on the stand out of habit, but then remembered that he was here to take Tornow to the funeral. The cadet was the only one heading out to Schönholz Cemetery with him; Gräf, Henning and Czerwinski were on duty.

'Where's our trainee got to?' he asked.

Erika Voss nodded towards the connecting door. 'He's in there. Herr Tornow had to take care of a telephone call.'

To Rath's great surprise on entering, he was confronted by a uniform cop: Tornow himself, reading a newspaper at Gräf's desk.

'What's going on?' Rath asked. 'I thought you'd left Uniform?'

Tornow folded the newspaper and stood up. There wasn't a single crease in his trousers; his buttons gleamed. The man was impeccable.

'When our colleague was murdered, I was still a cop,' he said, very solemnly. 'I think it's appropriate that I pay my final respects in uniform.'

Rath nodded and, all of a sudden he, too, was in funeral mode.

'Let's go, shall we,' he said, to break the embarrassed silence.

This time he had parked the Buick in the atrium. The rain hammered down on the enormous glass roof.

'Hopefully it'll pass,' Tornow said, and gestured skywards. The men got in.

'What lousy weather,' Rath said, switching on the windscreen wipers. 'Can I drive you back too?' The cemetery was out of town, in Pankow.

'Thank you, no,' Tornow said. 'That won't be necessary. I think I'd like to spend a little time with my ex-colleagues. If you don't mind . . .'

'Of course not. As long as Gräf can live with the fact that he'll have to write up your joint operation on his own. I don't need you today.'

'I've already spoken to Gräf.'

'Then that's settled. How did yesterday go?'

'Depends on how you look at it. A lot of work for not much result. Most likely Goldstein parked the ambulance where we found it and continued with the S-Bahn or tram. He could be anywhere.'

'Did no one see anything? Nothing from neighbours, workers at the freight depot?'

'Just one. A worker who says he was surprised that the ambulance driver wasn't wearing white, but didn't know which way Goldstein made his escape, or how.'

'He's brazen enough to have taken a taxi.'

'Gräf was going to check that today with the Taxi Drivers' Guild.'

'It's not much to go on. Even if he finds the taxi driver, it's unlikely he was dropped off outside the hotel door.'

'You think he's hiding out in some hotel?'

'There are enough flophouses in Berlin if you need to disappear.'

Tornow shrugged. 'Our witness did mention one other thing. Apparently Goldstein has a rip in his coat. A corner's missing.'

Rath nodded.

It took a long time for them to reach Pankow. The rain had stopped, but the sky was still grey. A few hundred metres from the main entrance, Rath applied the brakes. Outside the cemetery was chaos. Half of Berlin seemed to have arrived on foot—or bicycles—to pay their final respects, and it wasn't just police officers, but any number of private citizens. Perhaps there was hope after all. There were days when Rath thought this entire city was conspiring against the police, but today showed there were other people out there too.

He parked and the two men walked to the cemetery entrance. Tornow took his leave before they reached the gate. 'Thank you for the lift,' he said. 'But I have to be with my people now. One last time . . .'

Rath gazed after him as he mingled with the uniformed officers, greeting colleagues with a handshake. An unhappy occasion to don the uniform for the final time, he thought, and looked around. Cops were everywhere. Only when the hearse rolled into view did the crowd settle. Rows of blue uniforms led the cortège, marching behind Deputy Police Commissioner Weiss and Uniform Commander Heimannsberg. Weiss was dressed entirely in black, Heimannsberg in uniform like his men. A police orchestra played funeral music.

Rath joined the procession when the plainclothes officers began to pass, recognising his colleagues from A Division, among them Gennat and Böhm. A few metres ahead of the homicide investigators was the delegation from Vice, including the division chief himself, as well as several of his inspectors and chief inspectors. Werner Lanke shot Rath an angry glance over his shoulder; evidently Lanke junior had squealed about his recent visit.

It wasn't just police officers paying their final respects but a huge number of ordinary Berlin citizens; members of the Reichsbanner, the SPD's paramilitary wing, kept the flag of democracy flying, while the press had also sent its representatives. Emil Kuhfeld had been a Social Democrat and, increasingly, evidence indicated that a Nazi, rather than a Communist, had fired the fatal shot. This revelation made few headlines.

When the throng was gathered by the grave, Magnus Heimannsberg took the floor. The uniform commander wasn't much of an orator. Next up was Bernhard Weiss, who didn't need a megaphone to gain the crowd's attention. His light Berlin brogue could be heard everywhere, and he had no difficulty striking the right note. The pens of press representatives, which had been stationary during Heimannsberg's speech, suddenly began to take notes.

Weiss briefly mentioned events in Frankfurter Allee, before turning to the dead man. 'Emil Kuhfeld is not the only man to sacrifice his life in the performance of his duties,' he said. 'He is not the first. Nor, I fear, will he be the last. As we stand by his grave, we call upon our fellow countrymen to present a reasonable, decorous and humanitarian front that regards uniformed police officers as human beings, as opposed to fair game.'

Weiss had used similar words at Alex, in front of CID colleagues, but here, at the grave of the dead officer, they were a hundred times more powerful. All were moved, including those civilians present, and among mourners there was an unspoken feeling of togetherness. It didn't matter whether uniform cop, CID or ordinary citizen, all felt they were taking a stand against the violence and terror on the streets. Berlin was fed up with Communists and Nazis, and anyone else who confused politics with Wild West shoot-outs. The mood offered hope that Emil Kuhfeld might be the last police officer to be killed for political reasons for some time.

Perhaps, Rath thought, this city wasn't quite the hopeless case he had taken it for, since arriving in the spring of 1929.

82

The municipal hospital in Friedrichshain was almost like a small city, made up of impressive brick buildings on the edge of the Volkspark. Andreas Lange opened the door to Male Surgery where, a year and a half ago, SA-Führer Horst Wessel succumbed to gunshot wounds, and subsequently became a Nazi martyr.

With the aid of a porter, he found his room. A uniformed officer waited outside the door with a man in a white coat. Lange didn't have to show his identification, as the doctor and the police officer recognised him.

'Five minutes,' the doctor said, before opening the door. 'No excitement. The wound needs peace and quiet to heal.'

'Is the injury that bad?' Lange asked.

'The boy was astonishingly lucky not to damage his intestines.'

Lange went inside to find a burly young lad with a pale face lying on the bed. His pained expression didn't suit him. Lange pulled out his notebook and sat down.

'You wanted to make a statement, Herr Krahl?' he asked. The boy turned around.

'That's right, Officer.' The voice sounded strangely weak.

'Assistant detective. Assistant Detective Lange.'

'I hope you find that whore soon.'

'Let's start from the beginning. What is it you want to tell me?'

Lange pulled himself together. He was sitting at the bedside of a known petty criminal, who had been admitted to hospital with a serious slash wound. When someone like that was ready to make a statement, it was best to proceed with caution. The most pressing question was why someone who'd usually be loath to tell a police officer the time, should suddenly be so eager to talk.

'I'm here,' he began, 'because I have been informed by colleagues that your statement is linked to the KaDeWe break-in. I hope that is correct. I can be pretty nasty when people waste my time.'

'Alexandra Reinhold,' the boy said quickly. 'She's the one you're looking for. It was her in KaDeWe.'

'We know that already.'

'Do you know how dangerous she is, the little tramp?'

Krahl pulled back the covers and pointed to a heavy bandage they had wrapped him in like a mummy. There hadn't been quite enough material to go round.

'She cut me open, the bitch. I had to have stitches.'

Lange pricked up his ears. 'That was Alexandra Reinhold?'

Krahl nodded. 'She's dangerous. You need to be careful, you and your men.'

Lange wasn't inclined to believe someone so eager to get the police involved, but, when he remembered the wound on Jochen Kuschke's face, the boy's statement didn't seem quite so absurd. This Alex was a dangerous customer, and there was Charlotte Ritter making as if she had just gone off the rails. Was she even aware of the danger Alex posed?

'Where did you sustain these injuries?'

'I found her hideout. Some shitty little hovel on the grounds of the slaughterhouse. She cut me open. Without warning, just like that.'

'Because you found her hiding place? Nothing else happened?'

'What else could have happened, chief?'

'That's what I'm asking you.'

'Nothing.' Krahl looked innocent as a fawn. 'Left me lying in my own blood and disappeared.'

'Do you know where?'

The boy shrugged. 'She used to stay in the abandoned axle factory, in Roederstrasse, but not for a long time.' He made a face as if thinking— a mode of expression that was clearly unfamiliar to him. 'But,' he said, 'there was someone from Welfare or the courts helping her. You should sound her out. The Welfare Office shouldn't be shielding criminals, should it?'

Lange nodded. He could well imagine what this supposed welfare officer looked like, and he did, indeed, intend to sound her out.

83

Here she was again. Out of sheer boredom she had ordered a second breakfast, a bread roll with cheese, although she could have had it cheaper at Tietz, where Lange would have paid. She'd been here over an hour now, her third cup of tea and fourth newspaper in front of her, staring at the rain-soaked house front. The writing was still visible on the wall though Kuschke had made every effort to wipe it off, the rain also having played its part. It was still just about legible. REVENGE FOR BENNY S. Pig's blood, Alex had said. How fitting. It would probably need a new coat of paint, or three weeks' constant rain.

Let's be sensible here, Charly thought. The rain has only just stopped. What a dreadful summer! The weather had been better during the Kaiser's reign, or was she simply imagining it? When he abdicated she had just turned eleven; when, perhaps, all you remembered were the sunny days.

Right now, at any rate, it was pretty bleak outside, and Kuschke still hadn't put in an appearance. Why should he come out in this weather if he didn't have to? He was probably taking advantage of his leave to catch up on some sleep. Perhaps he hadn't even seen the papers?

If he had, would the latest development throw him into a panic? A police report saying a witness was being sought? Lange was gambling on Kuschke trying to find out who this witness was, so that police could collect a little more evidence. That was the theory. In practice all it had achieved was a great, fat nothing.

The CID appeal was carefully formulated. There was nothing to suggest a police officer was suspected of murder; it merely mentioned an *important witness* who might have observed the *fatal incident at Kaufhaus des Westens*, and whose description had been provided by another witness. Alongside was the sketch that nearly all papers had printed. Sadly, it really was a generic face. Were Lange's suspicions justified? Was it possible that this witness didn't actually exist, that Alex was leading them all on?

Charly didn't know what to make of the girl. On the one hand she trusted her; on the other, she sensed the deep mistrust Alex felt in return, in contrast to Vicky, who seemed to view Charly as a kind of maternal friend.

Yesterday evening, before she went to bed, Charly had been cautious enough to disarm the Bayard, removing the magazine as well as the rounds still in the chamber, and placing the cold pistol under her pillow. It was an excessive measure, as it turned out. The rounds hadn't been touched, and the two girls even made breakfast for her when she got up. 'A little thank you,' Vicky had said, with a shy smile. 'For everything.'

Alex said nothing at first, simply poured coffee, a strong brew that Gereon might have liked, but which Charly could barely drink. She complimented them on the jet-black sludge all the same. Finally, Alex spoke.

'We won't impose on you any longer. We'll find somewhere new.'

'You're not imposing. Stay a little longer if you like.'

Alex nodded, but didn't seem to take Charly's offer seriously. Whether it was the tail end of her mistrust or simply a desire to be independent again, Charly couldn't say. She'd have to wait and see. Either the girls would still be there tonight—or they wouldn't. She hoped they didn't get any silly ideas in their heads. The truth was, it was probably no bad thing for her to keep an eye on Kuschke, in case they had cooked up some plan.

Something was happening in the house opposite! The front door opened and Jochen Kuschke emerged. A little better dressed than yesterday, and he was clean shaven too. He had replaced the bandage on his face with a few, discreet, little plasters. The wound seemed to be healing well. In addition to a light-grey suit, he wore a broad-brimmed hat and carried an umbrella.

Excitedly, Charly folded the paper, almost spilling the pathetic little puddle of cold tea still in her cup, and stood up. She left money on the table again, before retrieving her umbrella and leaving the cafe.

'You should think about a tab,' the waitress called after her. 'Seeing as you're always in such a hurry.'

Charly didn't have time to react, because Kuschke was in a hurry too. He moved towards Winterfeldtplatz, using his umbrella as a walking stick. She followed him discreetly from the other side of the road, looking at the displays in the shop fronts whenever his pace slowed, but always keeping him in view. She was becoming a surveillance expert. Perhaps she should start her own agency.

Kuschke kept glancing at his wristwatch. Well now, Charly thought, perhaps we have jolted him into action. Who knows? Instinctively she checked for her pistol. Kuschke proceeded to the tram stop where a few people were waiting, or else Charly wouldn't have felt safe. She didn't think he'd seen her, but knew he had a fifteen-year-old boy on his conscience, and had opened fire on a girl in broad daylight. She studied the timetable while watching him out of the corner of her eye.

The tram rumbled into view, the 3, both cars full to bursting. Kuschke climbed into the first and Charly sprang onto the rear platform.

The tram rattled along, north past Nollendorfplatz and Herkulesbrücke and on through Tiergarten. The rain had stopped; perhaps Kuschke was out for a stroll? But he didn't get out until Hansaplatz, when they had already left the green of the Tiergarten behind. What was he doing in an up-market neighbourhood like this? Did their mysterious, bespectacled witness live here somewhere, and Kuschke had discovered his address?

Charly stepped from the platform and pretended to cast her eye over the timetable at the tram stop, playing the country girl while keeping Kuschke in view. Moving down Lessingstrasse, he was heading for the church, the same Kaiser-Friedrich-Gedächtniskirche on the corner of the Tiergarten that she remembered from Sunday outings with her parents and brothers. On the way back they had always stopped at Buchwald on Moabiter Bridge, for *Kaffee und Kuchen*, cocoa for the children, before returning home. She had loved those family Sundays, at least for a time.

She followed Kuschke at a distance. There wasn't much going on around them, so she had to take care that he didn't spot her. She fell back a little. Before the church he turned right onto Händelstrasse. She accelerated again. Lessingstrasse appeared infinitely long, and she hoped that Kuschke wouldn't vanish before she turned the corner. The houses on Händelstrasse were beautiful, offering an uninterrupted view of the park. Accordingly, they were much in demand: her father had always dreamed of owning one, but had never made it out of Moabit.

She had almost reached the end of Lessingstrasse when a uniformed policeman came around the corner and, for a moment, she felt as if she had been caught out, even though she wasn't doing anything illegal. The cop folded a handkerchief and stowed it in his pocket. By now she had reached Händelstrasse.

She peered around the corner and almost jumped back, so great was the shock. Kuschke hadn't vanished into one of the houses, or the Charlotten-hof, the outdoor restaurant at the edge of the park, whose outside tables were currently rainsoaked and uninviting. No, he stood not ten metres away, leaning against a streetlamp as if needing to take a quick breather.

Luckily he had his back turned and hadn't seen her. It didn't look like there was anyone else around. She positioned herself behind the advertising pillar on the corner. As she squinted to the side to keep Kuschke in view, she stole a glance at the posters. *The Marriage of Figaro* at the Kroll Opera House—hadn't it been closed in the meantime? She realised she was nervous, waiting for Kuschke to continue walking. He stood, not moving, one hand on the streetlamp and the other holding his stomach. What was wrong? Did he have a sore tummy?

Next to the opera poster was a police appeal from the Castle. WANTED. ABRAHAM GOLDSTEIN. Gereon's fugitive gangster.

She grew more nervous. What was wrong with Kuschke? Should she overtake him, but then what? Use the trick with the make-up mirror? What if it was a trap? What if he was just waiting for her to do that—because he'd already recognised her?

Only now did she realise what it was that so puzzled her: the umbrella. It lay by his feet, and he was making no effort to pick it up.

She decided to abandon her cover and approach him when his bulky figure lurched so suddenly it was as if a puppet's strings had been cut. He slid down the streetlight and sank to his knees as if in prayer.

She moved as quickly as she could, heard Benjamin Singer's alleged killer panting, his breathing heavy and frantic, but it was only when she reached him, when she saw his horrified eyes framed between the brim of his hat and the fresh plasters, and his blood-soaked shirt, that she realised what had happened.

She couldn't understand it, but neither could Kuschke who stared at his blood-smeared hand in disbelief, at the butt of the knife jutting out of his breast, then at her, at Charly. She knew he was a killer, possibly even a sadist, but his dying man's gaze cut her to the quick. His breathing grew faster so that it seemed as if the air were being pumped out rather than into his lungs. He tried to say something but couldn't, and then, before she could catch him, he collapsed to the side, striking his head against the pavement.

84

Back at the Castle things were no more than getting by. Half the officers were either still at the cemetery or out eating lunch. Rath was glad to have disappeared after Kuhfeld's coffin was lowered into the ground, having slipped away as the police orchestra was still playing, before Böhm could get his hands on him. He had returned to Alex in the Buick.

Vice was almost as deserted as last night. The clattering of a typewriter came from a single room, a lone secretary at work. All was quiet behind the door leading to DCI Krüger's office, where Lanke had his desk. If Rath was unlucky he would still be in the canteen; if not, he could give the porn lover a good, old-fashioned fright. He reached carefully for the handle, took a deep breath and threw the door open with a jolt, using his full force.

'Well, hello!' he yelled into the room, as brazen as Werner Lanke himself. He was in luck.

Gregor Lanke gave a start. This time he didn't have a chance to clear the photos off his desk but gazed back red-faced, as if his heart had skipped a beat. Another organ was beating in its place, visible in the bulge of his trousers.

'Have you gone mad, startling people like that?' Lanke junior groaned. His erection shrunk in record time.

'What have you got there?' Rath leaned over the desk to get a better view. The picture on top showed Old Fritz engaged in oral sex. Rath confiscated it before Lanke could react. 'They're over two years old, those ones. I didn't know you were still working on the case?'

'I . . . we,' Lanke stammered.

'I don't mean to boast, but we were a bit quicker in my time.'

'What the hell are you up to, damn it?' Lanke counterattacked.

'You're a CID officer, man. Have you no self-respect?'

'That's none of your fucking business. What do you want from me?'

Rath threw one of the photos he had taken from Lanke's desk last night onto the table: a strapping young lady, naked and on all fours, behind her a man toiling single-mindedly away with one hand on her arse cheek and in the other a modern 35mm camera, perhaps a present from Uncle Werner. In the mirrored wardrobe doors, it was possible to make out not just the bored face of Marion Bosetzky, but also that of the photographer.

Gregor Lanke gazed at his own likeness.

'I take it these aren't your new passport photos,' Rath said.

For the second time that day, it took the detective a moment to rediscover his voice. 'Where did you get that,' he gasped. 'Have you been . . . ?'

'This isn't about me,' Rath interrupted. 'It's about you. You've been having sex with a prostitute who's also on the E Division payroll. Illicit sexual relations with dependants, you could call it. Not that it matters if it constitutes a criminal offence, nor, indeed, what it's called. It's enough, I think, for the press to be aware of the sense of duty you evince in your dealings with prostitutes. This sort of field study would certainly have been unusual during my time with the department.' Rath paused, enjoying Gregor Lanke's face. 'Knowing your uncle as I do, I wouldn't want to be in your shoes if this gets out.'

'What do you want?'

'I think you already know. I'd like to hear a little more about the young lady you are evidently so fond of. I take it you have your own lab at home, or someone who develops these dirty little snaps for you?'

Lanke said nothing.

'Where's Marion Bosetzky?' Rath asked, his tone so sharp that Lanke started.

'I don't know where she is. It's as if she's vanished from the face of the earth since the weekend.'

'How did she end up working in that hotel?'

'How do you think? She applied for the job, simple as that, or are you one of those who thinks: once a whore, always a whore.'

'I see. You're helping a fallen woman reintegrate into society. Who's going to believe that?'

Lanke squinted at the door, as if hoping his colleagues would soon return from the funeral, or, even better, his uncle Werner, to bring this highly embarrassing line of questioning to an end. No one came.

Rath held the photo under Lanke's nose. 'Now, answer me, so that I don't have to use my contacts in the press. Why did you smuggle Marion Bosetzky into the Excelsior? Did you allow for the fact that she would help Goldstein escape, or was that an occupational hazard?'

Lanke was sweating. He seemed to find it hard to come out with the truth. 'Occupational hazard,' he said, finally. 'We wanted to keep an eye on Goldstein. So that we . . .'

'Who is we?'

'Myself and a few colleagues,' Lanke said at last. 'We heard about the Yank—one of us knows the lady from the teleprinter's office that received the news. We wanted to catch him doing something red-handed and take the credit.' He looked up at Rath like a wounded deer. 'Do you think it's easy to get promoted when you're the division chief's nephew? Not with this commissioner, anyway.'

'Don't make me cry. The officers you arranged this with, are they similar poor souls who have been hit by the moratorium?'

'Make as much fun as you like. It's how it is.'

'Give me names.'

'I can't do that.'

Rath waved the photograph.

Lanke shook his head. 'I can't! It's all gone south anyway. What do you want the names of the others for? I won't snitch on my fellow officers. I'll take the fall for this.' He adopted the expression of a man of honour or, at least, his interpretation thereof.

Rath left it there for the time being. Young Lanke had deviated from the straight and narrow, launching investigations of his own so that he could climb a few steps on the career ladder . . . It was familiar enough to Rath, but he'd never have thought the apathetic Lanke capable of such ambition. Perhaps he had been talked into it by one of his more zealous colleagues who knew about Goldstein and needed Lanke's informant to keep an eye on him. It hadn't worked, and if anyone was to be brought to account for Goldstein's disappearance, Rath swore it would be Lanke junior's head on the block. For now though, he would watch how things developed. As long as he feared exposure, Lanke could still prove useful.

Which was why Rath issued a little threat by way of goodbye.

'If I should discover that you do know where Marion is, I promise the big city press will do such a job on you that your uncle will have to return to the beat with you.'

'Believe me,' Lanke said. 'I really don't know.'

Rath left the office after giving a sinister final look, but in the corridor had to suppress a smile. He left Vice in the best of spirits and started towards Homicide. His expression didn't match his mourning suit, but it didn't matter. The funeral was over.

The door to Homicide opened and Assistant Detective Lange emerged. Rath gave a polite greeting, and the man from Hannover said 'hello' in return. He was another Rath would have liked in his team in exchange for Czerwinski. Behind Lange, another face appeared in the door. Rath's smile froze.

'Cha . . . Fräulein Ritter!' He gave a slight cough. 'What are you doing here? After such a long time.'

Charly looked even more startled than him, although she must have guessed this might happen. It was his workplace after all. Perhaps it was the mourning suit and unfamiliar top hat that made her look at him the way she did.

'Good day, Inspector,' she said, smiling. 'Nice to see you again.'

She was quickly back under control. Her strength of nerve really was a thing of wonder. Rath felt a tingling sensation, triggered by her last sentence. Perhaps it was because he'd have liked nothing more than to touch her, but couldn't, not here at the Castle in the presence of colleagues. He gazed at her face and knew that the sentence wasn't intended to sound erotic. When he looked closer, he saw that she was actually upset. Something must have happened.

Hopefully it wasn't Alex. Money gone. Jewellery gone. Alex gone. Something like that. Perhaps it was a good thing she still didn't have her ring.

He realised that Lange was looking at him expectantly, while Charly gazed at him in confusion. They were waiting for him to say something. Rath gestured towards his top hat and black suit. 'Just back from a funeral, didn't have any time to change,' he said, and continued on his way. When he reached the door to his office he turned around again. Charly had disappeared with Lange into one of the interview rooms.

What on earth was going on?

85

The man gazed up at Charly, just as indifferently from under his shako as all the others. 'No, it's not him either.' The man disappeared, and another took his place.

She shook her head.

Lange leafed patiently through the photographs and placed the next image before her. Another unidentified shako-wearer.

'How many police lieutenants are there in Berlin?' she asked, having shaken her head for the umpteenth time.

'We'll be finished in a moment.' Lange attempted a smile. 'At least with Tiergarten and Moabit.'

She had been sitting in this interview room for an hour, poring over images. Not the police mugshots that witnesses were shown, but the personal files of uniform cops.

'Are you certain it's a cop you saw?' Lange asked.

'I didn't imagine him. He was there, and he emerged from the street where Kuschke was killed. He must have seen something. If not the murder itself, then the murderer.'

'But you didn't realise straightaway. That Kuschke had a knife in his stomach, I mean. He didn't cry out or behave suspiciously in any way. Why shouldn't it be the same for this officer?'

'I only saw Kuschke from behind, and was so busy making sure I wouldn't be spotted that I noticed everything else far too late.'

'You're implying that this officer must have seen everything you missed . . .'

'I don't know,' she said, and let her shoulders droop. 'It's just that . . . sometimes I get the impression you don't believe me, and I can't stand it. At least, not right now.'

'Well, you're just going to have to,' Lange said, his voice sounding strangely cold. '*Right now* I don't know that I can believe you.'

'Pardon me?'

Lange stood and leaned with both hands on the desk. 'Does this police officer actually exist, or did you invent him to distract from your protégé, and keep me occupied?'

Charly's blood ran hot through her veins. The kind, harmless-seeming Andreas Lange had grown unexpectedly aggressive, and she pitied the men he grilled in these rooms. The stupid thing was, she was the one now being grilled.

'I haven't invented anything. I thought we were working together.'

'That's what I thought too. Why didn't you tell me what happened at the slaughterhouse?'

'I didn't think it was relevant to our case.'

'A person was seriously injured, evidently by Alexandra Reinhold, and you conceal it from me! How much further are you prepared to go to protect her?'

'She didn't injure anyone!' Charly shouted back. 'I wanted to gain her trust, that's why I didn't call the police. I made sure that the injured party received medical attention.'

'Why didn't you tell me anything?'

'Because it would have been a breach of trust!'

'What about my trust? Superintendent Gennat's trust?'

'She was raped, for God's sake! Do you have any idea how hard it is for a girl to talk about that? In front of a police officer into the bargain?'

'I'm sorry, I didn't know.' Lange lowered his voice again.

'That bastard, who is, clearly, now trying to sell her out, raped her; him and his whole crew. Someone else slashed his stomach. Defending her.'

'Did you see it?'

'No.'

'What's his name then, this knight in shining armour?'

'I'm not going to tell you.' She was furious. 'Sometimes I wonder who it is we're protecting in this country. Criminals, or those who show civic courage.'

'You call cutting someone's stomach civic courage?'

'The way you're behaving confirms that I was right not to tell you anything.'

'You made a mistake and don't want to admit it. You should have let us arrest the little brat.'

'So Alex would be at the mercy of Kuschke and his accomplices?'

'Right now it looks like Kuschke was the one at the mercy of Alex and *her* accomplices!'

'You don't really believe that?'

'I know she injured him pretty badly, perhaps even slashed a boy's abdominal wall.'

'She didn't do that.'

'You didn't see anything, remember.' Lange gazed at her with a look she couldn't bear. 'Anyway,' he continued, 'perhaps Alex enjoyed cutting the boy up so much that she wanted to do the same to Kuschke, only her knife slipped.'

'That's speculation.'

'There's a lot more evidence for it than for your mysterious police lieutenant, of whom there isn't a trace in the files.'

'Have you considered that it might not even have been a police officer, but Kuschke's killer? Someone dressed in uniform to get closer to Kuschke without drawing suspicion. To make it easier to flee the crime scene. Now that I remember, the man stowed a handkerchief in his pocket, with red spots on it. If he'd been a civilian I might have thought it was strange, but not a uniform cop.'

Lange waved her away. 'I don't want to hear any more of your theories. Bring this Alex in now, whether it suits you or not. The girl's a murder suspect. It's time you thought about that.'

Charly already had, which was why, after she notified Lange and he finally appeared at the scene, she had returned on foot to her flat, which was no more than fifteen minutes away. In theory it was to change her blood-smeared blouse, but it also allowed her to see whether Alex and Vicky were still there.

They weren't.

She had been expecting as much, and didn't know whether it spoke in the girls' favour or not. More than anything, she'd have liked to ask them directly whether they had anything to do with Kuschke's death, but that was no longer possible.

After changing her blouse she headed to Lange's office at the Castle where, inevitably, she ran into Gereon. She still didn't know how much she could tell him. He had seen Alex at her flat and most likely drawn his own conclusions. Hopefully he had kept his mouth shut. She had so much on her mind . . . but couldn't tell him a thing.

'I think we're done,' Lange said, packing away the personal files. 'Have you anything to add?'

Charly shrugged. 'Such as?'

'Such as where we might find Alexandra Reinhold.'

'I wouldn't be sitting here if I knew. You can count on that.'

86

They were coming out again, casket-bearers at the front. Jakob Goldstein lay in a simple, unadorned coffin carefully shouldered by the men. Next came the family, and Abe instinctively withdrew a little when he saw his black-bearded cousin, lowering his head and turning slightly away. He hadn't gone into the synagogue, which in any case was full. His grandfather must have been a popular figure in the community.

They stood on a large burial ground, next to the synagogue. Waiting among the crowd for the formalities to end, Abe looked at a simple, stone monument, and read the inscription carved into the white stone. TO OUR FALLEN SONS. THE JEWISH COMMUNITY OF BERLIN. The war had left its mark everywhere. He remembered how badly his parents had been treated, above all by the Irish and the Yankees, before the United States entered the conflict. All because they spoke Yiddish and the Paddys couldn't differentiate between the two languages, so had lumped them together with the Germans.

The trees at the Weissensee Cemetery stood close together, but Abe had resisted the impulse to seek refuge there. Lurking behind tree stems or bushes, sooner or later he'd have been spotted by someone; the crowd was a better hiding place, even now as the cortège resumed its procession. He remained at a distance, far away from the family, among men of his own age. There weren't many long-bearded caftan wearers here. Aunt Lea's family were in the minority.

Again and again, the procession came to a halt. Abe didn't like this Jewish custom, which was supposed to symbolise the mourners' reluctance to approach the grave. A specialist in quick goodbyes, he hated anything that dragged out the mourning process.

After what felt like an age the procession reached the grave dug for Jakob Goldstein. His grandfather would have approved, Abe thought. The plot was a little off the beaten track, away from the main road and in the shade of a wall. The eulogy was brief, which would have pleased his grand-father too. The cantor began a psalm as the coffin was lowered into the ground.

The family was the first by the graveside, each member throwing three handfuls of earth over the coffin. Abe recognised his aunts and their fami-lies from the hospital, all with a tear in their collar as a symbol of mourn-ing. Abe hated this custom too. He had refused to wear one at his mother's funeral, likewise his father's, which he had disrupted more than attended. Around a dozen men approached the open grave, among them his black-hat cousin. Abe knew what was coming and prepared himself. While the men were still grouping around the grave, he stepped to one side, behind one of the big family plots in the shade of the trees. He didn't want any onlookers to see him. He positioned himself so that he kept the men stand-ing by his grandfather's grave directly in view, and when they began their age old prayer, passed down the centuries, he prayed quietly along too.

The Hebrew and Aramaic words came so easily to his lips it was as if he had learned them yesterday, rather than twenty years before. Abe mouthed the words quietly so as not to attract attention, but loud enough for God, if he existed, to hear. His grandfather too, should his soul be journeying from one world to the next.

He had fulfilled both of the old man's dying wishes.

While the family accepted condolences, Abe noticed two men who didn't seem to belong. The mourners, perhaps recognising them as Goyim, gazed curiously in their direction, but Abe knew they were cops. They hadn't sent Detective Rath, probably so that Abe didn't notice them straightaway, but it had backfired. It was the cops who hadn't spotted *him*. His black mourning suit meant he was indistinguishable from the group and, since the majority of those present kept their heads bowed, they hadn't seen his face under the brim of his hat either. Thus far, the pair hadn't attracted too much attention, but as the funeral drew to a close they sprung awake, and set off in front of the mourners. Abe knew not to underestimate them.

As the procession started back he kept himself as far as possible from the family. The funeral complex had an additional chapel and further out-buildings. The detectives took up position in the portico leading out of the cemetery, closely monitoring everyone who exited the grounds.

Abe dropped into the throng to gain a little time. He couldn't leave, not now. Even if the pair hadn't seen him, they would recognise him as he passed, thanks to that blasted sketch.

He took up position in front of the basins where mourners washed their hands before leaving the cemetery. While he awaited his turn, squinting at the portico out of the corner of his eye, he had a sudden flash of inspiration.

He wasn't the only guest to make for the toilets, but he found a free cubicle all the same. He bolted the door, sat on the seat and waited. He would have to be patient, but that was OK. Initially, there was still a great hullabaloo, but gradually the noise died, until the only sound was the echo of water dripping on the tiles.

Abe remained where he was for a moment, to ensure the detectives had taken their leave. And what if they hadn't? He felt for the Remington in his jacket. He shouldn't have brought it here, but knew his grandfather, if he were watching, would understand.

When he had listened to the water dripping for at least fifteen minutes—it felt like hours—he stood up. He hoped he wouldn't have to shoot his way out, but wouldn't hesitate if the situation demanded. His legs had gone to sleep. He waited until he felt them return to life, opened the door and stepped out.

Everything went smoothly until he entered the washroom and almost jumped out of his skin. He hadn't heard him come in; he must have been stealthy as a ghost.

The man with the black beard and black hat gazed at him in surprise, more curious than hostile, just like a few days ago on the street outside the hospital. He didn't say anything, but Abe could see from his eyes that Joseph Flegenheimer knew exactly who stood before him.

87

'Please excuse the late interruption . . .' The caretaker stood outside Charly's door wasn't being sincere. He would have called again later, if necessary. 'Many apologies,' he said, 'but I've tried a few times this week and no one's been home.'

'That's fine, Herr Maltritz,' she smiled. 'It's not your fault I'm out so often.'

'My apologies.'

'You're only doing your job. Someone has to collect the rent.'

'If you would be so kind, then. Twelve fifty, please. Your receipt is ready as always.'

'Just a moment.'

She disappeared inside the flat, not having so much as thought about the rent, which was due on Mondays. Normally she had the money counted out beforehand, to keep the weekly process as brief as possible, but, what with this week's chaos, she hadn't thought of such trivial details as the rent. On Monday she had accepted Lange and Gennat's special assignment, said yes to Heymann and met with Gereon. Life hadn't been any less busy since.

In the kitchen she opened the crockery cupboard, freezing as she looked inside the earthenware pot. It was empty.

For a moment she considered frantically what she could have done with the money, but soon realised what had happened, and who had stolen it. To think, she had trusted the girls, and all because they hadn't pilfered her gun. Alex must have taken the money while she was making coffee at breakfast, as Charly naively praised the undrinkable sludge. One hundred and twenty marks! Rent and housekeeping—everything she had set aside for the coming weeks. She had been planning to go shopping tomorrow, buy a guidebook for Paris, as well as a dictionary to brush up on her rusty French.

Alex, you rat!

She went back to the door. 'This is very embarrassing, Herr Maltritz,' she said, 'but I completely forgot I wasn't at the court today. I won't get my paycheck until Monday now. If you could possibly wait until then.'

Hans Maltritz didn't look pleased—he was already a little dubious about two women sharing a flat—but he put a brave face on it. 'Fine,' he said, 'I'll turn a blind eye this time. Because it's you. But I need the money on Monday, otherwise I'll have to charge interest. Backdated!'

'Of course.' Charly gave a winning smile. It helped. Maltritz tipped his hat and bid her good night. On the steps he turned around again. 'Monday,' he said, and Charly nodded, smiling at him all the way down the stairs.

Damn it, she thought, as she closed the door. Damn it!

One thing was for sure: Alexandra Reinhold was a cunning little minx. Charly had been deceived. What a fine judge of character you are, Fräulein Ritter. Gereon had been absolutely right; Andreas Lange too.

88

It was a grey morning, even though the sun had risen much earlier, and a thick layer of cloud hovered over the city, threatening rain. The Mühlendamm was humming with activity, with five ships waiting at the locks. The lockmaster chewed on a second breakfast of bread and dripping as he opened the sluice gates for a barge loaded with scrap metal. Since he needed both hands for the job, he held his breakfast sandwich between his teeth. Gradually the vessel moved inside the lock chamber. Four men stood on board and kept the lock wall at a distance with long wooden poles, ensuring the vessel didn't scrape against the algae. Two of them manned the ropes, mooring the barge in the lock chamber while the lockmaster cranked the wheel to shut the gate.

The lockmaster finished his sandwich, and the iron sluice gates closed more quickly than they had opened until, all of a sudden, they stopped moving altogether. Something was snagged against the gate. Hopefully it wasn't a piece of scrap metal from the barge. Whatever it was, it resisted.

'Damn it,' the lockmaster cursed, cranking the wheel back. Opening the gate just a little usually helped. The things that floated down this way! They had found all sorts: oil drums, a rusty bedstead, a traffic light, the frame of a pram, even a half-decomposed cow. Everything got caught here, at the Mühlendamm, and with some items it was impossible to say how they wound up in the Spree at all. He had no idea what it was this time, only that the river needed cleaning again soon.

Cranking the wheel back seemed to help. Whatever was caught underwater detached itself, and the sluice gate moved with a gurgling squeak.

'There's something in there,' shouted one of the men on the barge, leaning on his staff. The gate was by now almost closed again. The lockmaster gazed into the water, and saw something glimmer just beneath the surface. The optical refraction made it look as though it had been steamrolled. If the lockmaster had known what it was, he probably wouldn't have looked so closely, but he didn't realise until he saw the eyes staring back at him out of a face so pale and swollen it no longer looked human. But human it was, the skin waxy and green with algae, hair swaying like seaweed. There was a deep, but bloodless—and therefore all the more hideous—wound on the man's face, which exposed half his teeth and made it look as though he were snarling. He was staring at a corpse.

His knees grew weak, and he felt his stomach turn. He sank to the floor, retched once, and threw up both first and second breakfasts in the dirty black water of the lock chamber. It was six forty-five on Thursday morning.

89

The atmosphere was eerily reminiscent of the week before. Again Bernhard Weiss stood on the podium, and again the deputy commissioner made a serious face. Another uniform cop had been killed, in the Hansaviertel this time but not, this time, in the line of duty. He had been stabbed to death while on leave of absence.

'The circumstances remain a mystery,' Weiss said. 'It seems unlikely to have been politically motivated, although we cannot rule that out. It appears that, on this occasion, it wasn't the police uniform that was targeted, but the man himself. Jochen Kuschke.'

Tornow swallowed. 'Damn it, that's one of my colleagues from Wittenbergplatz.'

This was confirmed moments later when Ernst Gennat replaced Weiss on the podium. Buddha explained that underworld involvement couldn't be ruled out, since Sergeant Major Kuschke had taken part in the KaDeWe operation two weeks before—the same operation which had famously resulted in the death of one of the young intruders.

'It is possible,' he continued, 'that it was an accomplice of the dead intruder, or indeed the mastermind behind the robbery, taking bloody revenge.'

Damn it, Rath thought. Was Charly's Alex a murderer too, on top of everything else? He hadn't breathed a word about her yesterday evening, and Charly hadn't mentioned anything either, but keeping quiet was no longer an option. What the hell was going on? Was she so up to her neck that she was covering for a murderer?

'We are pursuing all lines of enquiry,' Gennat said. 'Since this case is now our priority, we will be reassigning certain members of the homicide team.'

It was unusual for Buddha to lead an investigation himself. Looking around, Rath could see that even the department's old hands were nervous.

They wanted to be in the team. Rath, too, felt restless. You could always learn something from Gennat and, apart from anything else, it was good for your standing. He would even be willing to partner Wilhelm Böhm, the first name called. Next up were Grabowski and Mertens, followed by several assistant detectives he didn't know. Rath came away empty-handed, and Gräf didn't make the cut either. Plisch and Plum weren't even in the room. No sooner had Buddha assembled his team than they learned why.

'A corpse was fished out of the water at the Mühlendamm early this morning,' Gennat said. 'I've given it to Henning and Czerwinski.'

Gennat had now reassigned most of the officers working on the Kubicki case, leaving just Rath, Gräf and Tornow. Most likely he felt that Rath and Gräf still had to make good on their error at the hotel, as Abraham Goldstein remained the prime suspect for the SA man's death. At least with Tornow they'd have an additional colleague—unless, of course, he was being returned to Warrants? But no, Gennat had explicitly requested that Rath, Gräf and Tornow attend a subsequent briefing.

Once there, Böhm handed them the Kubicki documents, which already filled two heavy lever arch files. 'I almost filled one myself,' Gräf said, with a sour smile. 'Pages of useless statements, made by so-called witnesses.'

'At least we know what we don't have to read,' Rath said, wondering whether the old Jew had returned to repeat his statement. It didn't sound like it. He gave the first file to Gräf, the second to Tornow, and was just about to leave when Böhm waved a third in his face.

'This is for you too,' he said. Rath gazed at it curiously. 'Looks like there's a second corpse linked to this case. Rudi the Rat mean anything to you?'

'From the Nordpiraten?'

'Correct. They found a corpse a few days ago at the dump, out at Schöneiche. Kronberg has identified him. Bullets to the head and chest. Same weapon as Kubicki, apparently.'

'Damn it,' Gräf said. 'Do the Nordpiraten know?'

'Not yet.' Böhm looked suspiciously at Rath. 'My advice would be to find Goldstein before the Nordpiraten get to him first.'

Rath glared at the file. It looked almost as if Böhm's men were trying to get rid of anything that had to do with the case.

'I have what might be a lead,' said Grabowski. 'I've discovered where Goldstein bought his cigarettes. The tobacconist recognised him from the sketch. He says a man fitting Goldstein's description bought a large quantity of American cigarettes from him at Stettiner Bahnhof on Sunday morning: Camel.'

Rath looked inside the file at a long list of addresses. It looked like a hotel directory of Greater Berlin. 'What's this?'

'All hotels within a kilometre radius,' Grabowski said. 'They're sorted according to distance rather than price category. He might be lying low somewhere. There are a lot of flophouses in that part of town.'

That part of town was the Poetenviertel, near Stettiner Bahnhof, but the only thing poetic about it were the street names, named after Germany's great Romantics. Otherwise, the area was devoid of both poetry and romance. It was a railway district: dilapidated house fronts, dim rear courtyards, dive hotels, prostitution, drugs, the whole shebang. It was also Nordpiraten turf.

Barely an hour later, Rath was forced to park outside the newly completed yellow-brick commuter line station that looked like a miniature version of Stettiner Bahnhof, but was treated like its inferior cousin. There was a great to-do by the main station as tanned holiday makers encountered pale city dwellers desperate to escape the rainy summer. He had requested an Opel from the motor pool, as the Buick was too small for three people and he didn't want to consign Gräf to desk duty.

Before they got out of the car, he distributed the lists, having asked Erika Voss to sort the addresses according to location. Most of the hotels were to the south of Stettiner Bahnhof. Rath took those in the southwest, while Gräf handled those in the southeast. Tornow took everything north of Invalidenstrasse. Thanks to Grabowski they had more than enough to get on with.

'Right, men,' Rath said. 'We'll meet at the station restaurant at one. If either of you find Goldstein, place him under arrest and notify the nearest precinct. Even if it's before lunchtime.'

The men fanned out and Rath gazed with envy at the tanned Baltic Sea holidaymakers streaming out of the station. Was the weather on Rügen so much better than in Berlin? It certainly looked that way. What it would be to go on holiday with Charly now, and reprise their miserable summer. Perhaps he'd visit her in Paris in the autumn, when there was less going on in the Castle and they could take time in lieu. He wondered where she was now and hoped her fugitive girl hadn't had anything to do with this latest police murder.

Tornow had been quiet all morning; you could see from his face that the cop's death affected him. Perhaps he had been a friend. Rath hadn't wanted to ask, but sensed that Tornow would rather be part of Gennat's investigation than searching for some Jewish gangster.

Which was probably exactly why Gennat hadn't picked him.

Rath hoped the work would help take his mind off things. Anything was better than sitting crouched in their office. He glanced at the list. The first hotel was in Eichendorffstrasse.

90

The flat was furnished and looked as though it been cleaned the day before. It was tidy enough, but lacked anything that made a place homely. Clearly, a bachelor lived here. There were no pictures or plants, and it appeared that the only woman the flat had ever seen was the landlady. Right now she was making no move to leave, regarding Lange with suspicion as he opened the wardrobe containing Jochen Kuschke's uniform. The shako lay on top of the wardrobe.

She stood directly behind Lange, and Charly could see that she was making him nervous. Finally he lost patience.

'Frau Stock,' he said, planting himself in front of her.

'It's Fräulein. I'm not married.'

'Fräulein Stock, you must have washing to take care of, or carpets to beat? We don't want to keep you.'

Fräulein Stock only needed a moment to understand. She didn't like to go, but went all the same.

A few minutes later she could be heard beating carpets in the courtyard. Either it was pure coincidence, or the landlady's Royal-Prussian spirit was so dominant that she interpreted Lange's suggestion as a command. Charly opened the top drawer of the desk and looked across at Lange, who returned her gaze with a grin.

She had accompanied him at her own request. It was agreed that, afterwards, she should stay away from the Castle. 'If there's anything you can do for us, Charly,' Gennat had said, 'we'll be in touch.' Buddha had tried to make her feel as though she were needed, but Charly sensed that they had pushed things too far, and he was keeping her at a distance. If she appeared too often in Homicide, people might ask questions.

One person above all, Charly thought.

She still hadn't told Gereon anything. Although he had seen Alex in Spenerstrasse, and most likely drawn his own conclusions, he had said nothing, leaving it to her to come clean. She hadn't, and the secrecy Gennat and Lange had sworn her to was beginning to cause problems. On the one hand, she was happy Gereon hadn't probed, and thus spared them an awkward situation. On the other, her silence had begun to feel sordid. He didn't approve of her taking the girl in, but if only he knew the full story . . .

How much longer would she be able to remain silent? She was doing exactly what she always reproached him for, being cagey about work while serving her own ends. Admittedly, it was with Superintendent Gennat's backing, but did that really make a difference?

She leafed through the papers she found in the drawers. Nothing. She couldn't help thinking someone had already been through them. The mess here wasn't natural, an existing order had been destroyed.

A few books were turned upside down. If you looked closely there were signs that a search had been conducted. The flat's spotless appearance couldn't change that. Lange seemed to think likewise. He opened the window, called the landlady's name and, two minutes later, she was back in her tenant's flat with a look that said: You see! I knew you couldn't manage!

'Please excuse me for interrupting your work, Frau . . . Fräulein Stock.' Elfriede Stock's expression softened. 'We have another question for you: was anyone in the flat after Herr Kuschke left on Wednesday afternoon?'

'I was. To clean, this morning.'

'I mean anyone else.'

'Your colleague, but I'm sure you already know about him . . .'

'What colleague?'

'It was one of Herr Kuschke's colleagues, to be exact. A man in uniform.'

Charly could see that Lange was excited, but managing to keep himself under control. 'When was this?' he asked.

'Yesterday, late afternoon.'

'What did he want?'

'Just to pick up a few things. Herr Kuschke was about to go away, he said, and had asked him to collect his suitcase.'

'Did he really just collect his suitcase? He didn't take a look around the flat?'

'I don't know. I was making coffee next door.'

'You were making coffee?'

'The officer was so kind. I thought maybe he'd like a cup, but he didn't have time.'

'You just let him into the flat like that?'

'He was a police officer, not just anyone. I don't let in all comers, you know!' She sounded indignant.

'Of course not.' Lange remained amicable. 'The fact remains that you don't know exactly what this officer did in the flat.'

'He collected Kuschke's suitcase, at any rate. I saw it. He had it under his arm when he knocked on the kitchen door to say goodbye. Said thank you too.'

'Do you know what was inside the case?'

'Whatever you take on a trip, I suppose. A few shirts, trousers, underwear, socks, toothbrush and so on.'

'How can you be sure?'

'I didn't say I was sure. It's just what I imagine.'

'You said you cleaned here, didn't you?'

She nodded. 'And changed the sheets. Since I thought he was on holiday.' She seemed to remember that the man was dead and fell silent.

'Did you notice anything suspicious? What about Kuschke's toothbrush?'

The landlady hesitated. 'It's still in the glass.'

'Could it be that this police officer wasn't here to collect a suitcase, but to look for something?'

'Like what?'

'Perhaps Herr Kuschke mentioned something.'

Elfriede Stock pressed her lips together. She was holding something back.

'Fräulein Stock,' Charly said. 'Is there anywhere he might have hidden something?'

The landlady shook her head vigorously. 'No, no. He didn't *hide* anything here.' She smiled mischievously and gazed across at Lange. 'He did ask me to look after something though. Shortly after he moved in.' Lange and Charly looked at each other. 'I really don't know if I can give it to you,' she continued. 'He expressly said that I shouldn't give it to anyone, above all the police.'

'Taking a promise like that seriously does you credit,' Lange said, 'but I think the change in circumstances frees you from your obligation. Sergeant Major Kuschke is dead, and we're investigating a murder. He'd have wanted us to have anything that helped find his killer.'

Charly was astonished by how patiently Lange spoke with the old lady.

'It's a box,' she said. 'He would ask for it every few weeks, then give it back. "It's safe with you, Fräulein Stock," he always said.' The short, dry sob that followed was no doubt an expression of her grief. She pulled out a pristine white handkerchief and began dabbing her face.

'What's in this box?'

'Should I go and get it?' she replied, and Charly could tell from her curiosity that she didn't know.

'If you would be so kind,' Lange said, with a note of mild irritation. Elfriede Stock disappeared. Lange said nothing, but Charly could guess what he was thinking. The landlady returned, a little out of breath, with a wooden casket that looked almost like a treasure chest, and placed it on the dining table.

'Here it is,' she said.

The box was locked.

'You don't happen to know where the key is?'

'Herr Kuschke always kept it on him, I think.'

'This item is hereby seized. I'll happily provide you with a receipt before we take it away.'

'Don't you want to open it here?' she asked, her disappointment plain.

'I'd have to force it open,' Lange said, in a tone of deep regret. 'Surely you can't expect that of a Prussian officer.'

91

The porter shook his head, more bored than trenchant. 'Never seen him before.' He turned back to his crossword.

Rath had heard the sentence at least half a dozen times, but this was the first time he didn't believe it. It wasn't because of any uncertainty in the porter's voice; or that he spoke too quickly, usually the sign of a pat answer. Rather, standing behind his rickety table, or reception counter as it was supposed to be, the man wasn't merely disagreeable but utterly loathsome. Rath had thought the lead would be a waste of time, but the man was visibly thrown by the picture of Abraham Goldstein, much as he tried to hide it.

'Underworld river in ancient Greece. Four letters, ending in "x"?' he asked.

'Styx,' Rath said.

'How d'you spell it?'

Rath tore the paper from the man's hand and put it gently, delicately almost, on the table. He placed Goldstein's picture over the crossword.

'Take a closer look,' he suggested in a friendly tone, which evidently confused the porter.

'Like I say, I don't know this man.' The porter reached for the paper again.

There were electric lines showing through the wallpaper; it didn't look like the work of experts. It wasn't the cleanest hotel Rath had seen either. As for the accounts, well who could say?

'Listen here,' he said, still friendly, 'what do you think it would take to get this fleapit closed down? A call to the public order office? Or the board of public health? I'm pretty sure the financial office would do the job. A little tax audit. Yes, best to be sure.'

The porter put the paper down again. 'Let's talk. What do you want to know?'

Rath pushed the Goldstein sketch under his nose. 'Is he staying here?'

'No,' he said. Rath was just about to make for the telephone booth on Oranienburger Tor, when he added: 'He checked out a few days ago.'

'When?' The porter shrugged his shoulders. 'I hope you're not expecting a bribe. Either you talk, or I make the call.'

'Yesterday afternoon.'

'Where did he go?'

'I don't know. He just didn't come back. I've no idea where he's staying now.'

'What about his luggage? Is that still here?'

'No, otherwise he wouldn't be checked out. Someone came to pick it up.'

'Male or female?' A blank look. 'His companion. Did *she* pick up his luggage?'

'It certainly wasn't a woman! He had a beard this long.' The porter made a gesture with his hands. 'All in black. A strange type. With a caftan, you know.'

'*What* do I know?'

'You know. He was a Jew. Anyway, it was him who came to pick the stuff up. Just the one suitcase, settled the bill too. So, all's well that ends well.'

Rath nodded. He wasn't listening anymore.

Forensics didn't find anything. The cupboards were empty, and Goldstein had left nothing behind. The only item was a bible in the drawer of the bedside table. The room was much larger than Rath expected, probably the best a flophouse like this had to offer, but, compared with the Excelsior, it was a hole. The room hadn't been cleaned following Goldstein's hasty departure, and so, at the very least, the ED men were able to lift a number of fingerprints, enough to prove the Yank had been here, even if, by now, Rath needed no confirmation.

The most pressing question was no longer where Goldstein had spent the last few days, but where he was now.

Around four o'clock all three men were back at the Castle. In the absence of a third desk, Rath fetched a table into the office from next door and placed a visitor's chair in front of it. He couldn't offer Tornow his own extension, but had been only too glad to place his typewriter at his disposal. What was a cadet good for, if not the paperwork his boss despised?

While Tornow typed his report, to be checked by Rath before Erika Voss made a fair copy, he and Gräf went through Gräf's interrogation records hoping that, among the rubbish, they would find a few serious statements. Which, of course, they didn't. They highlighted the odd account pointing to sightings around the Poetenviertel or the area by Stettiner Bahnhof. It might help to pay these witnesses another visit but it was probably just coincidence. Someone claimed to have seen Abraham Goldstein in pretty much every neighbourhood in Greater Berlin.

Later, when Rath was sitting in the outer office going through Tornow's report, the telephone rang. He ignored it, having no desire to be yelled at by Böhm, the only one who ever dialled him directly. Everyone else went via Erika Voss.

Gräf and Tornow exchanged glances. Gräf likewise made no move to answer, so Tornow got to his feet, went over to Rath's desk and picked up.

'Tornow, Inspector Rath's office.' He listened for a while before handing Rath the receiver. 'For you. A Herr Liang.'

With everyone listening . . . Rath took the call.

'Yes,' he said innocently.

'I take it this isn't a good time,' he heard Marlow's Chinaman say.

'That's right.'

'Come to Borchardt's tonight at eight. Französischer Strasse. The Doctor would like to speak to you.'

'About what?'

'No doubt you already knew, and were just about to notify the Doctor.'

'Pardon me?'

'You didn't? Your colleagues have found Hugo Lenz. He's dead.'

'I understand.'

This time Rath wasn't sure he'd managed to sound casual and noncommittal, but neither Gräf nor Tornow had noticed anything. He hung up.

'Who was that?' Tornow asked. 'Someone Chinese?'

'My hairdresser. I had to cancel our appointment.'

'Then find a German hairdresser,' Tornow said and grinned. 'You could use a chop.'

92

If Rath had known what awaited in the Flegenheimer home, he might have postponed for another few days. The door to the flat stood open when he arrived but, for a moment, he lingered in the fabulously ornate stairwell. When he heard voices and no one responded to his tentative 'Hello', he entered.

Lea Flegenheimer and her husband were in the living room, just as before, but this time they were crouched on the floor, on small uncomfortable-looking stools. Four visitors, evidently friends of the family, were speaking with the Flegenheimers, in reverent, hushed tones. Rath entered with Kirie on her lead, and was met by six horrified faces.

Ariel Flegenheimer said nothing, he didn't even stand up. An elderly guest, like his host clad entirely in black, approached in his stead.

'What you are doing here?' he whispered, pulling Rath into the hall-way. 'This is a house of mourning.'

'CID,' Rath said. 'The Flegenheimers know me. I have a few more questions.'

'When someone is sitting Shiva you visit to offer your condolences, not to ask questions!'

'Offering condolences isn't in my job description.'

'What questions do you have then? Perhaps I can relay them to Ariel.'

Rath shook his head. 'I'd like to speak to him myself, and his wife. I'm sorry for the inconvenience.'

A hallway door opened and Joseph Flegenheimer emerged, starting back when he saw Rath. He closed the door behind him and entered the living room in silence.

'You can see what's happening here,' the elderly man said. 'Can't you come back in a few days?'

'I'm sorry, but the matter is urgent. I'm afraid police work often is.'

The man gave up. 'Fine, then,' he sighed. 'But leave the dog outside.'

Rath pressed the lead into the man's hand. 'Thank you,' he said, and went back into the living room.

The looks that Ariel and Lea Flegenheimer gave him were no more friendly than before. Rath waited until a guest had finished speaking before crouching alongside the two mourners on the floor. 'Please excuse the interruption,' he said. 'Might I start by expressing my sympathies once again.'

'But that isn't why you're here,' Ariel Flegenheimer said.

'Just a quick question and I'll be on my way.'

'Then ask away. You've disrupted our mourning enough.'

'I wanted to ask about your nephew again. Has Abraham Goldstein been in touch with you in the last few days after all? Has he made contact with you or any other members of your family?'

'Neither with me, nor my wife. Was that all?'

Rath turned towards Joseph Flegenheimer, who stood next to his parents. 'What about you?' He could still scarcely believe he was speaking with Abraham Goldstein's first cousin. 'Has he been in touch?'

Joseph Flegenheimer shook his head. 'No,' he said. Rath sensed that young Flegenheimer knew more than he was willing to reveal.

'You didn't see him anywhere?'

'Where would I have seen him?'

'Or do him a good turn?'

The face behind the black beard was motionless. Joseph Flegenheimer held himself in check.

'Be that as it may,' Rath said. 'Call me if he gets in touch.' He handed Flegenheimer his card. 'I won't keep you any longer.'

With that he left the mourners, reclaiming Kirie in the hall and descending the steps onto Berchtesgadener Strasse. In the Buick he lit a cigarette and waited.

About quarter of an hour later, Joseph Flegenheimer stepped out onto the street. Rath waited until he had reached Wartburgstrasse and was no longer in view, before starting the engine.

It wasn't hard to keep the black figure in sight. Halting at the Wartburgstrasse junction, he waited until Flegenheimer reached Martin-Luther-Strasse. There was a tram line here, but Flegenheimer continued down the street towards the Schöneberger town hall. Rath watched while he crossed Rudolf-Wilde-Platz and continued down Mühlenstrasse. Following as slowly as possible, he caught up outside a large Catholic church which fitted seamlessly between the house fronts, like so many churches in this city. He was looking for a parking spot when Flegenheimer did something unexpected.

Dressed entirely in the garb of his forefathers, he opened one of the church doors and went inside.

Rath pulled over. What could this mean? He didn't want to follow him into the building, as Flegenheimer might grow suspicious. Even so, he'd have liked to know what business an orthodox Jew had in a church.

He had been hoping that Flegenheimer would lead him to whatever flophouse Abraham Goldstein was staying in, but apparently it wouldn't be that simple. All the same, he was certain it was Flegenheimer who had collected his cousin's things from the hotel in Tieckstrasse and settled the bill.

He remained in the car to smoke an Overstolz, but Flegenheimer didn't reappear. At length he threw the cigarette out of the window and restarted the engine. It was already late. He had to keep moving if he didn't want to miss his appointment with Marlow. He wrote down the name of the church: Saint Norbert's.

93

The room had no windows and was seldom properly aired, hence the musty smell. A uniformed officer led them past a long line of shelves. It looked like an arms dealer's warehouse, an arms dealer with a sideline in bric a brac: pistols and weapons of every design, knives, sabres, brass knuckles, carpets, candlesticks, oil paintings, record players and even a welded safety deposit box.

Charly held her hand over her nose and watched Lange as he examined a light-grey suit covered in congealed blood. Against their original plan, she had returned to the station out of sheer curiosity. Lange had not, in fact, forced the wooden casket open, neither in the flat nor in the car. He really was a model of Prussian rectitude. Perhaps her father had been right when he claimed that Hanoverians were more Prussian than the Prussians themselves.

They hadn't spoken much on the return journey, but both were now certain that Alexandra Reinhold was no longer their prime suspect. Lange appeared just as relieved as Charly, not that it made the case any simpler. The cop in Kuschke's flat must have been the same one Charly had seen in the Hansaviertel, and he must have something to do with the murder. What a nightmare: a murdering policeman, killed, himself, by a police officer. So far the dead man in the Hansaviertel hadn't been accorded many column inches. The Castle had kept things under wraps, above all the man's identity, deciding to release the information in stages, ideally in conjunction with reports on the state of the investigation.

The problem was that their findings had shed an increasingly disturbing light on matters.

After Charly failed to crack the box's lock with a paperclip, they went to the evidence room. Lange fished a key out of Kuschke's wallet and raised it triumphantly into the air.

Charly handed him the box: a fit.

At first she couldn't make head or tail of the sheet of paper Lange took out of the box: a passport photo showing Jochen Kuschke in uniform, albeit not the uniform of a sergeant major; rather one that, for police, was strictly forbidden. Even before she read what was printed next to the photograph and saw the stamped symbol, she knew this wasn't something they could give to the press.

Lange whistled through his teeth.

It was a membership card, confirming that Jochen Kuschke had been a member of the Berlin-Brandenburg SA-Gau since 12th December 1930, and held the rank of Oberscharführer. It was signed by Walther Stennes, the former Berlin SA Chief who had since been expelled by Hitler.

Grzesinski and Weiss would do everything in their power to ensure the press didn't get wind of this. Who knew what would happen if word got out that, despite the strict ban issued by both the Interior Ministry and police commissioner, a Berlin police officer had not only become a member of the SA, but allowed himself to be photographed in their uniform.

They didn't know what to make of the other items, except that Kuschke clearly felt they were as worthy of protection as his SA membership: a black patch with a white hand stitched on, a similarly designed lapel badge and a few photos of Kuschke with other men, none of whom were in police or SA uniform, but plainclothes.

They packed everything up and were about to leave when Kronberg from ED peered around the corner. 'There you are,' he said to Lange. 'Fräulein Steiner said I'd find you here.'

The 'you' referred to Lange alone. He didn't so much as glance at Charly, but reached into an envelope and placed a photograph of a bloody knife next to the wooden casket.

'The knife used to murder Kuschke,' Charly said. 'Have you found anything?'

'It's a dagger,' Kronberg corrected, giving Charly a condescending glance. 'A trench dagger, to be exact. Made for trench fighters in the war. Every veteran owns one.'

'So?' Lange said.

'So, it can be difficult to identify the owner of such a weapon. But . . . in this case, I believe we have managed.'

'Yes?'

'The dead SA man in Humboldthain was stabbed to death with a weapon just like this, his own. Until now, the weapon's been missing without trace, but if you ask me . . .' Kronberg gestured towards the photograph. 'This is it here.'

94

Johann Marlow held a bottle of chilled white wine. F.W. Borchardt was one of the most exclusive gourmet establishments in Berlin, where fine cuisine was fused with an impeccable wine cellar. Marlow had taken a table in a booth where they could talk undisturbed. Liang was there, and they had laid a place for Rath too. As much as he despised Johann Marlow's attention, he was in no position to refuse. After all, what could he say? *No thanks, I've already eaten?* His stomach was making far too much noise for that. He hadn't taken any food on board since wolfing down a meagre lunch at Stettiner Bahnhof with Gräf and Tornow; Kirie likewise. He was almost refused entry with the dog but Liang, waiting by the door, handed a note to the man at reception, and soon a boy emerged to take her. Kirie went willingly, instinct telling her there was food on offer.

'Do sit down,' Marlow said. 'Wine?'

Rath nodded. Liang poured.

'I'm sorry about Lenz,' Rath said. 'Perhaps it will comfort you to know that Rudi the Rat was found dead at a rubbish dump.'

Marlow slammed his fist against the table. 'Damn it,' he said. 'Why didn't *you* tell me that Lenz was dead? Why do I have to hear from Teuber about your boys showing up in Amor-Diele, shouting about how Hugo's mortal remains have been fished out of the Mühlendamm Lock?'

Rath lit a cigarette. If he had learned one thing it was not to be intimidated by this man. 'It's not my case; I only heard about it from Herr Liang here.'

'Well, we picked the right man to have at the station.'

'I'm not your man. I'm doing you a favour because I owe you a debt.'

'I asked you to investigate the background to Hugo's disappearance.'

'I've already told you that I think he fell into a trap, at the Osthafen, and that he probably didn't survive.'

'Probably. So, who laid this trap?'

'I've spoken to colleagues working on the case.' Plisch and Plum had been only too happy to tell him what they knew, especially Czerwinski, who was proud to be leading an investigation that gave him the chance to order his friend Henning around. 'Pathology has confirmed that Hugo Lenz didn't drown,' Rath continued. 'He was shot. Bullets to the head and chest, just like Rudi Höller. They think Lenz's corpse drifted around the Spree for a few days before surfacing at the lock. They're assuming he was thrown into the water somewhere upstream. They don't know where.'

'But you do.'

'Like I said a week ago, we know that Hugo Lenz went to the harbour area, but that no one saw him return. The next day his car was still parked where he left it. Then, there are the shots the night watchman claims to have heard near the cold-storage depot.'

'You searched my warehouses and found nothing.'

'I still believe that's where it happened. Hugo Lenz was shot by whoever agreed to meet him at the harbour, and he would feel secure at a Berolina warehouse. It's the same MO as Rudi the Rat, only *he* was disposed of in a rubbish dump.'

'Both corpses were still found,' Marlow said.

'Perhaps they were meant to be. Mutilated and disfigured as a warning to you and the Nordpiraten.'

'Who's behind it?'

Rath shrugged. 'Another Ringverein. Or someone you haven't bargained on.'

Marlow made a pensive face. 'And this someone hired an American contract killer?'

'More likely it's someone trying to lay the blame at his door. That's what it seems like to me, as if the whole thing's been staged.'

'You surprise me, Inspector, protecting a gangster like this.'

'It couldn't have been Goldstein. I had him under surveillance at the time.'

'I thought he gave you the slip.'

'Not on the day Hugo Lenz disappeared.'

'Whatever the case,' Marlow said, 'we have a problem. Now that Hugo Lenz has been confirmed dead, I have to act.'

'You want revenge? When you don't even know who's behind it?'

'Let's not misunderstand each other,' Marlow said. 'I'm not mourning Lenz personally, but his death is an affront against my organisation and, since the whole world thinks the Pirates are behind it, it'll be the Pirates who take the rap. They've been acting up for weeks, and who can say that Lapke wasn't involved.'

'He and Rudi the Rat were best friends.'

'And rivals.'

'Aren't you being a little hasty?'

Marlow gave Rath a cold, hard stare. 'I need to act, and if you can't tell me who killed Hugo Lenz, it'll be the Pirates who get it.'

'Do you know what will happen in this city if you move against them now? It'll be a bloodbath.'

'You think I can stand for this? If I don't strike back, Berolina will be on me before I can count to three.'

'Lay down an example for all I care. Have a few Pirates beaten up, kidnap them, lock them in a damp cellar, but don't risk open warfare until you're one hundred percent certain who has your business partner on their conscience.'

'Then it's time you delivered.'

'I'm working on it.'

'I'll give you three days,' Marlow said. 'Exactly seventy-two hours. On Sunday evening we'll meet again and I want to know for certain. One hundred percent.'

'You will.' Rath stubbed out his cigarette and stood up.

'Don't you want to eat?'

'We're too close to the station.'

'Don't worry, your colleagues can't afford this sort of place, and the commissioner's too tight for Borchardt.'

'No, thank you, but you could do me another favour?'

'Yes?'

'I need to speak to Christine again. You know, the dancer from Venuskeller.'

'I think that can be arranged,' Marlow grinned. Liang took a black note-book from his jacket and wrote down an address before tearing out the page and passing it to Rath. 'You can reach her there, but not before mid-day. Or you can go to Venuskeller tonight.'

'No thank you,' Rath said. 'I've got something better in mind.'

95

Charly hadn't heard anything more from either Alex or Vicky. The girls were still missing. She closed the door to her flat and went inside. Gereon still wasn't home. Luckily, she hadn't run into him again at the Castle. She felt guilty, but also relieved that she hadn't had to speak to him.

She found a half-open bottle of red in the cupboard, and sat at the table with her glass. The first sip felt good. She lit a cigarette. What was she involved in here? Police officers killing police officers? Underage girls seeking revenge. How she would have liked to talk things over with Gereon, if only she could. Her case seemed to hang together with his. The murder weapon: the SA man in Humboldthain had almost certainly been killed with the same knife as the police officer in the Hansaviertel. This same police officer was also a member of the SA. Was that a link? Was there someone going around town butchering SA men? More, was that someone Abraham Goldstein, Gereon's gangster? He was Jewish. Perhaps that was why he had crossed the Atlantic? Because he had been contracted to take care of a few brownshirts on behalf of Jews who would no longer stand for the abuse. It was an absurd idea but, on the other hand, it was often the absurd ideas that led to the solution. Somehow, it fit.

All this secrecy. Gereon might be used to it, but she wasn't—and didn't think she ever would be. With every hour that passed it grew worse. Should she try and get the green light to notify Inspector Rath? Then again . . . she knew only too well that Gennat had brought Böhm into their little team because he had been handling the Humboldthain case, and that Böhm just couldn't deal with someone like Gereon, who rarely accepted another person's authority. Charly didn't blame him for ignoring Gereon half the time, even if Gereon hated him for it. She had always got on well with Wilhelm Böhm, so it could be done, so long as you didn't take his surly charms to heart.

She heard footsteps in the stairwell. Could it be Gereon? She took another sip of wine and listened, almost anxiously, to the noise from outside.

96

Earlier that morning, Rath had sent Gräf and Tornow away to resume their investigation into Grabowski's list of Camel outlets. They seemed to get along, so now he could do what he enjoyed best: working alone.

He parked the Buick on a side street in Treptow. Christine's surname was the solidly middle-class, run-of-the-mill Möller, and she lived in far greater comfort than he had anticipated. Front building, first floor.

It took a while for someone to open, even though Rath had heeded Liang's advice and waited until after lunch. The Venuskeller's main attraction wore a midnight-blue, silk gown, as elegantly cut as the bathrobe she wore in her dressing room. She seemed to have recognised him, and looked at him like a lioness in her den, shy and belligerent in equal measure.

'I knew we'd be seeing each other again,' she said, opening the door. 'Please come in. I'm having breakfast.'

The smell of coffee hung in the flat. She led him into a sun-filled room with the skylight tilted open and noise entering from the street. A percolator in a dark-red cosy stood on a small table with two chairs, alongside a cup of steaming black coffee. A stubbed-out cigarette lay in the ashtray. Christine Möller's breakfast habits mirrored his own.

'Coffee?'

'Please.'

She poured.

'Why don't you take off your hat and coat.'

Rath heard the undertone in her voice and, despite everything, could do nothing to prevent his sudden erection. This time Frau Lennartz's flabby upper arms wouldn't save him. He took off his hat and coat and joined her at the table, took a sip of coffee and tried to avert his gaze from her bosom, which was plain to see under the midnight-blue silk.

'Thank you,' he said.

'Warm in here, don't you think?' Christine blew away a strand of blonde hair and leaned forward so that her robe opened to reveal a breast.

It was time to get down to brass tacks. He replaced the coffee cup on the saucer with a clatter. 'You don't just work for Johann Marlow,' he said. 'You work for my colleagues in Vice too.'

She remained astonishingly composed. 'Don't you work for Marlow and the police yourself?'

'We're talking about you here, not me.'

She shrugged. 'If you pay well, I'll work for you too.'

The subtext was clear enough. He kept looking at her as he tapped a cigarette out of the carton and lit it. 'Not necessary, thank you.'

'A shame.' She snatched together the ends of her dressing gown. 'Perhaps you should tell me who you're representing here. Dr M. or Dr Weiss?'

'I'm here for me.'

The more she avoided his questions, the more convinced he was that she had something to hide. The photos he had found in Lanke's drawer were no coincidence.

'But that doesn't mean something useful won't come out of this meeting for my employers,' he continued. 'It depends entirely on whether you tell the truth or not.'

'You're here to threaten me.'

'I'm here to warn you.'

'Perhaps it's me who should be warning *you*. What do you think Dr M.'s going to do when he hears you've been trying to blackmail me.'

'What do you think he's going to do when he hears it was you who lured Hugo Lenz into a fatal trap?'

'What are you talking about?'

Her horror, even if she attempted to hide it with studied self-assurance, was genuine. Rath had only been expressing a hunch, but her reaction told him he was getting close to the truth.

'You provided Hugo Lenz with his police contacts,' he said. 'Lenz envied Marlow, and hoped to settle Berolina's issues with the Nordpiraten by double-crossing them with the police.' Rath drew on his cigarette. 'It was you who fanned the flames. Perhaps it was you who put the idea in his head.'

'I really have no idea what you're talking about.'

Rath felt confirmed in his hunch. Christine Möller had stopped trying to seduce him. She folded her arms to keep her dressing gown closed. He could no longer even see her neck.

'You know exactly what I'm talking about. Herr Marlow, on the other hand, doesn't, and I think it's best if you keep it that way.' Rath paused to let his words take effect, and stubbed out his cigarette. 'Of course, it's entirely up to you. You tell me what happened and it stays between us, I give you my word. Dig your heels in, or if I find out you've been lying, and I'll leave it to Marlow to extract the truth.'

'You lousy bastard.'

'It's your choice. Tell me everything you know, here and now. Or tell Marlow, while you're tied up in a damp cellar.'

He didn't need to make himself any clearer. Christine Möller understood.

'I didn't know they would kill him. I thought they were just going to arrest him.'

Then she told him everything.

97

In person, Gerald Thiemann looked even more like Harold Lloyd than on the sketch. He seemed nervous.

'Thank you for getting in touch,' Gennat said.

Thiemann nodded. 'A friend told me that my picture was in the papers.'

Seated on the upholstered green living-room suite in Gennat's office, Buddha was at pains to make him feel at home. Trudchen Steiner entered with freshly brewed coffee to join the selection of cakes already on the table. Gennat served them out personally after she poured. First, the witness. Gerald Thiemann selected a small slice of nutcake, clearly impressed by the range on offer. Charly passed, a decision Gennat met with a look that was somewhere between pitying and sympathetic, while Lange took an enormous slice of Herrentorte that he stared at reverently. For himself, Buddha chose a slice of gooseberry tart. The tray was still more than half full.

Böhm was the only one absent. Gennat had sent him back out to the Hansaviertel, where two assistant detectives were canvassing houses for possible witnesses to the Kuschke murder. Charly knew it was better that Böhm wasn't present for awkward interviews such as this. He could be intimidating, even when he didn't mean to be, and this was no time to be intimidating witnesses. It was one of the reasons they weren't sitting in an interview room, but over coffee and cake in Gennat's living room office. Ignoring the fact that the upholstery was not only worn but like something out of Kaiser Wilhelm's era, you could probably say that Gennat's was the cosiest office in the whole of police headquarters. Rumour had it that even the police commissioner's official residence on the first floor—with its panoramic view of Alexanderplatz—wasn't as comfortably furnished.

All that could be heard was the clatter of cake forks and coffee cups, until Gennat posed his first question. 'What did you see at KaDeWe on the night in question?'

Thiemann set his cup back on his saucer. 'There was this boy,' he said, 'and this girl. At first I thought she was a boy too, until I heard her voice.'

'Please, start from the beginning. You were walking down Passauer Strasse . . .'

'That's right.'

'What direction were you coming from, and where were you heading?' Lange asked hastily. Charly registered Gennat's angry glance, which caused Lange to go red and fall silent.

'I wanted . . . I . . . I was on my way to . . .' Thiemann looked at Gennat uncertainly. 'Does this really have to be on the record?'

Gennat shook his head. 'For us, the only important thing is that you were there. Not why you were there. Even so, it would help if you could provide a detailed outline of what you saw.'

Thiemann looked relieved. 'So, I was coming down Passauer in the direction of Tauentzienstrasse, on the other side from KaDeWe, when I was surprised to see lights on in the department store. Not just the neon lights. I mean inside, on every floor.' He took another sip of coffee. 'I was looking over at KaDeWe when I saw this boy.' In danger of disappearing into his chair, he sat up and gripped the armrests. 'I thought he was about to jump, the way he climbed over the railings, but then this policeman came, and I thought it'll be OK, there's someone looking after him.'

'Did you see what happened next?' Gennat asked.

'Yes. I was rooted to the spot.'

'Were there any other people on the street?'

'Not where I was. It was just me and this girl. She stood on the other side of the road looking up. She had trousers on. That she had just come out of KaDeWe, that she was a thief just like her friend up there . . . well, I didn't work that out until later.'

'What happened next?'

'I don't know how long it all lasted, but the co . . . the police officer just stood there making no attempt whatsoever to save the boy. At first I thought, he doesn't want to rush things, he's trying to talk him down, that sort of thing. Then I saw him tread on the boy's finger with his boot, almost as if he were treading out a cigarette with his heel.'

'You had a good view of all this from down there?'

'Define "good view". The front was illuminated by the neon sign, and there was light coming through the windows. So, I saw what I saw. My eyesight's pretty good, even if I do wear glasses.' He took his glasses off with his right hand and pointed with his index and middle fingers at his pupils. 'Long-sighted.'

Gennat nodded as Lange took notes, neglecting his Herrentorte as a result. They had made do without a stenographer to keep the number of people involved to a minimum. Charly could have taken on the role—indeed, she had been expecting to—but Buddha had pressed the notepad into Lange's hand.

'What happened after that, Herr Thiemann?' she asked, as though Gerald Thiemann was a storyteller, and she were listening to him over coffee.

'The boy cried out a few times,' Thiemann continued, 'until at some point he fell.' He closed his eyes for a moment and shook his head. 'Terrible. As he fell, he didn't make another sound, didn't cry out, nothing.'

'And the girl?'

Thiemann shrugged. 'I wasn't looking at her, but I think she stood stock still, like me. She ran to him straightaway, as did I. She shouted at me to call an ambulance.'

Charly thought of the Alex she had come to know. Yes, that was a fit. 'That's what you did?'

'First, I had to look for a telephone booth. The closest one's on Wittenbergplatz, so it took a while. And, well . . . when I came back, your colleagues were there, standing over the boy. I think he was already dead. The girl was gone.'

'What about you. You weren't questioned by our colleagues?'

'No one paid any attention to me. I was just another rubbernecker. I waited for the ambulance to arrive and went on my way without speaking to anybody.'

'You should have, Herr Thiemann.' Gennat pushed his cake plate aside and looked at the witness through friendly eyes. 'What you have to say is important. Why didn't you mention anything at the scene?'

Thiemann sat helplessly, rake-thin and disappearing inside a chair that was far too big for a single person. 'I didn't want any trouble. I had spoken to the girl, a criminal, remember, and I didn't stop her, I just let her go. Because I went looking for the nearest telephone booth to call an ambulance.'

'No one could reproach you for that.'

'Maybe. But . . . there was something else. That man . . .' He pointed at Kuschke's portrait. 'I was afraid of how he looked at me.' He swallowed, as though it were tricky to utter the next sentence. 'And I was pretty muddled after everything that happened; I didn't know where I stood any more. With you . . . with your colleagues, I mean.'

Gennat gave an understanding nod. 'Why didn't you contact us later? When you were no longer so muddled, I mean.'

'Perhaps I still am,' Thiemann said. 'As a child,' he continued after a time, 'as a child, I always learned that the cops are the good guys, and the robbers are the bad guys . . . that was how we always played it anyway . . .' He looked around suspiciously. 'But maybe things have changed since the Kaiser's reign . . .'

'I don't think so,' Gennat said. 'We're still the good guys. The exception proves the rule.'

98

Rath parked at the same spot as before. The only thing distinguishing Saint Norbert's from the adjacent buildings were the two church towers and gable front that rose above the five-storey apartment houses which otherwise dominated Mühlenstrasse. The left-hand tower was kinked slightly to follow the bend in the road, and bordered directly on the neighbouring Norbert Hospital. The lower levels, with the round-arched portals (one of which served as the entrance to the courtyard), were veneered with dressed stone, while on the upper floors the façade was broken by a row of windows which seemed to conceal a number of rooms, perhaps where the priest had his quarters.

He had taken an Opel from the motor pool and left the Buick at the station. His visit yesterday had startled young Flegenheimer, who later visited the church. Why? The only thing that seemed halfway plausible was a dead letter box. Somewhere in the church, Flegenheimer had left a message for his cousin.

He thought back to Christine Möller's flat. The Venuskeller's main attraction had indeed betrayed Red Hugo, though she had stressed, again and again, that she had no idea she was sending him to his death. He still didn't know if he could trust her, but it seemed more likely that her instructions had come from the police than the Nordpiraten. She hadn't been able to give a name, or even a description; everything had been done anonymously, and mostly over the telephone. The only face-to-face meeting she'd had was with Gregor Lanke, who arranged the initial contact with this ominous stranger—or, at least, his telephone voice. Lanke had pressured her, telling her if she didn't do him this favour he'd have her sent down on drugs charges. Someone must have told him she took cocaine as he had shown up at her house one day and uncovered her supply. She had been paying for it ever since, less with information than with regular services. She didn't have to go into any more detail.

After months of sex in return for silence, Lanke had tried to engage her as an informant. 'He must have heard about me and Hugo,' she said, 'even though I'd only been with him a few weeks.' The instructions she received over the telephone were precise, which was how she'd been able to set up a meeting without Hugo connecting it to her. Red Hugo must have met his killer twice; the third meeting had ended fatally. Christine had never seen the man, but she still remembered the number she had called. Rath looked in his notebook: *STEPHAN 1701*. He had tried it just now in the telephone booth. No one picked up, but at least he had something to go on.

The booth was on Schöneberg's main drag, a few metres down from Mühlenstrasse. He looked at his watch and thought about trying again. Watching the church for over an hour, he'd seen no sign of Joseph Flegenheimer or Abraham Goldstein.

After checking to make sure he didn't recognise anyone on the street, he got out of the car. Walking down Mühlenstrasse he gazed into an undertaker's window that reflected the church façade. Saint Norbert's was still visible from the telephone booth if he opened the door and stepped outside. He chose not to, however, even though the cord was long enough. It felt as if he were wasting his time here. He asked for *STEPHAN 1701* and let it ring a long time. No luck: not a police station, then.

He lit a cigarette, gazing through the window at the coffins, and wondered whether it wouldn't be better to give up smoking. The prospect of returning to a cramped, smoky Opel was less than appealing. If the mountain wouldn't come to Muhammad . . .

Barely three minutes later, he stood in front of the Flegenheimers' front door, determined to interrupt their mourning for a second time. It took a moment before he heard footsteps and a woman he hadn't seen before opened.

'This is the Flegenheimer residence, isn't it?' he said, a little confused. She looked him up and down. 'Yes.'

'I'd like to speak to Joseph Flegenh . . .'

'He's not here,' she said, before he could finish his sentence.

'Who is it, Rikwa,' Rath heard a familiar voice. Lea Flegenheimer was home. Two seconds later she stood at the door surveying Rath like a troublesome insect. 'Haven't you pestered us enough already?'

'I'd like to speak with your son, Frau Flegenheimer.'

'I'm afraid you've chosen the wrong day.'

'Pardon me?'

'Shabbos,' Lea Flegenheimer said. 'The men are at synagogue. I'm preparing our shabbat meal with Rikwa.'

'I thought the Sabbath was on Saturday.'

'You don't have any Jewish friends, do you, Inspector?' Lea Flegenheimer said, and while Rath was still thinking about whether he'd describe Manfred Oppenberg or Magnus Schwartz as friends, or, indeed, if he had any friends at all, whether Jewish, Catholic, Protestant or even Atheist, she provided the answer. 'Clearly not, otherwise you'd know that Sabbath begins at sunset.'

'Thanks for letting me know.' The best way to annoy people like Lea Flegenheimer was to remain resolutely polite. 'Would you be so kind as to tell me which synagogue I might find your son in?'

'You're not going to disrupt the liturgy?'

'Don't worry, I'll wait outside.'

Rath took less than five minutes to reach the synagogue on Münchener Strasse. Naturally, he didn't go inside, and wouldn't have done so even without Lea Flegenheimer's warning. He stood in front of the portal and lit a cigarette. Dusk was falling; it wouldn't be long now. He contemplated the enormous *Jugendstil* façade, above which a cupola stood in solitary splendour, capped by the star of David.

It took two cigarettes before the men started to emerge. Only men. No doubt the women were at home preparing the food.

He looked carefully, not just because night was closing in, but because most of the men were dressed in identical fashion. Nearly all wore black coats and black hats, and all wore prayer shawls. Beards and sidelocks made it trickier still. He caught sight of the Flegenheimers among a group of men proceeding down Münchener Strasse towards Grunewaldstrasse, and followed at a distance until Flegenheimer father and son separated from the group at the junction with Berchtesgadener Strasse.

For some reason he couldn't bring himself to speak to Joseph Flegenheimer, or tell his father that his offspring had been seen entering a Catholic church. He didn't know whether it was the prayer shawls, or that they were celebrating the most important day in their faith, but there was something in the air, an almost intimate feeling of religion, that he didn't want to disturb. Perhaps somewhere deep inside he was simply too Catholic not to respect those who still believed in God, even though he was no longer capable of it himself—however much he might long to be.

He waited until the two had disappeared inside their house before walking down Berchtesgadener Strasse towards his car. It was time to go and collect the Buick from the Castle.

99

On Saturday there was schnitzel. Czerwinski had asked for an especially large plate, with extra potato salad. The workers in the canteen knew the detective's appetite. Rath and Henning were more modest and contented themselves with smaller portions.

Plisch and Plum were in good spirits. Reaching the weekend without incident was all that mattered to Czerwinski, and he had managed again. The pair thought nothing of Rath quizzing them for information. They had worked together so often that it felt normal when he enquired about the state of an investigation, even now, after Böhm had split them up.

They still hadn't formally identified the Osthafen as the scene of the crime, even though it stood on their shortlist along with several other remote areas by the shore. Nor could they say anything about the time of death. In other words, they had nothing. In the absence of any other leads, Plisch and Plum only had Hugo's reputation to go on, and they concluded that it was a gangland revenge. Meanwhile, Rudi Höller's murder fitted the picture perfectly, even if the pair couldn't say who was avenging whom, given the uncertainty surrounding the times of death.

'What's strange,' Henning said, 'is that the pattern in both cases was the same. Exit wounds to the head and chest. Even stranger, according to Ballistics, both Höller and Lenz were killed by the same weapon. The one that injured the dead SA man's foot.'

'Goldstein's Remington,' Rath said.

'It looks as if the newspapers were right,' Czerwinski said. Despite his enormous portion, he was already eating dessert. 'Our gangster's been working overtime.'

'I don't know.' Rath was sceptical. 'Don't you think everything points a little too obviously at Goldstein? I mean, how does the dead SA man fit in there?'

'Don't blame yourself, Gereon,' Henning said. 'None of us feels good about how he escaped, but we have to look the facts in the eye.'

Rath fell silent, stood up and took his leave. Earlier that morning he had been to Lanke's office several times, where he was brusquely informed that Lanke was 'out in the field'.

The man lived in Schöneberg, near the Queen-Luise-Gedächtniskirche. He stood wide-eyed when he opened the door to find Rath outside. He seemed to have been expecting someone else.

'You?' he said. 'What do you want here?'

'To talk to you. Aren't you going to invite me in?'

'I'm afraid this really isn't a good time. I'm expecting a visitor . . .'

'Your uncle?'

Lanke didn't take the bait. 'Please leave,' he said.

Rath stepped inside the flat. He knew he had Lanke where he wanted him. Looking round he noted that Gregor Lanke seemed to exist on more than a detective's salary. How else could he afford such a roomy front-facing apartment? The maid must have been here recently too; everything looked clean and tidy. 'Aren't you going to offer me anything?' he asked.

'You want me to make coffee now?'

'Just a joke.'

'My sides have split.'

'What telephone number did you give Christine Möller?' Rath asked.

'Pardon?'

'Christine Möller. Another girl from your impressive collection. You know it's quite astonishing what you ask of your informants. Pretty much everything, it seems, except for information, of course.'

Lanke turned pale and leaned against the doorframe.

'I don't know what you're talking about,' he said, but it didn't sound convincing. Lanke knew why Rath was here.

'Hugo Lenz, also known as Red Hugo was your plaything's lover. Is that the right way to describe it? Were you jealous? Was that why you arranged the meeting with your supposed colleague? I think it was you who shot Hugo Lenz, or did you hire someone from overseas?'

'I'm sorry?' This time he sounded genuine. Rath was surprised. 'It wasn't me. You have to believe me!'

'Then tell me who it was.'

'I can't. Don't you understand!'

'No.'

'I can't betray the fellowsh . . . the men. It would mean certain death.' Gregor Lanke looked like a man out of his depth.

'The story about how you wanted to get Goldstein by smuggling your informant into the Excelsior was a lie,' Rath said. 'You were acting on behalf of your comrades there too, weren't you?'

Lanke said nothing, but Rath realised he was on the right track. 'What's going on here, Lanke?'

Gregor Lanke gazed at his feet, saying nothing, but shaking slightly. Rath almost felt sympathy for him.

'You should think hard about cooperating, otherwise I'll make your dirty business public and that'll be it for your police career.'

'If that's what you have to do. I've got nothing more to say. Now, please leave my flat.'

Rath wouldn't get anything more out of him for the time being. The man seemed genuinely afraid. When the doorbell rang he looked at it like a deer in headlights. Rath opened and stared into a pretty face. He had never seen this young lady before, but felt certain she could be marvelled at in an illegal nightclub somewhere in Berlin. He tipped his hat and took his leave, wishing both parties 'a nice weekend', which, of course, neither of them would have. Gregor Lanke was soaked in sweat, no longer capable of anything.

Rath had no sympathy, now, for his successor. He'd never been able to stand the man. The question was, what was Lanke so afraid of that he'd rather see Rath destroy his police career than blab? When it came out that Lanke junior was consorting with prostitutes doubling as Vice informants, his career would be over. Not even Uncle Werner would be able to prevent that.

Rath stepped onto the road and moved towards his car when, at that moment, he saw a man with a shopping bag. 'Hello,' he cried across the street, 'taking care of the weekend shop, are you?' Sebastian Tornow looked at him wide-eyed.

'What are you doing here?' he asked.

'I was about to ask you the same thing.'

'I always do my shopping here. I live just around the corner, on Leuthener Strasse.'

'A coincidence then.'

'And yourself?'

'I was visiting an ex-colleague. Assistant Detective Lanke.'

'Lanke! I didn't know you were in Vice.'

'You know Gregor Lanke?'

Tornow laughed. 'Everybody knows everybody around here. You run into people all the time, even while you're out shopping.' He gestured towards the bottles clinking in his bag. 'How about a quick beer at mine? We can usher in the weekend?'

Normally, Rath would turn him down without thinking, but this time it didn't seem like such a bad idea. 'Why not?' he said.

Tornow didn't live in the same comfort as Lanke. His apartment was furnished, with a live-in landlady. Rath was reminded of his first Berlin flat on Nürnberger Strasse. True, Tornow was slightly better off, with two rooms: one for sleeping, and another for eating and working, albeit both had a sloping ceiling. There was a small dining table with four chairs, an armchair and a small sofa. On the desk by the window stood a typewriter and telephone along with a few framed photographs. Rath's gaze fell on the aquarium next to the sofa.

'You have fish,' he said, surprised. An aquarium didn't fit his image of Sebastian Tornow.

'A man needs a hobby,' Tornow grinned. 'Ladies are strictly forbidden at Frau Hollerbach's.'

'Sounds familiar, which is why I found another flat. True, it might be a little more expensive, and it's in a rear building, but I'm my own master. Frau Lennartz comes to clean, otherwise I could have a hundred women over without anyone taking any notice.'

'Apart from Vice perhaps,' Tornow said.

He took two beers from the bag and placed them on the table, clearing the rest of his shopping into the cupboard. The men flipped the lids open and clinked bottles.

'Thanks,' Rath said. 'This reminds me that I haven't made good on my promise to buy you a beer.'

'There'll be plenty of opportunities. Perhaps I'll get to know the legendary Nasse Dreieck that Reinhold's been telling me about.'

'He has, has he?' The Dreieck by Wassertorplatz was Rath's local, where he ended long working days with Gräf. 'I wanted to wait until I bought you that beer,' he said, 'but since we're here now . . .' He stretched out a hand. 'It's time we called each other by our first names. I'm Gereon.'

Tornow shook. 'Sebastian.'

They clinked bottles for a second time. Rath pointed out of the dormer window, at the imposing figure of the Schöneberg gasometer towering above the roofs of the Sedanviertel. 'Nice view you've got here,' he said.

'Can I tell you something?' Tornow said. 'Every now and then I do something illegal. Pretty often, actually. Almost every week.'

'You're a serial killer?'

'No,' Tornow said 'From up there, you get the best view the city has to offer.'

Rath put his bottle down. 'You climb up *there*?'

'It's where I think best, when it all gets too much for me down here.'

Rath would sometimes climb to Liebig's dovecote when he needed peace and quiet.

'The gasometer's like an animal,' Tornow continued. 'It breathes. Every night the bell falls, and every morning it rises again. There's something comforting about that.'

Rath gestured with his beer bottle towards the enormous steel framework. The gas holder had risen almost to its full height. 'How do you get up?'

'There are steel steps. Do you see the rings up there in the framework? They're for maintenance workers, but anyone can climb them and see the whole city from the top.'

'And that's illegal?'

'No entry for unauthorised persons, it says on the signs.'

'Police officers are never unauthorised. Remember that, Cadet.' On the desk was a photograph of a pretty, young girl, perhaps fourteen or fifteen years old, with a knock-out smile. 'Who's that?' he asked.

'My sister.'

Rath looked at the cadet. 'The reason you joined the force?' Tornow nodded. 'A pretty girl,' Rath said. 'Still so young.'

'It's an old photograph.'

'You still haven't told me the whole story. Why you became a police officer, I mean.' Tornow took a sip of beer and fell silent, just like a few days

ago when Rath broached the subject for the first time. This time he probed
further. 'Don't you want to talk about it?'

'I'm not sure you'll want to hear.'

'Of course, I will. Tell me.'

Tornow gave a forced smile. 'Actually I'm not sure I want to tell it.'

'It's up to you.'

'Alright, then.' Tornow cleared his throat. 'It was more than seven years
ago and, damn it, Luise was the prettiest girl in the world.'

'Was?'

'She isn't dead,' Tornow said. There was a pain in his expression that
Rath hadn't seen before. He was usually so upbeat. 'But perhaps it would
be better if she was.'

Rath didn't probe further. He let Tornow talk.

'We lived with my parents in Teltow, a small town to the southwest of
Berlin, and our own little suburban idyll, or so we thought. One day, in this
suburban idyll, my sister—she was fifteen at the time—saw two men climb
through a window into a warehouse. She called the police, but when they
arrived all they found was the broken window. Shortly afterwards, two men
fitting their description were arrested. Luise had got a pretty good view of
them, and had no trouble identifying them when they brought her to the
station.'

Tornow paused, as if needing to gather his strength.

'The whole family was at the trial, even Father took the morning off.
We were proud of Luise, who had shown courage and refused to be intimidated. She made her statement in court. The lawyer for the defence was
from Berlin, an expensive type. Unaffordable, really, but the two intruders
were members of a Ringverein. Anyway, this lawyer spoke very kindly to
Luise, and asked her to read a letter, which he passed across. She couldn't;
she needed glasses to read. Glasses which she seldom wore—you know how
girls are. By the end, the lawyer had made it seem as though she were half-
blind. On top of that, he dredged up a few old stories that painted her as a
busybody driven by a desire to be the centre of attention. Even being class
president was used against her. The piece of shit. My parents, myself and
my brother, had to sit and watch how this brave girl, who had only acted
out of a sense of public duty, was suddenly turned into a short-sighted, busybody little brat willing to send two innocent men to jail. At the end, the

lawyer presented the judge with a watertight alibi for both his clients, so that the pair, who had plenty of prior convictions, were acquitted.'

'That sort of thing happens all too often,' said Rath. 'Justice becomes a question of money, and the person who can afford the best lawyer is usually the winner.'

'We sat in disbelief,' Tornow said. 'My sister put on a brave face, but I could see she was close to tears. No wonder, given that this lawyer had publicly humiliated her, and not just in front of her family, but half the town. A number of Teltow residents had made the journey to the District Court, and they were all witnesses to her humiliation.'

'I understand.'

'No,' Tornow said, so gruffly that Rath was taken aback. 'You don't. The story isn't over yet.' His voice was less sharp now. 'Life went on after the trial, but things were never the same. We had lost faith in the state and its judiciary. And then . . . Luise came home one day and said that she'd seen one of the men on her way to school. No one believed her, either in town or in school because, by now, she was just some half-blind busybody. We were the only ones who took her seriously, but our insistence at school and with the police got us nowhere. Then . . .' He had to swallow before continuing. '. . . then one afternoon just before the summer holiday—I still remember how hot it was—she didn't come home. We looked for her everywhere, but eventually it was a walker who found her lying beaten half to death in the Hollandwiese, clothes ripped to shreds and blood all over her body. She hasn't spoken a word since that day, but we know who's responsible. The two men who ruined my sister's life.'

'How is she now?'

'She hasn't said a word for seven years, and no longer leaves the house. How do you think she is? She's a walking corpse.'

'I'm sorry,' Rath said. 'It's a dreadful story.'

'She's the reason I became a police officer. My sister, Luise Tornow.'

Rath couldn't help feeling guilty. He was one of those who didn't shy away from working with criminals, with Marlow and his Ringverein. Only today he had given a colleague what for, more or less at Marlow's behest. Had he ever thought about whether something like that could be squared with his original motivation for becoming a police officer? Yes, he had; he had thought about it a hell of a lot, only so far he hadn't found any answers.

He pushed the uncomfortable thought aside. 'What happened to the two men?'

'They died in a shoot-out before they could be sentenced. Some gangland dispute but, who knows, perhaps the courts would have acquitted them again. Maybe it was better that way. Maybe death was their punishment.'

There was more than a little satisfaction in his voice. In Tornow's eyes, the men who had ruined his sister's life had got their just reward. He was probably right, Rath thought.

They were silent. Rath hadn't been expecting such a grim tale; it occupied his thoughts for a time. Tornow managed to find a smile again.

'That was yesterday,' he said. 'What matters is the here and now.' He raised his bottle.

Rath did likewise. 'The here and now! Now that you're with CID, you can make sure people like that get put away.'

'Let's hope so.'

'How do you find the work in Homicide?'

'If you forget about how boring it can be sometimes . . .'

Rath grinned, remembering what he had had Tornow and Gräf doing these past few days.

'. . . then I think it's the most worthwhile thing a police officer can do.'

'I couldn't agree more.' Rath didn't know if it was the beer making him so garrulous, but here was a chance to sound Tornow out. 'What would you think,' he began, 'if I were to put in a word with Gennat so that you can join A Division? Assuming, of course, you pass your examination.'

Tornow looked at him in surprise. 'Assuming I pass,' he said, 'I'd like that very much.'

Rath placed his bottle on the table and glanced at his watch. 'Time for me to go.'

'I'd have thrown you out in five minutes anyway,' Tornow laughed. 'One beer's quite enough. Seriously, I need to take an S-Bahn in ten minutes.'

'Where are you going?'

'The West End.'

'That'll take you a while on public transport, won't it?'

'I suppose so.'

'My car's outside. If you like I can take you part of the way. I need to pick up two passengers at Bahnhof Zoo: a dog and a woman.'

'Bahnhof Zoo would be great. It's only six or seven stops from there with the U-Bahn.'

Rath asked Tornow for a glass of water to mask the smell of beer, followed his host's lead by washing his face and hands and combed his hair, and soon they were driving along Potsdamer Strasse.

As agreed Charly and Kirie sat on the terrace of the Berlin cafe on Hardenbergstrasse.

'Is it OK if I let you out here?' Rath asked.

'I can manage the rest on foot,' Tornow said. 'No need to accompany me to the platform.'

Rath grinned and switched on the indicator to park.

Charly hadn't seen him, but Kirie recognised the car. The dog could pick out the Buick from hundreds of engine noises. She started barking and, as he cut the engine, Charly spotted him too.

Perhaps he should introduce her to Tornow, he thought. After all, Tornow didn't know her from before. Until now they had kept their relationship a secret from everyone in the Castle. Not even Gräf knew about it, although he was one of Rath's few friends in Berlin. The problem was that he idolised Charly, and had done since the pair worked together.

By now it was too late to weigh up the pros and cons. Kirie dragged Charly towards the car, just as Tornow was opening the passenger door. Rath hurriedly got out, and went round to the other side to receive Kirie's rapturous greeting. Charly smiled at him, she liked how he was with the dog. Tornow looked on.

'Hello, you two,' Rath said. 'Now, that's what I call a greeting. I've brought a colleague along. Allow me to introduce Sebastian Tornow. I've told you about him before.' Tornow stretched out his hand and smiled his winsome smile. 'And this,' Rath continued, 'is Charlotte Ritter, prospective lawyer.'

He broke off when he saw Charly's frozen smile. It was as if it had appeared by accident in place of an altogether different expression, which Charly, somehow, was unable to find.

'A pleasure,' Tornow said, stopping short now himself. Charly didn't say anything more. 'I must push on,' said Tornow, letting go of her hand.

With a tip of his hat, he took his leave, but not before looking back discreetly. Rath couldn't blame him.

'What's the matter with you?' he asked.

She looked at him, apparently bewildered. 'Who was that?'

'I told you that already. My new colleague, perhaps even a new friend. A nice guy, anyway. Sebastian Tornow.'

'I think I've seen him before.'

'He's only been at the Castle for a week.'

'Not at the station.' She gazed through him, the only person on earth who could look at him like that. 'Gereon,' she said. 'There's something I have to confess.'

They had hoped to take a drive out to the countryside while daylight still permitted, but contented themselves with a walk over Cornelius Bridge to the nearby Tiergarten. The dog needed exercise, and Rath wanted to hear Charly's story. He could scarcely believe what she had to say. As they strolled northwards, she explained how she had spent the past week. Since Monday she had been working undercover for Gennat as part of an unofficial operation. She had been detailed to track down Alex and perform surveillance on a cop suspected of murder. This same cop had now been murdered himself. Rath knew Böhm was handling the case from Thursday's briefing.

'And you witnessed this murder?' he asked.

'Not directly. I followed him, and . . . it's best I just show you. We're almost there.'

Soon afterwards, they reached a church, behind which began one of the better residential areas in the city: nice houses, all with small front gardens, clean and well kept. In the Hansaviertel there was no sign of crumbling stucco on the house fronts.

Charly pointed towards an advertising pillar. 'That's where I hid. Coming down Lessingstrasse I naturally kept my distance. When I turned the corner, he was standing by a streetlamp, completely motionless.' She gestured towards a gas lamp six or seven metres away. 'I didn't know what was happening, and just tried to make sure he didn't see me.' She swallowed. 'It wasn't until I went over to him, that I saw the knife in his chest. Or rather, a trench dagger from the war.'

'What the hell was Buddha thinking getting you involved?'

'I think he has a guilty conscience. He probably wasn't expecting things to develop the way they have.'

'You were forbidden from telling me?'

'Gennat and Lange didn't mention you explicitly,' she said, smiling for the first time since Hardenbergstrasse. 'They said I wasn't to tell *anybody*.'

'So, why now?'

Charly took his hand and pulled him and Kirie past the advertising pillar. At the fourth or fifth house she halted. 'It was here,' she said. 'This is where I ran into a cop. Just before I found Kuschke mortally wounded. He was coming towards me, approaching from Händelstrasse, from around the corner.'

'So?'

'This cop ransacked Kuschke's flat on the same day. His victim's flat.'

'A uniform cop killing one of his own? My God, what a horror-story.'

'Until now we thought Kuschke's killer only used the uniform as camouflage, and to gain access to his flat. You know how most landladies go rigid at the sight of a uniform.'

Rath nodded.

'Gereon,' she said. 'The man I saw here three days ago was Sebastian Tornow.'

100

Now everything was quiet, Alex could venture out of her hiding place. She'd never have thought she'd shut herself in a department store again. The business in KaDeWe and Benny's death were only two weeks ago. Now it was Wertheim, of all places, but she didn't have any choice. She urgently needed funds to get out of this city. Cash, that she knew was lying dormant in this vast, confusing mass of buildings. It was spread across the whole store, on every floor, in every department. The tills would contain only change by the evening, as the day's takings were stored in Wertheim's private cellar vault. Cracking it was impossible. No safebreaker had ever tried, not even the Brothers Sass, though she reckoned the Wertheim vault contained more cash than most banks in Berlin.

Getting to the money in the registers was easier, however, especially if you knew where the keys were kept. The cashiers picked them up every morning before the start of their shift, and she knew exactly where.

Jewellery and watches were a no-go. Kalli was dead, and with any other fence she ran the risk of being handed over to the police. So, cash it was, and change above all. It would be a real grind, but it would be worth it. In every till was thirty marks' worth of change, and there were many tills in Wertheim, often several to a department. Alex didn't know how many exactly but it was at least a hundred. This was Europe's largest department store, after all. A hundred times thirty. It would mean a lot of shrapnel, and a lot of weight, which was why she had brought Vicky along. They would have to negotiate their escape together, above all, if they didn't want to leave the spoils behind.

She had no reservations about stealing from her former employer. This would be her last hurrah before leaving Berlin for good.

They had borrowed a hundred and twenty marks, having found the cash in an earthenware pan that still smelled of herring. So far they had only spent around eighty, on a few new items of clothing for herself and Vicky, hair dye and, of course, the digs they were staying in. They had rented the room to continue their campaign of revenge. She had hatched a new plan when she saw the article. She wasn't certain, since it was very vague, but Vicky's call to the station at Wittenbergplatz had settled the matter. At first they had said that Kuschke was on leave, but when she dug a little deeper, saying it was a private matter she needed to discuss with him at his home, the cop on the telephone explained. He was very sorry, he said, to be the one to have to tell her, he didn't know how close she was to Sergeant Major Kuschke, but unfortunately the man had died in tragic circumstances.

Someone had killed the sadistic arsehole!

At first, she wasn't sure if she should be happy or not. It felt as if someone had stolen her chance of revenge. She wouldn't have gone so far as to kill him, just to put the fear of death in him, but now the fucking pig was dead and she didn't know if the punishment was fitting or not. It wouldn't bring Benny back to life, but, then, her own revenge wouldn't have done that either.

Standing in her dark outfit in the dim light of the store's vast atrium, Vicky looked almost exactly like Benny had two weeks before. The night watchmen had finished their rounds. It was time. They wouldn't need more than an hour if they stuck to Alex's route, beginning downstairs in haberdashery.

101

They were the last customers in the Nasse Dreieck but Schorsch, the taciturn landlord, didn't complain. He simply placed beer after beer in front of them with the patience of a saint, every so often adding a short for good measure. A landlord who knew his patrons didn't have to talk much, or take orders.

Rath had imagined his evening panning out rather differently. It was a week since he had last sat here with Gräf, putting the world to rights, and he couldn't think of anything he'd rather be doing after his latest blazing row with Charly.

Why did they always quarrel at the start of the weekend? They would be better off squabbling on Monday or Tuesday, so that they could make up again by Friday, Saturday at the latest. That would be altogether more productive, especially since any reconciliation usually ended with the two of them in bed, which wasn't the worst way to draw a line under the working week.

This time the cause was Sebastian Tornow. He couldn't believe what she had told him. Above all he didn't *want* to believe it: Tornow was no killer. 'You saw this cop for maybe three seconds, and his face is branded on your memory?'

'His smile. It's his smile that's branded on my memory. It was the same man.'

'He's not the only man ever to have smiled.'

'Don't joke, you know it upsets me!'

That was when he knew it wouldn't just blow over. The more arguments he presented the more stubborn she became in her—flimsy—defence.

'Tornow hasn't been in uniform for almost two weeks. It can't have been him in the Hansaviertel.'

He made a triumphant face, but Charly remained unimpressed.

'Even so.' She folded her arms like a defiant child. 'It was him. Just believe me!'

'How can you be so pig-headed?'

'*I'm* not the one being pig-headed around here!'

Five minutes later he was sitting in the car with Kirie on his way to Luisenufer. The dog understood their quarrels least of all. She had been settling in for a cosy evening in Spenerstrasse when suddenly they left without her mistress. Even as she trotted dutifully after him, it was plain that she didn't understand what was going on. People were inexplicable. With dogs it was different. They sized one another up and, as soon as they smelled each other, got down to business. People are far more complicated, thought Rath as he looked at Kirie, curled up at the bar.

He clinked glasses with Gräf who was immersed in his own thoughts. Rath hadn't mentioned the quarrel. Even though Gräf was a friend, he never talked about Charly, just went drinking with him whenever they fought.

'What do you think about the new man?' he asked, offering Gräf a cigarette from his case.

'Seems OK. Why?'

'Just asking.' Rath also took a cigarette and lit it. 'I thought he might be one for our team when he's finished training. It could be worth mentioning to Gennat, don't you think?'

'He's a good fit,' Gräf said. 'Impressive powers of observation and deduction . . .'

'But?'

'But nothing.' Gräf sipped at his beer.

Rath already regretted the question. Gräf would see Tornow as competition and, besides, no one liked being used as a spy. That hadn't been his intention, but now he was curious. 'You don't sound like you're convinced.'

'Some of his opinions are a little out there. I think if it was up to him, he'd put all criminals away without trial.'

'That's exactly what you said the other day in the canteen.' Rath realised he was defending Tornow, but there was no way Gräf could know the baggage the man carried around.

'Maybe. It's frustrating when someone gets away with something. Or when you can't get them even though you know they're guilty. Last week, we had Goldstein on a plate, and now that we can actually prove he did something, he's disappeared.'

'It's something you have to get used to in our line of work. Where would we be without the rule of law?'

'Then I fear young Tornow has a lot to learn,' Gräf said.

'Are you about to sell out a colleague, or what is this?'

'You did ask.'

Rath gazed ruefully into his beer. 'I'm just surprised. I thought the two of you were getting on well.'

'We were until he started asking these strange questions.'

'What kind of questions?'

'Well, what I think of the fact that there are so many criminals at large, for one.'

'Questions like that always bother young officers. More experienced ones too. It's good that he asks questions. It means he wants to learn.'

'It felt more like he was sounding me out. As if he wanted to see if I shared his opinions.' Rath looked at him quizzically. 'He asked me if I thought a good police officer should be able to kill.'

102

Watching the churchgoers streaming out of mass, Rath felt something akin to guilt that he hadn't fulfilled his Sunday duty. Now that cynicism was his only creed, he rarely gave it a second thought, but these people had a different perspective. Believing in something other than the Great Big Nothing, they aroused his envy and scorn in equal measure. He scorned them for their naivety; he envied them their faith.

Having faith made you strong, which was precisely how he *didn't* feel this morning. Worse, he was unsteady on his feet. He had left the Buick at his new permanent parking spot, outside the undertaker's and diagonally opposite the church front. He couldn't request an Opel from the motor pool today without arousing suspicion. He was off duty so, whatever he did here, he was doing it for himself and, since his business didn't concern anyone in the Castle, it felt wise not to have his signature beneath today's date in motor pool records. He checked his watch. Sunday Mass had ended promptly. He surveyed each member of the congregation as they emerged. Joseph Flegenheimer wasn't among them, but of course not, he hadn't visited the church because he harboured Catholic sympathies.

Rath's head was still fuzzy from last night. In truth his quarrel with Charly suited him just fine. He had better things to do than idle the day away with his girlfriend and his dog. He had left Kirie with the Lennartz family, knowing that he couldn't expect her to sit in the car all day. He didn't fancy it much himself, either, but sometimes you just had to bite the bullet. The word 'bite' reminded him of his rations, and he took his first apple from the picnic basket. He still hadn't been at his observation post for five minutes.

An hour later his food supplies were dwindling and there was still no sign of Joseph Flegenheimer. One hour! It felt more like three. He looked down on a solitary sandwich and a hard-boiled egg. Boredom made for hungry work.

He opened the car door to take a stroll down to the main drag. It was pleasantly warm, a gentle breeze was blowing, a beautiful Sunday, and here he was dividing his time between the inside of a car and a telephone booth.

He sighed. He had no choice but to do Marlow's bidding if he didn't want to find himself in serious trouble later tonight. True, he had made progress since his conversation with Gregor Lanke's informant, but he had no desire to throw Christine Möller under a bus. Better to give Marlow a concrete lead on whoever was actually responsible for Red Hugo's death. If he had one by then, that is. If need be, he could always serve up Lanke, but even there Rath had his scruples. The man might be an arsehole, but he didn't deserve to end up in Dr Mabuse's claws. Rath didn't want to be responsible for another two people getting killed; didn't want any more demons haunting him at night.

He needed a concrete lead, but the only thing he had was the telephone number from Christine. How many times had he tried it now? And all because this mysterious number wasn't to be found in any telephone book. The proof of the pudding is in the eating, his mother always used to say. He just had to keep trying.

It was stuffy in the glass booth, a real greenhouse. Rath lifted the receiver and put in a ten-pfennig coin when a face on the other side of the street justified his choice of observation post. In the meantime the operator spoke on the line.

Rath automatically reeled off the number: '*STEPHAN 1701* please.' At the same time he kept an eye on the pretty lady turning into Mühlenstrasse. She must have got off the tram, and it couldn't be a coincidence that she was hanging around here. He followed her with his eyes until she disappeared from his field of vision. He opened the door of the booth to watch as she made for the church. A slightly scratchy voice announced itself on the line.

'Yes.'

He was a little taken aback. He hadn't been expecting to get someone on the line so quickly, after all the failed attempts yesterday and the day before. Back inside the booth, he closed the door, muffling the noise from the street. 'Who am *I* speaking to, please?' he asked. This idiotic custom of answering the telephone without saying your name! Just like Charly!

'Who am *I* speaking to?'

The subscriber refused to be intimidated. Damn it, Rath wasn't prepared for this. He had hoped whoever it was would give their name, so that he could hang up and take care of everything else through the civil register. Perhaps the name might turn up in the files of the Berlin Police . . .

'I find it incredibly rude not to give your name,' he said. He couldn't think of anything more intelligent to say.

'Gereon?' the voice at the other end said, and Rath felt something like an electric shock pass down his spine. It was no coincidence that the voice had felt familiar from the moment he first heard it. 'Is that you?'

He hung up with his mind racing. He lifted the receiver a second time and waited for the operator. 'Operator,' he said. 'Would you be so kind as to repeat the number you just connected me with? I'm not sure I gave you the right one.'

'*STEPHAN 1701*,' a mildly irritated voice said. Rath looked down at the scrap of paper he had used to write the number. There was no doubt. The telephone number provided by Christine Möller, which concealed the man who almost certainly had Red Hugo on his conscience, had been answered by a colleague.

103

Charly paced around her flat like a tiger in a cage. Even at breakfast she hadn't been able to sit still. She simply didn't know what to do. Telephone Lange on a Sunday? Or Gennat? It was unlikely to be a problem, but she wasn't sure it was urgent enough. Gereon's misgivings had driven her so dotty that she no longer quite believed what she had seen in the Hansaviertel. Had there actually been a uniform cop? And had he really looked like Gereon's new colleague? She was furious with him. He could never back her, not even this one time. He always had to play devil's advocate!

She knew how sensitive it was to accuse a colleague of murder. Because that was what it boiled down to. He couldn't be a harmless witness if it was the same man who had ransacked Kuschke's flat.

Damn it! She'd have felt happier with Gereon onside. Just with him being there at all.

She could always resume her search for Alex, but there was too much going on inside her mind since she had seen Sebastian Tornow smile and experienced her moment of insight.

The telephone rang.

Perhaps it was Gereon? Despite her rage she was happy to call it quits. It was all getting too much for her, and she could use him by her side. Then *why*, she asked herself, did you send him packing yesterday evening, you silly goose? She had wanted to borrow money off him, too, since Maltritz would be back tomorrow for the rent. Very well. If he wanted a reconciliation he could have it. Just not right this minute . . .

Come on, don't be childish, don't keep him in suspense. He's already called five times. She lifted the receiver. 'Yes?'

'Charlotte Ritter?' It wasn't Gereon's voice.

'Speaking.' In the same instant she wondered whether it was wise to confirm her identity. 'Who is it, please?'

'I'd like to speak to Gereon Rath.'
'He isn't here.'
'Then please excuse the interruption.'
'No problem,' she said, but the caller had already hung up.

104

Rath slammed his fist down and swore. Engaged! Did she have to be on the phone at precisely this moment? He hung up and the ten-pfennig piece jangled onto the change slot.

Marion Bosetzky had disappeared inside the church, and he was still standing in this telephone booth trying to reach Charly. He had to speak to her, now, as soon as possible, quarrel or no. He couldn't help thinking back to last night ever since he had heard Tornow's voice on the line. It didn't make any sense, but something here was rotten. His argument from yesterday resurfaced: *Tornow hasn't been in uniform for almost two weeks now.* But that wasn't true. There was a day last week when Sebastian Tornow had been in uniform, even if he was still a long way from the Hansaviertel: Schönholz Cemetery in Pankow, at Emil Kuhfeld's funeral.

He took the ten-pfennig piece from the coin return and put it back in the slot. Hopefully she wasn't speaking to the grinning man, or else this could take forever. Keeping the church portal in view he gave the number. Still no sign of Marion Bosetzky, illegal nightclub dancer, chambermaid and gangster's moll. At last, the dial tone! Charly picked up.

'Yes?'

Well, of course, she never gave her name, unless she was at work. Now he remembered why he found it so annoying. 'Charly,' he said quickly. 'Gereon here. I hope you're not still mad.'

'Gereon! I . . . what a coincidence. I was just . . .'

'Listen,' he interrupted. 'I'm in a rush. I'm sorry about yesterday. I'm a total imbecile.'

'You've finally realised?'

'Listen,' he said again. 'I need to know exactly when you saw Tornow in the Hansaviertel. What day? What time?'

'Wednesday about half past twelve.'

A fit! The funeral started at eleven, at which point he had said goodbye to Tornow. After that he hadn't seen him. The cemetery was right next to the S-Bahn. Changing once or twice, it would take no longer than half an hour, forty-five minutes, to get to Tiergarten.

'I think it really was Tornow you saw in the Hansaviertel,' he said. 'Something's not right. It's just possible he had something to do with Red Hugo's death too, and Rudi the Rat.'

'Pardon me?'

'Two gangsters. Right now I've got something else to take care of, but I can be at yours in an hour. Wait for me there.'

'But . . .'

'Just wait. An hour tops. Then we can get something to eat, and I'll tell you everything.'

He hung up, left the cramped, stuffy booth and walked quickly towards the church. On the way he debated how he could provide Charly with a plausible explanation for his knowledge of the Hugo Lenz case. Under no circumstances could she discover that he was working for Johann Marlow. He thought about Henning and Czerwinski. Unlike him, Plisch and Plum were actually involved in the case, and Charly knew that the three of them often worked together. Whether she believed him or not was of secondary importance. What mattered now was that they pooled their knowledge of Kuschke, Lenz and Höller.

Things here could be tied up quickly. Once he had Marion Bosetzky, everything else would follow. If need be, he could always cuff her and take her back to the station. After all, why shouldn't an inspector just stumble upon a woman who had been the object of a police search warrant for more than a week? Perhaps it would be enough to lean on her a little so that she led him to Goldstein's current pied-à-terre. In that case he'd save his handcuffs for the Yank and let Marion go. Both would earn him points in Gennat's eyes, although the Goldstein variant was clearly preferable. Something like that could make him quite a name at the Castle, especially since the man had twice given him the slip.

He entered Saint Norbert's through the middle door, crossing to a little anteroom before reaching the nave. He saw the holy water and, without thinking, dipped his fingers in it to make the sign of the cross. He hadn't been inside a church for a long time, but the rituals of childhood soon took over. He had never been sure about his faith, but there was no doubt in his mind that he was Catholic.

He took in the familiar smell of a Catholic church, the same the world over, everywhere you went a slice of home and childhood. Perhaps they were the same thing: childhood and home.

It was pleasantly cool as he made his way through the nave alone, his steps echoing against the white walls. There was no sign of Marion Bosetzky. Where on earth had she got to? He looked inside the confessionals: empty. He even popped into the sacristy: again, no one. Perhaps in the organ loft? She had to be in here somewhere, or he would have seen her leave. He climbed to the upper floors, to the section of building overlooking the street. It looked more like an office than a priest's quarters. Rath gazed around curiously. Had Marion Bosetzky disappeared inside one of the rooms? Was she paying the priest a visit?

He knocked on one of the doors. No one answered. He pressed down on the handle, finding the door unlocked. He opened it slightly and looked inside. The room was similar to their offices at the Castle: desk, telephone, roll-front cupboards, even a typewriter and a smaller table by the window. Only the large crucifix and pictures of the Madonna and the saints made it look any different from police headquarters. Instead of the obligatory Hindenburg portrait was an oil painting depicting a saint in Norbertine habit holding a monstrance. Out of his chalice crawled a spider. Rath could vaguely remember a legend in which Saint Norbert of Xanten had drunk a spider that fell into his communion chalice, displaying both death-defying courage and an unshakeable belief in God. It was one of many hagiographies that had been drummed into him as a child. He glanced out of the round-arched window. Below on Mühlenstrasse, his Buick glistened in the sun.

Aside from a saint with a spider in his chalice, there was nothing unusual here. He left the office and knocked on the door opposite. Again, no response. The room was dark. He was groping for a light switch when something jumped at him.

The blow to his chin didn't strike him flush, but only because he had turned his head to one side. A blow like that to the point of the chin would have knocked him out, but as it was, he just felt a hellish pain in his jaw and fell backwards against the doorframe. The figure was on him, dealing a second blow to the solar plexus that left him short of breath, before making for the door. Rath stuck out a leg and, in the light from the corridor, caught sight of his attacker.

Abraham Goldstein.

He didn't have time to wonder how Marion Bosetzky had morphed into the Yank. Goldstein was now running downstairs. Struggling to get his breath back, Rath gave pursuit, leaping as Goldstein reached the bottom. The pair crashed onto the stone floor with Goldstein taking the brunt. He was still dazed as Rath knocked him down with a right hook. He got up before toppling backwards into the nave of the church, his hands desperately searching for a hold, but succeeding only in tearing prayer books from a shelf.

Rath jumped after him to finish him off, as he had stupidly left his handcuffs in the car. As he was about to throw a second punch, Goldstein dodged, recoiled, seized Rath's arm and rolled over backwards. Rath didn't understand what was happening until Goldstein pulled him down with his entire body weight. He felt the Yank's boot against his groin as he slammed against the church pews, Goldstein having now let go of his arm. There was a loud thump as the wood struck his forehead and he saw stars, teetering like a ship on troubled waters.

Then Goldstein was on him again, pulling him up by the collar. Rath dodged the ensuing punch, and attempted a kick to the groin which momentarily gave Goldstein pause for thought. Just when he saw his chance to land the deciding blow and send the Yank into the realm of dreams, he felt a hard thud against the right side of his head and heard a loud, gong-like clang. There was a flash of brightness which seemed to light up the world before everything went black.

105

Charly paced her flat increasingly nervously. She had already smoked seven cigarettes, one after the other, not knowing whether she should be happy or even more furious with the bastard. He had barely let her get a word in.

'I'm in a rush', she imitated. What was he thinking? Snubbing her like that. At least he had conceded, but what was it he said about those gangsters? That their death had something to do with Kuschke's? Red Hugo had been found dead at the Mühlendamm, and, as far she knew, he wasn't Gereon's case.

For some reason his telephone call had made her even more nervous. Pacing up and down, she felt the need to do something, but hadn't the slightest idea what. He had told her to wait, but her curiosity was greater than her rage. Almost an hour had passed. Where was he, and who was it that had telephoned for him? Did it have to do with his latest discovery?

There, the doorbell!

She checked her watch. Gereon had telephoned forty-seven minutes ago. If he had shaken a leg to get here it was most unlike him.

Her rage subsided, her tension eased. She had wanted to be mad with him but, as was so often the case, when he finally showed up her anger dissolved into thin air. At least she had the self-discipline to wipe the smile off her face as she opened the door.

She froze.

It wasn't Gereon.

Sebastian Tornow was outside with an older man who looked familiar somehow, even if she couldn't quite place him. She only knew it was his pistol pointed at her.

106

His head hurt. In fact, his whole body hurt. It was an unpleasant awakening. He'd sooner have slipped back into unconsciousness. At first he didn't know where he was; he saw angels and saints in fluttering robes. Then he remembered: Saint Norbert's. Goldstein!

Carefully, he turned his head. He was still in the church, and on one of the pews sat a mildly overweight priest, holding a battered incense burner, the sort of canister Rath would have swung as a ten-year-old boy. Though not to knock anyone out, which seemed to be what the priest had used it for.

Rath felt his temples. He had a mighty bump above his right eyebrow. 'Did you do that?' he asked.

Only now did he see Goldstein lying a few metres away and looking a little worse for wear too, holding the back of his head where the canister must have struck him.

'I don't tolerate violence in the house of God,' the priest said, sounding like a teacher who had caught two young punks fighting in the schoolyard.

'That man's a dangerous gangster,' Rath said, pointing towards Goldstein. 'He's armed.'

'This man,' said the priest, 'has sought the sanctuary of the Holy Church, and he has been granted it. Besides, he is unarmed.'

'What did you say?' Abraham Goldstein, a Jewish gangster, had found asylum here, in a Catholic church? 'There's a warrant issued for his arrest.'

'This man is enjoying church asylum, and, as long as I'm priest around here, won't be surrendered to any secular justice system.'

Rath could almost have laughed if the situation wasn't so serious.

'Who says?'

'I do. Johannes Warszawski.'

'We're not living in the Middle Ages!'

'Ecclesia iure asyli gaudet ita ut rei, qui ad illam confugerint, inde non

sint extrahendi, nisi necessitas urgeat, sine assensu Ordinarii, vel saltem rectoris ecclesiae,' Priest Warszawski declaimed.

That went beyond Rath's knowledge of Latin. 'I'm sorry?'

'From the *Codex Iuris Canonici*. It means something like no one who seeks asylum in my church can be made to go with people like you. At least not without picking a fight with me first.'

'What does church law say about priests striking police officers with incense canisters?'

'You're a police officer?' Warszawski showed no contrition, despite this revelation. 'You don't behave like one.'

'He's telling the truth,' Goldstein said, taking up residence on a church pew.

Rath could do without his support. He ignored the Yank.

'This man is a murderer,' he said, struggling to his feet. 'He stabbed someone to death in Humboldthain and is alleged to have shot two criminals.'

'He's no murderer,' the priest said. 'He's simply wanted for murder. He's told me everything. That you and your fellow officers are wrongly pursuing him.'

'You believe him?'

'Yes, I believe him.' Coming from the priest, the words didn't seem so naive. Perhaps because Rath shared his opinion. All the same, Goldstein was still a contract killer, who killed at the behest of an American criminal organisation. At least that's what they said over there.

'Joseph Flegenheimer vouched for this man,' the priest said. 'That's enough for me.'

'How does a Catholic priest know an orthodox Jew?'

'I'm an old friend of Joseph's. You can have a good old-fashioned rough-and-tumble with him about questions of faith.'

'You can have a good old-fashioned ding-dong with most Jews,' Goldstein said.

'You're one to talk,' Rath said, holding his head.

'You weren't exactly pussy-footing about either, but that bump there,' Goldstein pointed towards Rath's head, 'is from the priest.'

'You only have yourselves to blame,' the priest said. 'There are two things that I won't tolerate in my church: one, that someone who's sought the protection of the Holy Church should be surrendered to the state's henchmen . . .' That was directed at Rath. '. . . and, two, that blood should be spilled here.' That was directed at Goldstein.

The pair nodded like a couple of candidates for confirmation.

'Where's Marion, by the way?' Rath asked.

'Long gone. There's a rear exit,' Goldstein said. 'You should have come in a different car, Detective. Marion recognised the Buick.'

'You should have gone with her.'

'I couldn't have known you'd sniff around the whole building. Besides, it's about time we spoke in private, away from the prying eyes of your colleagues.'

Priest Warszawski understood. He got up and took the battered old incense burner back inside the sacristy.

Rath took a seat on the pew next to Goldstein. Despite everything he was alleged to have done, he couldn't help but warm to the man. 'What is there to talk about that can't be discussed in an interrogation room at police headquarters?'

'A whole lot of things. I hope you have time.'

Rath looked at his watch. 'Not really. I'm already running late.'

'Then I'll keep it brief. Firstly: I did beat up those bastards in the park. They were trying to pummel an old man. I even shot one of them in the foot. It was dumb luck; the gun just went off.' Goldstein looked at him, as if trying to gauge whether or not Rath believed him. 'Secondly, I didn't kill anyone, simple as that.'

'That was the abridged version?'

'Yes.'

'Is that why you kept quiet about what you did in New York?'

'What I've done in the States is none of your business.' Goldstein gave him an angry stare. 'The only thing you can charge me with here is illegal possession of firearms, but you can't even prove that.' The gangster laughed. 'Pastor Warszawski has the Remington. That was his one condition, before he unfolded the camp bed.'

Rath looked at his watch. He should have been with Charly long ago. He knew how much she despised lateness, and there was no way he could explain that he and Abraham Goldstein had fought in a church and afterwards settled down for a nice chat.

'You're aware that the old man you helped is the only person who can exonerate you?' Goldstein shrugged. 'Take me to him. Do you know where he lives?'

'Of course. I walked him home. His name is Teitelbaum. Simon Teitelbaum. I don't think he's been here long. At least, he doesn't behave like it.'

'He didn't want to tell me his name,' Rath said. He took another glance at his watch and stood up. 'I really do have to go now.'

'Why should I trust you not to have the church here besieged by your Warrants unit?'

Rath shrugged. 'I'm Catholic.'

'The same goes for the Irish in Brooklyn, but I wouldn't trust them as far as I could throw them.'

'You trust the Italians, if I've understood your file. They're Catholic, aren't they?'

'Trust isn't a matter of religious affiliation.'

'Let's make a deal. Isn't that what you say in the States?' Goldstein looked surprised. 'I'll promise to leave you alone until you've taken me to this witness, if you promise me something in return.'

'I'm listening.'

'That you don't ship out on the next boat to the States.'

'If only it were that simple,' Goldstein laughed. 'You see, that's one of things I wanted to talk to you about but, sadly, you don't have time.'

107

What a beautiful Sunday, Alex thought as she stepped onto the pedestrian bridge across the Spree. For the first time since Benny's death, she felt like she was getting back on top of things, and not just because last night had passed off without a hitch. The bags, weighed down with coins, were so heavy that she and Vicky almost hadn't got them through the window. No, Alex felt good because she was finally fixing everything she had neglected so for long. Soon everything would be back on track, above all her life and Vicky's.

She had even purchased a ticket for the S-Bahn journey to Bellevue. She couldn't run the risk of being caught fare-dodging again, not now. Besides, money was no longer a concern at twenty pfennigs a pop. They hadn't got three thousand marks out of the Wertheim registers, but it was well over two, and she'd never earned that much stealing watches with Benny. She should have thought of it sooner, but her reluctance to break into Wertheim prevented her. She was through with this city now, with Wertheim too. The store owed her this parting gift for all the misery her dismissal had caused.

She reached the junction at Spenerstrasse, feeling nervous and not knowing what to say to Charlotte, the court woman. Secretly, Alex hoped she wouldn't be home. She could slip the envelope with the hundred and fifty marks and the little note she had written through the letterbox, and the matter would be resolved.

With a queasy feeling in her stomach she climbed the stairs and, for a moment, stood outside the door to the flat before pressing the bell. Nothing. She pressed again and laid her ear against the wooden door. Nothing doing inside. A noise made her spin around. The door opposite had opened and in the frame stood an elderly lady in her Sunday best.

'Good day,' Alex said, dropping a curtsey. She could be a good little girl when she wanted.

The woman looked her up and down. 'Good day, young lady,' she replied. 'Are you looking for Fräulein Ritter?'

Alex nodded.

'She left ten minutes ago.' The woman painstakingly closed her door, turning the keys twice before saying, in a mildly disparaging tone: 'In the company of several gentlemen . . .'

There could be any number of things a woman might do on a Sunday afternoon *in the company of several gentlemen,* and evidently she disapproved of them all.

'I have a message for Fräulein Ritter,' Alex said, pretending she had to write something on the envelope. She waited until the woman had descended the stairs before fetching a picklock, acquired for the Wertheim break-in, from her bag. Only when she heard the front door close did she take the picklock and prise open the door to the flat.

Perhaps it was bravado, but she wanted to surprise the court woman by returning the money to the pot. It was possible, of course, that she hadn't even noticed it was gone, and wouldn't realise the amount had increased by thirty marks. Alex was picturing Charlotte's face when she noticed the mess. The flat was like a bombsite.

All the drawers had been pulled out, their contents strewn across the floor. Books were torn from shelves, letters and files were scattered everywhere. Total chaos. It looked like a break-in, but hadn't the old woman said Fräulein Ritter had only left a few minutes before?

In the company of several gentlemen.

Alex racked her brains. What had happened here? Which gentlemen had Charlotte left with? Were they the ones responsible for this chaos? Perhaps they were cops who had found out she was sheltering a wanted criminal?

She put the envelope back in her bag and looked around, hoping to find an answer. There were no traces of a struggle, although someone had clearly been looking for something. It couldn't be the little handheld pistol that must have rolled out of some drawer or other, Charlotte's weapon from the tannery. Cops would have taken something like that with them, wouldn't they? She picked it up. The cool, heavy metal felt good. She pulled the magazine out. It was empty, though the rounds lay close by. She had to fiddle around, but soon the magazine clicked back into place.

She didn't want to leave the money in this chaos. Who could say if it would ever reach Charlotte? She left the envelope where it was in her bag and stowed the pistol next to it. It wouldn't hurt to own a thing like that, if Kralle's crew came looking for her again. She knew a handbag wasn't the best way to conceal a weapon, but there was nothing about her new summer dress that could serve as a holster.

She was just about to open the door when she heard footsteps in the stairwell. Since she didn't want to have to explain what she was doing coming out of an empty flat, she listened at the door. Someone was coming up the stairs with a heavy tread. A man. Another instant, and he would be past. The coast would be clear.

When the footsteps approached the door to the flat, she instinctively retreated a few metres on tiptoes. The doorbell rang and she tried to hold her breath.

There was another ring. Away, she thought, go away! Can't you see there's no one home?

A key turned in the lock, and her heart almost stopped. She fumbled for the pistol, looked for the safety catch and aimed, just as the man appeared in the doorframe. His hands were already in the air.

Rath had been prepared for anything, but not a girl standing in the hallway with a little pocket pistol trained on his chest. The inside of the flat looked as if a bomb had been dropped. 'What's all this then?' he asked.

The girl looked at him suspiciously. She was like a cornered beast of prey. Rath had recognised her immediately. The fake hair dye couldn't fool him, nor the smart summer dress.

'It's Alex, isn't it?'

Her answer was a tentative nod.

'Charly told me about you.'

'Charly?'

At last she spoke to him, but her pistol was still raised. He debated whether he could get to his Walther, but it was hopeless. He had to talk. 'Charlotte Ritter. The woman who lives here.'

'I see.'

He pointed his chin at the pistol. 'Does it have to be like this?'

She let the weapon drop. 'No, I just thought that . . .'

That was all she had time for. Rath made a full-length dive, reaching with both hands for her firing arm. He felt the little minx kick and punch, but absorbed the blows until he had control of the weapon, letting it slide across the hall floor into the kitchen and under the table. He held her arms tight and used his body weight to press her flailing legs to the floor. It was an unfair match, and the struggle was soon over.

'Now, how about telling me what you're doing in this flat, threatening me with a pistol.'

She spat at him and he dodged just in time.

'I've had enough wrestling matches for one day,' he said. 'Shall we bring this to a peaceful end, or do I have to spend the next three hours on top of you?'

Her eyes looked daggers. 'The first one,' she said.

He stood up and kept a close eye on her, but she made no move to punch, kick or spit again. He picked up her handbag.

Alex stood up and held her hand.

'I'm sorry,' he said, 'but it's what you have to expect when you threaten someone with a gun. It's no laughing matter.'

'I know that but, shit, life is no laughing matter.'

Rath couldn't help but smile. 'What are you doing here, and where's Charly?'

'I could ask you the same thing.'

'I'm her . . . fiancé.'

'What are you going to do? Are you going to call the cops?'

'I *am* the cops.'

He had said it casually enough, but noticed how she gave a start, squinting towards the exit as if she might hightail it at any moment.

'Don't worry,' he said. 'I'm one of the good guys. You don't have anything to fear from me. Charly told me all about you, and about the business in KaDeWe with the cop. I'm sorry about your friend.'

Rummaging in her bag he pulled out a set of picklocks, and his compassion came to a sudden end.

'Did you break in here?'

'Did you think I crawled in through the keyhole?'

'Are you responsible for this chaos?'

'I didn't take anything.'

'What's this?' He pointed to her envelope and fished out a dozen ten mark notes.

'I was returning it. I borrowed money from your fiancée.'

He shook his head in disbelief.

'Take a look if you don't believe me. There's a letter inside.'

He skimmed what she had written. THANK YOU FOR EVERYTHING, it said. I'M SORRY ABOUT THE MONEY. I FOUND IT BY CHANCE AND BORROWED IT BECAUSE I NEEDED IT. I HOPE THIS WILL MAKE UP FOR IT. SORRY.

'You *borrowed* it, did you?'

'I pay my debts. The money doesn't belong to you, anyway. Put it back in the envelope and give me back my bag.'

She had a big mouth, no doubt about it, but she was right too. He replaced the envelope and returned the bag.

'Take your time, and tell me what happened.'

'I've only been here a few minutes. This is how it looked when I got here. Maybe those men have something to do with it.'

Rath felt an alarm bell sound in his head. 'What men?'

'Your girlfriend went off with a couple of men. That's all I know.' Alex shrugged. 'Ask the woman, your neighbour. She saw them.'

'Frau Brettschneider?'

'Whatever her name is. The one opposite.'

'Frau Brettschneider.' Rath sighed. 'What exactly did she see?'

'She said that Fräulein Ritter left a few minutes ago: *In the company of several gentlemen*. That's all.'

The alarm bells were sounding even louder now but, knowing that he was to blame for the trouble Charly was in, he said nothing. Instead, he dashed across the landing, positioned himself on the doormat, and pressed the bell above the name *Irmgard Brettschneider*. Never in a million years had he imagined this. He rang a few times, but there was no one inside.

'You can ring as much as you like, she isn't home.' Alex was standing behind him, bag on her shoulders. 'I reckon she's taking her Sunday stroll or something.'

He was beginning to calm down again. Perhaps there was a logical explanation for all this. 'Where are you going?' he asked.

'Do you have a problem with me leaving?'

She was already on the stairs when he called after her. 'The fact that I'm turning a blind eye doesn't mean I approve of robbing department stores.'

Alex turned when she was halfway down. 'I couldn't care less. Keep your opinions to yourself.'

'They aren't my opinions; they're the law. Breaking and entering is illegal. Think about that.' Shit, he thought, you sound just like your own father.

Alex reacted like an obstreperous daughter. 'Right,' she said. 'Perhaps you should have a think about it too. I mean, what does a department store like that actually do? They buy jewellery and watches for I don't know how many tens of thousands of marks and put it in their display window and charge double the price. Ten thousand marks for putting something in the window? I do a lot more for my money, I can tell you.'

She was gone. Probably she isn't too far wrong, he thought. Figuratively speaking, any number of so-called pillars of the German economy did little more than window dressing to make their exorbitant gains.

He went back inside Charly's flat. They had made a real mess: books and papers were scattered all over the floor; only her address book was in its rightful place, next to the telephone on the chest of drawers, and open at the letter R. On the second line, under RAABE, KARIN, written in her fine, elegant hand stood RATH, GEREON, LUISENUFER 47, 1. REAR BUILDING. TEL. MORITZPLATZ 2955. Complete with address and telephone number. All that was missing was his shoe size.

It looked as if someone was about to pay him a visit. Perhaps he could still catch the bastards. Before leaving he looked under the kitchen table. The pistol was no longer there. Alex had outmanoeuvred him after all.

108

She didn't have the faintest idea where she was. The men had dropped a hood over her head as soon as they left Moabit, and hadn't removed it until they set her down on this stool.

It felt like she was in a bad film. What was happening? Tornow and his helpers had taken an ordinary civilian captive from her flat in broad daylight. She still couldn't believe it.

In addition to Tornow and the man with the pistol was a third man who had driven the car. She had identified it as a Horch, but hadn't been able to read the number plate.

The room was windowless, a cellar perhaps, but she couldn't be sure. Unlikely though, on reflection, since she could feel the heat of day. All three men sat behind a table. It felt like a tribunal, a Holy Inquisition, and she was the witch standing trial.

At least they hadn't bound her.

Tornow sat on the left, with the older man—Charly put him in his early fifties—in the middle. The pistol lay before him on the table. To the right was the driver, whose face she saw for the first time. Draped behind the three of them was a kind of flag or wall-hanging, a black cloth, which bore the silhouette of a great white hand, reminding her of the lapel badge and sew-on patch they had found in Kuschke's box.

So, there it was, the first link between Arsehole-Cadet Tornow and the deceased Kuschke. If she had any lingering doubts that Tornow was responsible for the sergeant major's death, they were now well and truly swept aside.

'Do you know why you're here, Fräulein Ritter?' the older man asked. Evidently he was the highest ranking of the three. Charly debated where she knew him from; she was almost willing to bet he was a cop too. The driver likewise.

Police officers who abducted a woman. Unbelievable!

'Why I'm here? Probably because you wanted to play a hand of *Doppelkopf* and you were missing a fourth man. Well, I'm afraid I must disappoint you. First, I'm a woman, and second, I only play skat. Seeing as you don't actually need me, can I go?'

'I have to admire your sense of humour in a situation like this.'

'Exactly what kind of situation are we talking about? So far, all I've seen are criminal offences: trespass, intimidation, false imprisonment. What the whole thing means, I'm still not sure. Are you trying to extort money? Again, I have to disappoint you there, my parents really aren't that rich.'

'That's a shame, but I would have thought our operation spoke for itself. We're trying to prevent you from making a serious mistake. It seems you sighted Police Lieutenant Tornow at a given time and in a given place, despite the many witnesses who would attest otherwise.'

'What an elegant sentence. You must be either a cop or a lawyer.'

The man smiled. 'Well, you're a bit of both, aren't you. With the emphasis on *bit*.'

Now Charly remembered where she had seen the man, although she still wasn't quite sure. 'Do you really think you're going to get away with this? You abducted me! I might not know where you've taken me, but I do know who I have to thank for it.'

'We're aware that you've already made Lieutenant Tornow's acquaintance, but he isn't here. Nor did you see him in the Hansaviertel.'

'I know who you are too, Chief Inspector Scheer. I hope you've seen to your own alibi.'

The man in the middle appeared genuinely thrown. So, it *was* him. Rudi Scheer. It had been a shot in the dark. Scheer had run the armoury at Alex, before being transferred out for weapons smuggling.

'You have good powers of observation,' Scheer said, 'but I'm not here either. Just like Sergeant Klinger next to me.'

He meant the driver. No doubt he had given the man's name and rank to demonstrate their certainty that no one would be brought to account.

'Since you're just imagining all this, Fräulein Ritter,' Tornow said, 'why don't you tell us what you know, and what Gereon Rath knows? And whether you have any proof? What did you find in Kuschke's flat?'

'One thing I do know: there's no way you'll get away with this.'

'There are certain influential people who move in our circles. Underestimate us at your peril!' Tornow smiled. How could he be so friendly in a situation like this?

'That's why you *imagine* you're above the law?' Charly was talking herself into a rage. 'Do you know what you are, Herr Scheer? You're nothing but a crummy arms dealer. They should have finished you off when they had the chance, instead of transferring you out to Charlottenburg.'

Scheer looked at her in amusement.

'You abducted me,' Charly continued, 'do you really think you're going to get away with it, or are you planning to kill me, to keep all this hushed up? Don't you think Gereon Rath already knows what happened and who's behind it?'

She certainly hoped he did.

'What Gereon Rath knows is what you're supposed to be telling us,' Scheer said. 'You needn't fear for your life. We aren't going to harm a hair on your head. We won't have to. Of course, we won't shy away from it if need be, but we're counting on your good sense. I'm sure you wouldn't want to make a fool of yourself, and risk your career.' He tried to smile, but didn't manage quite so well as Tornow. 'You won't be getting much sleep in the next few hours. That can make people rather talkative, you know.'

It didn't sound like they were going to release her any time soon.

109

Rath parked the Buick in Ritterstrasse, pulled his hat down and turned up the collar of his coat despite the warm weather. Only now did he approach Luisenufer. There were no suspicious vehicles near the courtyard entrance and the coast seemed clear. The yard was deserted, as always on a Sunday. What if they've laid a trap? he thought, stepping into the dim stairwell. What if they're waiting for you in your flat? He took the Walther out of its holster, released the safety catch and hoped he didn't run into Frau Liebig or her husband from upstairs.

He turned the key slowly, quietly, and stormed into the flat, weapon drawn, pointing the Walther into every room. Nothing. Whoever had been here was gone.

Rath had guessed what awaited him, but was still surprised at the havoc. It was worse than Spenerstrasse. Half his tableware lay shattered on the kitchen floor, books and papers fluttered on the floor. Flowerpots were tipped over and in pieces, the wardrobe was completely empty, and his mattress had been sliced open, along with his favourite chair. But they had saved the worst for the living room.

They had cleared out his record cabinet.

A great many of his records were broken, including some that were irreplaceable, having been sent over from the States by his brother, Severin. The bastards would pay for this; Tornow and whoever else was in cahoots with him!

He tidied as best he could, found a cup that was still intact and put water on for coffee. He had to collect Kirie from the Lennartzes in half an hour, and could use a shot of caffeine to help him think things through.

Two hours later, Rath was parked in Spenerstrasse again. Dusk was falling as he rang on Irmgard Brettschneider's door for the second time that day.

Beforehand he had taken another look inside Charly's flat, but nothing had changed.

The neighbour who had so often regarded him suspiciously, but never exchanged a word with him, now stared as though he were an apparition.

'What can I do for you?' she asked.

'Good evening, Frau Brettschneider. Would you mind doing me a favour?'

She gazed at him as if he were asking for a cup of flour and two eggs, and Rath realised now would be a good time to reach for his police identification. He took the document out of his jacket and held it under her nose.

'Rath, CID,' he said. 'It concerns Fräulein Ritter. She was seen leaving her flat this afternoon in the company of several men.'

'Has she . . . Is she . . .' Irmgard Brettschneider struggled to find the right words. 'Is it prostitution?' she asked finally. Rath didn't know whether to laugh or vent his rage on this careworn woman with the overactive imagination.

'Please! Fräulein Ritter is a judicial clerk.'

Frau Brettschneider gave a confused nod. 'Of course, of course. I just thought . . . with the police in the building. So . . .'

'It is possible that Fräulein Ritter was the victim of a kidnapping,' he said.

Brettschneider looked horrified. 'Those nice men? You must be mistaken.'

'You saw them?'

'Through the peephole,' she said, apologetically. 'Two well-dressed men. An older man, and a younger man.'

'Would you recognise them if you saw a photograph?'

She hunched her shoulders. 'I think so. Do I need to go to the station?'

'That won't be necessary for the time being. May I come in?'

She gazed into the stairwell, nodded and stepped aside. He entered the flat and she closed the door behind them, leading him into a meticulously tidy living room. A tea table with two chairs stood by the window overlooking Spenerstrasse. He could see his Buick at the corner. He sat and took a photograph from Tornow's personal file, which had been passed to his office by Warrants.

'That's a police officer,' Brettschneider said as she looked at the image which showed Sebastian Tornow under a shako wearing his best smile. 'I thought this was a kidnapping.'

'Was this man present?'

She nodded. 'In plainclothes, not uniform.'

'Undercover operation. Do you see?' He gave her a conspiratorial smile and she nodded.

'Are you . . . Is that why you're in Fräulein Ritter's flat from time to time?' she asked. 'Are you undercover as well?'

He nodded. 'Keep it between us.'

'Why should she have been kidnapped?'

'I can't talk about that.' Rath lowered his voice. 'Official secrets.'

Irmgard Brettschneider gave an eager nod. 'I won't say a thing, Inspector!' She was beginning to flourish; she ought to have been a secret agent. 'I have a number plate too,' she whispered, as if her flat was being bugged. 'I always take down the registration of whoever parks outside. You never know. It was a black sedan. I can't give you the make, I'm afraid, I'm not so good with cars. But I do have the registration if that would help?'

Rath nodded, wondering how often Frau Brettschneider must have watched him coming and going, in the stairwell, perhaps even on the street outside.

'That would be a great help.'

It was dark when he parked on Luisenufer, right outside the house this time. He had spent over two hours at the Castle trying everything to get into Road Traffic, but it was all locked on a Sunday, like most offices at head-quarters. He didn't dare use official channels and call in the division chief or the public prosecutor. What, after all, could he tell them?

He stepped inside the smoky hallway, hoping that Charly might have returned; that she had spent the last few hours waiting for him while he prowled around the station and her flat. Only when he stood at the kitchen door did he realise what was confusing him about the smoke. It didn't smell of Junos. In fact, it didn't smell of cigarettes.

It smelled of cigars.

Thus he was less surprised than he might have been, as he entered the kitchen and saw Johann Marlow with a cigar between his teeth, tickling the back of Kirie's head. The dog didn't appear to have moved since Rath had left the flat. On a second chair sat Liang. Two more men in summer coats stood by the dresser.

Marlow looked up. 'There was no one here when we rang the bell, so we took the liberty of letting ourselves in.'

'I see you've made yourselves at home.'

'As far as we could, but it's not exactly tidy in here.'

'It was the men who killed Hugo Lenz,' he said. 'They got wind that I'm onto them.' He took the photograph of Tornow from his jacket and laid it on the table. 'Sebastian Tornow. The other one's already dead. A Sergeant Major Jochen Kuschke.'

'Respect,' Marlow said. He looked at the two men by the dresser and said: 'You could take a leaf out of this man's book.'

'So far, there's no official investigation against Tornow. The evidence is pretty thin, and I've only just discovered he's responsible for the whole thing. Clearly, he's trying to provoke conflict in the underworld. He probably killed Rudi Höller too.'

Marlow nodded thoughtfully. It suited him that police headquarters still didn't know. 'Where might I find this Tornow?' he asked.

'That's just it. I'm afraid he's taken someone hostage.'

110

They were right. Sleep deprivation was the worst torture you could inflict on someone without actually injuring them.

So far, it was only one night, but they were just getting started. Charly had slept badly the night before too, as she always did when she fought with Gereon. What she wouldn't give for a little nap, but whenever she was about to nod off someone shook her awake.

They had alternated during the night: Tornow, Scheer and Klinger, and other men she didn't know. For hours at a time they had sat in front of her asking the same questions over and over. What do you know? What does Inspector Rath know? By their style of questioning, she knew they must be police, but it just didn't fit. She had always thought of police officers as the good guys—with the odd exception.

She couldn't help thinking of Gereon, the way he had reacted yesterday (or was it the day before? She could no longer remember), his disbelief when she told him about Tornow and what she had seen. He would scarcely believe this, either. What about the others: Gennat and Böhm? What if everyone she accused could provide an alibi? Perhaps Tornow and Scheer were right and no one would believe her. On reflection Gereon might, perhaps. What had he said on the telephone yesterday? Or the day before? Today? Her thoughts went round in circles as she began to doze.

Her body longed to fall into blissful sleep.

Until she was shaken brutally awake.

'Where did Gereon Rath get this telephone number?' a voice asked. Not Scheer, or Tornow, but one of the other voices that had been tormenting her. She didn't have any idea what they were talking about, otherwise she might just have blabbed.

111

The Road Traffic Department opened at eight thirty. Rath had been sitting on the wooden bench outside since quarter past. Shortly before half past, a man in his mid-fifties came down the corridor, moving irritatingly slowly. Furrowing his brow, he looked at Rath waiting outside his office, and took a bunch of keys from his pocket.

'Good morning,' Rath said, receiving no response, not even a greeting.

Once the man had opened the doors, he tried to follow him inside, but was forbidden from doing so.

'If you would be so kind as to wait,' the man said. 'We open in one minute.'

Other employees came down the corridor, other doors were opened, but still Rath had to wait until eight thirty on the dot, when the first officer poked his head through the door. 'Good morning,' he said.

All smiles now that work's started, Rath thought, showing his identification.

'A Division,' he said. 'I need some information. The owner of this vehicle.' He passed the officer a handwritten note.

The man put on his reading glasses. 'Have you put in an official request?'

'No, but I'm in a hurry. Exigent circumstances.' This was usually enough, but the man shook his head doubtfully. 'It's urgent,' he said. 'If you could help me out.'

'OK, I'll turn a blind eye this time.'

Rath waited at the desk, but the man showed no sign of moving.

'What is it? Was there something else?'

'The owner of the vehicle?' said Rath.

'Things don't move that fast. I'll call you.'

'Would you please hurry up! This could be a matter of life and death.'

The officer was unperturbed. 'Pretty much par for the course in Homicide, isn't it?'

Rath hoped the situation wasn't as serious as all that, but he didn't know. He hadn't slept. Uncertainty ate away at his insides. What had Tornow and his men done with Charly? They seemed to have their backs against the wall, and were responsible for at least two murders, probably more. He had told Marlow his theories yesterday evening: that a group of police officers was intent on sparking a gangland war between the Nordpiraten and Berolina. Evidently, some were prepared to commit murder. *Murders*, plural. All of which they hoped to pin on the mysterious American gangster the press already had its claws into—thanks to Stefan Fink.

It still wasn't nine o'clock when he arrived at the office. He was the first there. Damn it, that pen-pusher in Road Traffic! Hopefully he'd cough up the vehicle owner's name soon. It was Rath's only lead.

At some point Erika Voss appeared, which meant it must be nine. Shortly afterwards Gräf entered too. Rath was distracted; he said hello, but no more. Gräf assumed it was Monday morning blues, and didn't probe further. Rath sat like a cat on a hot tin roof, needing the vehicle owner, needing something to do. Why were they keeping him waiting?

'Where's Tornow?' Gräf asked, cautiously.

'He won't be in today.'

'Sick?'

Rath didn't respond and Gräf preferred to focus on his work, phoning his way down the list of outlets that sold Camel cigarettes. In a low voice.

Suddenly, the door to the outer office flew open and Rath thought his eyes must be playing tricks. Sebastian Tornow smiled at each of them as if nothing had occurred.

'Good morning,' he said. Erika Voss returned his greeting.

Rath could have strangled her as, not for the first time, she gazed adoringly at the new man. Even Gräf's friendly nod went against the grain. Rath muttered something incomprehensible, taking a moment to process the shock before he could react in a halfway normal manner.

Tornow hung up his hat and coat, and sat at his temporary desk. 'Good weekend?' he asked. 'Let's get started, then.'

'*What* are you doing?' Rath asked.

'Going through the Camel outlets,' Tornow said, pointing towards Gräf. 'Our colleague has already made a start.'

'Our *colleague* can take care of that on his own.' Rath said. 'You're coming with me!'

'Where?'

'Come on!'

Rath was so aggressive that Gräf gave a start behind his desk. Even Erika Voss looked intimidated, which was a rare thing. They seemed to be wondering what punishment Rath would mete out for being ten minutes late.

Rath dragged Tornow outside into the corridor.

'What's the matter?' he asked.

'Not here,' Rath snarled. A few officers were making their rounds.

'I thought we were friends.'

'Keep your mouth shut.'

Rath yanked Tornow into the toilets and closed the door, seizing him by the collar and throwing him against the wall. Tornow gasped for air. 'Where is she?'

'Wait a minute,' Tornow said. 'Can't we resolve this like civilised human beings?'

'There's nothing civilised about abducting a woman.'

'Let me go! Now, otherwise you'll never see her again.'

Tornow had said it quietly, but pointedly enough to paralyse Rath with fear. Tornow still had the upper hand. He let him go and asked again: 'Where is she?'

'The fact you're so concerned makes me think we did the right thing yesterday.'

'Who is we?'

'That's none of your concern.'

'Where is she, God damnit?'

'Also none of your concern. Let's just say that she's doing as well as could be expected under the circumstances.' Tornow straightened his shirt collar and tie. 'We'll deliver her safe and sound as soon as you've carried out a little assignment for us.'

'You want me to kill someone? That's what you lot do, isn't it?'

'It's very simple. You need to forget everything you know about me, or think you know. No one's going to believe you anyway. Then, and this is the important part, so listen up. You're going to see to it that Abraham

Goldstein is arrested and charged with the murders of Hugo Lenz, Rudi Höller, Gerhard Kubicki and Jochen Kuschke. Oh, and Eberhard Kallweit. I almost forgot about him.'

'How about I throw in Emil Kuhfeld and Gustav Stresemann while I'm at it? Special offer.'

'In your shoes, I'd be taking this more seriously. I'm not joking.'

'What are you saying? That Charly will be released when Goldstein is sentenced? Are you planning to keep her locked up for six months?'

'It will be enough when Goldstein is arrested and charged with these murders.' Tornow looked Rath in the eye. 'It's up to you how long we keep the poor thing locked up but, in your position, I wouldn't hang around.'

'If you have so much as laid a finger on her . . . !'

'No one's going to do anything to her. We don't believe in assaulting women, but she might not get much sleep over the next few days, which is unhealthy in the long run. Like I said: I wouldn't be hanging around.'

What kind of man was this? Why was he doing this?

'You'll never get away with it,' Rath said.

Tornow laughed. 'Funny, that's exactly what a female acquaintance of yours said. You're mistaken, the pair of you. You don't know how well connected we are. I advise you to tread carefully.'

Rath shook his head. There was nothing more he could say.

'Oh, and another thing . . .' Tornow smiled his smile, which now seemed more like a devilish grin. '. . . it sounds rather strange to be saying this to a police officer, but it applies just as well. No police. If you want to get your girl out of this alive. This is between us.'

Rath left Tornow where he was and exited the lavatory, slamming the door as hard as he could.

112

Ernst Gennat sat on the terrace of Café Josty with a slice of gooseberry tart in front of him. Normally it was him dishing out cake to his subordinates, but here it was the other way around.

'I hope you're not trying to bribe me, Inspector?'

'I wouldn't dream of it,' said Rath. 'Please tuck in, Sir.'

Rath had taken his hat and coat and left the office without another word to Gräf or his secretary. Let Sebastian Tornow explain. Before setting off, he had paid another visit to Road Traffic. The information his friend from this morning had provided made him uneasy. He had impressed upon the man how important it was not to share it with anyone else.

The owner of the black sedan used to abduct Charly was known to him. Rudi Scheer had run the armoury at Alex, until it was discovered that he belonged to a weapons smuggling ring operated by right-leaning circles in the police force and Reichswehr. Scheer had been put out to pasture, but avoided censure. Even back then, Rath thought it was a mistake.

Gennat hadn't touched his tart. 'I would be very grateful, Inspector,' he said, 'if you would please tell me why you have asked me here. On the telephone just now you gave the impression that it was a matter of life and death.'

'I fear it might be, Sir.'

Gennat listened so spellbound that his gooseberry tart remained untouched. 'You're not about to get mixed up in this extortion?' he said, when Rath had finished. 'Falsifying evidence!' He was indignant.

'I have another idea, but it won't work without your support. First we have to arrest Goldstein.'

'We have to find him first.'

'Taken care of! I know where he's hiding.'

'Have you been withholding information again?' Gennat let his cake fork drop and gazed angrily at Rath. 'So, you *are* trying to bribe me!'

'Absolutely not, Sir. I just want you to hear me out. Ten minutes, then you can decide for yourself.'

Gennat listened.

As expected, Marlow wasn't pleased when Rath asked him to pull off the men in and around Tornow's flat.

'He'll get his desserts, I promise you that but, if we lean on him now, we'll be putting someone else's life at risk. He has to think he's safe.'

'You're asking a lot of me, Inspector.'

'I know, but how would it be if you let the constitutional state do its work. No vigilante justice. Rest assured, the man will be punished.'

At length Marlow agreed. Another hurdle cleared, but it was the next one that mattered most.

In Saint Norbert's, Rath came upon Pastor Warszawski, but the man was not inclined to cooperate. 'I thought you'd be back,' he said. 'Which is why I took the necessary precautions.'

'Goldstein's no longer here?'

'Of course not.'

'Where is he?'

'Why should I tell you? Why do you suppose he's no longer here?'

'Could it be that you don't trust me?'

'I trust in God, not in people. Tell me where he can reach you and I'll set everything in motion.'

'I don't have much time, damn it! Someone's life is at stake.'

'Then you'll have to explain.'

Rath explained.

It wasn't a particularly original hideout, but it was unlikely they'd have found Goldstein without the help of the Catholic Church. Pastor Warszawski insisted on accompanying Rath personally. A seed of distrust remained. They drove southwest along the Reichsstrasse 1, turning left just before Zehlendorf. As they reached a peaceful, green street, the pastor told Rath to stop. On one side were nice little houses with gardens, on the other a seemingly endless green hedgerow.

'The Abendruh allotment gardens,' Warszawski explained. 'I have a plot here.'

Rath parked the Buick outside a pretty, detached house, the kind he always dreamed about owning, but knew he'd never be able to afford without inheriting his parents' estate. The hedgerow on the other side was broken at regular intervals by entranceways. Behind it he saw trees, shrubs, flagpoles and the roofs of allotment sheds: the classic hideout in a city like Berlin. It was nigh-on impossible to find anyone here if you didn't already have a lead, or a resident who'd reported something suspicious.

The allotment gardens were huge. Rath followed the pastor along a path that was straight as a die, with hedgerow on both sides. After making a few turns, always at a right angle, now to the right, now to the left, he began to feel as if he were in a maze belonging to a baroque castle estate. Warszawski came to an abrupt halt.

'Here it is,' he said, though he didn't seem too comfortable about it.

113

Barely two hours later, a truck, four green Opels from the motor pool and, lastly, the black murder wagon drew up in Elmshorner Strasse. Uniformed officers sprang from the truck and moved on the allotments using three parallel paths. A group of plainclothes CID emerged from the Opels. Ernst Gennat climbed out of the murder wagon, followed by Wilhelm Böhm.

On their way out west they had been caught in rush-hour traffic, but decided against using the sirens for fear of attracting attention. Rath cursed his luck; every hour Charly spent in the grip of Tornow and his men was one too many. He had to pass the whole journey sitting next to Sebastian Tornow and would have liked nothing more than to ram his fist into the man's face. Tornow behaved as if nothing had happened between them. Still, Rath had done his best to avoid talking to the man, indeed, had barely even looked at him. Gräf observed the inspector's reticence, and no doubt put it down to their conversation in the Nasse Dreieck, which was a good thing, although it meant the detective was suffering from a guilty conscience. Gennat had alerted all officers working on the Goldstein case, as well as any murders the gangster was apparently responsible for, more or less exactly the investigations named by Tornow hours before.

Rath and his men made for Pastor Warszawski's shed along the middle path, where Wilhelm Böhm awaited them, a bastion of calm. In his hand he held a megaphone.

'Rath and Tornow, you stay out here,' he barked. 'Goldstein has already given you the slip once. Let's not make it a second time. He knows your faces.' The Bulldog pointed towards Gräf. 'He knows you from the hotel, too.'

The rest of the CID officers were allowed past. Rath was familiar with the plan of action thanks to the briefing Gennat had held before they set off. First anti-riot police would surround the area, taking cover behind the hedgerow. To the right and left of the plot gate, two officers would be stationed with firearms at the ready. Buddha had warned them to make use of their weapons only in case of emergency. He and Böhm were the only CID officers on the front line; those left over would be deployed to help Uniform keep overly curious gardeners away from the operation.

Rath, Gräf and Tornow were the only officers stationed outside who weren't in uniform, and held themselves apart. They had even less to do than the uniform cops monitoring the entrances to the allotments. Most used the lull for a cigarette break, Rath likewise.

'If all we're doing is standing around, then why are we here at all?' Gräf said in irritation, returning to the Opel in which they had arrived. Rath was about to follow when Tornow addressed him. 'Nervous?' he asked.

'Do I look it?'

'Yes.'

'It's because I'd like to know when you're going to release her.'

'As soon as I'm certain that Abraham Goldstein is actually in there, and we lay our hands on him.'

'You don't trust me?'

'All this happened pretty fast.' Tornow smiled. 'Either you knew where Goldstein was hiding and decided to keep it to yourself, or this is just a massive ruse and the only things we'll be digging up here are molehills.'

'Just wait,' said Rath, who was still thinking of socking Tornow one. Instead he threw his cigarette on the asphalt and trod it out, as if it were a poisonous spider. Or Tornow's smile. 'You still haven't told me why,' he said. 'Why did Lenz and Höller have to die?'

Tornow's smiled vanished. 'Best you don't know too much about that. Not that they'll be missed. They were career criminals. The whole world knew it, yet no one was willing to take them to court.'

'Kuschke wasn't a career criminal. He was a cop.'

'Perhaps he made other mistakes.'

'Like leaving a witness behind?'

'Like I said, there are certain things it's better you don't know.'

Böhm's voice was distorted and amplified by the megaphone.

'Attention! This is the police! Abraham Goldstein, we know where you

450 | VOLKER KUTSCHER

are hiding. Come out with your hands up. Resistance is futile; the site is surrounded on all sides.'

For what felt like half an age they heard nothing, and Rath prayed it would all go according to plan. He couldn't help thinking about Charly; her life depended on the scheme he had hatched together with Gennat.

114

At times she couldn't remember where she was, or who was questioning her. She just knew that someone was *always* questioning her, that they hadn't granted her a single break. There was always at least one man asking questions, sometimes more. She found it harder and harder to concentrate. Sometimes she saw men who weren't there at all, more and more often something flashed at the edge of her vision: a familiar face, a man in a red pullover. On one occasion she thought she saw Gereon. Fatigue dragged her down like a dead weight, but still they wouldn't let her sink to the floor. Again and again she was forced to struggle against the burden of her exhaustion. She could no longer say how long this had been going on. Hours, days, weeks might have passed.

Her cheeks stuck to her gums because they weren't giving her enough to drink. Only when she was no longer capable of speech did they allow her a sip of water. In the meantime she got the hang of simulating a dry mouth, since not all the guards were so strict. Some were a little quicker to show compassion, and one had even let her nod off for a moment before waking her. Others shouted at her constantly, beating their fists against the table to intimidate her.

Though they didn't let her sleep and seldom gave her anything to eat or drink, they didn't lay a finger on her. No one would believe what these men had visited upon her, indeed that they had visited anything upon her at all. It was a kind of violence that left no trace.

115

Arresting Goldstein proved easier than anticipated. The anti-riot police had expected a Chicago style shoot-out, something with machine guns, or at the very least smoking Colts, but nothing of the sort had occurred. Not a single shot had been fired in anger.

Böhm repeated his instructions, Rath heard a clink (it later transpired that one of the uniform cops in the adjacent plot had knocked over a garden gnome in his nervousness) and Goldstein had emerged.

'Keep your hands where we can see them, Herr Goldstein,' Böhm bellowed through the megaphone.

'Gold-sstiehn,' the Yank said, and Rath almost let out a yelp of joy. It had worked. 'My name is Gold-sstiehn,' he continued. 'I'm an American citizen and I think there has been a misunderstanding.'

'Herr . . . Gold-sstiehn, I am arresting you on suspicion of the murders of Jochen Kuschke, Gerhard Kubicki, Hugo Lenz, Rudolf Höller and Eberhard Kallweit.'

'Then tell your men to come out and cuff me. My arms are going to sleep here.'

'That's all you have to say?' The surprise in Böhm's voice was plain.

'And that I'm innocent, of course.'

Tornow and Rath listened spellbound to the exchange.

It took a while to escort the gangster out of the allotments and for calm to be restored. First came CID and the uniform cops who had made sure that no innocent gardeners ventured into the line of fire, then the officers who surrounded Goldstein's hideout. Lastly, the pair shepherding the Yank between them.

Goldstein had his hands cuffed behind his back and seemed more or less unperturbed until he saw Rath, and possibly Tornow, although he ignored the latter. At the sight of Rath, his expression darkened, displaying first anger then outright contempt. He didn't say anything but, as he was led past, he spat onto the asphalt in front of the inspector. The two anti-riot policemen he was sandwiched between pulled him away and bundled him into the murder wagon. Clearly, Gennat wanted to speak with him on the journey back. Then came the man himself, Ernst Gennat, together with Böhm, who held the megaphone like a Teuton emerging victorious from battle.

'Good work,' Buddha said and clapped Rath on the shoulder. 'That goes for you too.'

He was referring to Tornow, whom Gennat now accorded a paternal glance.

The cadet looked a little confused.

'And now?' Rath when they were alone again, strolling towards the Opel.

'And now *what?*'

'We had an agreement. Goldstein has been arrested on five counts of murder. Now it's your turn.'

'Just be patient a little longer. First we need to go to Alex, then I'll head home where I can use the telephone, and set things in motion.'

'Where can I pick her up?'

'How stupid do you think we are?' Tornow shook his head. 'All that's left is to wait.'

116

MAJOR POLICE OPERATION
DANGEROUS GANGSTER BEHIND BARS

American gangster Abraham Goldstein was tracked down and arrested today as part of a major police operation. Rumour has it that Goldstein, who was hiding out in an allotment in southwest Berlin, attempted to escape before being overpowered by courageous German officers. The American gangster is alleged to have killed several people in Berlin, including a police officer, an SA man and a second-hand dealer. He is also accused of the murder of two major underworld figures in the city. Homicide Division Chief Ernst Gennat explained to Tag *that the evidence was 'overwhelming.' Also playing a significant role in the successful police measure: Detective Inspector Gereon Rath. 'It was Inspector Rath who managed to locate Goldstein's hideout,' Gennat confirmed.*

Most evening editions carried the story so that, tomorrow, a significant number of people would know Goldstein was in police hands. Sadly, it was only *Der Tag* that alluded to Detective Inspector Gereon Rath's rehabilitation. Had Weinert not been aboard the Zeppelin, it might have appeared in *Tageblatt* too. Even so, a single mention was enough. Gennat owed him a debt of gratitude, Bernhard Weiss even more so.

Tornow had advised him to be patient, but Rath hadn't slept a wink. He had headed with Kirie to Spenerstrasse, even started clearing away the chaos in Charly's flat. He had changed the sheets on the bed, in the process feeling a little like his mother, who had gone to similar lengths whenever little Gereon had returned after the summer vacation. She even used to bake a cake for the homecoming son. Admittedly he hadn't done that for Charly, though he had put fresh flowers in a vase. He looked around.

The flat felt almost habitable again. He hadn't sorted the papers, of course, as he didn't want to go snooping through her things, but he had returned the books and everything else to their rightful places.

Finally, he sat at the table with a bottle of cognac and a glass, thinking about her. Had they released her yet? Was Tornow deliberately keeping him in suspense, or did he have to speak to his accomplices? So many questions were swirling around his mind, the uncertainty made him crazy. The only thing he knew for sure was that he was going to need a whole lot of cognac to get any sleep. He savoured the first gulp, then drained the rest of the glass as though it were schnapps—in the end, this wasn't about enjoyment or etiquette.

Kirie had curled herself up and was looking at him out of sleepy eyes.

'Cheers, Kirie,' he said, raising a second glass.

After drinking half the bottle, he fell asleep, to awake from tangled dreams, his right cheekbone aching from being pressed against the hard wood of the table. For a moment, he forgot where he was, then remembered, sitting up with a jolt that started Kirie out of her light doggy-sleep.

The kitchen clock showed four minutes to six. Rath stood up. The bed was empty, of course. Be patient, Tornow had advised, *all that's left is to wait*.

Rath had waited long enough. He had to do something. After a shower, a quick shave, a cup of black coffee, a final cognac and two cigarettes, he grabbed his hat and car keys and set off.

Traffic was still light, so he made it from Moabit to Leuthener Strasse in quick time. In Tornow's attic flat, the lights were already on and the day seemed to be proceeding as normal. At this hour, that meant: *Police-cadet Sebastian Tornow prepares for duty.*

Rath left Kirie in the car and climbed the steps to the top floor. Tornow was knotting his tie as he opened, but apart from that, looked as spruce as ever.

'You?' he said, not particularly surprised, and stepped to one side as Rath pushed past him into the flat. Tornow closed the door, stood in front of the wardrobe mirror and continued knotting his tie. Rath slammed the paper he had purchased en route on the wardrobe. The *Vossische Zeitung*, already open at the page.

'What am I supposed to do with that?' Tornow asked, finishing his tie knot. It was perfect.

'It states that a certain Abraham Goldstein was arrested yesterday by police and charged with several murders,' Rath said.

'I was there, in case you had forgotten.'

'I was starting to think I had imagined it. What's happening with your end of the bargain? Where's Charly?'

'Not here, if that's what you thought.' He smiled, but by now all Rath could see was a provocative sneer.

'I don't think it's funny,' he said. 'Until now I've played by your rules. If I find out that anything's happened to her, or you've taken me for a ride, then I'll start playing by mine.'

'What is this? Are you trying to threaten me with Johann Marlow and your gangster friends? Trust me, they're on their way out too!'

Rath froze. How did Tornow know about his links to Marlow? Had Red Hugo blabbed?

'Stop stalling,' he said, 'and tell me where she is. Why are you still holding her, damn it?'

'We're not.' Tornow looked indignant. 'She was released at five o'clock this morning. I did say you'd need to be patient.' He looked at Rath pityingly. 'Hasn't she been in touch?'

'She isn't home, that's all I know.'

'We didn't drive her *home*. She'll have to find the way to the nearest bus stop herself.'

'Where is she? Where did you drag her?'

'*Drag* her? She was chauffeured.'

It was unbelievable. Tornow was still smiling.

'Where?'

Rath felt his anger wrestle against the bonds he had imposed on it.

'You really mean it, don't you?' Tornow made a magnanimous face. 'Very well, then,' he said. 'Onkel Toms Hütte. There's a toboggan run on the edge of the Grunewald. You should take a look there. Maybe she fell asleep in the middle of a clearing. She's certainly tired enough.'

Rath couldn't hold back any longer. He slammed his fist into Tornow's grin.

Tornow looked at him aghast, leaning forward so that his snow-white shirt wouldn't be soiled by the blood dripping from his face.

'You really are an arsehole, Gereon Rath,' he said, spitting blood. 'Is that how you thank me?'

'I've thanked you by not hitting you a second time.'

He left Tornow's flat as quick as he could, slamming the door and running down the stairs until he reached his Buick, where Kirie awaited him, tail wagging.

117

The road to Zehlendorf had never seemed so long. Half an hour later Rath climbed out of his car on Spandauer Strasse and attached Kirie to her lead. She was looking forward to her walk, although there were a few clouds above. On the other side of the road was a path leading to Onkel Toms Hütte, a restaurant popular with day-trippers that had lent its name to the area as a whole. To the right was the start of the Grunewald. A weathered sign pointed towards the toboggan run, a large clearing in a pine forest located on a precipitous slope. Only a ski jump hinted at its winter use. A few men were walking their dogs.

No sign of Charly. Rath called her name and listened. Nothing.

One of the dog walkers approached, bringing his German shepherd to heel with a sharp, 'Bismarck, sit!' Rath looked on in envy.

'Can I help you?' The man held his head slightly to one side as he spoke, and the dog did likewise.

'I'm looking for a woman,' Rath replied.

'Here in the wood?' The man looked up at the hillside. 'You'd be better served using the lonely hearts in the *B.Z.*'

He laughed and walked on. Rath was too taken aback to think of a humorous response, but the man stopped.

'Wait a minute,' he said, 'I've just remembered something. A young lady shuffled through this morning at the crack of dawn. She went past my window as I was getting up. She looked—what's the word—helpless. Is it her you're looking for?'

'Helpless? Yes, could be.' Charly's condition sounded graver than he had feared. Perhaps Tornow had been telling the truth, and they had tried to make her talk by depriving her of sleep. 'Where did you see her?'

'Riemeisterstrasse. Where I live. Beside the U-Bahn station.'

'Thank you.'

Rath shooed Kirie, who was upset not to be going further, back to the car, and drove to the estate that GEHAG had conjured out of nothing and, indeed, was still conjuring in places, if the piles of sand and planks outside the houses were anything to go by. Some of them still hadn't been plastered and very few had mown lawns. On the corner of the road stood pines and beech trees, so high they must have been planted long before building work commenced. Rath parked outside the U-Bahn station. The cafe opposite clearly had airs, labelling itself a Conditorei.

He fetched the dog from the car, and no sooner did he have her on the lead than he felt a tug. Kirie had picked up a scent and was suddenly very animated, holding her nose close to the floor, sniffing intently and pulling Rath towards a modern brick portal that served as the entrance to the U-Bahn.

'If this is another dead animal!' Rath said.

Kirie took no notice, but dragged him down the steps to the platform. Rath had to watch he didn't take a tumble.

She was lying huddled on a bench. Charly in her flowery, summer dress.

The other passengers barely took any notice, and those who did were more disdainful than compassionate. It was her, though. Kirie must have sniffed her from upstairs.

She had made it to the U-Bahn, only to fall asleep while waiting for the next train and the citizens of Berlin, accustomed to going their own way and never interfering, had let her sleep. Not even the noise of the nearby construction site had wakened her, in contrast with Kirie's tongue.

Charly opened her eyes, just a little at first, then wide with fear as she gazed into the face of the smiling, black dog. She sat up and recognised first Kirie, then Rath, who was standing alongside. She smiled blissfully and wrapped her arms around his legs, on the point of sleep again. 'I have a ticket,' she mumbled.

'We're taking the car.' He didn't know whether to laugh or cry. 'You just have to walk a few metres.'

That proved trickier than anticipated. Rath provided support, and Charly made every effort, but her circulation was so restricted that she had to pause repeatedly, above all when climbing the stairs.

'Come on,' Rath said. 'The car's just up here, you're almost there. You made it from the wood to the station!'

'That was before I fell asleep. Sleeping makes you tired.'

Rath debated whether he should get her a Turkish coffee from the cafe opposite, but decided against. Get her in the car, quick-sharp. He bundled her onto the seat and she was asleep again before he started the engine.

At Spenerstrasse he carried her over the threshold, otherwise he'd have had to leave her sleeping in the car. She lay soft and light in his arms as he bore her up the stairs. The hardest thing was turning the key in the lock, but he managed that too. He kicked the front door shut and carried her into the bedroom, laid her on the bed and undressed her as best he could. As he put the covers over her the doorbell rang. It was just before eleven.

He left Kirie with Charly and went into the hallway, took the Walther from its holster on the hall stand and reloaded. He crept towards the door, keeping close to the wall in case the person outside decided to blast their way in. He placed his hand on the handle and with a jolt, threw the door open, taking aim at the intruder.

A small man looked like he was about to collapse out of fear. Rath lowered his weapon. It took a while for the little man to calm down. 'Maltritz,' he said at last. It sounded like an apology. 'I'm the buildings manager here.'

'Please excuse me, Herr Maltritz,' Rath said. 'But I thought . . .'

'What did you think?'

'There was a break-in here a few days a go, which is why I'm on my guard. I'm a friend of Fräulein Ritter,' he said, 'and a police officer.'

He showed his identification, but the little man seemed unimpressed.

'Where is Fräulein Ritter?'

'Not at home, which I can understand, after everything that's happened. The break-in, I mean.'

'She really isn't here? I heard footsteps on the stairs just now.'

'Footsteps? Well, that must have been me.'

'You alone?'

'Me and my dog,' Rath said. 'What business is that of yours, if I might ask?'

'Fräulein Ritter is behind on her rent. She said she would have the money by yesterday evening. Only, yesterday evening she wasn't home.'

Rath remembered how Charly had asked him for a loan. No wonder he had forgotten, after everything that had happened. How they could use Alex's hundred and fifty marks now.

'You'll get your money, Herr Maltritz. Fräulein Ritter has . . . ah . . . asked me to settle up.'

'Good,' Maltritz said, looking expectantly.

'What is it?'

'I'm waiting for the money.'

'I don't have it for you *now*.'

'Listen: go tell your cock and bull story to some kids. Maybe they'll believe it, but *I* will not be taken for a fool. Wherever Fräulein Ritter is hiding, whether it's in this flat or somewhere else, please let her know that Hans Maltritz is not to be messed with.' He placed his hands on his hips. 'I don't care who pays, whether it's you, Fräulein Ritter, or your monkey's uncle, but if I don't have twelve marks fifty by tonight you'll see a different side to me. You wouldn't believe how quickly I can get hold of an eviction order.'

Twelve fifty! What a ridiculous sum to make such a fuss about! 'Don't do anything rash,' Rath said. 'You'll have your money. I'll go to the bank later today.'

'Are you being funny with me?'

'Nothing could be further from my mind.'

'Then you obviously haven't seen the papers. You won't be getting any money at the bank. I hope you've got another source of capital.' He looked Rath up and down. 'I don't care *how* you get it. Just make sure you do!'

Once the man had gone downstairs, Rath looked at his copy of the *Vossische Zeitung*, bought to rub the Goldstein article in Tornow's face.

It was a different story that had made the front page: a German banking crisis. He skimmed the article and continued flicking through the paper. The stupid buildings manager was right, getting money from the bank today would be impossible.

The Danatbank had hit the skids over the weekend and could no longer pay out to its customers. The Darmstädter and Nationalbank! But that was a perfectly reputable enterprise. Rath had his money elsewhere, in a postal giro account, though things didn't look too rosy for the other banks either. Fearing for their deposits, an onslaught of customers had attempted to withdraw cash, causing most banks to close their counters—only increasing the sense of panic. Rath felt himself worrying about the few thousand marks he had set aside for a rainy day. As if he didn't have enough on his plate already.

The Danatbank had been so badly hit that the government had been forced to guarantee all deposits. 'Aunt Voss', as the *Vossische* was known, wrote that *following discussions with the government, all other major German banks have declared that they view any government guarantees as superfluous, that they are fully solvent and capable of meeting all demands.*

Even so, all bank counters would remain closed for the next few days. Arrogant bastards, Rath thought. He didn't have much time for the financial industry, which he had never understood anyway. He knew even less about the financial crisis, which now seemed to have pulled the banks into its maelstrom. Only two years ago, any number of shares on the New York Stock Exchange had fallen through the floor, and speculators had jumped out of the windows of the city's skyscrapers. Why enterprises that had nothing to do with New York should be affected, honest German companies for example, even German public servants such as himself who had seen their salaries cut, was a mystery to him.

To the economics editor of the *Vossische* too, it seemed. WHAT WE LACK, was the title of his lead. WHAT HAS HAPPENED? THE FACTORIES, ON WHICH GERMANY'S ECONOMIC STRENGTH HAS BEEN BUILT, ARE STILL STANDING, AS THEY WERE FOUR WEEKS AGO. THE GERMAN SOIL HAS YIELDED THE SAME HARVEST AS LAST YEAR, IF NOT BETTER THAN IN MANY PREVIOUS YEARS. OUR RESERVES OF COAL AND IRON REMAIN INTACT BENEATH THE GROUND. IN ALL THESE WAYS GERMANY IS NO POORER, SO WHY THE ALARM? BECAUSE, ALTHOUGH THE GERMAN ECONOMY IS AS STRONG AS EVER IN ITSELF, WE LACK THE FUEL TO DRIVE IT FORWARD. WE LACK MONEY.

How true, Rath thought, we lack money. Isn't that what so many people have always lacked?

THIS CATASTROPHE IS UPON US, the journalist continued, AND IT WOULD BE COWARDLY TO TURN A BLIND EYE TO THE GRAVITY OF THIS UNIQUE SITUATION. THE COLLAPSE OF A MAJOR GERMAN BANK IS WITHOUT PRECEDENT IN THE COUNTRY'S ECONOMIC HISTORY.

WHAT WE ARE NOW EXPERIENCING IS NOT INFLATION, BUT ITS EXACT COUNTERPART.

Rath didn't quite know if that was good news or bad. At first glance it sounded good: no inflation. That was something, surely. Nevertheless, it didn't change the fact that money was in short supply. What a lousy world, he thought, remembering what Alex had said in the stairwell.

When he returned to the bedroom, Kirie was waiting eagerly. Charly was still fast asleep. 'You dogs have it good,' he said, stroking Kirie's fur, 'and not just when it comes to affairs of the heart.'

He sat beside Charly. She briefly opened her eyes and snuggled up to him, reaching for his hand. 'I didn't tell them anything, Gereon,' she mumbled, more asleep than awake. 'Not a thing!' She closed her eyes as Rath pulled the covers over her shoulders and kissed her on the cheek.

'I'm so sorry,' he said, though he wasn't sure she could hear him. At least it made it easier to admit his error. 'If I had believed you none of this would have happened.'

He sat on the chair next to her bed and placed the Walther on his lap. He gazed at her, fast asleep in broad daylight. No one would ever take her away from him again.

118

Dusk was falling as the police vehicles pulled up. The enormous silhouette of the gasometer stood against the westerly glow of the night sky. It had rained in the early afternoon, and the pavement was glistening dark and wet. A great number of people and addresses stood on their arrest lists, stretched across all four corners of the city. Even so, Rath had opted for Schöneberg, just like Gennat. Böhm had gone to the West End, which made the decision easier still.

Right now, police units were stationed at seventeen different locations throughout the city. At eight on the dot they would swoop, so that those under arrest would be unable to warn each other. At seventeen different addresses in Berlin, the illusion that police officers were above the law was about to shatter.

Rarely had Rath found the passage of time so torturous as in these last few days.

Even after Charly's release, little had changed. As far as possible he had kept his distance from Sebastian Tornow, though they had crossed paths on a number of occasions at work. Everyone was working with great zeal to make the chain of evidence in the case against Abraham Goldstein as tight as possible.

Everyone except Gennat, Böhm and Grabowski.

Rath was the only one who knew. Everyone else assumed they were looking into the Goldstein affair. No one suspected that they were actually conducting interrogations in an undisclosed location. Even less, that Helmut Grabowski was the man being interrogated by Homicide's two oldest hands. They had needed three days to crack him, but then Grabowski started talking. Seventeen names, and enough background information to justify today's arrests.

Now, they stood at the base of the stairs: Gennat, Rath and the squad leader with his men. They had taken a dozen uniformed officers along with them. Every so often the wooden stairs emitted a tired protest, as if unused to carrying so much weight.

Rath and Böhm had discovered that Assistant Detective Grabowski must be the Castle's leak at more or less the same time. Böhm, still angry that confidential information pertaining to the Goldstein investigation had been passed straight to the press, narrowed the list of suspects one by one. Only seven people had known what Abraham Goldstein looked like: Gereon Rath and his three men, Deputy Police Commissioner Bernhard Weiss, CID Chief Scholz and the female employee who had received the telex from America and passed it on.

At first Böhm focused on Rath and his men, whom he obviously thought capable of such indiscretion. He even briefly considered Weiss and Scholz for different, no doubt politically motivated, reasons. The one person he hadn't reckoned with was the girl from the teleprinter's office, an innocent in her mid-twenties. Eventually, however, she had been the only possibility remaining, and, after a marathon interrogation, had confessed to having mentioned Goldstein's imminent arrival to a fellow officer in the canteen.

That fellow officer had been Assistant Detective Helmut Grabowski. The same assistant detective whom the porter at the Scherl building recognised as the man who had delivered the mysterious envelopes to Stefan Fink.

At first Grabowski stubbornly maintained that he had acted under his own steam, but when Gennat confronted him, bit by bit, with the statements Lanke junior had already made, he cracked. Gregor Lanke, whom Rath had softened up the week before, appeared to be a relatively small cog in the machine.

Then there were the names Charly had been able to throw in. Over the past few days she had gazed at hundreds of police portraits. Gennat hadn't summoned her to Alexanderplatz but to a safe house. His co-conspirator was his trusted secretary Trudchen Steiner, with whom Charly continued to live for security reasons, and with whom she would stay until Scheer and Tornow were safely behind bars.

The picture they put together was shocking. *Die Weisse Hand*. The White Hand. A secret band of frustrated police officers, who were tired of the judicial system releasing people onto the streets after they had bust a gut to put them behind bars. Police officers who had resolved to go over and above the call of duty, and play judge, jury and executioner. Their aim: to eliminate the most notorious criminals in Berlin's underworld.

Police officers who were moments away from being arrested.

They arrived upstairs. Everything in the attic flat was dark. They hadn't switched on the light in the stairwell. Only a little twilight filtered through from outside. It took a lot of effort, but Rath could just about read the nameplate on the door. s TORNOW. Only a week ago, he had been here thinking he had made a new friend. How quickly things changed.

Gennat had paused on the stairs. Rath gave the squad leader the nod. He waved at his men and they stepped into action like a perfectly rehearsed ballet troupe. The first man kicked in the door and the second peeled inside, firearm at the ready, followed by three colleagues. Rath remained outside, his Walther primed, even if he didn't think Tornow would come out shooting.

The squad leader emerged from the flat shaking his head. 'No one home,' he said.

Rath cast a brief glance over the flat. It didn't look as if Tornow had fled. His gaze fell instead on the gasometer at the end of Leuthener Strasse. He exited the flat and the officers descended once more, frustrated as ever after a futile operation. Gennat was waiting for them at the foot of the stairs.

Rath shrugged. 'No one home, but I'd be willing to bet I know where he is.'

Perhaps Tornow had an inkling after all, Rath thought, as they approached the gasworks, although it wasn't public knowledge that Helmut Grabowski and Gregor Lanke had been arrested, let alone interrogated.

Rath had waylaid Gregor Lanke outside the canteen, using the pretext of a confidential discussion to lure him out to Schöneberg. The detective had been astonished to find Superintendent Gennat and Chief Inspector Böhm waiting for him in the priest's office at Saint Norbert's. Once he had recovered from the shock, Lanke had seemed genuinely relieved by the presence of Buddha, and unburdened his soul.

Grabowski, meanwhile, was part of Böhm's team. All the Bulldog had to do was summon him. The assistant detective from Homicide was, by far, the harder nut to crack, but Gennat's doggedness, allied with Lanke's statements and the names Charly had provided, finally broke him.

Rudi Scheer seemed to act as a kind of patron, placing the necessary means at the group's disposal for specific operations. Grabowski claimed that Scheer was still involved in weapons trafficking, though it would be difficult to prove. The only lead they had was an illegal arms dealer in Grenadierstrasse. Goldstein confirmed that was where he had purchased the Remington. He got the address from Marion, who at that time had been working on behalf of Gregor Lanke and *Die Weisse Hand*. Somehow, in the maze, Goldstein had become an important witness.

But that was another story entirely.

Even if Scheer had provided the money, the group's driving force was Sebastian Tornow, young as he was. The two hoods he had told Rath about, who had apparently lost their lives as part of a gangland war, the two who had ruined his sister's life, had been his first victims. In Rudi Scheer, whom he must have met in the early stages of his training, Tornow recognised a kindred spirit. From that point, the pair had surrounded themselves with men who shared their worldview. Gräf, too, had been sounded out by Tornow, when asked whether a good police officer ought to be able to kill.

In Tornow's eyes, the answer was yes. Jochen Kuschke, meanwhile, who had taken this principle too much to heart, had to die, because he had acted impetuously and become a danger to the organisation. His fate, so Grabowski said, had been sealed at a secret night-time meeting of group members. In the end Tornow took the job upon himself because Kuschke, his erstwhile superior officer and mentor, had trusted him the most.

They reached the site of the gasworks without any trouble. As Tornow had said, only signs forbade people from climbing the gasometer. They described such behaviour as *strengstens verboten*, the sound of which alone was enough to make would-be offenders recoil.

Rath was used to breaking rules.

'Wait here with your men,' he said to Gennat. 'I'll see if anyone's up there.'

Before Gennat could say anything, he was on his way.

Scaling dizzying heights was hardly the stuff of his innermost dreams, but this was personal. Tornow had taken Charly from him and made her suffer for two days. If he was crouched up there, admiring Berlin's night sky, then he, Gereon Rath, wanted to be the one to tell him he was under arrest.

The gasometer was a massive, barrel-shaped guide frame, a steel, half-timbered construction, around eighty metres high, in which the gas bell patiently went about its business. A kind of fire escape led upwards, a steel staircase the like of which could sometimes be seen in tenement houses. After four steps, Rath reached the first maintenance gangway, a steel ring of catwalk grating that extended around the whole gasometer. There was one every ten or so metres, but Tornow's spot was up on top of the gas holder, not on one of the maintenance gangways. Rath continued.

On the first landing he held to his resolution not to look down, but at one point he inadvertently took the risk, and instantly regretted it. He held on tight to the rail and hunkered down. Below he could see Gennat talking to a man, probably the night watchman. Buddha pointed skywards and Rath tried to look the other way, up inside the structure, to dispel the feeling of vertigo. The framework's interior was filled by an enormous steel cylinder that was in motion day and night, rising and falling, as gradually as the sun and moon, and just as inexorably, an irresistible, relentless force. Cantilevers with guide pulleys ran via tracks into the vertical steel ribs to ensure the gas bell breathed steadily. Rath thought he could see it slowly descending as the bell exhaled again, an operation that would last the entire night. The heavy telescopic bell descended at a speed that was barely discernible, compressing the gas into the network of lines and hoses that played their part in illuminating Berlin's night sky.

When he reached the topmost maintenance gangway he saw Tornow sitting on the enormous steel bell and the gas supply for half a city. Not just anywhere, but right in its centre, on a large valve that looked like a steel tree-stump and was the same size as a comfy stool. Next to him was a rucksack.

Rath climbed onto the gas bell using one of the cantilevers. Like the maintenance gangways, the slightly domed upper surface of the gas holder was secured by a wrap-around rail.

Slowly he approached the middle of the bell. It was like ascending a little hill, steadily sloping upwards. On top of the flat, circular summit sat the former uniformed officer, whose promising career as a CID inspector was over before it had begun. The man with the perfect smile: Sebastian Tornow, the fallen angel.

Rath came to a halt about a metre behind him.

Tornow, who had his back turned, took a brief glance over his shoulder, and turned around without saying anything. In his hand he held a half-finished bottle of beer.

'I've come to take you away,' Rath said.

'You sound like the devil himself.'

'I'm a detective inspector come to make an arrest.'

'An arrest? It's not forbidden to sit up here drinking beer.'

'No.'

Tornow raised the bottle to his lips. 'Let me finish my beer, then I'll come with you. You know how much I'm going to miss sitting up here.'

Rath nodded. Tornow offered him a bottle. 'You want one too?'

'No, thank you.' Rath shook his head. 'You know how it is: business before pleasure . . . I'll smoke instead.'

He took a cigarette from his case, lit it and sat next to Tornow. 'It really is beautiful up here,' he said, blowing pale cigarette smoke into the night sky.

'But that isn't why you're here.'

'No.' Rath looked across at Tornow, who was staring into the distance. 'Today is the day *Die Weisse Hand* is finally broken. Right now all across the city men are being arrested. You're one of them. You'll also be charged with the murder of Jochen Kuschke . . .'

'Kuschke, the fool.'

'. . . and with acting as an accessory to the murder of Eberhard Kallweit, Hugo Lenz, Rudolf Höller and Gerhard Kubicki.'

'I had nothing to do with Kubicki. That was Kuschke's idea. The same goes for the boy at KaDeWe.'

'Kuschke was in the SA himself. Why would he stab a fellow member like Kubicki?'

'I asked him that too. Apparently to pin it on Goldstein, but there were other reasons. For Kuschke, any SA men who didn't go along with his hero Stennes were just a bunch of fag boys. At least, that's how he explained it to me. The fact that he was in the SA should have been a warning. Recruiting him for *Die Weisse Hand* was the biggest mistake I made.'

'He was good for the dirty work, wasn't he? Hugo Lenz for example. Or would you have managed him on your own? Did he shoot Rudi Höller too?'

'What does it matter now? I thought we made a good team, Kuschke and I.'

'But you were wrong.'

'So long as he did what he was told, everything worked fine. The problems only began when he started thinking for himself. The man was a sadist, as I should have known. It was my mistake.'

'Here was I thinking that sadism was a prerequisite for your little troop. You kill people. Just like that.'

'We eliminate *criminals*. It has nothing to do with sadism.'

'You didn't kill Goldstein. Why?'

'Perhaps we wanted to shake the general public awake. Show them how dangerous it is to have a gangster roaming the streets of Berlin unattended, and that the laws which allow it to happen need to be changed.'

'He wasn't unattended. It was only through your expert help that he gave us the slip.'

'We were watching him the whole time. *Die Weisse Hand* isn't as dim-witted as Inspector Rath.'

'With the exception of Kuschke. He was only supposed to be keeping Goldstein under surveillance, wasn't he, not to be killing an SA man into the bargain?'

'He wasn't best pleased to see the man behave like a Boy Scout. So he lent a helping hand. To ensure the picture Berliners had of him was accurate.'

'That he was a Jewish gangster? One who's about to be exonerated in the press.'

Tornow looked into Rath's eyes, as if he could read the inspector's mind. 'He's in on this, isn't he?' he said, in a moment of insight. 'Goldstein is in on this conspiracy against *Die Weisse Hand*!'

'Conspiracy's the wrong word. These are criminal proceedings, and his role is not to be underestimated. Quite simply, because he didn't commit any of the murders your lot tried to pin on him.'

Rath thought of Simon Teitelbaum, Goldstein's defence witness. The old man had good reason to withhold his name and address: fear of deportation. Teitelbaum was in Germany illegally. It was only after Gennat set everything in motion to grant him citizenship that he had declared himself willing to repeat the statements he had made to Rath in court.

'You working with gangsters is nothing new,' Tornow said, 'but Gennat too! That was Buddha I saw down there, wasn't it?' Tornow pointed his beer bottle down towards Leuthener Strasse.

Rath shook his head. 'I just can't believe that you'd simply stab a man to death.'

'It wasn't simple, you've got it wrong there. It was *unavoidable*.' He looked at Rath. 'Believe me, I wasn't always this cold-blooded, but time teaches you. Having a sheet of ice around your heart helps. A carapace, like after a sleet storm.' He paused and gazed into the distance, towards the western horizon, over which the last of the daylight could still be seen, before the night finally took over. 'The ice set in the day we found my sister Luise in the Hollandwiese, when all that remained of her was her physical shell, and the person she had been only that morning was irretrievably lost.'

'You think that gives you the right to become just like the men who destroyed her?'

'I'm nothing like those bastards!' Tornow flashed him a look of such rage that Rath gave a start. 'I never will be!'

'You've become just as hard-hearted as them. Is that really worth striving for?'

'It isn't about whether it's worth striving for.' Tornow took a final gulp of beer. 'We don't get to choose whether we become hard-hearted or not.'

The bottle was empty. Tornow packed it inside the little leather rucksack, clinking it against another bottle. The one Rath had turned down. He stood up.

'Let's go back down,' he said. 'I don't have to cuff you, do I?'

Tornow shook his head and stood up, shouldering the rucksack and fiddling with its clasp.

'You've been very open with me,' Rath said. 'Why didn't you tell me all that a few days ago? You would have spared us a whole lot of trouble.'

'Because back then I didn't know I was talking to a dead man.' All of a sudden there was a pistol in his hand. 'You're a Catholic. You know what good it does to unburden your soul. Above all when you know that the seal of confession will be preserved.'

Rath gazed into the mouth of the pistol. It was a Mauser, he saw now, the same model he had once had. 'Don't do anything stupid. There's a squad of a hundred officers waiting below. You've no chance of escape.'

'Who says I want to escape. Perhaps I just want to shoot you.'

'In front of over a hundred witnesses?'

Tornow shrugged. 'So what? Have you forgotten that I'm already a police killer. One more won't make any difference.'

Rath shook his head. 'I don't believe you.'

'What is it you don't believe?'

'I don't believe you're cold-blooded enough to just gun me down. Besides . . .' He pointed towards the maintenance gangway encircling them. While they had been speaking the gas dome had descended by a few centimetres. 'At any moment this place is going to be surrounded by uniformed officers with loaded carbines. If you shoot me, they'll gun you down like a hare.'

Tornow looked to the side, which was all Rath had wanted. With a quick movement he was beside him, with both his hands on the pistol in Tornow's right hand. A shot resounded from the Mauser, the bullet flying high into the night sky.

The two men landed on the gently sloping dome of the gas holder. There was a muffled thud as the Mauser and Tornow's right hand crashed against the metal. While Rath focused his energies on the man's firing arm, Tornow kicked him hard in the groin, catching him off guard. Rath felt everything go black and for a moment couldn't breathe, but still he clasped the hand holding the weapon, slamming Tornow's knuckles against the steel gas holder. He absorbed the kicks and punches until Tornow's knuckles bled and he let go of the pistol. It slid a few centimetres and came to a halt. Before Tornow could retrieve it, Rath slapped it away as if it were a table-hockey puck, only to watch it skidding across the gently sloping metallic surface. It turned on its axis several times and finally, still moving at pace, slid over the edge of the gas bell. It didn't fall into the depths, between the telescopic bell and guide framework, as Rath had hoped, but flew across the gap to land on the catwalk grating of the maintenance gangway.

Tornow ran over, diving across the floor and lying face down on the edge of the gas holder, frantically stretching to take the pistol in his grasp. Rath rose unhurriedly to his feet, ignoring the pain from the blows Tornow had dealt him, and pulled his Walther from its holster.

He had just loaded the weapon when Tornow finally reached the Mauser. He had failed to realise that the gas holder was still falling. The handrail on the maintenance gangway hadn't moved, but the rail that fenced the edge of the gas holder continued its descent. Tornow had reached through both rails to grasp hold of the weapon. His eyes dilated when he realised that his right arm was stuck, jammed between them.

Rath needed a moment to work out what was happening. It was Tornow's initial, barely suppressed cry of pain that alerted him.

'Pull your hand away, for God's sake,' he cried.

'I can't! I can't!' Tornow's voice was already panicked. 'Stop the damn thing! Stop it.'

Rath looked around for an emergency switch, but that was nonsense: it was gravity pulling the gasometer down. Someone had to pump in more gas to reverse its relentless downwards motion. He climbed onto the maintenance gangway, ignoring Tornow's cries, and called down to the others. 'Stop it!' he shouted, as loud as he could. 'You need to stop the gasometer. Send it back up!'

He couldn't tell whether they had understood. Tornow was still screaming when he climbed back onto the dome and tried to lift him out of the trap. It was hopeless.

Tornow pulled on Rath's arm, but it was already too late. The two rails had wedged his forearm tight and wouldn't let go.

He screamed like a banshee as the bones in his forearm broke one by one. Rath tried to pull him away, but couldn't, the steel rails that were slowly moving apart had his arm firmly in their grip. The pistol slipped onto the catwalk grating; Tornow's hand hung loose and strangely contorted above it.

Tornow wasn't screaming any more. The pain had rendered him unconscious. Still, the gasometer descended relentlessly, millimetre by millimetre. Rath heard muscles and ligaments tear, bones crack, and despairingly tried again to pull him away. He didn't think about what he was doing, just pulled and pulled, knowing all the while that it was hopeless. Then, abruptly, and with one final, ugly noise that sounded like a curtain ripping, the gasometer released the cadet, and Rath pulled his body away from the handrail.

Dismayed and exhausted, Rath gazed at the unconscious Tornow, at his right arm, or what remained of it. From the shredded stump jutted fragments of bone, torn sinews and ligaments. Blood sprayed at regular intervals onto the metal of the gas bell. Rath took his belt and bound Tornow's arm, until the blood was no more than spitting from the horrific wound. He climbed onto the maintenance gangway, surprised, at that moment, not to experience any vertigo, and looked for Gennat and the officers below. 'An ambulance,' he shouted down. 'We need an ambulance, God damnit! Quickly!

PART III

CODA: ESCAPE

Saturday 12th September 1931

119

The announcement that grated through the loudspeaker sounded every bit as miserable as Rath felt.

'Attention please, the fast train from Hannover will shortly be arriving at platform 3. Please mind the platform!'

He stood with Kirie in the queue, waiting to buy a platform ticket. They had already checked in Charly's luggage, but even so, her nervousness was driving him mad. He had accompanied her to the station as a matter of course . . . but something told him it was a bad idea, and not just because he hated goodbyes.

'Come on,' she said, for at least the twenty-third time, 'or we'll miss the train.'

He rolled his eyes, but the gesture was only seen by the man at the counter, who assumed it was directed at him.

'Hold your horses! I'll be with you soon.' First he had to supply tickets to a family of five.

Rath winked at Charly and waved the ticket as if he had won first prize in the lottery, but she seemed to have left her sense of humour at home. Perhaps she had stowed it in one of the three suitcases that were making the long journey with her.

They made for platform two where the train to Paris (via Magdeburg, Hannover, Cologne and Brussels) was scheduled to depart in twenty minutes. Kirie pulled on her lead excitedly, sensing, as usual, that something wasn't quite right.

Potsdamer Bahnhof was where Rath had begun his own fateful journey, arriving in the crisp cold of March 1929. It was where he had received and taken leave of his few visitors since then; and it was where, in a station locker, he had deposited evidence that no one must ever find.

Yet never before had he felt so out of place.

They walked along the platform, hoping to avoid the crowds. Charly looked at her watch. 'Where has Professor Heymann got to?'

'The train doesn't leave for fourteen minutes. It hasn't even arrived yet.'

She wasn't listening, but rummaging in her handbag, looking for her passport for the umpteenth time.

'In the side pocket,' he said. 'Next to the ticket.'

He couldn't bear it any longer, and didn't know how he would manage the next quarter of an hour until her professor showed up. He had to take his leave now while they were still alone and a private, intimate goodbye was still halfway possible.

'Kirie and I had better go. We don't want everyone to find out that . . . you know.'

Charly nodded wistfully. She leaned down and ruffled Kirie's black fur. 'Well, my darling, look after this one for me,' she said. 'I'm glad he's still got you at least.'

She stood up straight and looked at Rath. He could hardly bear her gaze. 'Let's keep it brief,' he said. 'I hate long goodbyes.'

She nodded.

He took her in his arms. 'I love you,' he whispered in her ear, as a shrill whistle sounded from the platform opposite. He wondered if he had ever told her before, remembering an old saying: that love disappears as soon as you give it a name. You should never talk about love, simply live it. He could no longer remember which clever person laid claim to it, but all of a sudden it seemed horribly plausible.

'What did you say?' Charly asked, looking at him through eyes which seemed strangely different. The whole situation felt unreal.

'Nothing important,' he said, giving her a quick peck on the cheek. She hadn't heard, perhaps that was a good sign. 'So!' he adopted a confident smile. 'Safe trip. I'll call you tomorrow in the hotel.'

She nodded, but looked straight through him, as if she hadn't processed what he said. 'Oh, look, there's Guido,' she said and waved over Rath's shoulder. 'How nice of him.'

Guido, the grinning man? Rath looked around. Him as well! Time to leave, before her friend Greta showed up too.

He embraced her so tight it was as if, for a fraction of a second, he never wanted to let go, and kissed her. She didn't reciprocate, probably because

Guido was already close by. Rath looked at her for a final time, her face, her eyes, and turned around. He couldn't bear it, couldn't bear to stand here with Guido to wave her off. Greta, too, had always despised him. Charly must see that! He had pictured their goodbye differently. He didn't know how, exactly, just differently. The lump in his throat grew larger.

He met Guido with a mumbled greeting, and proceeded towards the milling mass in the station concourse, not wanting to turn around in case he triggered some catastrophe, like Orpheus or Lot's wife.

Passing through the platform barriers he gave in and, though he didn't turn into a pillar of salt, and Charly didn't glide off, never to be seen again, part of him felt as if they had parted for good. She didn't even gaze after him. Instead she chatted animatedly with Guido, who gave her a friendly hug and handed her a package, a book most likely, for the long journey. All of which reminded Gereon that he hadn't got her anything. Whatever, he had no idea about books, and you didn't give someone flowers at a train station . . .

He could no longer stand and watch.

'Come on, Kirie,' he said, jostling his way through the mass of people without really noticing them.

In the initial weeks following Charly's abduction he had felt close to her like never before. At the same time, her imminent departure had cast a cloud over everything. She would be in Paris for six months, and they hadn't even discussed seeing each other in that time. He didn't know what to make of it, only that he would have wished it otherwise.

Already he missed her, and debated whether he shouldn't wave her goodbye after all, but soon the thought of Guido, of Greta and Professor Heymann, and whoever else might show up, quashed the impulse. You arsehole! he thought, stop being so goddamn sentimental.

He drove back to Luisenufer and took a stroll with Kirie through the park, before going up to his flat. Inside, he didn't know what to do. It wasn't quiet enough to listen to music. He telephoned Gräf, but he wasn't home. Weinert had sent his apologies again. He seemed to be at a different reception every night, moving in circles to which Rath would never gain access. Since his return, Weinert's interest in police matters had noticeably waned.

Rath felt left out and, for a moment, considered coughing up for a

distance call to his friend Paul, if only to hear that familiar, sing-song Cologne accent. Stupid idea, he thought, and placed the receiver back on the
cradle.

He sat at the kitchen table and stared at the bottle of cognac. It stared
back, but he remained steadfast. Not a drop! Instead he lit a cigarette. Kirie
looked at him, her head tilted to one side.

'We're just going to have to get used to being on our own again,' he
told her.

The telephone rang. It was Gennat.

'What's happened?'

'It's Tornow,' Buddha said.

'Has he finally talked?'

Sebastian Tornow had been in hospital for eight weeks, but hadn't
spilled. On one occasion even Rath had tried, but all he received were hate-
filled looks. His organisation had collapsed around him, but still he remained silent, as if protecting someone. Legally speaking, what he had told
Rath on the gasometer was worthless.

'That would be a thing,' Gennat said. 'No. I'm afraid we won't have the
chance to make him talk any time soon.'

'What's happened? Has he . . .'

In the first few days Sebastian Tornow had almost died of blood poi-
soning.

'No, he's alive, I'm afraid.' It was rare to hear a sentence like that from
Ernst Gennat's lips. 'It looks as if he's escaped. He must have had help.'

'How is that possible? Wasn't he being guarded?'

'He was in a hospital, not a cell.'

'Isn't he helpless with just one arm?'

'The sister tells me he's become quite skilful at getting things done.'

'How did he make it past the guards?'

'He didn't have to. The two men have vanished as well.'

'From *Die Weisse Hand*?'

'That's what we suspect.'

'Now what?'

'We've put out an appeal. No leads so far. We suspect that he means to
go abroad, and are monitoring all border checkpoints. The alternative is . . .'
Gennat hesitated.

'The alternative is that he's after me. Is that what you were about to say?'

'He has reason enough to want revenge.'

'Luckily I've got company tonight, that I don't think he'd dare go near.'

'Sounds like you're having dinner with Hindenburg.'

'Even better,' Rath said. 'I have to say goodbye to someone.'

'I can guess who you mean.'

'On Dr Weiss's orders. Besides, Abraham Goldstein isn't as bad as his reputation suggests. So long as he doesn't shoot you.'

'Then make sure you don't get shot. And see to it that the man actually catches his train. He's been here long enough.'

'Twelve weeks to be exact, but only one at the state's cost. He's made a real effort to support the local tourism industry.'

'Maybe you should too,' Gennat said. 'I hope we'll know more about Tornow's whereabouts by next week.'

'Gladly, if the Free State of Prussia is footing the bill.'

'I doubt it will stretch to a suite in the Adlon. Or the Excelsior for that matter.'

'Shame. A room's just become free there.'

Rath took Gennat up on his suggestion. He packed a few things and some cash, dropped the dog off with the Lennartzes, and headed west. He'd had enough of the Excelsior for now.

The hotels in Charlottenburg weren't the cheapest but he could lay out a little extra from his own pocket. The Savoy in Fasanenstrasse was one of the most modern hotels in the city, and was located beside Kantstrasse and the Ku'damm. He took a single room for two nights and went upstairs to freshen up. When he emerged from the shower he felt rejuvenated. Perhaps not like a new man, exactly, but it was better than waking from a bad dream. In fact, it felt something like his arrival in Berlin, when he had also spent the first few nights in a hotel. Now, as then, he was alone. Perhaps he would throw himself into the city's nightlife, since neither Weinert nor Gräf had any time for him.

From his window he looked straight onto Delphi, a dance hall in Kantstrasse which he had previously visited on duty. There were other places too. He was spoilt for choice. He opened the window, breathed in the Charlottenburg air and suddenly felt completely free.

Dusk was falling as he stepped onto the street. A number of people had gathered outside the synagogue. It seemed to be some sort of Jewish feast day, though he hadn't any idea which.

Café Reimann wasn't known as a dance hall, but there was a band playing, and Abraham Goldstein held court as if he owned the place. He stood up when he saw Rath and stretched out a hand.

'Glad you could make it,' he said. 'It's not the most fashionable place for our farewell gathering, but it's become a real favourite of mine.'

'I'm more interested in seeing you safely on your way.'

There were others at Goldstein's table: to his left, Marion Bosetzky, former nude dancer and chambermaid, now gangster's moll. She gave a brief nod of acknowledgement.

Goldstein gestured towards the man sitting opposite him. 'Allow me to introduce Mister Salomon Epstein, an old friend from Brooklyn. We're going home together.'

Rath shook the man's hand. He looked like a scientist, thin as a rake with glasses and thinning hair.

'Were you here on business or as a tourist?' he asked.

'He doesn't understand,' Goldstein said. 'His parents didn't speak German in front of him, not even Yiddish. They wanted to make a good American out of him. That's why we're sitting here, while inside they're celebrating Rosh Hashanah.' He pointed towards the synagogue.

'Rosh hash what?'

'Jewish New Year.'

'Happy New Year! We can celebrate your departure instead. For a while, I was afraid you might apply for German citizenship.'

'I almost did,' Goldstein said, 'but dear Marion here will apply for US citizenship instead.' He laughed and winked at her. 'Do you know what, Detective? This city of yours is pretty damn crazy. Still, I'll be glad to leave it behind. You too, right Sally?'

Salomon Epstein, the man with the glasses, gave a wise smile when he heard his name.

'It's Sally you have to thank for getting rid of me,' Goldstein said in English, patting the man's hand. 'He's come to take me home.'

'You're welcome,' Epstein mumbled in his unexpectedly deep bass.

'Anyway, it's nice to see you, Inspector,' Goldstein grinned. 'I wouldn't have thought we'd end up as friends.'

'*Friends* is taking it too far. I'm here on duty. To make absolutely sure you disappear.'

'There was I thinking you had a higher opinion of me.'

'Let's not misunderstand each other. I'm extremely grateful for your help a couple of months back, allowing yourself to be arrested like that.'

'I had your word you'd get me off, and for some reason I believed you. It worked out in the end.'

'I think it was the second part of our agreement that did it.'

'My new business relationship? You'll understand if I don't divulge individual details, but it is lucrative, you're right in that sense. Above all, because I won't be pulling chestnuts out of the fire for other people any longer. Say hello to Herr Marlow for me.'

'I will.' Rath lit a cigarette. 'In spite of everything, I'll be relieved when there are several million cubic kilometres of water between us.'

'Let's drink to that.' Goldstein filled a line of champagne glasses in front of him. 'Our ship sets sail tomorrow morning.'

Rath lifted his glass. 'Here's to making your train, and the steamer tomorrow.'

The men drank. Marion just sipped. When the music came to an end, noise on the streets broke through. Loud cries. Men chanting something. Rath was surprised. The Communists didn't normally march in this area.

But they weren't Communists.

A troop of brownshirts marched past the windows, shouting something Rath couldn't make out. 'What was that you said? A crazy city? Just when you think it can't get any worse with these idiots . . .' he pointed towards the brownshirts outside. '. . . they go and surprise you all over again.'

There was a sudden, deafening crash as a chair was thrown through the window. The glass shattered into a thousand pieces, as a cold wind blew through the room and the chanting became louder still. *Wir ha-ben Hunger! Wir wol-len Ar-beit!* We are hungry! We want work! The door flew open and half a dozen brownshirts looked around aggressively. They couldn't have been more than twenty years old.

'Are you from the Glaziers' Guild?' Goldstein asked.

An old man near the entrance was knocked over along with his chair. A terrified waiter dropped his tray, there was a clatter and all was still. Everyone in the room stared at the intruders. A chair was thrown across the room. People ducked. A woman was struck on the head and fell to the ground, holding her hands over her bleeding face. The brownshirts bellowed with laughter.

Goldstein stood up with Rath and everyone else at their table. 'In this town the street gangs wear uniforms,' he said to Sally, planting himself in front of them.

'How about you lot scram and notify your insurance company so that they can start repairing the damage?'

The shouting stopped, and the brownshirt who had thrown the chair squared up to Goldstein. He was a thin, dark-haired man who looked like a Tunisian carpet dealer's apprentice. 'Don't get involved, friend. This is none of your business! It's the Jews we're after!'

'What if I happen to be one?'

'You don't look like one.'

'You don't look Aryan, and your queer Führer definitely not. Is it true what people say? That you lot are a bunch of queers?'

Goldstein was ready. He blocked the man's punch and dealt him a right hook to the chin, knocking him to the floor. He pulled the Remington from his pocket. 'Stay where you are,' he shouted, 'and put your hands up.'

The first two brownshirts obeyed, the three behind likewise. All five stared anxiously at the barrel of the gun.

'Let's get out of here,' Goldstein whispered to Rath, 'there are more of them outside, a whole army. We can't fight them all.'

Rath pulled Sally Epstein and Marion Bosetzky behind him, while Goldstein kept the brownshirts in check. Amazing how an automatic weapon concentrated the mind. But as they reached the rear exit a second windowpane shattered and two shots rang out. It had started again. The inside of Café Reimann was done for. Rath just hoped most patrons would escape in one piece.

Running through a series of rear courtyards leading to Knesebeck-strasse, he knew his hopes would be dashed. There were brownshirts everywhere, as well as a number in Young Stahlhelm uniform. Hundreds of them; everywhere chanting and shouting, accompanied by the sound of smashing glass.

Deutsch-land erwa-che! Ju-da verrek-ke! Germany awake! Die Jew!

Together with Goldstein, Marion and Sally Epstein, Rath made his way to the taxi stand on the Ku'damm. Strangely, they were left to themselves. Perhaps Goldstein looked too Aryan and Marion too blonde. On the Ku'damm, real-life hunting scenes were playing out in front of them. Innocent passersby fled crazed SA hooligans, who pursued them and beat them with long sticks until they lay on the ground bleeding. The uniformed thugs didn't even shy away from beating women and old men.

Marion fell behind to fix one of her shoes. Rath heard her cry out and looked back to see an SA man grab her by the hair and raise his stick. Goldstein reached for his weapon as someone said: 'Let her go, man,' almost horrified. 'She's blonde!'

With that they were on the lookout for new victims. Rath wondered how many blond Jews and black-haired Teutons were walking the streets. Hopefully a lot.

'Kill the Jews!' Social envy and racial hatred: a toxic combination.

Goldstein remained astonishingly calm.

'Don't you take this sort of thing personally?' Rath asked.

'Very much. I hope your police arrive soon to lock these crybabies up.'

'I'm a police officer too.'

'You think if you show your identification they'll toddle off?'

'I was thinking more of my Walther,' Rath said.

'If you pull out your gun, it'll be a bloodbath.'

'My colleagues will be here soon,' Rath said, more to reassure himself. 'That will put an end to it.'

Two uniformed officers were already there, but weren't about to step in. They observed the goings-on cautiously, behaving as if they had mistakenly wandered into the Schlesische Viertel and were at the mercy of Communists and criminal gangs. Only, this wasn't East Berlin, it was the Ku'damm, and scenes like this were unprecedented.

It shocked Rath to see this elegant, middle-class neighbourhood morph into a riot scene. Other pedestrians were shocked too, not believing their eyes until the toe of a brown boot caught them, or a fist landed in their face, until they had a bloodied nose or broken ribs.

The taxi stand was deserted. Either the taxi drivers had decided to protect their precious vehicles, or they were all gone, hired by fleeing pedestrians. They had to keep going. Marion took off her high heels and ran in stockinged feet next to Goldstein.

Then Rath saw something that gave the lie to later reports of a sponta-
neous uprising led by young unemployed men. This wasn't a disaffected
populace, not even a mob of brownshirts running wild. They were advancing systematically, giving each other signals, whistling and waving. The
commanders were directing them like troops in battle.

The general's vehicle looked unreal in the middle of it all, a chauferred
open car being driven down the Ku'damm. In the back sat a man wearing
a Navy cap with gold braid trimming like an admiral, and a brownshirt
who looked like his aide-de-camp. The man with the Navy cap kept asking for the vehicle to stop, waving over a Scharführer here, a Gruppenfüh-
rer there, and distributing orders.

Rath made a mental note of the number plate before hurrying after
Goldstein and his friends, shepherding them inside the U-Bahn. He hoped
it wouldn't prove to be a trap, and was relieved to see no brownshirts below ground. Everything seemed normal. If it hadn't been for the harried
faces of fellow passengers, he might have thought what was happening above
was a bad dream.

He decided to take his leave from Goldstein at the station. He would
be flouting his duty, of course, but he could hardly believe the Yank would
willingly stay in this madhouse. Goldstein's night train left in an hour and a
half. 'I need to take care of this,' he said.

'You do that,' Goldstein agreed. 'You're hosting the Olympic Games in
a few years. I hope you have that lot under control by then.'

'We will. This won't happen again in a hurry, I promise you.'

He wished the three a safe trip and waited until the train disappeared
before looking for the nearest telephone booth. He asked to be put through
to Alex and requested back-up.

'You aren't the first,' the watch sergeant said. 'It's on its way.'

'Well, it isn't here!' Rath shouted into the receiver. 'We're losing control
of the streets to this brown rabble. Isn't it bad enough that we've no say in
Communist areas? Now, get a move on.'

He hung up. There was a knock on the glass pane. Two brownshirts
stood tapping coins against the booth and grinning. Rath put them in their
early twenties, but one was as spotty as a sixteen-year-old. He opened the
door. 'What's the big idea?'

'You're a Jew's sow too, are you?' Spots said, while the other carried on grinning. 'Called your Isidor, did you, so he'd send the good old German police out to help?!'

'No need.' Rath showed his identification, drew his Walther and released the safety catch. 'You two brown arseholes will have nothing against accompanying me to the nearest station?'

They threw their hands in the air.

'You can't speak to us like that,' Spots said. He seemed to know his rights; probably a law student.

'Wrong.' Rath waved his gun, hurrying them on. 'It's *you* who can't speak to *me* like that. Insulting a public official is a punishable offence in Prussia. Insulting a couple of arseholes is not.'

Spots and his friend kept silent as they trotted down the Ku'damm towards the 133rd precinct in Joachimsthaler Strasse.

Rath had anticipated an evening drinking a few civilised cognacs at the bar in Kakadu, missing Charly, but at the same time, listening to the new houseband, which was supposed to have a very good drummer. Instead, he found himself escorting these two idiots to the nearest police station. At least they had resigned themselves silently to their fate.

Later, he emerged from the station and lit a cigarette. On the Ku'damm everything was quiet again, the shouting replaced by the sounds of the city's nightlife. On the other side of the road the neon of the Kakadu-Bar beamed into the night. He looked at his watch. The Nazis hadn't completely ruined his evening. He could still drink his cognac.

The red-gold saloon was full to bursting. In here, the mob felt like a bad dream. Only the black eye and slightly dirty suit of the man next to him at the bar reminded him what had happened. The man smiled at his female companion as if all was forgotten. The barman, too, was friendly as ever. Rath ordered his cognac and tried not to think of Charly, concentrating instead on the music and, yes, the new drummer was very good.

He drank hoping, when the time came, to fall pleasantly inebriated into his hotel bed. Meanwhile, the atmosphere in Kakadu was as riotous as ever, and he felt happy to be among these people who just wanted to drink, dance, listen to music and have fun. He wasn't interested in what was happening outside. Still, Abraham Goldstein was right about one thing: Berlin *was* a crazy city, and it was getting crazier and crazier.